Sylvie looked around, decided that she liked the bareness of the room. She would insist on keeping it that way. No pictures, no rug, no distractions. No bric-a-brac, nothing to identify her one way or the other. Spare as a confessional.

Margo was saying, "Am I to understand that you're fed up with office life and want a change?"

Sylvie hesitated. "Something like that."

"Well, look, that's good enough for me," Margo said. "I have really stong, positive vibes here. Can we say it's decided?" Her face, bright and encouraging, willed Sylvie to make an affirmative decision. "I have a feeling this is going to work out." Sylvie didn't know whether it would work out or not and didn't really care. She wanted to chance it for awhile.

STAYING AFLOAT

Muriel Spanier

FAWCETT CREST • NEW YORK

Library of Congress Catalog Card Number: 85-1913

ISBN 0-449-20881-8

This edition published by arrangement with Random House, Inc.

Manufactured in the United States of America

First Ballantine Books Edition: January 1987

FOR MARC
AND FOR ANDREW AND KAREN

PROLOGUE

I N Vermont that fall it rained for weeks. The roads and
highways, wreathed in mist, were bad enough by day,
worse at night, with the shoulder beds leached away, turned
into running troughs, and the shiny asphalt like glass.

This is how they imagined it happened: The trailer truck
hurled itself into an S curve outside of Brattleboro and never
found its way out. There was a long subhuman screech of
brakes, then a sudden sway and shudder as the tractor
whipped around and crashed on its side across the full width
of the road, its wheels still spinning.

According to the police report, a station wagon, speeding
along moments later, skidded to a stop. A young man jumped
out and ran to the overturned truck. He began screaming at
the driver, who was crawling, dazed, out of the cab, one arm
held against his chest. "Oh, my God! You're blocking the
whole damned road! We've got to get through! We've got to!"
He ran from one end of the sprawled vehicle to the other,
waving wildly in the direction of the station wagon. "She's
bleeding to death in there. For God's sake, help me! I've got
to *move*!" He fell on his knees in a crazed, imploring way

I

before the driver, who, astonished by his own escape, wondered whether he had caused a multiple accident.

Eventually the police arrived in a brilliance of revolving lights. Eventually the young man, the woman in the car and the truck driver were transported to the hospital in Brattleboro. There, a gurney was wheeled into place. Cardiovascular monitors, IV poles appeared. A medical team worked frantically to pump blood into the young woman's veins, to build up her pressure. Once they thought they had carried her over the peak. The palest rose blossomed for a few seconds in her cheeks, then disappeared. The miracle was that the baby was born alive.

The doctors, emerging from surgery, told the young man she'd opened her eyes twice. The first time she said, "This is so crazy . . ." The second time her eyes fluttered wide and she gasped, "Mother."

CHAPTER 1

SYLVIE Weyman swam early-bird laps each morning at the local health club near her home in Rosevale: three-quarters of a mile, the pool lights melting overhead, her primary senses flattening out and dimming.

At this hour—7:30 A.M.—the club was usually empty. There was only one attendant, visible through a glass partition in the wall, sleepily folding towels. After her laps, Sylvie floated face down in a chlorine trance, unwilling to rise to full consciousness. She imagined herself in her gray tank suit doing the dead man's float on and on, arms and legs splayed in the water. Recently—this week, last week, her days ran together in hopeless strands of time—the pool attendant had come running out across the tiles and poked her with a drag pole. "Good grief, Mrs. Weyman," she called, "why don't you try the backstroke for a change!"

Victor had said, "Courage, courage, my darling," whispering it as if it were a litany, a prayer. When she had failed some weeks before, on two consecutive mornings, to get out of bed and go to work, he had left his office at Apollo Life and Equity in downtown Manhattan, taken the Long Island Rail

Road and arrived at her house with the calm efficiency of a paramedic. He made hot coffee, rubbed her wrists and temples with ice cubes, poured the cologne he'd given her at Christmas on his handkerchief and touched it to the cleft between her breasts and to her hair, which hung like rope between her shoulder blades. He had brought bikini pajamas, to make her smile, he said. To remind her of how sexy a mature woman can be. "If I had known you as a teenybopper, we'd never have come up for air."

"Oh, please . . ." The thought of herself in those filmy wisps —it was the beginning of January, and she froze in flannel— made her want to laugh. But tears sprang to her eyes instead. "Oh, Victor, you're too much!"

He had answered, the faintest hint of Europe in his speech, "Unfortunately, I'm not enough."

She shivered and drew her robe tighter. "No, don't say that. You're so much better than I deserve."

He was sitting on her bed, balancing a cup of coffee in the palm of his hand as though they were picnicking in a Vienna wood. "Enough!" he said. "Another word and you'll have me calling for the violins."

But one morning at the health club Sylvie sank into a dead man's float more completely than ever before, slipping over the edge of the world into a new, compelling darkness. The floor of the pool shimmered and retreated beneath her, and in its depths she saw Angel's startled face. "How did this silly thing happen?" she was saying.

Sylvie and Victor had seen a film the night before about youth cults. There was one young girl, someone's child, with blond hair bleached white like puffs of cotton, who stared blandly into the camera and said, "The thing about living in the world today is that true passion is dead." And she pressed her mouth into a wry, knowing smile.

Victor muttered, "A lot that one knows about passion." But Sylvie had caught sight of Angel in the girl's look, in her deplorable innocence. Her heart beat wildly, and she rose suddenly and ran from the theatre. Victor caught up with her outside and held her against the building, speaking softly into her ear. "Just breathe deeply, good steady breaths. That's it." He'd bought a chocolate bar and pressed some between her lips. "Chew, for God's sake! Swallow! If your blood sugar were higher . . ." He shook her gently, as if she were a stopped watch, and finally said, "Come on, you need exercise." Leaving his car on the street, he walked her slowly down the darkened Rosevale roads to her house.

At the pool the next morning, lying face down in a dead man's float, she saw again, in a ripple of freeze frames, images of Angel repeated far below. Trancelike, she studied them with care.

This time the towel attendant jumped in after her and pulled her to the pool's edge. "You know, Mrs. Weyman, you could lose consciousness or something, holding your breath that way." The young woman was treading water in jeans and sneakers, one arm clutching Sylvie's waist. The pool manager came over and stared down at her, scowling. "Hey, you practicing to be a nonbreather? It's making us nervous. Next thing you'll be trying to walk on water." Sylvie apologized and dragged herself out of the pool.

IN Manhattan, in her office at Louden Realty, Sylvie tried to concentrate on putting the New Listings file in order. But her mind drifted. She noticed that someone, perhaps Tania Prince from Industrials/Commercials, had dropped a copy of a newspaper on her desk. During coffee break she thumbed through it, barely responding to what she saw. The newspaper was called *Upper East*; it had the usual local announcements and community topics in its columns. But in the Help Wanted section, an ad, framed as though it were a poem, with lots of white space and a scalloped border, caught her attention.

HOUSEHOLD MANAGER: Professional couple seeks mature, live-in woman with exceptional skills. Duties to include child care, occasional chauffeuring, bookkeep-

ing, other administrative duties. Also some supervision
of aged parents. If you are capable, gentle-tempered
and upbeat, contact at once. High salary.

Sylvie smoothed the paper open on her desk, a peculiar
heightened focus gathering in her. She suddenly imagined
this couple in a penthouse somewhere, trying to organize the
general uproar in their lives. What were they looking for, she
wondered—a stand-in to walk the dog, pay the dentist, shepherd the children to the planetarium, the music teacher, the
orthodontist, the Friday afternoon puppeteers? How well she
remembered her own bright, child-centered days. She didn't
really approve of surrogate parenting, that haphazard world
of hired help, and yet she found herself endowing these parents with affirmative, lighthearted traits. Their optimism
might be infectious. And if it came to it, she rather hoped the
agenda would include puppets. Years before, at the age of
seven, Angel had fallen in love with Stove-Pipe Pete, the
ruby-eared pirate of the Downtown Puppet Theatre, and
Sylvie and she took the train from Rosevale once a month to
see him. "Do pirates ever get married?" Angel had asked.

"Yes, especially pirates," she'd answered.

Now Sylvie stared at the ad, rereading it again and again.
Living in such a house might be a kind of abdication. One self
replaced by another—a foot-soldier self waiting for orders
from the top to filter down. With luck, it would mean psychic
rest in exchange for work. Not the worst of possibilities.

She took a container of yogurt from her windowsill and
began to eat. She wished there were a pool nearby for the
midday break. She liked to blank out underwater, dissolve.
She pushed her files and catalogues aside. NEARBY SUBUR-
BAN clattered to the floor, the index cards scattering in every
direction—Larchmont, New Rochelle, Port Washington.
There was a peculiar airy fizz in her head. How well she knew
what grief could do: make you crazy in a self-protective way.
She'd begun to imagine herself doing odd and terrible things.
Climbing onto the gabled roof of her house and keening into

the night. Making a pyre of her clothes in front of the Rosevale railroad station, the other commuters watching in shock. She imagined everything in flames, even her tortoiseshell combs, her leather shoulder bag, the Indian seed belt that Angel had given her just last spring. "It has a good-luck motif, Mother. I bought one for myself, too."

Oh, luck, that court jester!

CHAPTER 2

LUNCH at The Perfect Carrot. It was Tania's way of acknowledging Sylvie's current asceticism in food. There were radish boutonnieres and sprigs of scallion and rosemary on each table. Sylvie placed *Upper East* beside her plate and tried to concentrate on Tania.

"He just up and quit," Tania recounted for the hundredth time, dipping her finger into her sparkling cider and stirring.

Tania was thirty-five, younger than Sylvie by twelve years, and she could not stop talking about her husband, Larry, who had left her recently. "The thing is, we were perfect together. Edith Piaf could turn us to soup. I mean, the first note, and we were gone. I told him once, he had lazy sperm. It made him wild. He was eating ice cream, and he took a spoonful and flipped it in my face."

She ate a deviled shrimp, and Sylvie turned away. According to Tania, she and Larry had been trying to have a child for the past two years, going from one fertility doctor to another, she with her legs in stirrups, Larry shooting semen into little plastic cups. And their programmed sex life! Forget it, Tania said. All the tallyings and countings! "As if we were

8

in an agricultural commune!" But the verdict was unanimous. Low sperm motility.

Then one day Larry began to lose interest in sex. He said, "Christ, Tania, going to bed with you is about as spontaneous as doing push-ups!" And then he got down on the floor and did seventy-five push-ups! Tania sighed. "I guess I represented personal failure." Her eyes spilled over, sending streaks of mascara down her cheeks.

Sylvie was barely listening. She didn't know how to comfort Tania. Motherhood had come to her so swiftly, with Angel arriving almost unbidden, entering her life like an extraordinary gift. "I think I know how you feel," she said. "Still, you don't want to be too obsessive about motherhood. There are the traps, too, the pitfalls. Part of you becomes submerged and lost." But Sylvie had welcomed mothering, flinging herself into it the way a distance swimmer might fling herself into the ocean, confident that the rewards would be worth the stress.

"Oh, I don't know," Tania protested, blotting her eyes with a napkin. "What I really want to do is give away every bit of myself."

Sylvie pushed her salad aside. She ate next to nothing these days, as though shedding pounds might rid her of misery as well as flesh. Victor had said, "Even Meryl Streep must eat a banana now and then." But Sylvie liked the idea of holding back, filling her refrigerator with grapefruit, bunches of watercress, tofu. Denying herself food was a form of penance. There was that, and there was the swimming.

She had not slept with Victor for weeks.

Victor, who was enchanted by Meryl Streep, said Sylvie reminded him of her. Sylvie was older by some years, but with the same burnt-umber hair and exquisitely ironic smile, he said, when she chose to smile. And the suggestion of a fragile core. It was the fragile core that troubled him these days. One early evening recently, when he'd driven her into the city for a change of air, and they'd walked and walked, finally in the direction of Battery Park, he said to her, "This must come to an end, you know. This drowning in grief. Ultimately it's an addiction like any other."

It was windy and in the distance the Statue of Liberty rose like a defending goddess from the crumpled waters of the Bay. Garlands of light were coming on in the buildings around them. "You'll have to swallow this awful thing, Sylvie. She's *gone.*" The very word opened hairline faults in the wall of her chest. Her arms and legs seemed to loosen in their sockets. If she had been in the pool, the attendant would have had to scoop her out with a net.

"In the end you'd say it's just statistics, I suppose," she said bitterly, staring off at the statue, whose crown, host to a flock of gulls, appeared to shudder in the declining day.

"Yes, in the end that's exactly what it is."

SYLVIE touched Tania's hand. "Larry will come back, and then you'll try something else. You'll adopt."

"No," Tania said quietly. Her bangle bracelets hung limply on her wrist. "He says he doesn't want a family now. He says it came to him like a revelation, just in time. I know what will happen next. He'll find someone else. . . ." She squeezed her eyes tightly shut. "So who needs sperm!"

Sylvie empathized with Tania's feeling of injury and loss. Her own husband, Arthur, had died eight years before of a heart attack one afternoon on a quiet, tree-lined street in Queens. Little boys on tricycles found him collapsed against a privet hedge. He and his young law associate had been at a meeting with an action group—the Flaming Spear or the FALN—she had always been confused about the details. The associate, Scott Rudick, was still in the house when the little boys rang the bell. He came flying out, carried Arthur a block and a half to a taxi stand and rushed him to a hospital.

"Beware of impassioned idealists," her father had told her long ago.

Now, ignoring Tania's dishevelled face across the table, she found herself thinking of Angel. Angel, fourteen years old and sitting beside her at the chapel during Arthur's funeral, listening to a eulogy that invented and then praised an Arthur they had never known ". . . a sober, devoted family man . . . a man dedicated to the public cause, yet whose loved ones were at the very center of . . ." Scott sat with his face buried in a handkerchief, sobbing. Angel's chilled hand was clasped in hers. Afterward, Scott kept saying, "I'm sorry, Sylvie. Oh, please listen to me, I'm so sorry for everything . . ." even as she turned away.

Sylvie had trouble swallowing. Tania had finally stopped talking and was sipping the last of her apple drink. Her auburn-tinted frizz gave her the look of a distracted Zulu. Sylvie wanted to feel more tender toward her, but she had lost the power to understand other people's suffering.

Tania suddenly said, "I'm ashamed about carrying on this way, as though I were the center of the universe." She laid a hand over Sylvie's. "Now it's your turn. You've been so damned patient. Do you want to talk?" she asked hesitantly.

Sylvie shook her head. A marionette's head, disconnected from her body. She sipped her Perrier. What was there to say to Tania, who had become as strange to her as the findings of an anthropological study. Tania, who was young and would one day recoup her losses. Was it worth saying, You'll find a man, you'll have a baby? When all of it was chance. Victor had strolled across her path by chance, two years ago; her own widowhood had hung heavily for nearly seven years before that, although there had been men here and there briefly flaring into her life like brushfires. She met him at a Mostly Mozart concert in Lincoln Center. Strolling along the perimeter of the central mall, she became aware of someone persistently trailing her. It was Victor, in white chinos and a striped silk shirt rolled at the sleeves. Two ice-cream cones were dripping down his wrists.

"I beg your pardon," he said, tilting the briar in his mouth, "but that fellow over there, the one under the ice-cream umbrella, insisted on selling me two of these. Do you suppose you could relieve me of one?"

She looked at him carefully. He had a good face. Somewhat longish nose. Stubby moustache, tobacco-scented. He was too well dressed to be considered rugged. "Actually, I was struck by your necklace," he continued. "African?"

"No, New England college," she said, fingering the chunky wood-and-silver beads that Angel had made.

They managed to sit next to each other during the concert, with Rampal and Yo-Yo Ma creating a flood of music so piercingly sweet that at one point she was moved to murmur, "Oh yes."

And Victor, beside her, whispered, "Exactly."

Now Sylvie made an effort at drawing Tania into her field of vision. She removed a scallion from the bud vase and carefully shredded its stem. "Did you happen to leave this newspaper on my desk today?" she asked, pointing to *Upper East*.

Tania sighed. Her lips were trembling. "I suppose so. Yes, as a matter of fact, I did. The boutique called Stellar Nights with the French ribbon sweaters and the satin vestlets from Zagreb, did you notice?" She looked away. "I once had an emerald vest with funky silk fringe. I'd wear it at home with nothing on underneath. Zilch. God, it seems long ago. Anyway I thought maybe you and I could prowl around tonight after work, buy some little image-shattering thing."

Sylvie didn't think so. She had neither the energy nor the interest. Victor would be at her house for dinner tonight. Besides, she disliked boutiques, and ribbon sweaters were not for her. She was too tall and, despite her slender frame, full-bosomed. Victor said her cleavage was biblical.

"It's not possible," Sylvie said, swallowing. The vegetable salad had formed a lump in her throat. "I'm doing Scarsdale listings in the over-$200,000 class, and it will take forever. Anyway, I'm going to try to make dinner for Victor. . . ." She paused, slowly framing her words. Tania's face seemed to be drifting off, like a balloon on a string. "There was something else, though, that caught my eye." She opened the newspaper flat. "This."

Tania read the ad and looked surprised. "What's so special about that?"

"It seemed special, that's all. Don't you wonder about people who need assistants just to keep their private lives in order?" Sylvie broke some rosemary off its stem and held it to her nose. The penetrating scent stirred her brain.

Tania was saying, "They're rich, that's all. And the rich are different. Our very own Zack Louden calls for his Mercedes to take him around the corner to the barber's every day!"

Sylvie thought of how it might be, entering another family's life, giving up control, everything laid out, provided for, decided on. Like entering a peacetime army, or a country with a benevolent dictator. All the same, the whole experience could easily be a disaster. And there was Victor. What would Victor say? In bed at night, on the nights he stayed over, he often held her fingers to his lips as though blowing nourishment through straws. "I'm here," he'd say. "We're doing this together."

At first she had cried a great deal. Tears streaming down her face became a natural condition. She often went to the library in Rosevale, and standing in the darkest stacks, Angel's shadow in her head, and a star-glimmer of the infant Sean, she'd bend her head and sob. Even when she felt strong enough to go back to work, she'd sit at her desk, scanning new apartment listings, and suddenly find her face wet with tears.

Tania was saying, "Of course, where Louden is concerned, it's a matter of having money to burn. Sweetie, are you OK?"

Sylvie touched a napkin to her eyes. "Yes," she said. She thought of Zack Louden, the absentee monarch on the penthouse floor, whose well of sympathy had undoubtedly run dry. He had sent flowers, baskets of fruit, a note in a self-consciously flowery style urging her to take as much time off as she needed. "Heal yourself and then come back to us," he'd said. But she knew that as far as Zack was concerned, the time for healing was gone. He was capable of firing Sylvie in a minute, denying her commissions earned, if he guessed what she was contemplating. But she couldn't be bothered thinking of him, or even of Tania and her troubles with Larry. She wished it was morning again and that she was in the pool blindly swimming laps.

CHAPTER 3

THE kitchen was in disarray. A partly eaten half grapefruit was glued to the counter in its sticky juice. Dish towels and newspapers were scattered around. Sylvie had always been reasonably neat, but now neatness seemed an arbitrary convention.

These days, Victor straightened things up when he arrived. He would not only hang up his own coat, he would move through the house putting Sylvie's belongings in order as well. Sometimes he would even vacuum before dinner, removing his tie, rolling up his sleeves. Tonight he would probably arrive around eight o'clock, depending on the vagaries of the Long Island Rail Road, and Sylvie, nervous because of the news she intended to impart, had planned curried veal and rice pilaf, his favorites, for dinner.

Although they did not actually live together, Victor stayed with her several times a week and most weekends. His beautifully tailored suits hung in her closet; his cuff links, brushes, English pomades, were in her bureau drawers or on her bathroom shelves—small surprises that pleased her when she came upon them. His electric razor had displaced her electric toothbrush. "You don't want to do violence to your gums, do you?" he'd asked. This was before she had begun to fast and to swim each day.

His fishing gear hung in the back of the downstairs hall closet—old dungarees, a shiny yellow foul-weather jacket, rubber boots—a striking contrast to the polished image he showed the world.

"My place is moldering," he'd said, after they had known each other a few months. "Don't you think it's time we joined forces?" He lived on the Upper West Side in a spacious old-fashioned apartment facing Central Park. As a Louden listing—one bedroom, one and a half baths—it would, if thrown on the market, easily command thirteen hundred a month. But he had lived there for years with his former wife, Mona, before she went to Cuernavaca, where she was now weaving fabrics. "Vivid stuff—lots of jungle flowers and birds," he said. "The New York decorating world found her and made her very rich." He paused and continued with some bitterness, "She became the all-time feminist—always ready to be told how 'put down' she'd been. I, of course, didn't quite see how. She insisted our karma was all wrong, or our stars in conflict. I'll be damned if I remember which. And maybe she was right. She was so confidently Episcopalian, and there she was, married to an evanescent Jew."

Sylvie dipped the veal in flour and set butter to melt. She'd planned on a small piece of sole for herself, but when she took it out of the refrigerator, the smell, delicate but distinct, assailed her. She didn't like the odor of fish. Victor would be furious about what she intended to do. . . . She thought of Larry flipping ice cream in Tania's face. But that was not Victor's style. He would fume. But he would control his anger. He was too fine-grained to express violence of any kind. And five years younger than Sylvie, a fact that left her with a vague feeling of disquiet. He was forty-two, with curly graying hair and a secretive smile, a feline smile that suggested that he knew more than he cared to reveal. He was not in the least effeminate, however; he was lean and wiry, with strong tight bands of muscle across his chest and shoulders —a hiker and a fisherman—with a narrow aristocratic head, and lips made slightly mysterious by that thick, neatly trimmed moustache.

She mixed rice with boullion and put it on to simmer. She tried to keep her own calorie intake to around 900. Someone once told her that fasting was better than amphetamines for producing a high—a state of being she could no longer even remotely imagine. But it was not so much a high that she was seeking as a form of transcendence. Simple relief from the weight of her own self.

She set the table. From the large armoire in the corner of the dining room she took out two crystal wine glasses, a legacy of her European babyhood. Her parents had left Budapest for New York before the war, like migratory birds with a keen instinct for survival; Sylvie had been two years old.

She didn't need to think about dessert. Victor would bring something outrageously rich for himself. He always did. Angel had loved sweets too. When she came down from Vermont, she gobbled his whipped-cream pastries and then licked the tips of her fingers as though they were also delicious. "Victor, king of schlag!" she teased.

"Schlag? Would that be a small Central European country about the size of Liechtenstein?" he asked.

Angel had gone to Vermont with Gary after they both were graduated from college. Sylvie had been relieved that the relationship seemed to be one of those loose, "liberated" alliances. She found Gary disturbing. She suspected he was the sort of person who attached himself too quickly to new ideas and ideologies in order to fill an inner vacuum. It was holistic medicine when he and Angel were in school. He railed against antibiotics, injections, even dentistry. He spoke about going to Katmandu on a retreat. When he was excited, his voice rose in pitch, like a tenor scaling a difficult passage.

"It's the everyday hype that gets to him," Angel explained. "He has the heart of a purist, that's all."

"Or an extremist," Sylvie suggested.

"Come on, Mother! All right, he climbs on these bandwagons. But I can calm him down."

Gary had taken an apprenticeship in bookbinding in Brattleboro. Angel was working with silver. To hear Angel describe it, their life was one long bucolic idyll. She never mentioned graduate school or future plans.

"But what are you going to live on?" Sylvie had asked on one of her long-distance calls. Gary had answered the phone. "Welfare, if necessary. The way I see it, the body politic owes us."

Sylvie hung up, shocked.

In Brattleboro, Angel created pendants and earrings that looked like astral fallout, luminous bulky pieces that hung heavily from the earlobe. She had given Sylvie a pair for Mother's Day.

"Are you sure these aren't meant for a New Zealand bushwoman?"

"Oh, funny! Woody Allen could really use you."

Once, at the movies, when Angel was six, she'd pried at Sylvie's ear and placed a piece of popcorn inside. On the screen the queen was asking the mirror, "Who is the fairest, the fairest?"

"You," Angel had whispered, her lips shiny with butter.

Along with the jewelry-making, Angel raised weimaraner pups. One room in the house had been turned into a kennel with shredded newspaper on the floor.

SYLVIE made a little pitcher of Campari and lime juice for Victor. She hoped his mood would be good. Not that he was intimidating. It was his belief in boundaries that put pressure on her. "We can go so far, and then we fall off the edge of the world," he once said. "So it makes sense to have a rational plan." He would not acknowledge the fact that she had already fallen off the edge of the world.

When Angel died, Victor was a lion at her side. His constant presence was a barrier between herself and the unthinkable. During those first terrible weeks, whenever she opened her eyes, his face was before her. He would draw her to her feet and, with his arm around her waist, walk her through the rooms of her house, as if they were tourists at a place of interest.

"I want to die too," she told him.

"Great! And leave me behind?"

According to Victor's odds, there should have been only the minutest percentile of risk. Not more than 6.4 women in every 100,000 die in childbirth, no matter what their condition or circumstance. The number is higher among black women, lowest among white females between the ages of eighteen and twenty-four. But Angel had chosen to play Gary's game and lost. When she called in January to announce that she was pregnant, Sylvie had felt the heat flame to her cheeks. Gary's thin impatient face rose before her. "So are you two married, or what?"

"I don't necessarily want to be married. Does it surprise you?"

"Yes, as a matter of fact . . ." Her heart stood still.

"These days having a baby out of wedlock is no big deal."

She tried to understand. Was it Gary, with his bent for the outrageous, who had mesmerized Angel with another of his dubious plans? "What's so great about having an illegitimate child?" she had asked. "Prostitutes and bereft little teenagers do it all the time." Angel banged the phone down.

During a later and calmer phone call, Sylvie asked pertinent questions. "Have you seen an obstetrician?" It turned out that Angel had not. She was taking courses in hatha-yoga, in the nutritional advantages of grains and legumes. She was taking long walks in the woods. They were going to have their baby at home, with a midwife to assist and the kitchen of their rented house as a delivery room.

"We've joined the ranks of the pure and simple of heart," Angel said over the phone. "You know Gary! He feels technology has made people forget what they can do with their own two hands. And he may just be right. Remember what you told me about the physicist's son who moved to Vancouver and lived in a tree house?"

"It was an anecdote, not a prescription."

She made a trip to Brattleboro to see what was going on. It was the end of February. They climbed the ski trails of nearby Hogback Mountain and sat on a rock in the sun. An occasional skier hurtled by. Angel, newly pregnant, took off her tasselled hat and shook out her hair. It was a nimbus of light. Her given name was Marisa, but in a burst of parental pride they early on began to call her Angel, as if conferring celestial grace. "Brat," Sylvie murmured, pulling her child's head to her shoulder. "Terminate it," she said. Her voice was barely a whisper.

"What?"

"If you have doubts about marrying him, why have his baby? It doesn't make sense."

"Mother, I can't believe you're saying this."

"But I am saying it. I do say it."

Angel's face seemed to congeal. Sylvie knew that look. She had seen it before during Angel's progress into adolescence. Once, at the age of eleven, she had backed the family car out of the driveway and driven it, honking, around the block, toppling garbage cans along the way, narrowly missing the neighbor's cats. Even Arthur had allowed himself to be dragged from his preoccupation with Malcolm or Martin to dispense punishment. "No allowance for three months, young lady!" he'd boomed.

When Victor arrived, he had his movie camera with him. It was a Viennese model, ". . . better than any of the Japanese brands, otherwise, you know, I wouldn't spit on the Viennese." In certain ways it was obsolete. Eventually he would replace it with video equipment, he said.

He looked around the kitchen. She had managed to get the counter wiped clean. The curried veal was in a casserole in the oven. He held two long-stemmed roses wrapped in green tissue. "Some sweet young thing in Ptolemaic chains and leg warmers was selling these at Penn Station." He lifted his head. "It smells damn good in here. I'm starved."

He went upstairs to change, and she tried to visualize her room. Had she made the bed? She knew the bathroom was a mess, her wet bathing suit and towels flung under the sink. The mornings were the worst. Her motions were so heavy, it was as though she was swimming breaststroke through a resisting medium in her effort to get first to the pool and then to the train.

She put the roses in a vase and set them on the table. Upstairs, she could hear Victor moving around, opening closets, straightening things. He had this penchant for order. "In defense of the Platonic ideal," he once said, apologetically. She saw it as a reaction to the disorder of his early youth. He had been born in Vienna at the beginning of the war, and he still carried a flame of rage and bafflement over that particular corner of his history. During the war, he had lived in the south of France with a family who pretended to the neighbors that he was their little Aryan nephew from Vienna, an orphan. Toward the end he did, in fact, become an orphan.

When they first met, these fragments of European childhood created an instantaneous bond. "I think we were meant for each other," he had said during intermission, that first time at Mostly Mozart. "I'm amazingly intuitive—unforgivable in an actuary, you know—about things like that; our being meant for each other, I mean."

"But what will my daughter say?"

"A daughter? Ah, the plot thickens."

At another time he said, "But you were only two when you arrived on these shores. You're as American as pumpkin pie."

"And you were nine. Do you feel so European?"

It was not that, he said. It was something else. Something dense and puzzling that had to be figured out. Perhaps for that very reason he had become a statistician with an insurance company, an actuary, pushing blocks of numbers around, a cartographer of risk, he said, smiling wryly.

AFTER dinner, he prowled the house deciding on a good location shot. He had changed to corduroys and desert boots and looked particularly boyish. The clothes that Victor wore, with their eccentric elegance, were at odds with his personality, which was direct, formal and faintly abashed.

Victor's game was to turn her rooms into improbable stage sets and photograph them. Last week he had urged her into being Cezanne's woman, sitting in the bay window with a bowl of apples in her lap, and he panning in, using a wide-angle movie lens, doing a scene of her holding apples in a bowl, taking dripping, juicy bites. "We're carrying the artist's intention a few steps further by answering the question 'What happens to the apples when the artist turns his back?' " He was trying to amuse and revive her. He was posing cinematic riddles. Perhaps he was trying to excite her, too. Once, last spring (it was before Angel's death, which had become a cataclysmic divider of time, like B.C. and A.D.), he had suggested that she take the part of Renoir's nude stepping out of a bath.

It was a comic scene. A wet robe and scattered towels. Victor on his knees in a soapy puddle.

"You're a clown," she said indulgently.

He was peering into the camera, and when she rose, dripping, holding a loofah mitt modestly before her, he said, "Too poignant, my darling! You're like Venus at the mercy of the vandals." And pinning her to the tile wall, announced, "And I am the vandals!"

VICTOR had enrolled in an evening film course at New York University and planned to take a leave of absence from Apollo one day to do a modest film, if he could get some money together.

He believed that a good short film, like a dentist's drill, could touch an exquisitely sensitive nerve. Tonight he wanted to make movies of her as a counterwoman in a diner. He had something in the style of Edward Hopper in mind. A seedy diner. The woman staring straight ahead as though a cosmic eraser had just rubbed away her landscape.

He was in the dining room fussing with lights. The dining table would be the counter. He said, "Put on one of those loose caftans and boots. We're in SoHo, you know. The counterwoman might easily wear boots. I'll show her coming around and sitting at a table, having coffee with a customer. The beauty of moving film is that we can show more than the artist knows." He bloomed with enthusiasm. "I believe life is a chain of freeze-stops imbedded in ongoing motion. That's why stills done from moving film are often so shocking. Look at the evolving frames of a smile, sometime. It's scary. So what do you think?" He lit his pipe and gave her a long serious look. "Sometimes we're caught in a really bad freeze-stop," he said, holding her hand tightly to his heart.

She went upstairs to look for clothes, found her Zero King storm boots and put them on. They reminded her of snow. Of Angel alive and in Vermont last winter. She had written a letter to Sylvie saying, "Nearly three months pregnant, and all is well. Not to worry. I do a little cross-country skiing. We have a snappy second-hand snowmobile now, so we really travel in style. Gary is learning to do glorious watery endpapers. He has invented a glue that resists time. I've made some gorgeous pieces using azurite on a silver wire. My reputation grows, along with my belly. It's crazy, but the New York skiers are wild about the stuff. And there are four new pups (four!), gray and silky like those Victorian gloves women used to wear. Peace, Mother. Please!"

Sylvie made another trip to Brattleboro, this time with Victor. They arrived after a two-foot snowfall and parked at the bottom of the rutted driveway. In the crystal day, the house seemed miniaturized, as if afloat in a paperweight.

Victor filled his lungs. "One could turn devout in a place like this."

Gary made lunch—stone-ground bread, a salad of alfalfa sprouts, whey cheese and bulgur wheat.

"We grow the sprouts ourselves," Angel informed them.

"Very salutary," Victor said.

"We're not all that holy," Gary said. "We gorge on pizza and tacos, too."

Sylvie was looking around at the large bare kitchen, the

linoleum worn so thin in spots that the rough wooden planking showed through, and the table—throne to her grandchild's birth? The nearest hospital was ten miles away.

There were a half dozen books covered in rough-textured materials on a shelf. Clearly Gary's work. Sylvie suddenly said, "If you're serious about bookbinding, Gary, it seems to me you should be living in a large city where book manufacture is done. Otherwise I wonder whether anything can ever really come of it." She realized too late how she sounded—pushy, insensitive—and wished she'd said nothing.

Gary flushed. "I guess I'll have to handle that in my own way."

"I only meant that it must be hard to sustain . . ."

"Oh, yes, sure . . ."

Victor interrupted, "The fishing up here in summer must be terrific."

"If you like fishing. I happen to think it's a big yawn," Gary said. He was tall and slope-shouldered; all the planes of his face seemed to come to a point. He had the sharp-eyed look of a fox, and a sudden beautiful smile. His smile took Sylvie by surprise, made her feel she had to reexamine her attitude toward him. He seemed to have something more to say to her, but Victor was interrupting.

"There's a metaphysical side to fishing, you know. I would have thought you'd be interested."

"Well, I'm not. There's too much else to do." He had narrowed his eyes, red-rimmed from the strain of his work, as he watched Sylvie butter a slice of wheat bread. Then suddenly rising, he took a handful of sesame seeds from one of the jars of herbs that lined the windowsills and sprinkled them in a wide arc on the salads. Some fell like snow to the table.

Angel scooped them into a pile. "Gary, you beast!" she cried.

"I've blessed you with sesame. Don't knock it."

"Are you dispensing magic?" Victor inquired, lighting his pipe. But Gary had left the table.

Later, Sylvie and Angel fed and watered the puppies and

took a walk down the snowbanked road. The plows had frosted the ground with salt and gravel. Angel chattered away, uneasily, Sylvie thought. "You know, you're really being hard on Gary. He feels things in a very deep and serious way, and I don't think you understand that . . . I don't think you see it at all." She had linked her arm to Sylvie's, but now she stopped and faced her. "He never really had parents," she said. "His mother was in and out of hospitals with some progressive nerve disease for years until she finally died; his father couldn't cope. Gary stayed with his grandmother for a while, and then he actually lived in a foster home all through adolescence. I mean, that kind of experience can either destroy a person or deepen him. I think, with Gary, it's the latter. Can't you see?"

She hadn't seen. Perhaps the vacuum was in herself. "I'm sorry. I think I hurt his feelings. I ought to apologize," she said.

But Angel was still talking. "He was planning for a while to go to law school, and then he said, no, there'd be no peace because his whole life would be spent preparing arguments for or against some dumb thing. You see, he's not competitive that way. Won't put himself on the line. He told me there was a time at the foster home when his father didn't visit or write to him for three whole years. He said he never felt sure of his effect on anyone after that. His self-image just sort of decomposed."

Sylvie looked at Angel standing in the snow, this grave, utterly assured young woman, the merest hint of belly discernible beneath her parka.

"What is it, Mother?"

"Nothing, just thinking." They had always known each other's minds. Where was her baby cheerleader, animal lover, ombudsman for the rights of ill-used pets? In high school Angel had thought she'd be a veterinarian, had scanned college catalogues for appropriate courses. "Well, the empathy between you two is fine, but what's happened to the animal doctor in all of this?" Sylvie asked.

"It could still happen," Angel said. "There's Cornell with

a really terrific program. We might eventually move to Ithaca, when Gary gets his act together. Well, it's Gary's act first, then mine. In the meantime the weimaraners are fun." She looked away. "What does Victor say—I mean about everything?"

"You can guess. He hates the idea of saddling a child with illegitimacy."

VICTOR placed cups and saucers on the dining-room table that was supposed to be the counter. He had composed a sandwich of two pieces of bread and a ruffle of watercress. He suggested that Sylvie place it on a serving tray. She felt vaguely ill. The smell of veal lingered dangerously. She had knotted the Indian spread, from Angel's bed, around her waist, but now she pulled it off. There were times when she believed that Angel was not completely gone, that her essence had been snatched back somehow and implanted in another being. It gave her a peculiar nervous alertness that was exhausting.

"I'm wearing the Zero King storm boots that were in Brattleboro last winter," she said to Victor. "Will they be visible behind the so-called counter?" She tried to manage her voice, which teetered precariously.

Victor answered, "Of course." He was rearranging the lamps. He said, "In this light your hair is pure gold."

As Victor's camera hummed, she poured coffee into a cup, but it spilled on the sandwich. "Oh, this is too stupid." She felt light-headed. Perhaps she ought to eat a Yogi bar for quick energy. She said, "I'm fainting, Victor. Let's stop right here."

"Are you serious?" he asked quickly, putting the camera aside. She had poured herself a glass of milk and was drinking it as if it came from a survival kit. She had the copy of *Upper East* and pushed aside the coffee cups to spread the pages on the dining-room table.

She said abruptly, "Victor, I'm thinking seriously about

this." She pointed to the ad. "I'm tired. Don't give me an argument too quickly."

Victor read and was silent. His face changed from instant to instant. Finally he said, "But this is absolutely absurd, of course. I don't get it."

"Don't ask me to explain. I'm worn through. You'd call it psychic exhaustion. You're the analytic one."

Victor started to speak, but she interrupted. "Look, I need something—shelter, a place to crawl off to. When I saw the ad, I thought, Why not the shelter of an anonymous family? Is that really so fantastic? The way I see it—well, it's survival of a kind, to be pulled into the belly of other people's lives and digested, somehow. . . . Anyway, I can't keep going like this. As if I were on downers and uppers at once. My head full of craziness. It can't go on. And the ad—if you'd only think about it, it's not so farfetched at all. . . ."

"Not so farfetched!" His voice seemed to thunder in her ears. "But you have a job, real work. You could put your mind to those low-rent cooperatives that your agency is getting into. That's socially useful, at least. Or are you punishing yourself, by any chance? Is this like your recent food habits, another eccentricity to hide behind in that rush of yours into oblivion?"

"Oh, God, don't be reasonable," she moaned. He had once told her, "Your only priority is to pull yourself together." It was when they had first tried to find Gary. Someone told them he might have gone to the Yucatan, and she wanted to fly to Mexico at once. She had visions of a burning sun, desolate landscapes, the baby turning the color of a fig. Victor made dozens of phone calls. He left descriptions with the Mexican police. "When you're truly on the mend, we'll go out ourselves and explore . . ." Gary, too, had fallen off the edge of the world.

Now she said, "People do things. Listen, I know a dentist who, after the death of his wife, gave up his practice and went out West to measure monadnocks. Plateaus, small flat mountains—"

"I know what monadnocks are!" he snapped.

"Besides, this is only temporary. Maybe sometime in the future it will even seem amusing. Something to laugh about. You'll see."

"Marvellous. I'm laughing already." His lips were pressed together. "By the way, do you think your housekeeping skills measure up, to say nothing of your mood? Upbeat, the ad said? Are you trying to pass yourself off as upbeat? An honest girl like you?"

He tried to light his pipe but his hands shook. The packet of matches flared. He seemed to kiss his fingertips in pain, and this detail reduced her to tears. They had slept these last months with her body curved in the shadow of his, as though they had taken vows.

She wet a cloth and wrapped it around his hand. "I'll be back weekends," she was saying. "I'll tell them it's an absolute requirement."

He pounded his bandaged fist on the table. "I'll tell you this! The way you cling to grief—it's disgusting! I'm fed up." His voice had become thin. "I thought you'd come to me. I expected that we . . . Mona's divorce will be final in another few months. You knew that. I thought we'd go to Europe for a while until you felt better, after that we'd make plans."

But she had stopped hearing. She might have been floating face down in water. There was only the decision, already made.

CHAPTER 4

THE morning had its share of surprises. First, the house. Because it was located in the Eighties near Fifth Avenue, Sylvie had assumed it would be an apartment, perhaps overlooking the park. She had never imagined this town house with its cool ultramodern façade.

The second surprise was the woman who answered the doorbell. Margo Kort was much younger than Sylvie expected, small, boyishly slender, uncertain, dressed in baggy jeans and pullover, her eager face framed by a wisp of bangs. When she introduced herself, she held out her hand and took Sylvie's in an energetic grip.

Walking up the stone steps a few moments before, Sylvie's heart had plummeted. She felt like Gretel at the edge of the wood peering into the shadows. Victor and she had made a truce of sorts that morning. She had skipped the pool and eaten the toast and poached egg he had made for breakfast. He had kissed her good-bye when their train pulled into Penn Station and said, "Well, anyway, call me and let me know if the folks at the manse approve."

Now Sylvie wanted to turn and run away from the house,

and the young woman who was talking with such strange earnestness.

"You're Mrs. Weyman? I'm really glad we could get together so quickly."

It was mid-morning. Sylvie had phoned the office to tell them she'd be late. Tania had answered the phone. "I'm wearing a vestlet," she reported mournfully.

The young woman walked ahead, up the stairs, chattering. Her slim hands flew about, punctuating her words. "Just to be brief, the job is five days a week, weekends off." (Good, Sylvie thought.) "You've seen our ad, so you know what we're interested in." They were on the parlor floor. A large black poodle was sprawled on the couch. Enormous, with eyes like two embers stuck in his woolly head. An electroperk bubbled on a side table, and Margo Kort immediately poured coffee. "Frankly, I'm getting a very positive first impression," she said, breathing deeply and smiling at Sylvie. She had grabbed the dog by the collar and pulled him gently to the floor. "Good boy, Zorro, go find your munchies." She looked up, her face bright and open. She had light brown hair, freckles sprinkled across her nose. One could imagine her living a frivolous life—rounds of lunch, shops, tennis—except for a nub of unexpected seriousness woven into her manner. "So far, the women who've contacted me were mostly Spanish-speaking. They seemed perfectly capable and all, but there was a communication problem. I have—well, really complicated requirements." She sat back. "Now if you could tell me something about yourself."

Sylvie drank quickly. The coffee might steady her, lift her. Or it might have the opposite effect—palpitations, a heightening of panic. She held the cup carefully. She had sunk into the couch and seemed to be falling farther into its claustrophobic depths.

"That couch is broken," Margo said. "If you're not comfortable . . ."

Sylvie sat up straighter. The worn furniture was at odds with the architectural impressiveness of the house. "I must have a place to swim in the early morning," she heard herself say. "It starts my day . . ."

"Oh? The aerobic effect, I suppose," Margo replied.

"Is there a pool nearby, or a health club?"

"A pool? Let's see . . . There's the Y not far from here, but I don't know how good the facilities are. Of course there are private health clubs all over the place." She looked at Sylvie. "It's that important, is it?" But Sylvie was thinking that any pool would do, even an oversized bathtub.

"I jog in the mornings when I have time," Margo Kort was saying. "It's not a *must*. A cup of strong coffee does the trick."

Too nervous to sit, Sylvie got up and moved around the room. The dog, leaning now against his mistress's knee, got to his feet and followed Sylvie. He put his muzzle in her hand; a slab of wet tongue explored her fingers. "Oh, Zorro, relax," the young woman said. "Here, wait . . ." She bent and poured some coffee into a saucer and set it before him. "Actually he freaks out on coffee. It puts him to sleep. Something to do with animal metabolism." Sylvie had a wild image of herself having coffee with the dog. She looked around. The living room was friendly but indecisive, like Margo. The furniture, a mixture of oriental and modern pieces, seemed to be a holdover from another life. Yet the house held fast to its vintage beauty, even though the old moldings and plaster friezes had been removed. Balls of light were reflected off several glass and metal surfaces and were buried in a softly tinted dhurrie rug, stained, it seemed, by something yellow. Finger paint? Urine? The floor was a mosaic of woods, worthy of being carved, framed, hung. A cloisonné oval held the portrait of a child. Yes, there was a child.

As if following her thought, the young woman said, "Jessica is six. She's in school now." Then she said, "I guess you'd take her afternoons to any of a half dozen places. There are so many things kids do these days. She has flute, drawing at the Junior Museum, karate—she can topple a child almost twice her weight. And there's her Little Chefs group. . . ."

She paused and shook her head. "Our freezer is packed with crazy malformed cupcakes." Her voice had a thick, happy quality. "She's really a great little person. If you don't mind my immodest ravings."

The child is precious to her, Sylvie thought, precious in a consciously felt way. She found the woman endearing, perhaps not so indecisive after all.

"Well, anyway, let me try to sketch out the job," Margo was saying. "Jessica in the afternoons. I've told you about that. I also have two fairly ancient parents. My mother is senile, arthritic, diabetic, the works. My father is merely partially blind and considerably deaf, otherwise OK." She spoke blithely, as if the right tone could lighten the facts. "We have sufficient nursing care, of course, but there are all the administrative details. Medicare forms, doctor's appointments, physiotherapy, sick-room supplies, fresh air on occasion. It's endless. You do drive a car?"

"Yes, I do." Private woman Friday. In another era, she would have been the maiden aunt, pecking at the crumbs of someone else's life.

"I think you could handle that end of things—my parents' requirements—maybe one or two mornings a week. Also, I'm opening an office in my house. I'll need help there, eventually. Clerical chores, if it all works out. At the moment it's a pretty loose plan. I hope I'm not overwhelming you." She tried to catch Sylvie's eye to establish something companionable between them. Smiled briefly. "It sounds more complicated than it is." But Sylvie chose to look away. She thought Margo's good nature floated too easily to the surface, possibly concealing something brittle and abrasive from view. It bothered Sylvie. Such a young woman to feel so pressed to keep a decent front on things.

Margo was saying, "Of course, you would sleep in Mondays through Fridays. Does that present a problem? If so, we can rearrange the hours somewhat; maybe do three or four nights a week and an occasional weekend. At night it's mostly baby-sitting. I'm afraid I take the business of baby-sitting very seriously." She lifted her palms as though offering hidden weaknesses for review. "These days—I don't know—I want someone thoroughly responsible around Jess at all times."

"That's all right, the part about living in," Sylvie said, thinking it was the whole point, after all, to be the stranger submerged in the everydayness of their affairs. She could imagine Victor groaning in the distance, his true feelings hidden behind a quip, "Oh, spare us, Saint Agnes of the hearth!"

"Do you have a family of your own?" Margo was asking. Her clear brown eyes held Sylvie's for a moment.

Sylvie sat down abruptly, stretched her legs—long slender legs in textured stockings—the legs that challenged Meryl Streep's, according to Victor. She said, ignoring the question, "I just want to be clear about one thing. I would have to be allowed to make my own decisions about the things I'm responsible for. I would hope executive initiative is expected, not subservience. I'm interested in your child, and your parents, and did you say you're starting a new career?"

Margo's eye's widened apprehensively, and then she said, "But of course. That's exactly the kind of arrangement I had in mind. That's what I expect to be paying for." She returned to her original question, "I would like to know something about *you*, why you—why you're here. You're obviously qualified for any number of more important things. Do you have a family? I suppose I'm asking, Why have you answered my ad?"

"I don't have a family," Sylvie said. "My husband is dead —that happened eight years ago."

"Children, then?"

"Children?" Sylvie's eyes felt very bright, as if shards of light had pierced her pupils. "No," she finally said, and waited for her lungs to fill. "It's just this. There's something comforting in the idea of being part of a family now. I'm at loose ends, and it was the perfect moment to read your ad and be attracted. Do you find that strange? You must have had someone like me in mind."

It was the right answer. Margo seemed pleased. A tint of pink flushed her cheeks. She had a scrubbed, mindful look—good bones, the body of a dancer, that kind of pliant thinness. And yes, so anxious to please. "We could moderate those sleep-in nights . . ." she had said. A good girl who would grow old trying to fulfill someone's prescription of being good.

"I think we'll get along," Margo said. She jumped to her feet. "Come, let me show you the rest of the house."

First, downstairs, the street floor, which held the kitchen and dining room. A sunny space filled with greenery. The kitchen atrium was a beautiful idea. Sylvie admired the cascades of hanging plants. There was something so jubilant here. A well-designed atrium could add twenty percent to the value of a dwelling, that she knew. One of her own clients had confided that the atrium saved her marriage. "It was easier to stay together than decide who gets the seventy-year-old dwarf conifer."

An asparagus plant, dry from direct sunlight, hung in the kitchen window of her own house. It seemed to have taken on the prevailing mood. She watered it as often as she could remember to, which was not often enough these days. Victor stirred the potted soil with a fork and sprinkled a blue fertilizer that looked like sugar crystals on top. He had said to her only recently, "If we have any luck with this reluctant thing, I'll make you a wreath of spider. You'll look like Athene, blooming at last after a long illness." Victor the romantic—so sweet and silly, so unexpectedly formal at times, stretched out on her couch in his houndstooth vest with one of his current movie-making tomes propped on his chest and a brandy in his hand. She wondered why he'd put up with her this long.

Margo was opening the refrigerator. "You could take your meals however you please. Just tell us what you like."

"I don't eat much. Mostly vegetables and fruit juice." She turned her eyes from those packed shelves.

They passed through the dining room with its long Palladian windows. An enormous modern abstraction in a blaze of color covered three-quarters of a wall, diminishing the room, squeezing out the light. Margo, following her glance, said, "Overpowering, I know. My husband, Michael, loves it, though. It's called 'Joseph's Coat,' and it would look great on a museum-size wall or inside an office building. It's the sort of work I'm moving toward: finding and selling decorative art for commercial spaces." Sylvie was thinking about this husband, Michael, with his taste for immensity.

There was a copy of the morning paper on the table. Bank robbery in Litchfield. Teenagers. A shoot-out, with politically inspired killings. A photograph of a girl in a ponytail stared from the front page. Sylvie paused to glance at it. Margo, watching her, said, "Can you imagine the way the mother of *that* young woman feels?" Sylvie could imagine. She imagined all too clearly. Parenthood's crooked road, the many stations of stress.

When Angel was sixteen, she was stricken with acute hepatitis. For six weeks it was touch and go. In bed each night, Sylvie clutched herself and prayed; but to whom? The force that makes apples fall? The Madonna in charge of young souls? Arthur had been dead for two years. She was like someone in an egg cup on a vast choppy sea. Afterward, during Angel's long, uncertain recovery, she felt that her child was being returned to her in exchange for fealty to some set of ideals of her own choosing. And in a fiercely obsessive way she tried to be more decent and disciplined. She dissolved relationships abruptly because they seemed shallow. She terminated a complicated love affair with Gordon, Angel's pediatrician, who had a wife and family of his own. "I will not cause grief to children," she told him quietly on the phone and refused to see him again. She could not get into bed at night unless she stood at the window and scratched the panes of glass several times with her right index finger for luck.

She had done free-lance library research for years, had

helped editors and writers find the reference materials they needed for their work. But with Angel convalescing, she wanted a reliable income. She switched directions and, aiming for a more practical course, enrolled in a program in real-estate management. The free-lance part of her life was reserved for odd hours. There was Angel, first and foremost.

Margo, looking grave, was saying, "Even blood ties don't matter these days, and it's frightening." She told Sylvie that her husband had returned from Rome last month and mentioned that the minister of state there had been stabbed in the eye with a Mont Blanc pen by his daughter, a college student, after a violent political disagreement. "It's like some sort of disease. Patricide. Matricide. You hear about everything these days." She stared down at the newspaper, a gust of worry crossing her face. Was she thinking of her own Jessica, grown-up, unreachable, lost? Sylvie wondered, moving out of the room away from Margo's unexpected inwardness.

"I was never an activist myself," Margo was saying, closing the glass-and-bronze dining-room doors behind them. "I was in high school during Vietnam and all that. A cheerleader, wouldn't you know?" She smiled apologetically. "I've always felt there was some deficiency in me that made those years seem so removed, sort of like a theorem in geometry that I'd never get to use. Wearing the scruffiest and most miserable Frye boots seemed more important than anything else. I have a friend, though, older than I am, who was drawn right into it, into all that campus turmoil, and it made a difference in his life for a while." Sylvie thought she heard a dropped beat as Margo mentioned this friend.

Margo seemed to be waiting for some equivalent bit of revelation. Sylvie chose silence. If Victor were here, it would be another matter. He had a cynic's view of history. Heroes and villains were not always so easy to distinguish, Margo might be interested to know, except for the few outstanding examples. These last weeks Victor had been hinting more and more about the film he intended to do. "Which is the stronger emotion," he'd asked, folding the cuffs of his Armani sweater, "compassion or revenge?" The film he was planning was not quite James Bond, he'd told her, but it had its moments.

Sylvie, on the other hand, took note of political happenings from a safe distance. Her father had been a lecturer in economics—the youngest member of the faculty—at the University of Budapest. In New York, deprived of social status and academic rank, at sea in the manic swell of New York life, without contacts, he was forced into unsuitable jobs—running a knitting machine in a stocking factory; pushing a rack across the jammed sidewalks of Seventh Avenue into Macy's stockroom. He was thirty-two years old; those were still the Depression years; his language skills were poor.

He had got rid of most of his books before he came to America. "Kicked them out of the house," he said. "If great ideas fail to persuade, what ever will?" Sylvie had come to feel that people who had experienced the impersonal cruelty of history, even at second hand, tended to be drained of idealism. She forgave herself for sitting in the park near Rosevale Harbor, reading *To the Lighthouse,* or *Herzog,* or *Everything That Rises Must Converge,* instead of carrying petitions door to door. Just sitting, soaked with pleasure, watching Angel play in the children's sand pit nearby.

Following Margo up the floating spiral stairway past the living-room floor and on to the bedroom level, she was thinking that idealism and cynicism were luxuries of civilization that surface only after the gross business of survival is attended to.

THE bedrooms were vast: large uncluttered areas, again apparently furnished as an afterthought. Bare floors, shades but no curtains, except in the master bedroom, which, despite its veneer dresser and bureau, had a beautiful old brass bed.

"A place to breathe deeply in," Sylvie said.

"Space does it," Margo answered cheerfully. "A large space with the fewest possible objects. The Michael rule! Michael and I haven't really gotten around to replacing and refurnishing yet. We haven't been here that long, barely two years. Frankly, this house needs to be tamed or it will rise and swallow us." She paused to look around. "Isn't the stairway amusing? It was Michael's idea. There are times walking down those stairs when I feel like an actress about to deliver some very false lines." She laughed, a small pensive sound, but Sylvie's temples were throbbing. Overall, it was such a static environment. There was nothing to fix on.

Then she saw there *was* something to fix on. Four large framed photographs hung in the hallway. They were of boats anchored offshore, decks and dock piled with cargo. Someone was obviously fond of waterfronts. Victor too loved the ocean, loved fishing. He had a photo of himself standing in a sprawl of flounder.

"My husband builds ports," Margo was saying. Builds ports? Sylvie wondered whether she'd heard correctly. It seemed such an overreaching specialty. Perhaps her own technological ignorance was at fault, she who marvelled at the wizardry of can openers. She glanced at Margo, who seemed suddenly smaller, more delicate, a tendril of hair curled around her ear. She had thrown open another door.

"But since all rules are meant to be broken," she said, "how about this?"

Jessica's bedroom. There was a ruffled canopy bed, white furniture with decals of Snow White scolding a pack of love-sick dwarfs, a rocker, and sitting in it, a life-size Ballou doll, tough and ugly, wearing a boa, ankle straps, rhinestone ear-rings.

"The neighborhood streetwalker. Every child should have one," Margo said. "Michael's idea of a joke."

Scrambled in the middle of the floor were crayons, books and a T-shirt with the message "I'm Daddy's Lollypop." A large wolf cutout from the Bronx Zoo hung on the wall, and on the dresser was a triptych of an infant in a silver frame. Jessica at the age of four months? Angel's baby would be about that age now. Her heart skipped a beat, and she leaned against the dresser. *Sean,* Gary had written on the birth certificate, a name that immediately conjured up green eyes,

freckles, the soul of a poet. Why had he chosen so Celtic a
name, she wondered? For a hero in the IRA, perhaps, someone who had starved himself to death on principle. By the
time she had had the emotional strength to deal with the
baby, even to walk a few steps in the Brattleboro air without
collapsing on Victor's arm, Angel's funeral was a week past,
and Gary had claimed his infant son at the hospital nursery
and disappeared.

"Feliciana hasn't gotten here yet, so this place is an unholy
mess," Margo observed.

"I don't think so," Sylvie said. "I would call it cheerful
chaos."

A look of gratitude touched Margo's face. "I think you like
children," she said. Sylvie thought the young woman was
going to reach toward her and squeeze her hand, but instead
she turned and moved ahead along the densely carpeted hall.
"Now this . . ." She opened the door of a room that faced the
small back garden. Sylvie saw a gray metal office desk, new
file cabinets, a painted floor. A wall of shelves held neat stacks
of magazines with names like *ContempoDesign, Graphics
Mode, Art Forum.* A charcoal drawing of a nude, so muted
and generalized it could have represented either sex, was
tacked to the wall. "I'm establishing an inventory, and organ-
izing a file of possible clients," Margo was saying. "Institutions are discovering it's not really more expensive to have
decent art on their walls than decorative junk." She spoke in
a quick burst of enthusiasm. "Anyway, you could help me
with dealer catalogues, putting together a file on the younger
painters, et cetera. Right?" She stood in the room and gave
it a quick approving glance.

"Looking through the Sunday real-estate pages for new
buildings would be a real help. Just *knowing* that Trump
Tower and AT&T were on the drawing board," Margo explained as they climbed a short flight of ordinary stairs.

"Well I *do* know something about the real-estate pages,"
Sylvie said, almost to herself. She would ask for a four-month
leave of absence, tell Louden it was urgent, a personal matter.

They had arrived at a half-landing; to the left was yet another bedroom and bath. Not quite the maid's quarters, Sylvie realized as she looked around. It was a square, decent-size space. One large window framed a new residential tower nearby. She recognized it as a Louden's listing. Expensive. Three hundred dollars and up per square foot. Margo partially lowered the shade.

There was a no-nonsense, utilitarian feeling here. Sylvie liked it. The double mattress was snug in its envelope of sheets and blankets; there was a mahogany bureau, a reclining chair with a reading lamp and a TV on a chrome swivel pedestal. A transplanted motel room; just right.

Margo sat on the bed. "Do you think you could be comfortable here? We might add another chair and some bookshelves."

"It's nice," Sylvie said. "And yes, bookshelves are always useful."

But she sensed problems in this house. There was something in Margo that was divided and unclear. If she was so consummate a mother, why this elaborate need for a stand-in? An unforgiving mood stirred in Sylvie. You can't have it all ways, she thought to herself. No one can.

Sylvie remembered she had almost never left Angel with hired help when she was little. Arthur worked for a small public-interest law firm in those years. His clients were people with low incomes. Sylvie had been proud of him, of what she perceived as the impassioned generosity of a man who cared. "Possibly a misplaced passion," her father had warned. "Possibly an engorged ego in its latent state." He stared at her over his spectacles. "Do you think Mrs. Socrates was so overjoyed at her husband's obsession with the public good?"

"Oh, God!" she'd exploded.

She had met Arthur at a wedding reception in a restaurant in Little Italy. The bride had been her closest friend at the city college to which they both commuted. Arthur played clarinet in the five-piece band, and during intermission he singled her out. He had just graduated from law school, he told her, pouring Chianti for them both. He intended to do important things. Work for people, not corporate institutions. Music was his hobby, but the law was his mistress, he said with an embarrassed grin. He spoke in an undertone, holding her hand lightly, his fingers twined with hers. When he took her home, they stood in the outer corridor of her apartment building and kissed and kissed. A few weeks later he asked her to marry him. She accepted almost immediately. She was so driven by her instinct to love, by mindless desire, so eager to step away from the European shadow of her family's life—from the heavily curtained windows that faced out on Riverside Drive, the fake oriental rugs, the antimacassars on the overstuffed sofa cushions, the crowded cabinets of glass and china picked up at a discount to represent the genteel life. Her father eventually found a part-time job teaching social studies at night at a small college in New Jersey. During the day he was a salesman of orthopedic shoes.

But the house leaked memory. Her mother, a woman grown pale as if the good rich blood of expectation had been drained from her, would say things like, "When you stop to think of it, in all of America there isn't a single castle." Sylvie intended to have her own castle.

MARGO was leaning toward her. "I wonder if you could tell me about your most recent job?" She asked it almost apologetically as if she'd overstepped a boundary. Sylvie sank into the reclining chair, wondering again why she was here. Whatever she'd hoped to gain suddenly seemed so ephemeral.

"These last few years," she said evenly, "I've worked at a large midtown real-estate firm finding homes for people. Before that I free-lanced. I did library research for writers and others. Sometimes I tugged at the facts slightly. Nobody ever complained. Even the truth benefits occasionally from a little careful embroidery." Sylvie paused. She was telling more than she should, throwing out a screen of trivia, a smoke screen behind which the subject that most needed talking about lay buried. She sat in her chair and held herself in. Margo was clearly fascinated.

"Oh, you may be bored with us, with what you'll be expected to do," she said, as though she could perceive a future in which Sylvie was becalmed and restless in the fold of their family life.

Sylvie shook her head. "I assume that the salary you'll be paying will overcome boredom." She looked around, decided that she liked the bareness of the room. She would insist on keeping it that way. No pictures, no rug, no distractions. An opaque shade at the window for nighttime privacy. No bric-a-brac, nothing to identify her one way or the other. Spare as a confessional. The image seemed right. She had become like a nun with all her disciplines, with the renunciation of desire.

Once, there had been so much. A hot, bright center that burned. Arthur lit the flame, then ran. After his death there was Gordon, with his antiseptic sweetness and unquenchable lust. They'd been happy for a while with their brief stolen trysts—Gordon, who had lasted nearly two years—until, with Angel so morbidly ill, she had eliminated him abruptly with a phone call. A sacrificial act. "You have the heart of a terrorist," he'd said when he understood. And then the long sexual solitude until Victor came along. The dear inquisitor.

"Do you think women with red hair and cat's eyes are as dangerous as they look?" he'd asked.

"Cat's eyes?"

"Well, yes, as a matter of fact. Your eyes do this funny thing—they glow in the dark."

The first time they had gone to bed together he covered her with his body as though sex were a nurturing process and he was the provider. Afterward he said, "This first time I wanted to be polite."

"However, just to get things clear," Margo was saying, "you won't be required to do housework. What I want is something else . . . administrative help, general household management. Jessica! This is a time in my own life . . . well, I'm sometimes really at a loss, these days." She had lifted her hand and now it fluttered quietly in her lap. "Things have a way of getting out of control. Of course, Jessica is the most important element in all of this, so I truly want someone responsible, and I think you're that person." Then, as if pulling at a loose thread, "Am I to understand that you're fed up with office life, and want a change?"

Sylvie hesitated. "Something like that."

"Well, look, that's good enough for me," Margo said. "I have really strong, positive vibes here. Can we say it's decided?" Her face, bright and encouraging, willed Sylvie to make an affirmative decision. "I have a feeling this is going to work out." Sylvie didn't know whether it would work out or not and didn't really care. She wanted to chance it for a while.

CHAPTER 5

Margo turned on the tape recorder, hoping to snare her mother's attention, but it was impossible. Celia's brain was tuning in and out, like a radio with dying batteries. Concentrate, Margo ordered silently. She was in her parents' apartment in Queens, in her mother's bedroom. Celia was in a wheelchair, Margo on an ottoman at her knee.

Blondell, who took her job seriously, had dressed Celia carefully, and braided her fine white hair with pink ribbon. It was no use; her mother looked like a ruined doll tilting sideways, her hands clawlike and petrified in her lap.

"What kind of oral history will this be, if you won't try to remember anything?" Margo said. "The last time I was here you told me about going to Coney Island on a trolley when you were seventeen and meeting a young man named Stanford. The one who turned out to be a dentist and brought you a satin garter with a diamond ring stitched on."

A feather stroke of worry touched Celia's face. "We must have been engaged, or he wouldn't have had the nerve," Celia finally said; but her memory was evaporating as she spoke, and she gazed aimlessly around, listening for sounds from the kitchen, sounds of Max and Blondell up to no good. As a young girl Margo had heard the story again and again. Even her father, Max, told it triumphantly. "The dentist's loss was my gain. Some bargain!"

The truth was, Stanford's mother made him call the whole thing off. She wasn't going to hand over a dentist with a fully equipped office to a little nobody without a dime. "He begged me to wait until he could figure things out," Celia said nostalgically through the years. But then Max came along, flamboyant and unsentimental. "I was ready to play my cards," Max explained. "How could she refuse a firm offer?"

Margo remembered hearing all this, in disbelief, as a child. Steeped in the romantic simplicities of fairy tales, she assumed love always found a way. And now these two were burdened with age, her mother by far the worse with her crippling arthritis, her drift on and off into senile dementia. The doctor had suggested an activity to engage her flickering attention. "Make her talk, tape it, let her listen to her own voice."

Did love ever find a way? Probably not. It seemed a sentimental notion, like "Truth will out" or "Every cloud has a silver lining." Michael wasn't sentimental. Firm in mind and body (as he saw himself), he cut a swath through the underbrush of their daily lives, making most of the family decisions. *Mea culpa,* she would remind herself when she felt overwhelmed by dismay, thinking about how it was *she* who *allowed* herself to be led. He was the one who had come up with the idea of advertising for a household assistant.

Michael was full of closely held opinions, including the notion that they should have only one child. "One really great kid we can fully concentrate on," he'd said, reaching for the fifty-pound weights in their bedroom, then mounting the stationary bike for his daily five-mile stint. Lately, she found herself pitted against him in a subtle, unspoken way. She ignored his money, couldn't bring herself to think about its meaning in their lives. On Madison Avenue she had recently seen a glorious bauble—a Chinese theatre, in porcelain and gold, meant to be hung on a wall. It cost five thousand dollars, and she thought with a start, I could buy that if I wanted to. I could just walk in and tell them to wrap it up. But that was not the direction in which she chose to go. She had quietly taken the first steps to set up her art business, and she had hired a household assistant, Sylvie Weyman. who had just started to work for them.

Thoughts of Michael brought on vagrant images of Brill. She had the sudden picture of Jessica and herself listening to him talk about wolves at the museum. That odd and funny man, she had thought, in his climbing boots and windbreaker, his spectacles pushed up and buried like owl's eyes in his thick hair. "They're really the flower kids of the animal kingdom," he told the audience, referring to the social organization of wolves; there were ripples of laughter. She had gone up to him afterward and asked him to repeat the lecture for the children at Pritchard, Jessica's school, and he agreed, amiably pulling down his specs so that he could see her more clearly, smiling, as if her suggestion was laced with humorous possibilities. That invitation was the first misstep, she supposed. If only, she thought, we carried invisible alarm systems sewn inside us like pacemakers, to send out warning beeps at the first sign of trouble.

He gave the talk at Pritchard, and afterward she and the Parent Association chairwoman invited him for coffee at a neighborhood café. At the last minute the other woman couldn't make it. She and Brill went on alone. He slipped into the booth, unzipped his windbreaker and said he would pass on coffee but have a beer. He spoke easily. He was a zoologist of sorts, he said. "Shared behavioral patterns in man and beast; that's my kick right now." He had a close-cropped curly beard glinting with threads of red and gold, and dark blue eyes refracted behind metal-frame spectacles. When he reached for the matches, his hand grazed hers, and she felt alerted in a disconcertingly pleasant way. He played with his cigarette case, then dropped it with deliberate care into his jacket pocket, holding his hand over it as though he were holding his heart. "No," he said staring at her so intently that a flood of warmth crawled up her neck. "I will be disciplined. Anyway, back to the subject, if you're interested. Are you?"

"In the similarities between wolves and men?"

"For the moment. You're a great-looking woman, you know. Nice. There's niceness in your face. I hope you don't mind this bit of species notation. Anyway, I think your children are lucky . . ."

"Child. One."

"Ah. I like what I suspect about you . . . concerned mom, thoughtful, empathetic. I bet you have a pet with a human name, like Wally or Celeste."

"Oh? What would that prove?"

"I don't know, something good. Tolerance, maybe. A yearning for human perfectibility transmitted to subhuman creatures." But he was smiling. "Wolves, by the way, are the most moral beings alive. They simply do *not* eat living creatures as a matter of course—if you'll forgive the pun. It places Red Riding Hood rather under a cloud."

"Well, that's a relief—in case I'm ever out at night on the Russian steppes," she said.

She visited him once at his office in the museum, to collect a few reference books for Jessica's school. And he came to her house once, after his Pritchard talk, to give her some additional material for a parent project on wolves. He brought a Bronx Zoo poster for Jess that time, and standing in her living room, looking around, he said, "So this is the way the *riche* live."

"Or the *nouveau*—which, for the record, we are."

Zorro, newly groomed, sniffed at his ankles. "And an elegant hound; what's he called?"

"A pet," she said without blinking.

He looked at her for a moment and burst out laughing. "I see."

A jade medallion—Michael had brought it home from Singapore last year—rested under a glass dome on the cocktail table. Brill made a globe of his hands and placed it on the glass.

"This looks edible, like an oversized Necco wafer, the kind I ate by the score as a kid."

He seemed ill at ease, and she realized she had probably immobilized him by inviting him to her house. "We can do better than Necco wafers . . ."

They had lunch down in the breakfast room. Feliciana had set out plates shaped like lettuce leaves, each piled with shrimp. "And your own private rain forest," he said, glancing around at the palms massed near the window and the giant dieffenbachia, whose leaves were like parasols. Pots of hanging spider plant grazed the tops of their heads. "Very nice." His glance touched Feliciana, who had paused to rearrange the serving spoons.

"Nice but recent," she said, relieved when Feliciana disappeared into the kitchen. "My husband did one thing really well, and the world made a track to his door." She was telling him more than he had any right to know.

Brill reached up to touch a plant that swung in a low arc above them. "Which one thing?"

"Oh, well, they're called offshore ports. Ports that float, or tunnel underwater. Unique conceptions for moving freight from ship to shore. The low-tech countries appreciated his ideas and fell to their knees."

"Ah, the low-tech countries." He pulled a spider from its stem and set it in his buttonhole. "Plenty of serving persons from the low-tech countries. This damn thing may make me sneeze." She disliked his condescending tone and wondered whether it was meant to equalize what he perceived as the economic distance between them.

But he was smiling at her, a friendly interested smile. "I lived in a greenhouse once, on and off, during my college years. Sneezed a lot in those days. I was in love with a botany major, and I used to visit her on campus. We'd just slip away with my sleeping bag and her hot plate for a day or two—when she had the greenhouse key and nobody was around."

"Sounds like *The Blue Lagoon.*"

"Not exactly. It was a leafy paradise, though. So warm and humid you could grow potatoes in your socks. But it was 1968 —remember?—and my love was making tin-can poppers and tallow incendiaries in the same little greenhouse. It was a passionate time, all right. An innocent math student working late one night in the science building was accidentally killed by one of those incendiaries. For me, it was the end of Eden."

"And after Eden?"

"The Peace Corps. Remember?"

Margo remembered. She had wanted to go on a nutrition teach-in to Ecuador with an American Friends group when she was in college. It was impossible. Celia was in one of her deep depressions, those prolonged episodes of despair that hung darkly over their family life. But even if she had been in a so-called normal phase, the answer would still have been no. To Celia even then, peril was everywhere—in innocent places like darkened movie houses, in sunny playgrounds, and always in the company of strangers. She had been forty-two when Margo was born, and she experienced motherhood as a trick. "I expected menopause, not a baby," she would sometimes say, looking like the injured party.

"I did a stopover in Africa," Brill continued. "Ended up for a while in Alaska, where I was introduced to *loup*. Wolf, to you. Did you know wolf pairs stay bonded for life?"

"Not really. Although I'm not surprised at loyalty in animals." She nudged Zorro, who was underneath the table, resting his head solidly on her toes.

Afterward, over coffee, he said, "We could move from wolves to something else. Rocks and stones. If you Pritchard moms are of a mind." He gestured at a few of the books he had brought. He was available, he said. He had a few specialties he was noted for. And then before she knew it, he was getting ready to leave. "Well, I have to get back to my beasts." He was standing at the door and scribbling his phone number on a card. "I'm not *always* available," he added, holding her hand between both of his as though it might flutter away.

He cleared his throat. "There is usually one perfect moment for almost anything, you know . . ."

HER mother had fallen to one side like a tip-toy, and Margo got up and resettled her. She placed both her hands on her mother's cheeks and stared into those glazed elliptical eyes. "Mother, where are you?" she murmured, a phrase echoing from her childhood. "Where are you? Come back!" as though her voice was magic and could draw Celia away from darkness and into light. She had been in a custodial relationship to Celia from adolescence on, going from doctor to doctor when Celia's depression settled in. Seeking and finding insulin therapy, electroshock, a whole warehouse of drugs, taken, tested, discarded. The depression would last a year or two, to be replaced by Celia's "normal" personality, argumentative, suspicious, always in a rage over Max's suspected shortcomings. "Without me he would have been a has-been before he even got started!" The drug lithium proved to be the final reprieve, eliminating the depression but leaving Celia with her suspicions intact and further distorted by the inroads of senility.

Fortunately now there was the necessary money to deal with all this. Michael had agreed to buy a new automated chair with levers, switches, buttons for every possible body adjustment. "If she wants to play canasta on her stomach, this chair will allow for it," the surgical supply salesman had said when he came to the apartment.

"I shit on canasta," Celia remarked to the startled man.

Last month it was a new electric bed, a stainless steel commode on swivel legs, a hoist with a web of straps and pulleys to move her from chair to bed, a traction frame hanging from the ceiling.

Her father slept in a little study next to the living room in his own electric bed, which he had conned the doctor into prescribing. He loved displaying mastery of the controls; he

pressed buttons, and the mattress rose as if filled with yeast.
"It's like being the captain of a dirigible," he said with a small
laugh.

Margo never asked herself why her parents were here and
not in a nursing home. The answer seemed clear. There were,
after all, moments when Celia, opening her hazy gray eyes,
found her surroundings real and recognizable; and Max was
able to shuffle around from room to room, cranky and demanding in his scarves and sweaters, riding his bed, his hear-
ing-aid dangling from his ear. But in his own home, he'd say,
banging his cane against the couch in a lordly way, calling
out for his glass of wine. "Blondell! Open the Asti Spu-
mante!"

She and Michael paid for all this—a thousand dollars a
week for nursing aides, equipment, doctors, medicines. It was
Michael, with his new-found and very legitimate wealth, who
made such extravagant home care possible. He would be
going to Brazil soon—a ten-day trip—and he wanted her to
go along. She felt the cold thud of apprehension without
knowing exactly why. If she said, "There's too much going
on at home right now," he wouldn't interfere; he never did.
He held to the democratic ideal of people being allowed to
fulfill their needs. A civil engineer, he had become the darling
of the shipping giants almost overnight. Contracts poured in
from Asia, from Europe, from South America. He had estab-
lished his own consulting company, and they had suddenly
found themselves with enough money to make her feel a
peculiar kind of dissolution, as if her old identity was evaporating before a new one could take shape. In a month or two
he would be going to Jidda. "Jidda!" she said, astonished,
when he told her. He spoke about a classy idea he had for
moving construction lumber. "Imagine a long umbilical cord,
a snakelike conveyor connecting ship to port. The ship stays
out in the harbor, no dockside jam-up . . ."

"But Saudi Arabia! Getting involved *there* seems so . . ."
Ideologically barren was what she wanted to say. When Max
wanted trees planted in Haifa, after the Munich massacre, she

had personally started a fund. There was a glade in Mt. Elath bearing her parents' names.

"Jesus H. Christ!" Michael had said, angrily. "Even the Israelis sell aeronautical parts to the Arab world!"

"So let me add more to the story." Her mother's eyes had opened wide, and she was looking at the tape recorder in Margo's lap. "When he said good-bye, it was, 'You are my true and only love.'"

Margo turned the tape on and tried to pay attention. "Well, you must have found Dad really attractive to have given up on Stanford so quickly."

"He wasn't too bad. Except he once killed a cat with his bare hands. A cat that used his shoes for a toilet."

"Max did that? Tell me more!" But Celia's attention was again filtering away; she stared at her hand, bunched around a therapeutic rubber ball.

Blondell came into the hallway and called out in her honeyed voice, "Anyone in there want anything?"

"Tea later," Margo called back.

"Bitch!" Celia muttered into her bib. She insisted, these days, that the nursing aides were really Max's girl friends.

"Prostitute bums," she ranted to Margo on the phone, the phone held to her ear by one of those very aides. "They take down their pants, he puts it in. Don't think I'm deaf and dumb."

Innocent Blondell. Short-tempered Jolene, who was always sneaking into the bathroom for another smoke. Gertrude, whose son wanted to be a rock star and who moved through the apartment dusting and vacuuming with a Sony Walkman dangling from her neck. The three of them rotated hours, always at the receiving end of Celia's addled rage.

Last week Jolene phoned Margo, bristling with indignation. "I'm a married woman with a good man. We Seventh Day Adventists, and not even allowed to *dance*!"

Margo consoled her. "You're a professional. You're not supposed to take anything she says personally." She gave all of them bonuses, holidays off, perfume, fur-lined gloves.

Now her mother was leaning forward, bird-bright eyes fixed on Margo's face. "I heard them again last night, the bed thumping . . ."

Margo, deciding to be literal, said to her mother, "But he's such an old man. *How?*"

"Don't ask me how! They do it with a little rubber hose and some wire. Do you think I'm a dummy?" Her mother shrieked and faded. It was eerie.

"Par for the course," the gerontologist had said. "These old girls can cook up some pretty hair-raising stuff once the repressive trigger goes." He doodled thoughtfully on a little pad. "And with her record. All those shock treatments, the drugs, her age, well, the confusion she's showing is no big surprise." There seemed to be nothing more to say. He prescribed Navane, which turned Celia into a drooling glassy-eyed wraith. Her delusions disappeared, but so did the last remnant of her personality. Max flushed the Navane down the toilet.

Margo could hear sounds of Blondell at the sink in the kitchen, peeling vegetables for dinner, her father's brittle voice grumbling that his afternoon milk had a funny taste; Blondell responding, her words punctuated by a laugh, or was it a sob? She ought to go to the kitchen to see. Lately, her father had said, Blondell was doing a lot of crying. He would find her in the living room or coming out of the bathroom, sniffling and wiping her eyes, the crying alternating with hysterical giggles. "I don't know what's going on," Max said, his squint magnified behind thick lenses. "These women are making me crazy." Maybe Blondell was in love. Brill floated through her mind again. Not as large as Michael, he had the rugged sunburned look of someone at ease with the outdoors. She imagined him crashing down the Colorado River in white water, his rubber raft rocketing over exposed rock, like a picture on an Outward Bound poster.

Her mother lifted her head and stared with dawning recognition at Margo. "You don't look well," she said, as if noticing her for the first time.

"I feel pretty good."

"Your hair is too short, it gives your face a monkey look."
Pure tone after so much static. Was her mother entering an
interval of clarity? But Celia immediately said, "Does *your*
husband run around with every little twit-ass he can find?"

"Oh, for heaven's sake, Mother!"

"Maybe you're one of the lucky ones." Margo braced herself for more obscenities, but Celia only asked, "How's Jessica?"

"Jess is fine. I'll bring her over next week to see you, if
you're OK." She let herself think about Jessica and Sylvie
Weyman. Were they at Peewee Karate? She felt uneasy. Jessica was tough, but still she'd urged Sylvie to be vigilant about
the size and weight of Jessica's opponents.

It had been only two days since Sylvie came to stay. Margo
still wondered about her. She seemed intelligent, the way she
looked their house over quietly, absorbing everything with
the smallest nod of her head—a graceful head, her hair
caught up and wound in a high tight knot—yet she had
offered so little of her private self, had deflected Margo's
questions with quiet, oblique answers. Some women were like
that, preserved an air of mystery. They'd fry an egg and make
it seem like a clue to something more. And were there truly
no children, or was she speaking metaphorically, the way
parents sometimes do out of a sense of betrayal?

Margo thought she would reserve judgment. There was
something about Sylvie that was, well, resonant. It might be
nice just having her around—an older woman, someone to
talk to in a confiding way, to develop a sympathetic friend-
ship with. Still Margo couldn't believe that Sylvie would stay
for any length of time. Already she was prepared to hear her
say, "This isn't really working out." But everyone was enti-
tled to a change of heart, to privacy, the kind of privacy that
doesn't require defense or explanation. She thought of Brill
again. He had given her the head of a wolf carved in soap-
stone. "Eskimos use it as a good luck charm. Keep it in your
purse," he said. At Christmas she had known him only four
weeks, and she didn't know what was happening to her or

how it had come about. Did she believe in magnetism, in
bodies randomly rushing together? What did she see in him?
Or for that matter, he in her? She was too small, too quiet,
too culturally stereotypic. She felt disturbingly unsure, at
risk. Her friend Alessa, forever involved in a new romance,
had said, "But darling, *risk* is as fundamental as air, as
earth."

Her mother was nodding off, and Margo put the tape
recorder in its case. She felt regret for the mythical Stanford,
who sat like unbudged rock in her mother's memory, flashing
signals in times of crisis: ". . . if you had only waited."

Margo started for the kitchen, and the ambiguous sounds
became clearer. Blondell was indeed crying. She was sobbing,
small choked sounds between heaving gasps of breath. Max
stood by, patting her shoulder, looking both bewildered and
desperate. "Well, what do you think?" he said to Margo. "All
this excitement and upset. Is this for a man of my years?"

Blondell lifted her tear-soaked face. "Oh, I am sorry. I am
so sorry to be causing you this bother. It just overcame me.
My trouble. It just ran away inside me." She got up and
rushed to the bathroom.

"What's all this about?" Margo asked. She felt a sinking
sensation. Blondell, the youngest, had been with her parents
for a year. She was a peaceful young person, good-humored
in spite of Celia's insults.

"I'll tell you what's going on right this minute, young
lady," Max said. "If you want the lowdown, here it is. She's
going to have a baby." He took a deep breath and clung to
the kitchen sink as if the impact of his words would make him
swoon. "The young man doesn't want to know from nothing.
Won't have any part of it. Claims there's no proof it's his
baby to begin with. That's the way young people are these
days. Like rabbits behind every bush and never mind the
consequences. Let Uncle Sam pick up the tab with the tax-
payers' money, the Medicaid, the abortion clinics. And she
doesn't have a dime for it. Came to me and said, 'Mr. Max,
what should I do?' I told her right off, 'Blondell, I'm ashamed

for you.' " He sat down in exhaustion, his eyes like tiny fogged lamps behind headlight-thick glasses. He had dug his earpiece into place, waiting for a response.

"I hope you weren't cruel," Margo said wearily. "Mother told me you once killed a cat."

"She'll say anything. Don't I know? She has it in for me because I'm not the long-lost lover, the fairy dentist. Have you got her story down on tape?" He wagged a finger, looking as though he, too, might burst into tears. "Remember, equal time. I want my day in court . . ."

Blondell came out of the bathroom with brimming eyes and sat on the couch. Margo tried to comfort her. The girl couldn't have been more than twenty-two. Her skin had an ochre gleam. With a camelia behind her ear she'd look like one of those airline ads that urge, "Come to Aruba, to Trinidad."

"What are you going to do, Blondell?" Margo asked.

"I just don't know what to say, Miss Margo."

"Well, do you have plans?"

"Are you saying do I think to keep what is inside me?" Her voice had thinned to a whisper. "My answer is yes, I believe I do. I don't know how else. I don't have it in my heart to do anything else."

"What about money? Won't the man—the father—help?"

"There is no man," Blondell said in a choked voice. "It was a mistake on my side to think there was."

Max had come into the room. "I promised her three hundred to tide her over. More when the baby is due." He leaned over and peered in Margo's face. "Did I do right?"

"Yes, you did right, but let's not mention any of this to Celia, please."

Blondell was sniffling into her handkerchief. "Oh, Miss Celia, she'll surely have the fits."

Max was laughing under his breath. "I'll tell you one thing. With the way your mother's head is now, she'll think I did it. I'm the snake in the grass."

"Well, anyway, just try to relax," Margo heard herself say

to Blondell. "Whatever you decide, we'll help as much as we can."

"Didn't I say she was true-blue," Max cried. "My little Margo. A prize. We waited long enough for her—into our middle years. But when she came, no disappointments." Still grinning, he went off into the kitchen, where he would read his large-print newspaper, studiously holding a magnifying glass over each letter, as though examining a gem for flaws.

Margo turned on the lamps and the room swam before her. Old-fashioned but not seedy. The arms of the worn couch bulged like a fat woman's thighs. There was tan wall-to-wall carpeting that had turned the color of mud, and a breakfront stuffed with tourist trinkets from Atlantic City and Lake George. There was a miniature stuffed grizzly from Yellowstone Park, an enamelled plate of the *Maid of the Mist* purchased at Niagara Falls, and a framed retirement plaque from La Brava Furs, where Max had worked for thirty years.

"True-blue," he had said. The burden of being the good girl had been loaded on her from day one. Max, boasting of her achievements: "A ninety-eight in algebra!" Celia's immoderation when her psyche was in its "up" mode: "That child . . . first in the spelling bee . . . I tell you, nothing but pleasure from her . . ." Hanging even now in the hallway was a crayon drawing of children at the seashore that she had done in the sixth grade.

Well, she didn't feel true-blue. She felt she was part of a hoax that would one day be revealed, and she looked forward to the revelation with perverse pleasure. It was Jessica who had made her know how truly human it was possible to be. But she would not go to Brazil. Michael would have to live with it. She would stay at home and get down to work. She thought of Brill, and again it was as if she had entered a tunnel where the air was close, the light bad. She was glad she couldn't summon up his face, which remained a floating composition of specks, his voice unformed. A perfect stranger. Not quite. She had slept with him once. Fled. Returned. Perhaps one day she would know Sylvie Weyman well enough to discuss these things with her. "Is it possible to fall from grace gracefully?"

Blondell, on her way to prepare dinner, said, "I am one grateful person, Miss Margo."

At that moment Celia came to life and called from the bedroom, "I'm sitting in something wet!" Blondell rushed to help her. "Keep your hands off me, prostitute!" Celia shrieked.

Blondell sang a hymn, her voice pouring over Celia in a stream of sweetness: "The lambs are one in the sight of the Lord . . ." She tried to use the hoist to lift Celia from the wheelchair to the commode, but Celia still in a dream rage, fought her off, screaming, "Don't touch me, filth!"

"The lambs nest 'neath the wing of . . . ," Blondell sang as she cranked the hoist.

In the struggle, Celia slipped from the canvas seat and fell to the carpeted floor. Blondell and Margo tried to lift her, but she was dead weight. The doorman, summoned, came to help.

"Jumpin' creeps," he muttered, reaching for her.

Seeing him, Celia cried out, "Are my private parts covered?"

Max, his earpiece dangling, had come, tapping his silver-headed cane, to the doorway. "What parts? Is there something I should know?"

"No! For God's sake," Margo cried, trying to keep the hysteria out of her voice. The doorman was helping Blondell drag Celia to the commode. "Please go away! Read your newspaper! Everything is under control!"

CHAPTER 6

SYLVIE'S first days in the house were strange. There were so many threads of activity spinning at once. She wondered if she could make herself care enough to function. Michael grasped her hand the evening of the day she arrived and held it firmly in his. "Glad to have you here, Mrs. Weyman. Hope you'll be comfortable." When he had returned from work, his vibrant basso calling out to Margo and Jessica filled the house. "Where are my women?" he boomed. Jessica leapt into his arms. Margo stood by and watched pensively. "I'm told we're a lovable crew," he said to Sylvie, staring down at her, beaming an open friendly grin. "Wild but lovable. Everything all right?"

"So far," she said.

He was a big man. All his movements were large. He ripped off his tie and jacket and dropped them on the chair. Feliciana ran to pick them up. He grabbed her arm. "Hey, stop that. I pick up my own trash." Sylvie liked him at once.

The place hummed. In the days that followed, Sylvie could see there was a great deal going on. Not all of it harmonious. Michael obviously travelled a lot. His conversational asides frequently had a global reference: in Qatar . . . in Goa . . . in Valdivia . . . He waved his hands for emphasis. Margo often seemed to be thinking of something else. She had long phone calls with her friend Alessa, who lived nearby but ran a picture gallery, weekends, in Woodstock. Alessa was helping Margo build up a folio of contacts. Sylvie overheard bits of conversation about corporate parameters for art, designer networks, noncontroversial subject matter, neo-objectivism in large public spaces. Margo's voice would drop to a murmur, wander off the subject.

There were frequent references to "him."

And then there was Jessica. Sylvie hadn't been prepared for Jessica. The obstinate standoffishness of a six-year-old. The personality, at once trusting and hypercritical, penetrating Sylvie's heaviness like a hook. "*My* mother puts on eyeliner and shadow when she goes out," Jessica said, examining Sylvie's face—no powder, a touch of lipstick—with disapproval.

And the insatiable curiosity, too, came as a surprise. Yet how could Sylvie have forgotten. "What makes tokens work, Mrs. Weyman?"

"Tokens are cut by one machine and made to fit into another machine, which activates a rotary gear system." She wondered if she had it right.

"Well, maybe." Jessica stood on one foot, biting her lip. They were coming home on the subway from the downtown Children's Book Fair. Jessica held a clutch of animal books in her arms. She was trying to decide which she wanted most for her next birthday, a pair of gerbils or a dog-training course for Zorro. "I want to say 'Sit' and make him do it," she said emphatically. "He's still a baby, you know, and pees on the carpet. It makes Daddy see stars."

The child had a small pert face and the brightest blue-green eyes. Dark hair caught in a rubber band hung down her back. The tip of her tongue pushed at the inside of her cheek when she asked a question or listened to a response.

"You're funny, Mrs. Weyman," she said when Sylvie told

her about the chameleon who fell dangerously in love with the color purple, thus making himself visible to his enemies, and about the toad who came to his rescue. "What happened when the toad got hungry?"

"He had a longing for purple chameleon pie but managed to control himself."

Victor called several times that first week, ignoring her admonition that *she'd* phone *him*; what she didn't want was the Korts speculating about her personal life.

"What are you doing?"

"Just quietly trying to stay afloat."

"That's a relief. I had this vision of you with a rag tied around your head and a scrub brush in hand. It made me want to laugh." She heard anxiety behind the banter. "You're not being molested, I hope."

"By whom? Jessica or the husband, Michael."

"You tell me."

"Neither. Although the dog worries me."

"Lucky beast. Be safe, darling." Then, "Are you managing?"

"I don't know. There's snow in my head most of the time. It's hard to think." She wanted to say, I'm dead weight. I'm sinking.

"Is there a pool nearby?"

"I suppose so."

"Well, swim. And try hard." His voice was completely serious now. "You know I care."

In those first days Sylvie often moved aimlessly through the house. Feliciana left at five or six. Dinner was usually prepared and waiting in the refrigerator for Margo to heat and serve. An odd household, Sylvie thought, remarking on the haphazard furnishings, the way the opportunities that wealth offered were ignored. Except for the stairway, which hung in midair like a mobile and must have cost a fortune.

Margo had suggested to Sylvie the things she ought to do, and Sylvie tried to comply. There were telephone calls to art galleries from a list that Margo had left. Cortelli's told her

they had some new work by a young Indian from Albuquerque. Huge blood-colored abstractions, still inexpen-
sive, they said. She jotted down notes for Margo. Then she
went through trade journals and magazines for additional
leads. Called a few interior designers whose specialty was
corporate decor.

She brought the checkbook up-to-date—the one that was
kept separately for Margo's parents. *That* whole arrangement was impressive. A mini nursing home in an apartment
in Queens. She had been right, she thought; Margo was a
good person, a good daughter. But Sylvie wondered about
her, about how she organized her days. She seemed willing
to give Sylvie the briefest instructions and then go her way.
In a while it would be time to pick up Jessica at school.

She passed through the kitchen to the dining room, where
an old-fashioned baker's rack faced the gigantic painting on
the opposite wall. A large bowl centered on one of the shelves
seemed to be filled with pebbles. But on closer inspection she
saw they were not pebbles at all but teeth. Animal teeth, she
guessed, in a variety of sizes and shapes. Some white, some
yellowed, spotted, discolored as though from nicotine. A
cigarette-smoking moose? Was this Michael's hobby, or
Margo's? Was it a joke? A fetish? When Michael grinned at
her from his tall, muscular height, his lips parted to reveal
white, squared-off teeth of his own. The teeth seemed sincere
enough. It was hard to put up a defense against a broad white
smile.

But since teeth were often symbols of strength and power,
she wondered what this bowlful on the baker's rack meant.
Was it Michael making some sort of statement? When she
was little, her Aunt Milla, her mother's youngest sister, had
had all her teeth pulled out over an unhappy love affair. "A
real Casanova," her mother had said. "He burned women
like kindling and swept up the ash." Milla needed to do
something terrible because she felt so full of blame, so worth-
less, her mother had added. She was only thirty-eight, but she
committed violence against her own mouth—"made the den-

tist go along because she screamed that her mouth ached day and night."

Sylvie remembered Milla walking around with that caved-in look and later with her new teeth, which clacked faintly when she spoke. Another person might have chosen a shorn head. Van Gogh had hacked away an ear. She, too, seemed to be in a rough contest with her own body. She had found a swimming pool at one of the East Side racquet clubs that opened early in the morning, and in a narrow marine-blue swimming lane did endless laps, making a paw of her hand and slamming the water, holding her breath, kicking, her heart bursting, until finally she ended in a long dead man's float.

Her minimal diet kept her light-headed. There was often a dazzle of light before her eyes. She enjoyed imagining her flesh melting, her bones glistening; she saw herself approaching, piercing, entering a tightly furled bud of revelation. She remembered being told about someone who said he wouldn't drink another cup of coffee until he mastered Rubik's cube. She understood that kind of obsession. Angel was dead. She clutched the dining-room table, frightened. The dining-room wall, as if made of foam rubber, seemed to bend toward her, and with it the huge painting, arched, bowlike. Nothing was safe, she suddenly thought. Certainly the child, Jessica, wasn't safe. Not with her. What was she doing in this house? She sank into a dining-room chair and waited for the feeling to pass, stared at the bowl of teeth. She wondered whether there were human teeth in that bowl. Jessica's first incisors, perhaps? Somewhere in the disorder of Sylvie's own bedroom, wrapped in surgical gauze and placed in a tiny velvet ring-box, was Angel's first eyetooth; it had been tucked under her pillow, for the tooth fairy, and magically replaced by Sylvie with a thimbleful of dimes.

She turned from the table and went into the kitchen. Leaning empty-headed against the refrigerator shelves, she spooned yoghurt into her mouth. She unscrewed the cap from the peanut butter used earlier for Jessica's lunch, spread some on a cracker, took a bite and then threw it away.

There were lots of odds and ends from the Orient scattered around the living room—elaborately filigreed ivory figurines, jade carvings, a Chinese garden stool. None of them provided a defined personality in this harum-scarum setup. It was a room that cried out for some stamp of identity. Near the fireplace there was a Barcelona chair, filled, she saw now, with Zorro's huge sprawling bulk. "Off!" she said to the dog, who lifted a long curly ear and stared up at her in friendly insolence. When viewed from behind, sitting in a chair, he looked like a small dark woman with a page-boy haircut.

Sylvie had seen body-building magazines lying around on the hall secretary. Arnold Schwarzenegger in the pose of the decathlon hero. Michael was already graying at the temples. And always somewhat formally dressed in good suits and colorfully coordinated shirts and ties, his shoes buffed to a mirror finish. "Natty," Victor would have said. But this time Victor would have been wrong. "Stylishly bewildered" would be more to the point for Michael, as though, not yet having found his "look," he fell back on certain clichés. In the early morning she could hear him pedalling on his stationary bike, the grinding rhythm of those wheels held steady for twenty minutes or more before slackening off. She could imagine him pumping away, glazed with sweat, the mini TV at his elbow, even before she slipped out of the house for her own trial by water.

Sylvie went upstairs and paused in Margo's study, wondering where Margo had gone that afternoon. There had been some mention of a visit to her parents. On her desk was a list of artists whose work was of interest. There was one young man whose name was underlined. Bob Fleet. He lived in Vermont, in Cozzens, not too great a distance from Brattleboro. Her vision blurred, and again she felt a lightness in her head, as though she were being deprived of oxygen. She had invested so much—she had imagined Angel would grow up to be independent and in firmer control of her life than Sylvie had ever been. Gary was the first surprise.

There had been other hints, however. Once, in Angel's early adolescence, she began to worry that she was adopted. She skipped classes, sat alone in the back of the study hall, refused to eat anything that had walked around on "feet." "Are you sure I'm really yours?" she asked.

"Baby, of course you're mine, Daddy's and mine. How could it be any other way?"

"Suzanne's adopted. She told me her parents went someplace and filled out an application, like for a car loan, and after a while they got Suzanne."

"That has nothing to do with us!" Sylvie said, wondering where this was coming from, this crack in Angel's absolute knowledge of who she was. Was it that Arthur was away so much?

SYLVIE checked again through the list on Margo's desk. Cozzens. She wondered how far it actually was from Brattleboro. How far was Brattleboro from the Yucatan? Gary had disappeared so totally. He and the baby. Sean, mythical child. She tried to imagine him. Elfin, delicate, like the infants in those English Peepside books that she had bought for Angel by the score. For an instant, Angel's infant face merged with his. Blond and rosy. Faintly almond eyes, a nose more cleanly defined than was typical of a new baby. Victor had only recently sent a photo of Gary to a tracing agency in Mexico City. No response as yet. Sylvie knew that Gary would never get in touch with her. He was too wounded and frightened, denounced by her implicitly, as though he were a murderer.

He'd met with Victor once, right after it happened, while Sylvie lay drugged and stupefied in her motel room. He threw his arms around Victor's neck, Victor told her later, and wept.

IT had turned colder outside, raw January weather, and she went into Jessica's room for an extra sweater. She would be picking Jess up at school in half an hour. The room was filled with white light, cloud puffs of curtains at the windows; pale blue shades with Muppet pulls brought the sky indoors. The whole colorful spillage on the shelves and carpet had a certain style.

It was the only room in the house that seemed to have found its true tone. A child's room, light, carefree. She straightened up some of the mess of dolls and games still on the floor. Got down on her hands and knees to find the missing parts of a jigsaw puzzle. Zorro, who had followed her, sat on the ABC rug, his furry tail thumping. And then, believing there was some sort of game in progress that included him, he bounded over and slathered her face with his tongue. She pushed him away, muttering, "Save your flattery," and suddenly found herself in tears. Angel's room in Rosevale floated before her. Dolls graduated according to size, games in tidy stacks, cubbyholes for everything. Angel would play seriously, her blond head tipped toward the project at hand, and afterward just as seriously return the toys to their places. Years later, Sylvie would wonder where it all went—the conscientiousness, the wish for order and system in things. But perhaps order and system, like beauty, were in the eye of the beholder. Perhaps they had been there all along in her life with Gary.

Walking out of the room she was aware, as always, of the Bronx Zoo poster on the wall—the head of a wolf, jaws open, fangs bared, yet somehow not menacing. The wolf, in fact, looked as though it was smiling. Was it wolves or the entire zoo that Jessica was drawn to? Perhaps Sylvie could take her on a pet-shop tour one of these afternoons, to those specialty shops around the city that feature unusual animals—civets, rhesus monkeys, mynah birds, rare lizards. Angel, whose interest in animals had included even lizards, once told Sylvie that the blood temperature of an iguana in winter could cool a glass of milk. Standing in Jessica's room, Sylvie felt the chill of the iguana's bloodstream in her own veins. Her teeth chattered with a deep subliminal cold.

"It was all so quick," Gary had sobbed to Victor. "Sud-

denly all of her so still . . ." The placenta tearing, gushing
. . . Sylvie stepped jaggedly out of the room, touching the door
frame to balance herself. She would be late.

JESSICA'S school was in the Sixties off Lexington Avenue, a
square brick structure that looked as though it might once
have been an iron foundry. Jessica was waiting on the front
steps with a group of children and a teacher's helper. She was
smaller than the others, daintier. Dainty despite loose-fitting
OshKosh engineer's pants turned up at the ankles, her little
feet in warm-up boots planted firmly in first position. A
tartan beret with a big pom-pom was perched on her long
brown hair.

"Jessica," Sylvie called. The child bounced down the steps
toward her. "Are you chilly? I brought another sweater." It
was Wednesday, flute day. But the instructor had called and
cancelled because she had the flu. They weren't due at Peewee
Karate until five. Perhaps she'd cancel that, too, and take the
child for a hot chocolate and then home.

"I'm never cold," Jessica was saying, as she stuffed the
extra sweater into her book bag. The other children were
getting into cars and minibuses and driving off. Some of the
older ones were walking down the street to the public bus
stop. "Well, sometimes my fingers get chilly. But then I bite
on them, or if Zorro is along, I stuff them into his mouth,"
she said, giggling. Sylvie wondered whether she was being
baited, didn't want to find out. She hoped to keep something
akin to professional distance between herself and this bright-
eyed child whose little face, even as they walked, had become
noncommittal.

They went in the direction of Central Park and turned
south. There was a doll fair at FAO Schwarz. They could do
that. The air was brisk, but the wind had died down.

"Are you sure you're not too cold to walk?" Sylvie asked.

"Walking's good for us," Jessica answered crisply. Again
Sylvie looked down to see if some sort of mimicry was in-

tended. But Jessica was adding, "I miss my flute lesson. I miss Mrs. Beerbohm."

"We'll go right home and you can practice."

"It's not the same. Last week she brought me a paper daffodil. She pinned it in my hair and let me wear it through the whole lesson."

Schwarz's looked crowded, and they continued on to Fifty-seventh Street and turned west. When they came abreast of Henri Bendel's windows, Jessica stopped to admire the life-size puppet people, gorgeously dressed, turning and bowing on invisible guide wires. She stood in front of the window, one mittened thumb in her mouth. "These are some *dolls!*" she breathed.

An idea was taking shape in Sylvie's mind. "Come with me," she said, pushing Jessica through the revolving doors.

Inside the store, they were caught in a shower of reflections bouncing off the glassy walls. "Look at me!" Jessica exclaimed, pointing to her accordion image in a mirrored column. "I'm a sparkly fan!" Merchandise was scattered around like minor treasures dropped by people who had more important things to think about. The ultimate boutique, Sylvie thought. Tania would have been in seventh heaven going from counter to counter here. Poor Tania. Sylvie had phoned her that morning. "Where are you?" Tania complained. "Why are you being so mysterious?"

"Don't make me explain again. I'm just calling to be sure I've left no loose ends. You can reach me weekends at home."

"Our own Zack is fit to be tied because of you."

"He'll survive, with profits intact. How about you, Tania, anything new?"

"You mean Larry? Nothing. We've met a couple of times for dinner. . . . Oh, everything is so lousy, Sylvie. It's Ends-ville for me."

"I'd like a Spanish shawl for Mrs. Beerbohm," Jessica was saying. Now that she was inside the store she was all business. "And a carved green wolf for my mother."

"Why green?"

"It's her good color. Daddy says her eyes are simpatico to green. Sim-pat-ico . . ." She paused, thinking of something else. "Mr. Wallace knows a lot about wolves. He's our friend and gives speeches about wolves at school."

Sylvie suddenly wondered about the zoo. Was it Margo's interest or Jessica's? But she said, "And a gift for your father?"

"Oh, him!" Jessica turned up her hands in frustration. "Maybe another model boat for his next birthday, or a pair of running-in-place shorts."

Sylvie was looking around for the cosmetics department. There had to be one. She remembered taking Angel, who had been thirteen at the time, to a Macy's branch near Rosevale. Passing the cosmetics section, Angel had said, "I'd love to shave off my eyebrows."

"What an awful thought. Why?"

"Do I have to know 'why' to everything?" she said, trying on a lipstick dark as fudge. "You always want reasons," she said years later about quitting school, about moving into the country, about Gary. "Sometimes things just *feel* right."

A salesperson dressed as though she were going to the theatre asked if she could help. "Cosmetics?" Sylvie inquired. She used cosmetics sparingly. A brown pencil to darken her brows, which only recently had begun to silver. A touch of lipstick to turn her from ghost to person. Her skin was fine-grained, still firm. She liked the pallor.

So did Victor. He had said, perhaps as recently as last week, "I like your marble look. In fact, I think Virginia Woolf might have worn that face." He had wrapped his arms around her, rubbed his cheek against hers.

"Cosmetics, yes, of course." The saleswoman pointed to a far wall.

Sylvie saw the pink archway and, taking Jessica's hand, moved toward it. We'll show you, Mrs. Beerbohm, she thought. But Sylvie didn't really know what propelled her. The room was a blur of pastels, the counters filled with expensive offerings by L'Oreal, Lauder, and foreign names she had never heard of—tissuey creams from Icarus of Sweden, a special offering from Madeline Mono. *Mono,* as in mononucleosis, she thought, skating drunkenly backward in time. It had been a virulent hepatitis, instead. Angel lay limp against the hospital pillow, the whites of her eyes the color of egg yolk. Sylvie's terror had been profound. Arthur was dead. Friends didn't help. When Angel recovered, she'd felt they'd somehow passed an extraordinary test and time now stretched limitlessly before them.

A young man leaned over the counter. "Hello, loves," he said cheerfully. "Madeline has a gift for you. Thirty dollars' worth of purchases will get you a complimentary makeup." He wore a frilled shirt over skin-tight pants; his kohl-stencilled eyes and lavender lips made his face seem like bisque. Sylvie thought he looked like the pictures she'd seen of Nijinsky in *Afternoon of a Faun.*

"Maybe," Sylvie found herself saying. "And what about my friend here?"

"Oh, this little doll? Touch her up a bit with peppermint rouge and she'll go for a fortune at FAO Schwarz."

A look of delight had spread over Jessica's face. "I could be in the doll fair!"

They sat on high stools with white bibs tied around their necks. The young man laid out long-handled palette brushes, tiny pots of tints, pastel powders. He flitted before them, smelling of some important fragrance. "Darlings, you're to be still as the Sphinx, both of you. Now first a foundation cream . . ." The effect was unreal. Perhaps it was the lighting.

Sylvie looked at her face, all the lines and shadows removed, as if she'd been reconceived at a younger, simpler time. Simultaneously Jessica, with her lip line erased by a white cream, was a baby clown in the works. Her eyes were stars; her hands jumped in her lap. Then a dusting of chrome rouge for both of them, a flare of deeper pink close to the hairline. "Now for the really serious nitty-gritty." Dew had collected in the corners of the young man's mouth. "The eyes. What effect would you like to achieve? Subdued or dramatic?" He asked this almost shyly, as though afraid of being too intrusive.

"Dramatic," Sylvie answered. "Yes, dramatic." Why bother at all unless the outcome was startling?

"Oh, bravo! And the child? Is she taking part in some sort of theatrical production?" Jessica sat wide-eyed on the stool, fake roses radiating from cheek to forehead. Sylvie gave her a detached and faintly conspiratorial look. "In a way . . ." she answered.

"Then we'll go dramatic," the young man said exuberantly, grabbing a hand mirror and examining his own exotic face. Three shades of eye shadow came next, one blending into the other and applied with scrupulous care. Sylvie's eyelid had begun to flutter involuntarily. "Steady now, darling. This won't hurt a bit." Then a waxy kohl pencil to make her eyes and Jessica's look as if they'd been drawn in charcoal. A smattering of something gold and sparkling, taking the shape of harlequin frames, flared up around their lids. "Ah, this looks so lovely on you both. It's called Arabian Light. Brings Scheherazade to mind, yes? And you know how successful *she* was." Finally lip gloss like pink butter, and they were done.

Outside, they walked quietly down Fifth Avenue, Sylvie carrying the small, splendidly shiny bag filled with facial stuff she would never wear. Although she might surprise Victor some night when he was in his movie-making mood. Slink down the stairs like Cher, like Dietrich in *The Blue Angel.* In previous centuries, women used chimney smudge to darken their eyes, wild-berry stain for their lips. Life was cheap. Mothers did not necessarily expect their infants to survive the first year, and so they must have mothered from an emotional distance. A plateau of withheld love.

Victor was brooding these days. He might find the kohl pencil amusing.

It was late afternoon, and the streets were crowded. People turned and looked back at them. Sylvie stared straight ahead and tightened her grip on Jessica's hand, glancing down from

time to time at the little painted face, its babyhood erased.
They looked like two hookers, one a miniature of the other,
strolling along after an afternoon's work. She hoped they
wouldn't meet Margo or Michael on the street.

Jessica giggled, whispered, "You do funny things, Mrs.
Weyman. I feel famous. Like a famous actress."

"You look a little bit famous," Sylvie said.

They passed a frozen-yogurt man, oddly misplaced in January, leaning over his wagon in a wool hat and windbreaker.

"Aren't you past your season?" Sylvie asked, realizing
suddenly that she hadn't been able to fit swimming into this
morning's activities or yesterday's. And today she'd done
everything backwards, taken Jessica to Bendel's instead of
Peewee Karate, and now they were walking downtown instead of up.

"There's no one season for frozen yogurt, lady, you know
that. Everyone loves it, summer, winter." He pressed two
scoops of raspberry into cones. "Here, you should live a
hundred years on this product, like the people in Azerbaid-
zhan."

A hundred years, when a hundred hours seemed more than
she could bear? "Eat carefully or you'll mess up the fancy
paint job," she said to Jessica, as they continued slowly down
the avenue.

But Jessica's tongue was making a trail around the cone.
Her lips slurped yogurt, and when she wiped them an una-
dorned smile appeared.

At Fifty-third Street, Jessica began to lag. Saint Thomas
Church was on the corner, with its apron of stone steps
fanning outward from the great bronze-studded doors. A
flock of pigeons paraded in search of food. Next to the railing
an old woman in sweaters and vests layered over her coat sat
eating a banana and whispering seriously to herself.

"Do you want to rest? Take a bus? Call a taxi?" Sylvie
asked Jessica. The child looked up, the sparkly upper part of
her face like a party mask. "Rest."

They sat together, eating their cones and watching the

crowds hurrying past. Now and then some passerby would do a double take, giving Sylvie an inkling of what they must look like. Middle-aged woman and child sitting on church steps as forlorn and eccentric as the bag lady nearby in her tattered clothes. The old woman turned and stared at them. Her gray hair hung in girlish braids. She held out a half-eaten banana. "There's good potassium in this thing. Vital for liver function."

Sylvie said, "No thanks. My liver's all right."

"Well, watch out for your gallbladder. There's a tricky devil." The woman fished in her bag and came up with a water-filled jar in which speckled objects like marbles floated. "My gallstones," she said. "They have magical properties. I rub the jar and sometimes things happen." She looked closely at Sylvie. "From the color of your face, I'd say your gallbladder is planning a big surprise for you."

"I hope not," Sylvie said. "Come along," she said to Jessica, starting to her feet. "We've got to get home and wash this stuff off before it becomes permanent."

Jessica had wormed her hand into Sylvie's. "I bet your gallstones have magical properties too," she said, in a puffy little burst of confidence.

CHAPTER 7

BRILL'S apartment was on the seventh floor of an old brick building on the Upper West Side; it was in a lively neighborhood. Falafel, X-rated videotapes, McEnroe tennis shoes were sold in nearby shops. A Japanese restaurant promised "serious" delicacies. Margo loved the vitality in this part of town. She would have preferred the lighthearted bustle of an apartment here to their brownstone.

When she had first visited Brill here—was it six, no, seven weeks ago—she had felt a peculiar sense of adventure. He had called and asked if he could return her hospitality. Would she meet him for lunch at a little Indian place he knew? With barely a skipped beat, she agreed. The restaurant was under the Fifty-ninth Street bridge, that grim span leading to Queens, to Celia and Max, Blondell, Jolene and Gertrude. It was the day she had heard about Max planting an avocado pit in his urinal, and Celia screaming from her wheelchair, "Now you're growing flowers for the whores." Jolene had threatened yet once more to quit. Gertrude wanted to borrow eight hundred dollars for urgent private business. And Blondell had begun her fits of weeping. Margo willed them all into oblivion.

Seated, she said to Brill, "I was wondering. Why not gather some simpler, less threatening wolf fables for the younger children? What do you think?"

"Ah yes, the younger children," he said. He was wearing a down vest, khaki work pants, boots. He looked like someone you might meet on a mountain trail, someone who lived on leaves, nuts, berries. He ordered the tandoori special with flat bread for them both, and then proceeded to shred the bread to splinters on his plate. She guessed he was acting out the same turmoil she felt.

She sipped her wine, conscious of the look of appraisal in his eyes. Her voice sounded a bit gravelly when she said, "And something slightly more sophisticated for the older students. I'm told it's stylish to dig *Beowulf* these days."

"Right, *Beowulf.* And maybe the good beast Grendel." There was a flicker of a smile in the corners of his mouth. "You sound very conscientious."

"Unconscientious, if you knew me better . . ."

Brill spoke slowly, "I'm going to suggest that we go back to my place." He had piled the splinters of bread into a mound on his plate.

She answered with equal care. "Look, just to set things straight, I don't need or want complications. My husband's ego is huge. And you see, I have this dependency . . ." An image of Michael when she first met him drifted across her mind. She saw him materializing from a landscape of striped umbrellas at Jones Beach. She had twisted her ankle running. He wrapped her foot in ice from his Igloo chest, unscrewed a thermos and poured stingers for them both. "I'm Michael Kort," he said, as though merely announcing his name settled everything. He had taken charge. It was reassuring. He had taken charge ever since.

"We can probably avoid complications," Brill said, looking out of the window at the snake of cars on the bridge. "If we're lucky. If it matters."

"Of course it matters."

"Well, anyway, you might like to see my digs. Just seeing

where a person lives is a kind of intimacy. I've already seen yours."

"Mine?"

"Your house. It's very nice, although not quite you, I suspect. I mean, all the oriental stuff. It's as though you're the custodian of a public trust or something. Where is the modern? The eclectic? Someone like Georgia O'Keeffe? Or Marisol? Or am I off limits?"

"Pretty much, now that you mention it." She hadn't been sure whether he was teasing or criticizing, but she was certain that she didn't like either. "We haven't done much with the house yet," she said stiffly.

"Don't be annoyed," he replied, leaning toward her. "This banter is all wrong. I really feel quite serious about knowing you. If it's not too much of a hassle. For you, I mean."

Riding with him to his floor that day, she was aware of the docile way she had allowed herself to be led. She had never been drawn to quick flirtatious thrills, unlike Alessa, who lived on that kind of high. Still she found herself silently repeating again and again the word *easy, easy,* as though it were a mantra.

"Stark but decent," Brill said as he flung open the door. She had a moment of surprise. She didn't know what she'd expected. She was in a single large room, ablaze with light. The blinds had been pulled to the top of the window frames. A dog rushed toward them, growling. "Spunk!" Brill called out sharply. "Hey, baby, cool it. This is not the hamburger thief." The dog looked like a mixture of Irish wolfhound and German shepherd; he stopped in his tracks, baring two rows of white picket teeth. For an instant she appreciated Zorro's benign worship.

Brill lowered the blinds slightly, and the room snapped into focus—a sun-washed cave. Hair rugs like touselled wigs were strewn around. There was a vast blown-up color photograph of El Capitan, snow-capped and dazzling, rising from the valley floor of Yosemite. There were stuffed replicas of arctic families, wolves, grizzlies, giant-tusked walrus. Eskimos in furry hoods were grouped on tabletops. A poster of a pocked western landscape, surreal as the moon, hung above the fireplace. THERE ARE NO BADLANDS, the cautionary legend said. On one side of the room was a glass-fronted case with shelves on which minerals were displayed—emerald skyscrapers, melon-shaped rocks sliced open to reveal clusters of amethyst crystals clinging like marine life to a reef—each with a description on a small white card.

"I like your place. Nothing is left to the imagination," she said. The couch was earth-color, strewn with issues of *American Zoologist, Sierra News, Wildlife* bulletins.

"Is that supposed to be a compliment?"

"I think so." She made a place for herself, sat down and picked up a magazine. Spunk quivered, his lips pulled back.

"Turn it off, fella!" Brill called sharply. "My bodyguard and sidekick," he said, pulling the tips of the dog's ears. "If I didn't own him, I'd probably hire him." He bent and stroked the dog, who growled in a more temperate key. "I have this habit of prowling the less fortunate neighborhoods in the Bronx, yoked to Spunk." He explained he did volunteer work for a community services organization. "Sociological indenture of sorts, like in the old Peace Corps." He said it was his attempt to tame the wolves on those very mean streets, show them how to get their bread from the Feds. "Nevertheless, I'm not exactly considered the apostle of Southern Boulevard," he added. "Ergo, Spunk."

"Sounds like a busy life," she said. "Zoo, museum, community service . . ."

"I like feeling breathless."

"I think I do too." He seemed to be gauging her reaction out of the corner of his eye. He took a few quick strides to the kitchen alcove and brought back beer. Kirin, she noted. A brand Michael favored. Brill moved swiftly. He had the body of a dancer or an acrobat, that sort of restlessness. His hands were constantly in motion.

He offered her a bowl of raw cashews, which he proceeded to eat in nervous handfuls. She wandered over to a wall of

books, ran her fingers idly along the bindings, pulled out
Wolves and People and saw pictures of wolf families, as con-
ventionally grouped as figures in an old-fashioned tintype.
She turned a page, and there was a photograph of a wolf boy.
"Mythology?" she asked

"Probably. I'll tell you . . ." He described Gault, child of
wolves, who'd arrived out of the wilderness one day in a small
town in Albania, naked and speechless. Brill had an air of
authority as he spoke. He lit his pipe. There were so many
points of light in his face. The fractured light of his eyes
behind glass, the curly gilded threads in his dark beard. The
sun made rosy pools on the floor and walls. The couch was
sunk in light. It was a room that hid nothing. Inquisitors
could grill their victims in such a room.

She ought to leave, she thought. Instead she said, "People
have always done that, looked for the anthropomorphic connection, the magic fix. Historically it goes all the way back,
doesn't it? You know, talking fish, frogs, bears who have
superhuman powers. Helpless in the universe, that's what it's
always been about. Don't you think?"

"Are you?"

"Am I what?"

"Helpless in the universe. I know I feel it—my own insig-
nificance. Sometimes at the zoo, among certain animals, I get
this picture of myself . . . only a tiny spark of human intellect
separating us. Me from them. It's humbling."

She ignored this, steering him back to Gault, as though
everything he said was dangerous. "I think the children will
be enthralled. Is there a happy ending?"

He seemed to be coming from some interior distance but
finally he said, "Actually, no. I think the poor lad was stoned
by the townspeople, who believed he was an evil spirit in
flight from darkness, which, to them, was the same as hell.
But never mind. We could give it a happy ending. We'll have
him washed, clothed, taught to speak and read and forced to
make weekly visits, carrying baskets of food, to his wolf
mother in the forest." He reached out and covered her hand
with his.

"Yes, the loyalty of wolves. It fits the model you told the kids about," she said, quickly starting to gather her things. "No orphans among wolves, you said. It was touching. Touched Jessica." But it was Margo who had been touched by the simple kindness and gentleness he expressed as he reminded his young audience of the dignity in nature. "Jessica said the wolf in Red Riding Hood was probably a crazy and belonged in a wolf jail," she added, snapping and unsnapping her shoulder pouch. She couldn't bring herself to meet his gaze. "Well, anyway, now that I've seen your place . . ."

Spunk got to his feet and stared. His parted lips revealed those razor-sharp incisors.

"I think your dog has decided I'm not his type."

"His bad luck." Brill had gotten up too, and stood in front of her, one hand on her arm.

She forced herself to look at him and said, "May I borrow your book, just for a few days? I'll send it back."

He said, "No rush." She didn't know whether he meant the book or her on the way to the door. But then his hand was on her chin, and he was tipping her face toward him, his mouth on hers, and she went momentarily blank. Just a long inverted gasp, a balloon of air trembling between them. She'd forgotten to breathe. He seemed so strange and new with the sturdy bulk of him so close. She realized he was only a few inches taller than she. Medium-size but strong. She felt herself sinking; Brill's breath and breathing fogged her brain. She thought, I've never been good or honest in my life. She thought, Now I *will* leave. Too late. There was the business with clothing. "Here, I'll do that." He was tugging at snaps and fastenings; his mouth returned to hers. She had a glimpse of Spunk's outraged eyes, of Brill levitating toward her. There was the magnified landscape of his face close up, the pits and gulleys; his nose too large compared to the finely chiselled chin; the glinting frizz of his beard. And then his hand on her inner thigh. Just the pressure of his thumb was enough. She was gone, thrashing in her own pool of warmth like some dazzled bit of marine life.

Afterward, she went into the bathroom and threw water on her face. His terry robe was hanging on a hook, and she patted herself dry with that. His terry robe. His soap. She held the soap to her nose, breathing its flat resinous scent like a victim of a street accident who needs to be revived. In the living room she started to dress, her sweater nearly over her head, but she wasn't quick enough. "Not yet," he said drawing her back to the couch.

"We can't do this," she breathed. Such hollow protestation. But he seemed not to have heard. His hands spanned a frail compass of ribs; she shivered beneath his touch as though ice cubes were sliding down her spine.

WHAT had life been like before Brill, she wondered now, entering his building and taking the elevator up. Comfortable, untroubled. If there were intimations of discontent in her, she smoothed them away by concentrating on her small family constellation. (She was not like Alessa, thank God, who pursued "exhilaration" as if it were another art form.) She adored Jessica. Believed herself in love with Michael. Paid attention to the terrible concerns of her parents. She'd certainly get high marks for domestic servitude. But Brill was like a reward. In her secret heart she believed she deserved him. Deserved him for now—this new and private delight. He made love to her as if she were rare. He made her feel *unearthed*. She didn't allow herself to dwell on possible grim scenarios in the future. What if Michael found out? Or if Brill wanted more, or possibly less of her. For the moment she seemed to be in control. She had Sylvie Weyman to give her the additional freedom that she needed. Michael, frantic with his own plans, had never been more satisfied with his life. Her parents were in a holding pattern. So why this uneasiness, this gathering sense of dread?

When she rang the bell, Brill flung open the door and swept her toward him. Spunk merely growled. "You took forever," he grumbled in her ear. "How come your new household help doesn't leave you free as a breeze?" She saw that he'd brewed herb tea for her. There was an unopened bottle of Kirin for himself. Spunk had done a belly-crawl back to his lair behind the couch.

"I was in SoHo. There's a young artist whose work I wanted to see."

"I hope he had horns and a foul breath . . ." He lifted her hand, entwining his fingers in hers, and kissed her knuckles one by one. "Well, so much for civilized social discourse." He nudged her toward the bedroom. Undressed, he seemed something else: unexpectedly vulnerable, in a primal way, perhaps because of the furred nap on his shoulders and chest, soft and glinting like the down on a very young calf. When he reached for her, she felt silvery; she floated in a suspension lighter than air. They made love ferociously. He said, "Every time I see you, I don't know . . . it's like I've been stuck on a raft in the middle of the ocean, waiting. . . ." She smiled at that. They lay in a steamy tangle. She felt as if she had been scraped to a fine finish. She imagined her bones gleamed. Alessa would say she'd been very adequately fucked. When they returned to the living room he poured her tea, patting the couch beside him.

"Come sit," he said. "I missed you." He had put on his pants, but his chest was bare. She had replaced her sweater and skirt but not her shoes and stockings. He pushed some papers to the floor. She saw it was his most recent request for a foundation grant. He used his time as he pleased. Had an office at the Museum of Natural History, another at the Bronx Zoo. He had just finished a paper on the wolf in captivity. The mating fervor remains remarkably undiminished, Brill said, when you consider that wolves can feel a kind of sadness akin to the depression found in dogs. Except for Zorro, she thought, who seemed to operate on a perpetual canine high.

Brill bent, kissed, then licked her toe.

"I can't bear that."

"But these are nice. I'm a toe man. Wolves go for ears. If

you see one wolf chewing another's ear, you can be damn sure he's making an important statement."

"Is your fondness for my toe an important statement?"

"Yes." He swallowed his beer and gave her a lengthy serious look. "I want you to go away with me," he said slowly. "Not this minute, but soon."

Her stomach did a swift free fall. "It won't work," she said quickly.

"Think about it," he persisted. "I've been asked to set up a study in Montana. Coyotes. A small group associated with the university there wants me to get the project off the ground."

She leaned over and wound her arms around his neck. "I can't just leave."

"Sure you can. As I understand it, you can be scouting that part of the West for a couple of weeks, looking for talent."

"A couple of weeks!" She sank back against the couch. "Brill, I'm not able to allow for even one night." It was true. She'd seen Brill only on those few afternoons, sandwiched between his work at the museum and at the zoo. They had never been together overnight.

"I don't understand," he said, looking annoyed. "You have this admirable woman working for you who should be able to take over. Your husband ought to be tolerant—he's away so much himself. Tell him it's business. Part of it will be."

"*Probably* admirable woman." She was speaking almost to herself. There was something so elusive about Sylvie, a pale signal light flashing. The way she left the house for the pool each morning punctually at seven with her carry-all, like a doctor making house calls, and returned by eight-thirty to get Jess ready for school. Quietly preoccupied, her face like porcelain. "I don't really know her yet. I almost feel a little intimidated." Jessica had mischievously pulled a comb from Sylvie's hair that morning, and Margo witnessed a shoulder-length fall of coppery gold framing that whittled face. Sylvie had been, still was, a beautiful woman who seemed indifferent to her own physicality. She had bent and rewound her hair and replaced the comb. "Please don't do that again," she said firmly to Jessica.

"Maybe you're picking up some valid reason to be intimidated. Go with your instincts. Get rid of her," Brill suggested.

"That's taking it too far. She's interesting. I'd like to know her better. And besides, my household's so complicated . . . and you're part of the complication." He had a grouchy, rumpled look. She reached up and tried to soften his chin with a kiss. "Give me time," she sighed.

He was staring into the flush of sun at the window as if gathering illumination into him. And indeed he glowed. He held her close. She tried to relax but felt threatened by some obscure convergence of things. The doctor had told her that Celia's low blood count would require a bone-marrow test. Michael was going off to Brazil without her and afterward to Jidda. "Jidda," he had said, baring his teeth. "Think of me in a burnoose, gathering a harem of my own." Sylvie Weyman perversely kept her personality under wraps. And now Brill was withdrawn and hurt because she didn't leap to his notion of flight. Her life seemed strange and unwieldy.

She turned his head toward hers and kissed him once again. "I will think seriously about everything," she promised.

CHAPTER 8

S HE had been at the Korts' for five weeks when Victor
announced one weekend that they were going to drive
out on Long Island in the early morning for a walk on the
beach.

"In winter? Victor, I can't handle it." She was at low ebb,
carrying out her duties at the Korts' as if it were all a dream.
Even her recent life at Louden's seemed befogged. When
Tania called her the previous weekend and spoke about snag-
ging a buyer for a forty-acre farm in western Connecticut
after only a ten-minute phone call, Sylvie had asked vaguely,
"Is that good?" There was an instant of amazed silence,
before Tania had said, "Sylvie, are you on dope?"

But Victor prevailed. He arrived at the Korts' on Friday
evening, rang the bell, then sat in the car and waited.

Jessica escorted Sylvie to the door, holding a package mes-
sily wrapped in white tissue paper behind her. In the doorway, she yelled, "Surprise!" and stuffed the package into
Sylvie's hands. Unwrapping it, Sylvie found a pair of red felt
earmuffs attached to a metal clip, with gummy bits of sequin
and ribbon pasted on them.

"I made these for you in crafts," Jessica said.

"They're lovely. But shouldn't they be for your mother?" Sylvie asked. She was determined not to become entangled in this child's affections.

"Nope. When it's cold, she wears a hat with tassels. These are all yours."

Victor, waiting at the curb, flung open the car door and pulled her toward him. It was cold and he smelled winey and fresh. He was wearing a dark beret tipped over his forehead and he had a certain look, European, like her father's but without the bitter rind. "Are you all right?" he asked.

"I'm working on it . . ." She held the earmuffs in her hand and looked at them, trying to block out the memory of Jessica's small, trilling voice. She wondered whether she had enough presence of mind to continue with this job, whether she was even minimally reliable. The other evening she had drawn a bath for Jessica and then forgotten about her, until the child appeared at her door in pajamas with straggly wet hair complaining, "We were supposed to finish *Charlotte's Web* tonight!"

Victor was saying, "I missed you."

"What's to miss?" she said, feeling that she was too much to be borne.

They had dinner at home. Victor had prepared everything the night before. Bisque with fennel, baked sole, fresh strawberries.

"I may be sick," she said apologetically, looking at the food, the table set with linen place mats and wine glasses.

"Give it a chance," Victor said. "Eat lightly, in small amounts. You'll feel better, believe me. Think of food as medicine, as a form of antidepressant. It's very effective." Yes, she thought. She remembered hearing Balanchine on TV describe how he sometimes cooked Russian delicacies for Stravinsky just to keep him in a beautiful mood.

Victor paused to let his words sink in. "And the same holds true, you know, for wind and sea. It has to do with oxygen to the brain . . ." Again, he mentioned his plan for an early morning walk on the beach.

"Must we . . . ?" She looked around. Her house was orderly, dusted, swept. The armoire rose like a battlement against the dining-room wall, its glass front revealing numerous shining objects inside—wedding gifts from a former age, the little glass animals Angel collected as a child. Sylvie sipped the bisque and asked quietly, "Have you moved in, by chance?" But of course his clothes and general presence had been there all along.

"It seemed sensible," Victor said. "Put the papers out. Take in the milk. You don't want your house to look abandoned."

In bed that night, he moved against her. His breath warmed her neck. She felt his lips on her spine. "It's years between weekends," he murmured. "How long will all this go on?" She turned back to him and drew his arm across her shoulders.

"Let's sleep late tomorrow, please."

"Let's imagine we're sleeping late."

THEY drove out on the expressway in the early morning, past the turnoffs to Seaford and Amityville, past Brightwater and Bay Shore. Sylvie, bewildered, said, "I thought you had Jones Beach in mind, or Babylon."

"Oh, we might as well go the limit," Victor said. He seemed secretly pleased. "You can't compare Montauk in winter to anything else."

"Montauk!"

"Why not? Let's do the thing right. It's only another hour or so in the car."

When they picked up the Montauk Highway, the light gave an opalescent sheen to the landscape. Bright green potato fields planted with winter rye sparkled emerald in the distance. Victor had taken his Minolta, and from time to time he stopped and snapped photographs through the open window of the car—a farmhouse framed in marsh grass with a pickup truck standing in front, motels closed for the winter, a house with a shrouded boat on a trailer in the driveway. The sun had risen, burning away strands of vapor, but it was cold. Gusts of wind scudded against the car, rattling the windows.

Prodded into wakefulness by the elements, she felt strands of anxiety being plaited and tied inside her, and she thought how tenuous everyone's connection to life is. If Angel had even *once* considered the possibility of her own mortality . . . But even if she *had,* she probably would have said, "Who, me?"

When they passed Shinnecock, Sylvie sat up and looked around. "This is insanity, Victor—driving all this distance just to walk."

He didn't answer. "I'll pose a problem," he said at last. "It will pass the time—is it possible to forgive someone who condones murder, even the murder of children?"

It was an effort for her to listen. Her attention was drawn to the smell of salt in the air and the cold—a fizzy cold like dry ice. What on earth was he talking about? The murder of children? "You sound a little bit like my father," she sighed, "the way he used to leave everyone speechless with his . . . his rhetorical wanderings." She took a series of shallow breaths and tried to concentrate, but she was thinking of another time, and she could hear Angel's laughter, and Victor's, and her own. It was the summer before last; Angel was down from Vermont, alone, for the weekend, and the three of them had driven out to the end of Long Island for the day. There was a sweet giddy mood in the air. Victor turned off the highway. "We'll rent a boat and try for some fluke," he said.

Angel said, "I'd rather try for the real thing."

Victor reached over and pulled her hair. Sylvie laughed aloud. It was a hot day, and the sunstruck waters of Peconic Bay were a deep metallic blue. They fished for a while with no luck. "Nothing's biting," Sylvie said. Victor bent and took her hand in his teeth.

"Aha, the piranha strikes," Angel cried, and the three of them doubled over with laughter, rocking the boat.

"This levity must stop," Victor said sternly. Just then a gust of wind lifted his hat from his head and sailed it overboard. And they collapsed in a spasm of aching howls. Everything seemed so hilarious.

Now Victor was saying, "Well, all right, not *forgive* so much as view differently, on a wider personal screen. *Panavision,* where everything is so attenuated you imagine seeing through to the other side. How about that?" He reached out and placed a gloved hand on her knee, but she could barely feel it through her layers of clothing. She was thinking how, after fishing that day, they had walked along a deserted stretch of shore, looking for a place to swim. Victor brought out his camera and focused on Angel, who had stripped down to knee socks, bikini and sweatband. "We could do a mock-up of *Suzannah and the Elders,*" he said. "Do you mind crouching in the beach grass, young lady?" He advanced toward her.

"Victor, you old lech!" Angel cried.

They made a train in the water, the three of them, floating along the shore; later they had cold chicken and coleslaw on the beach. Victor produced a bottle of wine. "I never want to go home," Angel said, burrowing in the sand.

"We *always* have to go home," Sylvie said. "It's a universal law, like . . . like entropy."

"Oh, Gary would go for that. He's in Boston this weekend doing something that will probably add to the general confusion." And then she added, "I meant, I never want to go home *today.*" She held up her chicken leg and said, "The bone in this thing is like the femur in people."

"Well, thanks for absolutely nothing," Victor said. And they were off again, their laughter filling her ears.

Victor was saying, "Are you listening?"

She wanted to ask him if he remembered that perfect day, the summer before last; but she was too busy trying to grasp his meaning. "I don't understand what you're getting at," she said, "this business about condoning the murder of children."

"Ssh, I think I'm trying to be profound. The children are just an example." He relit his pipe and the maple-scented tobacco turned the car into a cave. Hibernating animals could curl up in comfort here. She wished she too could sleep for months, for years.

Victor had opened the window a crack, and streamers of air mingled with the smoke. He continued. "There is this story. I saw it in the *Times* a few years ago. I nearly leapt in the air with the paper in my hand when I read it. The effect was electric. It made me slightly crazed. It made me think about so many things—good, evil, guilt, the modifications of guilt. I mean, it was my own reaction that shook me up." He glanced at her.

"Yes?" she said. "Go on."

"There was this former Nazi officer, a Colonel Kesselmann, imprisoned in Italy for crimes that he'd authorized against the local population during the war." Victor spoke in a low excited voice. "Documented killings, the most despicable kind. The work detail he authorized for children, alone . . . He was born in West Germany, had a wife he'd married while he was in prison. They'd been married only eight years when the event I'm about to describe took place. There was a stepson.

"Well, at about this time, the old dog developed terminal cancer and had to be moved to a military hospital in Rome. Now, visualize this, if you can. The wife, who was a physiotherapist—I would cast her as a stocky, raw-boned type, still relatively young, not really over the hill, perhaps in her early fifties—she gets special permission to come to Rome to visit her seriously ill husband, and she brings with her a large suitcase, supposedly filled with supplies for him. Let's say her visa allows one and only one visit at this time. She enters his room—a hospital cell with perhaps a guard outside the door —and stays with him for a few hours. Nurses come and go. Perhaps one comes in and tries to comfort her. 'After all, Frau Kesselmann, he is not in pain!' When she leaves, she, of course, takes the suitcase with her. The guard, I expect, offers to help, but she waves him off. No! She is capable. She is a trained professional, used to handling heavy weights. It is only a suitcase, after all. She has taken the precaution of having a car waiting, but nobody in the hospital knows this. An hour or so later, when the nurses again enter the patient's room, he is gone. Naturally, the wife has stolen him. Has kidnapped her husband, carted him down the hospital steps —the enormous suitcase banging against the risers, gouging her ankles, her shins; her strength has to be extraordinary— and taken him back to his own country, his own city, to die."

Sylvie raised her head and stared at Victor.

"Now don't ask me about extradition, or any of those practical matters. For me the story ends here. What do you make of it?"

"She actually did that? Carried her husband away in a valise?" Victor nodded. "The woman sounds heroic," she said, fully roused. "Is this the film that you've been hinting at?"

"But why heroic?" Victor asked, ignoring her question. "Her husband was a monster. Why not bring her up on charges for interfering with the legal process?"

"Because her effort was humane. Well, in the context of her life, it was. And unreal—like something in a fable. After all, she didn't authorize the killing of children, did she? So what would you do? Stone her?" Her voice rose.

"Don't get excited. Actually, the point of all of this is that despite everything, my own experience, everything I've always felt, I lean toward your view." He was biting his pipe stem so hard that it stuck out of his mouth like a semaphore. "One's feelings do curious things. All of a sudden, there you are, all tangled up in something sticky like compassion, when the idea of revenge should be absolute."

The story continued to fascinate him, he said. He could not let it go. What would it take to make her, the wife, less than a heroine? Or was it possible that she was "good"? Very confusing. He intended to join a film workshop and go on from there. Learn about scripts, casting, production. Eventually he would try to find a small production company. It might be good to get away from the dryness of his usual work. Yesterday he had prepared a statistical study that showed that golf-players who were married had a shorter life span than golfers in the general sample. "Earthshaking!" He threw up his hands and the car swerved, causing Sylvie to observe her possible doom, for an instant, in the headlights of an oncoming truck. "After a while it's pretty stale bread," Victor said. "My neighbor in the adjacent pew is writing a biography of Rilke."

She slumped in her seat, tried to empty her mind. She didn't have the emotional reach to deal with him yet, his history, his obsession, the boy he once was, living with a farming family in Théoule in the south of France, his parents, sister, older brother, floating away from him in dreams. But he had managed, he said. He had a pet pig named Judith who would stagger to her feet, giddy with excitement, when he came into the yard. He loved her in a way, as if she were an overstuffed dog. All this described in a wry whimsical tone meant to conceal the sadness running through him. He told Sylvie that at Apollo he often finished his daily tasks quickly and then spent time writing letters and essays. He did something for the *New Republic* once on why Günter Grass was on the wrong track when he described Germany in the thirties as being diseased, when it was in fact more like a congenital deformity. But he tended not to talk about these things head-on—the catastrophes of war and politics; he approached them obliquely, wearing his private mask of derision, of mockery.

THEY were on the old Montauk Highway and the bleak landscape of winter loomed ahead. Victor guided the car off the road and into the parking lot of the nearby state park. She could see the ocean beyond, and the beach with its lacy tatters of spume.

He pulled her from the car. The chill morning air gave his

cheeks an instant bloom. In his puffy down jacket and pants he looked as if he could soar away. She supposed she looked the same.

"Breathe deeply," he urged, taking noisy breaths himself as if to show her how. They walked along the beach, arms locked, heads down against the wind. There were other strollers about, who acknowledged them with a glance as they passed, as if they were all members of a secret order. "Tell the truth," he insisted. "Don't you feel as if your blood is being renewed? Can't you imagine deranged people returning to sanity just by breathing this stuff in and out?" Down the beach, a Frisbee slashed the air and a collie leapt to retrieve it.

She tried to smile at him, but her face felt as if it would crack from the cold.

They walked for miles along the deserted shore, two specks in motion under the inverted bowl of the sky. The sun was high above them, but the wind was still very strong. They passed an old man in a hooded poncho sitting on a stool with a sketch pad in hand, staring out at the empty sea. Was he drawing a mythical boat, a fish, she wondered. "In the spring, he'll be standing there casting into the surf," Victor said. "He'll be pulling in bluefish and bass."

She had stopped in the sand and leaned against him. "I don't think I can manage any more fresh air. I'm simply frozen."

He peered at her, pulled her wool hat farther down on her face, touched his lips to the tip of her nose. "By God, you're right," he said. "Let's find some place to eat."

They drove down to the docks, past empty slips and moorings. The large *Viking* party boat had left hours before on its ocean tour. On one of the poles a sign saying *Cod* flapped in the wind. There was an open café just beyond.

The interior looked like a ship's cabin. Polished hardwood and brass. There were old-fashioned ship's lanterns attached to the wall, mounted fish, shelves of liquor bottles behind the mahogany bar. The laminated place mats on the tabletops looked like old sea charts.

Victor settled her in a booth and went off to order food. She stared out the window at the whitecaps being whipped slantwise as far as the eye could see, and felt the turbulence of all that motion inside herself. At the next table a woman loosely held a young child in a harness and reins. "Hi," the woman said cheerfully.

"Hi," Sylvie answered. Suddenly swamped with weariness, she placed her head on her folded arms on the table.

"You OK?" the woman asked. Sylvie lifted her head and nodded. The toddler, dragging his reins, came over and stared at her. His eyes had a limpid, puppy glow. He held out a bag of Fritos. "Takim."

"Thank you," she said, pretending to eat. The child snatched the chips away and ran back to his mother. Sean, somewhere, might have that face, that chubby seamless baby look. She was in a twilit state. The restaurant seemed to have taken on the undulating motions of a ship. Neither awake nor asleep, she saw movies of her life on the screen of her closed lids. Angel's high cheekbones, bright inquisitive eyes, the bridge of her nose sprinkled with freckles the color of bran. More talkative, more self-willed as she grew older. She had once taken an anniversary issue of the *National Geographic* and cut out the pictures. Scotch-taped a group of gorgeously photographed New Guinea tribeswomen to the wall of her room. "How could you do this!" Sylvie had cried. "This is not just *any* magazine to be cut up in pieces. You know that! It's a real *publication,* for God's sake!"

Angel looked at her, the look of a child who doesn't have to give reasons. Sylvie made her peel the pictures off the wall —dark ovoid heads with elongated necks and elaborate facial paint. "You're a terrible mother," Angel shouted.

Arthur took sides. "If you can't reason with her, you've lost her," he said. Sylvie wanted to explain that she hated to see things willfully destroyed, as if possession justified blind license. She didn't want Angel to be that kind of unreasoning person. But Arthur's mind was already on something else. He had gone to his room. There was work to do. He represented the Hillsdale Four—young blacks accused of pouring acids into the neighborhood water supply to protest their slum housing. She followed him into the study. He was at his desk, and she came and rested her hands on his shoulders.

She said, "I've been offered a job, if I want it—research on an English history text. I don't know. I'll be out of the house in libraries a great deal."

He seemed to shift beneath her touch. "Well, it's up to you, of course."

VICTOR came back with two large bowls of chowder. "There's a guy over there talking about going out on a tuna run in the spring." He chattered away. At one point he offered her some chowder from his spoon.

"Oh, Victor . . ." She turned away.

"I'd really like to see you have something hot," he said in a mothering voice. But she didn't want to be mothered; she wanted to be left quietly to herself. He went for coffee. When he returned, he said, "So what did you think of Kesselmann?" The coffee mug burned her hands. She had taken off her hat, and her hair had fallen to her shoulders.

"Kesselmann," she repeated, trying to rouse herself. "I don't know. I'm not sure that I see what you're trying to get at. For one thing, why film? Why don't you write a book?"

"Because my thoughts are too visual." He took a deep swallow of coffee. "I happen to think in filmlike segments. Cut—close-up—fade. I can't deal with verbal metaphor. My transitive verbs stink." He sat back and looked at her as if she were from a foreign country and he were trying to guess her mother tongue. Then he said, "Interesting, the way we can almost love what we have been conditioned to despise. I mean, look what's happened to my perfectly ordinary thirst for blood. After I read that story, the woman was separated from her own history. If I met her on the street, I might have kissed her hand and shouted bravo. *Me,* with what I know! But I could see it all—the way she lifted the frailness that was her husband from his hospital bed, folding him into the valise, maybe speaking some little endearment, 'Liebchen, not to be frightened. I am here,' then lugging the damned valise down the hallway. Anyway, the whole episode has disturbed something. I feel somehow naked. Certainly strange. Not quite healthy. I keep thinking, why should it all have become, so, well—*porous*—even though I want to feel permanently enraged. Do you see what I mean?"

"I'm not sure." She had never heard so much from him on this subject before. He usually said less rather than more. Never sentimental, he tended to laugh at himself. But this leap into abstraction frightened her. It was wholly private and obsessive, like his home movies, which tended to pose problems and nothing else. To her shame, she was filled with irritation. She wanted to say, "This coffee tastes like engine sludge. We could have had a long talk at home, for God's sake." But she tucked her arm in his and leaned against him. Their jackets were insulation, a fire wall that interfered with the heat of her need. She kept thinking, What about *me*! What about *me*! She said, "I just wonder what you hope to achieve, that's all."

"Nothing too important, I guess." His voice had a hollow sound. He got up and said, "I'm going to pay the check." He was losing patience. She watched him move across the room. A man with a large reel in his hand came up to him and seemed to be explaining something. Victor was smiling at him. Last weekend when she came home, Victor had met her at the door, grabbed her, held her against the hallway wall, his mouth on hers. She tried to pull away. "Victor, what . . . ?"

"Oh, I don't know . . ."

They went upstairs. He removed the pins from her hair and pulled her face to his.

She was speechless, watching from a distance. His shirt and trousers were on the bedroom floor, his tie rakishly on a bed post. Her mind closed off sensation. She was afraid to allow her body to warm, to feel . . . afraid she might set off the earthquake that was inside. He moved over her, and for a moment she felt the sweet steam of his body. Before he slid away he muttered, "Sorry—sort of Neanderthal, I guess . . ." He slept fitfully; but she studied the cracked and flaking ceiling as if it were scrolled in code. All that whirling in her head, making it imperative that she try to focus on almost anything. And Victor turning toward her, even in sleep, grasping her hand and anchoring her.

She watched him pay for their food. His easy serious look with the counterman, as though each moment deserved attention. Again last night she had wanted to say, "Not yet . . ." He held her at arm's length and lit cigarettes for them both, murmuring in his beautiful voice, "Perhaps I shouldn't be around you so much."

The baby was toddling in her direction once more, clutching his bag of Fritos. "No, Brian!" his mother called out. Sylvie laid her head on her arms and pretended not to see. If he comes near me, I could do anything, she thought.

CHAPTER 9

O N Monday they rose early to get to the commuter train. Sylvie's head ached. She was still recovering from Montauk. The trip back had seemed endless. When they left the café, they had driven into a region of woods and ponds where pheasants paraded in the marsh grass and deer loomed suddenly among the trees and leapt away. When they got out to take photographs, the wind flung her against the car door.

"Was it so bad?" Victor asked, as they sped west on the expressway.

"It was just so cold."

"That *was* rather the point."

But more than the cold, she was thinking of the toddler's face, and the strange mood that struck her, at the very last, when the child came stumbling toward her. She turned the car heater up.

Victor lit his pipe with one hand and puffed away. "Maybe it was the story of Kesselmann that got to you."

"I don't know. It's the kind of story that has the makings of a folk tale or a ballad. Are you sure you read about it in the *Times*?" She thought of the woman with the valise, but saw instead a child inside it, the woman running. And she sank deeper into herself, zipping her collar to her nose and clamping Jessica's unravelling earmuffs over her hat.

Victor was staring straight ahead, his chiselled features turned away from her. "Well, *I* thought it was riveting."

Now it was Monday morning, and he was in the bedroom doorway, his face lathered, a towel around his neck, his shorts making a shiny blur on the threshold. She had begun to sneeze, and he said, "I'll put up a pot of tea in a minute."

But she suddenly found herself making a devastating, un-premeditated little speech: "Victor, please, I'd like you not to live here anymore. Not right now—not while I'm at the Korts'." His mouth was erased by the shaving soap, but his eyes were narrowed and bright. She couldn't believe what she was saying, couldn't bear to see the slowly gathering coldness in his face. "Oh, God, don't look at me that way. Can't you see? Your being here somehow defeats things. I don't want to be helped. I don't want to feel grateful or lucky about you or anything like that. I don't think I want to see you for a while. And I know it's too much to expect you to understand. I don't even want you to understand."

He stood there soapy and aloof. "Funny you should jump the gun," he said. "I was planning to make a little exit of my own. Temporary, I'd hoped. I thought I'd just wait around for a while, at some distance, and watch myself being sorely missed . . ." His voice was leaden. "I think I've just discovered something, though. You have a very ladylike strain of the bitch in you. And I've just about *had* it, my love! Up to my ears! All I care to take!" He mopped his face and flung his towel aside. "All this goddamned tiptoeing around you as if you were damaged china or something. I mean, I can't wait to get the hell out of here, if you want to know the truth!" He threw his clothes on in a white heat and left. Left without breakfast, without saying good-bye. Left the bathroom in a mess, the morning papers strewn about, his shaving can open and oozing.

She was dressed for the city but decided to stop at the pool in Rosevale anyway. What did it matter? Her hair would dry behind her newspaper on the train. Victor's condemning voice thrummed in her ears, frightening her. She had set such an artificial distance between them now. What had possessed her?

At the pool, she slipped into her suit and plunging in, swam fiercely. His angry face rose above the uproar in her brain. She sliced the water, head submerged, until her lungs hurt. She felt slightly mad. Weren't all zealots mad? "You ought to know!" Victor would have said.

There was another swimmer at the far side of the pool. A man. She watched him, his bare shoulders like those of a water mammal breaking the surface, then submerging. The towel attendant had an eye on both of them. She came out of her cubicle and called out to Sylvie, "How are you doing? Haven't seen you around here for a while." Sylvie heard but ignored her. She had stretched into her dead man's float, face down, still as driftwood, trying to block out the hammer pulse that was building behind her temples.

When she finally lifted her head, she noticed that the towel attendant was partway into the pool. "Jesus!" the young woman said, staring hard at her. "You must be practicing for an Olympic event I've never even heard of." The other swimmer was also emerging from the water. He was a solemn-looking youth, bone thin, with stringy hair plastered to his forehead. He reminded her of Gary.

"It's all right," she said to the towel girl.

Afterward, she sat in the sauna room. The benches were like the surface of a grill. She sat on a thickness of towels, wondering where Gary and Sean were. The tracing agency in Mexico had come up with nothing. Perhaps they'd gone somewhere else—Oregon, Vancouver. She had tried to seal her mind against the child, tried not to think about the connection between them. Often, when she slept, he seemed to be reaching toward her through a morass of dreams. Gary's baby now, but not exclusively his.

* * *

SHE arrived at the Korts' at nine o'clock. Jessica had left for school, but Margo and Michael were at the breakfast table. "Ah, the lady of the lake . . ." Michael said. And Sylvie involuntarily smoothed back her still-damp hair. "Good weekend?" He was in fine humor, dressed for the day, oxford shirt, screaming tie. His papers were spread on the floor, and he was sorting through them, stuffing things into his attaché case. He was leaving for Brazil that evening. Margo's face glowed with some hidden source of animation. Sylvie had heard her singing one morning in full voice. And she had the image of her, alive with song, standing in front of her bedroom mirror, brushing her sleek cropped head, wearing a secret smile as she stepped into the shower. The phone had rung, and Sylvie answered it. A man's voice. "Is Mrs. Kort home?" Then a moment of hesitation when she said, "She can't speak to you right now. Is there a message?" A flicker of uncertainty. "Well, just tell her, the Mongolian wild horses. She'll know." An odd message. When she mentioned it later to Margo, there was a small breathy pause. "Oh yes, of course," she said, her voice too smoothly casual. "No name or anything, right?"

Sylvie went upstairs, first to Jessica's room, where she picked up clothing, set some aside for the laundry, folded some and put it in the chest of drawers. There were drawings on the bed, and Sylvie gathered them up to put in Jessica's toy closet. There was a crayon drawing of a woman's head: a round face, red hair. "My Sylvie," the caption said. In spite of herself, Sylvie was touched. Quickly she stuffed the drawings into a bottom drawer. She made Jessica's bed. That was Feliciana's job, but Sylvie had begun to take over all the chores that involved Jessica. She glanced at the appointment calendar. Tiny Tumblers tomorrow, karate again on Friday. The karate lady had been teaching the children the art of self-protection. "There are things kids can do if a stranger acts funny with them. Kids can scream, bite, kick shins. The important thing is not to be afraid of adults just because they're bigger than you. Just open up your mouth and *yell*. OK, kids? Let's hear you scream 'NO! GO AWAY!' "

"You'd better not act funny with me," Jessica had said to her in a hoarse little voice, afterward. A dentist's appointment was marked in red for the end of the month. Would she be here at the end of the month?

She went into Margo's office. More jottings in Margo's hand about the artist Bob Fleet. "Young, stylistically abstract. Works in acrylics and plastic paste—like sculpted metal. Ceremonial. Good for church, other public buildings, boardroom! Could buy direct from gallery on Prince Street, or if lucky, arrange to see artist's work in studio and bypass gallery markup. Have good contacts for new Lowitt building . . ."

Margo's scribbles were clean and confident. Sylvie made a note to send a letter to the Lowitt people summarizing Margo's conversation with them. There were telephone calls to other galleries. An appointment to be arranged with an interior designer who had told Margo he could use all the representational, low- to medium-priced canvases that she could find. He had sent a memo, "Under fifteen hundred dollars, love. The market is wild about fruit and flowers in porcelain bowls. Go find an artist and tell him to paint nectarines on a kitchen table—all the canvases he can do. They'll fly out to Scarsdale by themselves."

AT noon, Margo took Sylvie to Queens to visit Celia and Max. "You might as well see the source of all those Medicare forms and surgical-supplies order sheets you've been busy with," Margo said.

As they drove over the bridge to Queens Margo said, "I grew up here. I worked as a baby-sitter after school, if you can believe it. My father was a fur buyer. But money was always scarce." She drove into the bustle of neighborhood traffic. "He used to add fur trim to my clothes. Little muskrat collars on my jackets and dresses. I felt like a freak at school. I would tear the collars off and blame it on some roughneck kid."

Celia was in the dining foyer finishing her lunch. The bib around her neck was spattered. She looked up at Sylvie when they came through the door. "Another one for the harem?" she asked Margo, ignoring Sylvie and making a face at Jolene, who was on her way to the kitchen. Max came toward them quickly, leaning forward on his cane, bowing, dipping one knee like an Old World count. "So pleased to make your aquaintance," he said. Sylvie thought his twitching fingers were about to whirl the cane at her. "Anyone my little daughter puts the OK on is fine with me," he said, smiling with determined mirth.

Jolene was brewing a pot of fresh coffee for Margo and Sylvie, grumbling angrily to herself, "A person needs four hands and a pair of wings around here."

Margo touched Jolene's shoulder in encouragement and turned away.

Celia clawed at Margo's sleeve. "In my sleep I was thinking of the next chapter." Margo was bewildered. The next chapter? Oh, God, the oral history. She wheeled her mother into the bedroom. The room had the ammonia smell of incontinence, mingled with Breath-o-Pine. The dresser was crowded with snapshots of an incomprehensible time: Max on horseback in flared breeches and boots, her mother playing miniature golf at a mountain resort, girlish in a leghorn hat, pictures of herself as a little girl, on a tricycle, in a white carriage drawn by ponies with ribbons in their bridles. The last reminded her of an old French film in which the tiny heroine is driven through the Bois de Boulogne in a similar carriage, toward a mysterious destination. She couldn't remember where the ponies had come from, or why she was in the carriage.

Celia sounded as if she were speaking through a damaged microphone. "Uncle Arnie, who owned the Club Mitzi on Fourteenth Street. Remember?" In her excitement at this fragment of recall she leaned forward and nearly fell out of the wheelchair. Margo pinned her in securely with a bath towel. "Some gangster in Arnie's club sneaked him a Mickey

Finn. You know what that is? It's Irish and you take it with seltzer. Then they took him to the docks." Her mother rolled her eyes. "The police came, and when they searched his pockets, what they found was a terrible drug that makes people crazy. Then the police smashed his face. They did things like that in those days. Just kicked you down the stairs if they felt like it. Arnie was good, the way Stanford was. Both of them, gentlemen . . ." Jolene passed the bedroom on her way to the linen closet, and her mother interrupted herself to yell "Bum!"

Margo put her hand over her mother's mouth. "Behave!" she ordered.

IN the living room, Max was showing Sylvie his personal papers. His ebony cane lay across his thin knees. "Here are my letters to the world's great furriers. Ben Kahn, Revillon Frères. I write, and they answer. You'd be surprised. The bigger people are, the more they can't afford not to be polite. I once wrote to Kissinger and said he was all wet on Hanoi. As a Jew, he ought to be ashamed. He answered immediately."

Sylvie's own father had died when Angel was two. Her mother moved to Michigan and lived with a cousin in a small town near Ann Arbor. The two of them developed a knitting business in their sunroom and parlor. They created bulky cardigans and scarves that were popular with the students. Every Christmas Angel got a new wool hat and mittens with colorful reindeer and snowflakes. Once her mother devoted a whole letter to describing the surrounding farm country. "It's like the Bavarian meadowland, as I remember it. The grass is almost blue. But the picnickers here make sandwiches from a bread like wet Kleenex." She wondered whether such packaged abominations were sold in Germany too today. "Kiss Angel," she ended. "I hope you teach her to respect good things!"

But it was her father who had left a lasting imprint. He was the itinerant in the family household, a household that included Sylvie's brother, Jeffrey, younger than she by two years, who at the age of seventeen gave up trying to win his father's approval, lied about his age and enlisted in the Korean War. After the war, he decided to open a Big Burger franchise in Seoul; he eventually owned three Big Burgers and a string of Mini-Malts, and wrote home approvingly of the "much maligned" Park family.

While they were growing up, her father came and went as if set in motion by some mysterious inner signal. He stayed out of the house for days, took trips to libraries and research centers in other cities. He wrote monographs but felt little satisfaction even if they were published. "They will be buried in some musty archive soon enough." He was once gone for ten days—his longest stretch—and when he returned he merely said, touching Sylvie on the head, picking Jeffrey up and hugging him, "I was holed up in the library at Yale. Slept in the men's lounge. Picked up some slops at Dunkin' Donuts. I survived."

Burning with the injustice of his condition, he turned nasty. "In America there are channels, hierarchies of power." He was wild with frustration that these channels eluded him, and blamed it on the American concept of upward mobility. "It's not what you are that counts. It's how you sell yourself." When Sylvie was older, she realized that it was his personality, caustic, condescending, that had been his worst enemy.

He languished at Fowler Community College until the end. Tall, gaunt, with faded tufty hair that had once been the color and thickness of Sylvie's, he passed judgment on Sylvie's marriage to Arthur, on Arthur himself. "Save us from the sweaty fervor of a civil-rights lawyer. In a way it's worse than being an ambulance chaser!"

"You're being snotty," Sylvie said with weak bravado.

He bent to kiss her cheek. "I'm concerned because I happen to know you're deep and beautiful, and capable of throwing your life away."

What would he have thought of Victor, she sometimes wondered. He might have approved. She suspected that Victor's attraction to the Kesselmann story would have touched something perversely dark in her father.

"ANOTHER thing I do," Max was saying, "is start plants from scratch." He pointed to a leafy stalk. "That's an avocado. And there's a rubber plant. My daughter, Margo, bought me a stick. It looked like a nothing. I put it in water and presto, after eight weeks, a rubber plant! My interests also run to the cabala. Dybbuks and golems." He was giving her a Cook's tour of his personality. "With my magnifying glass, I can read anything. Although, sometimes, I'm afraid that a dybbuk has entered my wife's soul and is causing an uproar."

"If only there was some magic to fall back on," she said distantly.

He leaned forward solicitously. "Do you have a family?" he asked.

"Not now."

"Not now? Then a boyfriend possibly? An attractive woman like yourself?" He radiated musty, innocent charm. In his youth he might have been the sort who wore a boutonniere in his lapel and tipped his hat to women on the street.

Her own father had seemed indifferent to women, yet she believed he had loved her mother. She once saw them from a distance walking down Broadway. They seemed so separate from the real world, fading in and out of the crowd of shoppers, as though viewed through a stereopticon. They were holding hands. There was a look of wildness about her father. It might have been his hair or his clothes, in perpetual disarray. Her mother, always in high heels, hurried to keep up.

Years later, her father died in his sleep. Heart failure. The result of a severe asthmatic attack, the doctor said. He had been rereading a lecture for his class at Fowler, and his papers had spilled from the bed to the floor. A large bottle of allergy pills at his bedside table was mysteriously empty. The doctor examined the bottle for a moment and drew her mother aside.

She heard her mother say, "No! No!" Then her mother said, "He probably had an attack and *found* the bottle empty."

MARGO had just come in from Celia's bedroom when the doorbell rang. It was Gertrude, ready to take the afternoon shift. Gertrude hung up her hat and coat; the Sony Walkman dangled from her arm like a pocketbook. "When it gets good and quiet around here, I'm going to let you hear my Langston's new tapes. They're so good, they'll just about break your heart."

"You're not exactly an impartial judge," Jolene remarked, buttoning her squat body into her coat. "You're the mother. And what you don't have is distance." A cigarette was pasted to her lower lip. "Anyway, good luck with the Vice Squad in there."

Margo saw that Sylvie had taken her father's hand. "Someone is taking good care of your nails," Sylvie was saying to him seriously. Her father was beaming at her. She's a caring person, Margo thought, caring in a severe and complicated way.

Her father was carefully framing his words. "In my youth I cut some figure. The girls flew to me like butterflies." It was the stillness in Sylvie's face that struck Margo most. The overlay of bleakness, as though the gravity pull of thought was enough to make her features go slack. She had dared to say to Sylvie recently, "When you smile, your face changes remarkably. You're someone brand new." A cautious feeler. "I must remember that," Sylvie said.

And there was a man, Victor, who left messages on occasion and who, Margo knew, often picked Sylvie up on Friday nights. Oh, how Margo wanted to pry into that life.

Gertrude was standing over Margo, saying, "Now you tell me if this isn't *real* art." She had slipped the Walkman over Margo's neck and adjusted the earpieces. A blare of noise filled Margo's ears. A man's voice singing, "Oh, baby, get going! I says get, get going!" a Pink Floyd voice, drowning in a background of electronic harps.

"Very good," Margo said, removing the headpiece, an echo still racketing in her ears.

But Gertrude had taken her aside and was speaking in a quiet confidential tone. "The thing is, a person of special talent needs backing, a helping hand. How do you think Diana Ross and those Supremes got started? Good hard cash did it, you can bet! Now I was thinking, if you could lend me—"

"Well, I'm not a backer," Margo said before the discussion could get off the ground. "But if you'd like to borrow a small sum for Langston and pay it back out of your salary . . . ."

"You think Stevie Wonder got somewhere on a small sum?" She stalked into the kitchen to make Celia's afternoon tea.

"Who's out there?" Celia yelled, spying Gertrude from her bedroom.

"Tea in a moment," Margo called back.

After a while Gertrude came out of the kitchen. "No hard feelings," she mumbled. "All a person can do is ask." She fished in her shopping bag. "Actually, I have something for little Jess." It was a large stuffed bear in neon pink. "I won this bowling, just last night."

"That's terrific," Margo said. "Jessica has an elephant, a tiger, a marvellous wolf, and a huge wolf poster from the Bronx Zoo, in her room. She's getting to be quite a specialist." Her voice was relieved, lighthearted, her face was flushed. Listening, Sylvie was reminded of something else— the man on the phone with his cryptic message for Margo. "Tell her about the Mongolian wild horses." A nearly extinct species, Sylvie suddenly realized, probably on display at the Bronx Zoo. And hadn't Jessica mentioned a Mr. Wallace from the zoo, who lectured on wolves and was their friend?

Sylvie observed Margo: her brown eyes, bright as mica, the relaxed tilt of her head, her quick, very rich laugh as she bent down and straightened Max's scarf. No, Margo would not be going to Brazil with Michael, Sylvie thought, oddly incensed.

Max was asking them both to come into his little bedroom.

He closed the door and turned to Margo with elaborate seriousness. "Blondell says she will be due in a few months now. She says she didn't know how far along she was."

"She didn't *know*!" Margo dropped abruptly to the bed, inadvertently causing the electric mattress to begin to rise. "She will have to be replaced. That's all. This is not a halfway house!"

"Not so quick, Missy," Max said. "Shoving a girl into the cold is nothing to be so proud of. Surely we can knock our heads together and come up with something better." He apologized to Sylvie, saying solemnly, "Since you are my daughter's assistant, I think you should know the facts."

But Sylvie already knew the facts. The fact of Margo, duty-bent, struggling to hold her parents' lives aloft. Somewhere someone said that the family bond, no matter how ragged, was the toughest, most indestructible fiber in the universe. And it was true. Her eyes were suddenly brimming, and she thought of Victor. Oh, Victor—he was surely finished with her now.

Margo jumped to her feet, gave Max a hug. "Keep cool, sweetheart, we'll straighten out everything."

She went to Celia's bedroom to say good-bye. In the dimness, her mother was like a puppet whose strings have gone slack. Such an insubstantial shadow to be burdened with so much rage. Yet the bone-marrow test had been normal, offering a reprieve in the midst of all this disorder. Gertrude came in to put Celia on the commode. "There's only one thing I ask," Celia whispered to Margo. "If you are really my daughter, you'll pack up the whores and get them out of this house."

"I'll work on it, Mother," Margo said, keeping her voice low. "We'll manage something. I'll talk to you about it next week. We'll put it on tape."

Her father hung on her arm in the foyer doorway. He bowed to Sylvie. "I hope we haven't caused you to have a bad impression of us . . ." To Margo, he said, "Never turn your back on a person's trouble. I wrote to Mayor Koch telling him to start a plant-a-tree campaign in all the boroughs. Get people to do their part, beautify things. As yet, I haven't heard from him."

In the elevator at last, Margo turned to Sylvie. "Well, I guess you have the picture."

Sylvie nodded. "But they have vitality, even your poor mother . . ."

Margo wanted to say, "Yes, but what do you really think? What do you know?" She held her tongue. Sylvie was looking away. She seemed luminously close to tears.

When they reached the lobby, out of the blue she said, "Do you mind if I stay on weekends too, for a while? You don't have to increase my salary, or anything like that."

Margo, troubled, said, "I suppose so. Sure, why not."

CHAPTER 10

SYLVIE telephoned Tania. She needed contact with her former life. She hadn't seen or spoken to Victor since the Montauk trip, three weeks ago. She had tried reaching him recently at Apollo, but his secretary told her he was out of the office on private business. She called him at home without success. She had even taken a taxi to his apartment and pushed a note under the door. "Victor, enough! I need to speak with you." She had only asked to be left alone for a while, not indefinitely, not completely; surely he understood that. But there was no response.

Tania squealed when she heard Sylvie's voice. "Oh, this is so eerie. I had a dream about you last night. You were in a subway train crowded against the door and you were wearing a tank suit and looking as cool and calm as if you'd just won the Olympic high dive. I was absolutely thrilled for you. Listen! Can you meet me for coffee today?"

"Yes, but early. I have to be on my way before three.

They met in the underground mall of VITACORP. Zack Louden had managed part of VITACORP's rentals when the building was first built and Sylvie remembered his excitement when he'd concluded the deal—champagne for the whole office, white orchids on all the desks. Sylvie recalled Tania saying, "For a guy like Zack, money not only talks, it filibusters!" And she'd smiled, a pale twist of a smile, implying that she had problems that money couldn't touch.

Tania had found a small canopied table under a mass of potted palms overlooking the fountain, and she waved happily to Sylvie when she saw her. Sylvie was amazed by her appearance. She seemed toned-down, quieter, her hair less teased and puffed. No false eyelashes, gold bracelets or multiple rings on her fingers. The staccato high in her voice was smoothed out.

Tania ordered blueberry muffins and tea for the two of them and then grasped Sylvie's hand. "So how's it going, with whatever it is that you're doing?"

"Fine. I'm all right."

"Louden told me to pass on the word. When you're ready to come back, Middle-income Suburban is yours."

"I'll remember."

But Tania was clearly hurrying through the amenities. When her tea came, she poured, stirred, gave Sylvie her most radiant smile and said, "OK, listen to this. Are you ready?" She sat back, took a long, deep breath and said, "I'm having a baby!"

Sylvie stared at her. "Incredible!" she finally breathed. "I can't believe it!" Only two months ago everything had seemed so bleak for Tania. "What luck!" she said, not taking her eyes from Tania's frantically happy face. "Then you and Larry are back together again? Wonderful!"

"Well, almost wonderful. Almost everything. I've missed my period, but I have to wait another ten days before I can take a pregnancy test. However, I *feel* absolutely sure. You know, breasts swollen . . . tummy bloated . . . Remember?"

Sylvie remembered. She reached out and touched her teacup to Tania's. "See what happens if you're patient and hopeful . . ."

"And inventive," Tania remarked. She quieted down for a

moment and leaned toward Sylvie. "I've got something to tell you. I would have called you today even if you hadn't called me. I must confide in someone or burst, and I know you're the sort of person who won't blab. If anyone knows what heartache is, Sylvie, it's you. So what I'm about to say . . ." She gave a little unburdening shrug and took a swallow of tea. Tipping her head toward Sylvie, she said, "The father is *not* Larry! I took matters in my own hands. I thought if the issue of childbearing hadn't become so unreasonable and huge and sickening, Larry and I could have made it together. Sure, there were other problems. But this was the big one. The one that simply had to be solved." Another large swallow of tea, then, "So I went places and met people and looked for a solution . . . Get it?"

Sylvie wasn't sure she was getting anything at all. She turned away and studied the fountain, which had become a giant plant spouting silvery fronds of water toward the skylight. "What exactly are you talking about?"

"Saving my life, that's all. And don't look that way—as if someone was pouring Perrier down your dress."

"Sorry . . ."

"Anyway, at one of those schizy parties in Chelsea—you know, where people come dressed in old World War II clothes—I met this really sweet, attractive, clean-cut guy. One thing led to another. I told him that along with real estate, I was into a sideline—consumer testing. Did he want to see how it works? Sure, he said. Well, I started with favorite colors, favorite foods. Then I asked if he thought he was outgoing or broody and silent, and what kind of music caused a mood change, and did eating chocolate give him guilt feelings. Then I crept into the important area. Family history. Any diabetes, epilepsy, cancer, mental disorders? On his mother's side? His father's side? No? Good! Did he have scarlet fever as a child? Hiatus hernia as an adult? Any antisocial behavior? Was he ever in prison? What about asthma? 'Hey,' he said, 'are you testing for President of the United States here?' Not exactly, I answered, feeling like a first-class freak. But he tested out perfecto. A nice guy. His wife was giving him a hard time. They'd split and come together again, and then it just blew up once more, over something sappy and domestic. He'd decided only a few days before we met to accept a job as manager of a canning company in Seattle. Well, we drank to that. Another bottle of wine at my place, and you can guess the rest. He stayed through the weekend. I had my fingers crossed, but all the rest of me open and available, the whole time. When he finally left, he said, 'Sweetheart, you have one powerful urge.' "

Sylvie listened, dumbfounded. "The father?" she asked.

"Darling, who else? I mean how many times do you think I could pull off a stunt like that?"

Sylvie just looked at her. "And Larry? How much does he know?"

"Enough, but not one shred more. We'd gotten together recently a few times. Very warm and loving. Always ended up in bed, reminiscing. But now that I've told him what I suspect—and of course he assumes the baby is his—he's sort of dazzled, as if we've been touched by a mysterious force. 'Someone up there wants us to hang in,' he said to me."

Sylvie's face felt like blank paper. She tried to smile, make light, congratulatory sounds, but there were all the moral implications that Tania skipped over so blithely: Larry being led down a garden path, the true father ignorant in Seattle. She wondered how Tania, so ordinary and nice, could be capable of such extreme and dangerous behavior, lifting her arm and daring lightning to strike. Like Angel, who had wanted to have her child at home on the kitchen table. "The risk! The risk!" Sylvie had said then, trying not to sound like a raving fool.

"Oh, risk . . ." Angel had answered.

Now Tania was saying, "All right, you've heard, but remember, you've heard nothing! OK? Listen, Sylvie, there's not another living soul that I'd tell any of this to."

Sylvie rose. It was almost three o'clock. She had to pick

Jessica up at school. She felt not quite anchored in space; her legs were hollow. She'd slept poorly. There was Victor's unavailability. And now Tania's bizarre news. She had visions of the surrogate father sniffing out the truth, even in Seattle, trailing Tania and Larry through life, standing on the periphery and monitoring their progress. A ghost with rights. But she kissed Tania on the cheek. "Don't worry, I'll be a sphinx. And success, anyway," she whispered.

When she picked Jessica up, the child was holding a hand puppet with a menacing, witchy face. The puppet darted its evil head at Sylvie. "Mrs. Weyman," the witch squeaked, "I've put a terrible curse on you."

"Not again," Sylvie said drily.

Jessica waved the puppet in Sylvie's face, stirring a little flame of anger. She had the unsettling urge to slap the child, make her back off. "Oh, I wouldn't let the witch get *you*, Mrs. Weyman," Jessica was saying. "I would protect you and see that you only have blessings." She stuffed the puppet in her school bag and slipped a mittened hand in Sylvie's; Sylvie looked at it as though it were a found object.

She had planned to take Jess on a tour of some of the city's more interesting pet shops. There was one uptown distributor listed in the *Village Voice* who sold small, trained woodland animals. His clientele seemed to be mostly animal-fair exhibitors, but in some instances they were people in search of unusual pets. Civet cats, night owls, squirrel monkeys, bright pearly-hooded rats trained to drive a roto-wheel. She had thought it might be interesting for Jessica, but now she didn't know. There was a chip of energy that programmed her, drove her on. Sometimes it failed. She had weighed herself that morning at the pool, and for one alarming instant thought that she'd gained two pounds. But no, the scale merely needed adjustment.

Looking at Jessica trotting patiently at her side she decided to keep to her original plan. There was plenty of time. Margo wouldn't be upset if they were late coming home. She was away most afternoons these days, and many evenings. *Busi-*

ness, Margo explained. There was talk of a painter in SoHo. There was someone else in Santa Fe. And then the artist in Vermont, Bob Fleet. Margo spoke to her friend Alessa with newly acquired wisdom. "You absolutely must find these people when they're on the way up," she said with authority.

Michael had gone to Brazil and returned. But there was the new and very sensitive trip to the Middle East coming. Sylvie had heard the two of them talking. Margo's lowered, anxious voice: ". . . and what about the French lawyer who was found in an alley in Qatar with his index fingers cut off?" And Michael's swift, confident tone: ". . . impossible!" Such a constant onrush of activity, Sylvie thought. How easy it would be for Jessica and her to slip through the net of family life. How many hours would it take for them to be missed if, for example, they didn't return for dinner? How long before Margo, disciple of devout motherhood, would even notice? But then, why should she care? Sylvie inquired of herself. The child was not hers. She must remain detached.

Transvaal Pets was on Broadway in the Nineties. A long, narrow shop, filled with the twitching sounds of caged animals. There were brilliant tropical birds, darting and screaming behind a wall of chicken wire. One looked as if it wore a ruby prayer shawl. "I love it," Jessica screeched. "Can we get it? *Please!*"

"We're not buying. We're seeing. Pretend you're at the zoo."

Jessica said, "I've been to the Bronx Zoo three times. Twice with my mom. Mr. Wallace showed us everything." She went off to examine stacked cages of baby armadillos and rhesus monkeys. "Aren't we going to buy *anything*?" She asked in exasperation. Her tightly drawn ponytail gave her face an egglike sheen. She knelt in front of the armadillos. "Here, babies." She said hopefully, "They're like funny turtles. Maybe they don't cost much?"

"I don't think your mother would find them funny."

Sylvie remembered a parade of animals in her own house. Arthur coming home once with a gerbil in his coat pocket.

And Angel, looking at him ecstatically, crooning, "Daddy!" She'd had a Mongolian sloe-eyed cat whose coat was bluish buff. Her uncle Jeffrey sent her small flat snakes, brown as whips, from Seoul. When she was nine, she'd had a mutt named Sloppy. The dog died when a bone punctured his esophagus, and Angel insisted on having him cremated. For years she kept Sloppy's ashes in a mayonnaise jar on her dresser, next to Arthur's picture.

But Arthur—how had she failed to realize that the glue would be so thin? They had been married only three years when there was a melting away of ardor. His focus changed. From poor people's law, he turned to causes. The house was always crowded with other lawyers, activists, politicians, people who burned for something never fully attainable. There were men in her living room, holding Angel on their knees, who would kill over the issue of busing; who applauded the monks who set themselves on fire in Saigon. There was a woman judge who sat on their floor surrounded by a rapt circle and discussed a legal position that would render the looting laws inapplicable to the Newark rioters. And in the midst of it all was Arthur's avid face with the narrow, preoccupied smile that hardened the corners of his mouth. Once in that earlier time, after too much to drink, too much of the endless harangues, the brocade of strategies, fall-back positions, bottom lines, she had lured him into the bathroom, and pressing him against the door, said in a wine-soaked voice, "I'm famished for you, darling . . ."

He looked foolishly surprised. He touched her hair. "Sylvie . . . when they're gone."

They were never gone. He travelled. He became famous for a certain persuasive outrage in his courtroom delivery. His law firm was more and more in demand to defend its clients against the state, the federal government, the law of the land itself. He took on a new associate, Scott Rudick, and bloomed with enthusiasm. "That guy can track down the most obscure, I mean *obscure*, point of law in the most minor judicial decision!"

He and Scott were gone for weeks, for months at a stretch, holing up in Georgia or Alabama or California with the local lawyers on their cases. When he returned each time, he and Sylvie were like friendly strangers trying to find ways to retake the lost ground between them. There were flashes of passion. He brought her a voile nightgown made by one of the local handicraft communes in the South. When she wore it to bed, he looked frightened. He held her in his arms. "God, it's been so long . . . I'm sorry . . ."

She wondered whether he was having an affair and tried to watch him more closely, appraising the missed dinners, the trips to other cities, the weekends off somewhere on business. She wondered who the woman could be. Was she different from Sylvie, more aggressively vital? She searched the pockets of his clothes, read his mail. Once she found a nosegay of dried flowers in his jacket pocket wrapped in a handkerchief. They looked like primrose and lavender. The little petals gave off a familiar brandy scent with a whiff of orange as though they'd been sprayed with Cointreau. When he came home that night, she held the handkerchief out to him. "These?" The word was like a bark caught in the back of her throat.

He looked at her for a long time and then said firmly, "It's nothing!"

She thought about leaving him. But why? For better sex? To be the object of someone's unfailing devotion? She rejected the latter as being morally infirm. He generated excitement. He was the type who could make small but significant changes in the universe—or so she believed. She clung to the possibility that his life would tame down. That they might come together, as before. He had said that one day the two of them would have to write a book on the decade of the sixties, the preposterous early seventies. But she had already lost hope.

Early on it became clear that Angel was the invisible wire threading their lives, holding them together. He sometimes made arrangements that included Angel and her. They went to Atlantic City and once to Las Vegas, where Angel, enthralled, stuffed quarters into a slot machine. In Las Vegas, in a mirrored bedroom, satin-poufed like a jewel box, he made love to Sylvie with so much tenderness and conviction that she wondered whether their life together was about to take a new turn. Of course, that was before the lavender nosegay, before his descent into a deeper, more permanent abstraction.

JESSICA came rushing down the fish-tank aisle. "That man over there says the baby armadillos cost sixty dollars. Is that too much?" She grabbed Sylvie's hand and kissed it, glancing up, her little mouth pressed into the familiar knowing look that would one day become arch. "Pleeeease!"

The shop owner was talking to another man at the far end of the store. Sylvie said, "Armadillos are not house pets. Zorro would be very upset."

"He wouldn't," Jessica pleaded. "He'd have a friend." Sylvie had the bizarre image of Zorro and the armadillo lapping coffee in the kitchen.

She steered Jessica down another aisle. A little squirrel monkey reached out and clung to Jessica's ponytail. The child shrieked, pulling free of the hairy clutching fingers, rubbing her head in astonishment. The two men had turned to look at them. "What about a monkey? I could train it to ride on Zorro's back, and we'd give a performance at school. Mr. Wallace could come and maybe bring a baby wolf." Jessica was in the clouds. She grabbed Sylvie's hand again. "I'd teach him to say, 'Good morning, everybody.'"

"Animals do not talk," Sylvie said sharply, trying to curtail some of the excitement.

"They do! They do!"

"Maybe some do, in their way." Angel used to come up with arcane wisdom about animals. Sonar speech in dolphins. The nudging, staring, turning, pawing of other species. Birdsong. Gary had chipped in, "I wouldn't be surprised to know that parsley screams when it's chopped to bits." Now Sylvie said, "No monkey will ever learn to say good morning anything! Possibly a parrot . . ."

The two men were moving toward them. The owner of the shop said pleasantly, "Can I help you?"

"We seem to want one of everything," Sylvie said.

"How much are the parrots?" Jessica asked, tilting her head and offering her most bewitching smile.

"Well, let me see—there's one old fellow over there . . ."

But the younger man was looking at Sylvie. "Mrs. Weyman?" he asked. She studied his face. A big, good-natured face. Blue eyes, wind-coarsened skin stretched flat on his high cheekbones. He was wearing patched jeans low on his hips and rubber-soled boots.

"Do I know you?" she asked. Then she remembered. It was Daniel Baum, the young man who lived in the next valley, west of Brattleboro, and who had known both Gary and Angel in college. In fact, it was Danny's enthusiasm for Vermont life that had encouraged those two to explore the area. And it was Danny, with his tractor-driven plow, who had helped them that first summer to break up the sod so that they could put in their vegetables.

Sylvie had grown very still, dizzied by the surge of blood beating in her ears. "Yes, I know you," she finally said.

"Are things going along OK . . . you know . . ." He stood before her embarrassed, the specter of Angel between them, his face taking on a ruddy polished tint. Had he been at the funeral? she wondered.

"Oh, I'm the way you'd expect . . ." She was not helping much. "What are you doing right now?"

"Farm-type things." He was very tall, with a clear direct gaze, and he leaned toward her, amiable and concerned. "I've drifted into making bread and yogurt under the label of Black Fox Orchards. The yogurt's going like hell's blazes. I'm in town to set things up . . . the distribution channels and all . . . the way I did in Boston. And also to add to my little game preserve." He reached out and clasped the hand of the squirrel monkey. "Summer stuff," he said. "While the mommies stock up on yogurt and ten-grain bread, the kids play with the animals.

"I've thought about you," he said, plunging on. "I bumped

into Gary the other day. It was so unexpected, with the way he'd dropped out of sight. I saw the baby, too. That's when you were in my mind."

"Gary!" Sylvie's heart churned, then froze. "I didn't know he was in New England," she heard herself say. "We understood he'd gone out West. We'd asked around . . ."

"He went to Baja California. That's sort of Mexico, but he came back, I guess. Anyway, he was in the Brattleboro area about a month ago." He looked at her closely. "He didn't get in touch with you?"

She shook her head. "And now, right now—do you know where he's living now?" She steadied herself by resting a hand on Jessica's thin little shoulder.

"I really don't know. He said something about staying in Cozzens for a while—that's about forty miles north of Brattleboro. And then he mentioned Montpelier. He was very vague about everything, not too anxious to talk, especially to me, I guess. He did say he's been doing bookbinding again. Good stuff, too; he showed me some really beautiful things."

"And the baby is with him? Sean?"

"As far as I could see. Gorgeous kid. Gary said he had some woman coming in to take care of the baby, the cousin of someone we knew at school." He was silent for a while stroking the squirrel monkey's arm, which hung out of the cage now like a length of furred rope. Then he said, "Gary did say something about winding up his affairs one of these days and pushing off again to an easier climate. Maybe back to Baja Cal. He thought it would be good for the baby. He seemed really turned on to the whole idea. Mentioned Ensenada and towns like that as being laid-back and welcoming."

Sylvie turned away. Jessica was looking eagerly at a cage of tiny marmosets.

But the shop owner was coming toward them with a brilliant mauve-and-green parrot hooked to his shoulder. "Here's a really decent little fellow," he said. "It's a lilac-crested amazon with very good speech potential. I could let him go for three hundred."

"Oh, let's give him three hundred," Jessica said excitedly.

But Sylvie was ready to leave the shop, needed to leave. She said good-bye quickly to Danny Baum, who seemed to be peering worriedly into her face. "I'd like to know how to get in touch with you," he said.

She was already on her way. "I'll be in touch with *you*," she said, her voice faltering even as she spoke. Clutching Jessica's arm, she marched her out of the store.

CHAPTER 11

S YLVIE stayed in her room for two days following her
meeting with Danny Baum. She felt feverish. The room
rocked. She closed her eyes and tried to steady her thoughts,
steady herself. She held the coverlet to her neck; held on.
Sean's imagined face, Gary's fidgety scarecrow look, both
rose before her. She tried to read, but the words trailed
off the page. It was a weekend, part of her revised arrangement—extended time on the job. Margo had been sympathetic. "Maybe you're getting a touch of the flu. Just take it
easy."

The sounds of the house filtered through. Jessica had per-
suaded Margo to go back to Transvaal Pets and buy the
parrot.

"Oh, really! Only three hundred!" Margo repeated, mi-
micking Jessica's breezy voice. Then she added, "Look, baby,
that's a real pile of dough."

But in the end Michael intervened. "This will be your
birthday present from us and from Grandpa Max and Nana."

Now Sylvie could hear Jess in the hall, talking to the parrot
through the fine mesh of his cage, repeating in her clear, high

voice, "Say, 'Good day! Good day, ma'am! Good day, Mrs. Weyman!' "

The parrot screamed, "Hak! Hak!"

Michael was operating at medium boil. His trip to Rio had fed into the Middle East connection. There was someone in Turkey who was an important money-mover. "That means the movement of goods—so they're very hot on me at the moment, naturally." He tried to stay away from government officialdom. Red tape, he explained to Margo, as though she were a student taking notes. He liked to move into a port, a city, install his systems, get paid and move out fast. One never knew when the local political fireworks might start. He didn't want to get trapped in *that.* Sylvie listened, heard Margo complaining.

"But that's just the point. You have a sub-rosa look. People can't figure out exactly where you're coming from, or who your backers are. In Teheran, they could just as easily tie you to a tree and let the birds peck out your eyes and then announce you'd been in a road accident."

"Unlikely. And we're talking Jidda, not Teheran." He sounded so sure of himself, Sylvie thought. "In Jidda there are more Mercedes per capita than in Beverly Hills."

Sylvie could hear them in the halls, at the breakfast table, when she went down to get her yoghurt from the refrigerator. The irritated cadence of their bickering was everywhere.

At one point, Margo stormed out of their bedroom. Sylvie heard her thumping down the stairs. "Oh, do as you please! You will, anyway." And then she walked back and said, before she closed the door behind her, "I may go off for a couple of weeks while you're gone . . . fly out West . . ."

Jessica had opened their bedroom door; Michael was saying in a lowered voice, "Do you think Sylvie can handle it?" and Margo answering crisply, "Don't you?"

SHE sat back in her recliner and tried to force herself to read. She had gone back to the nineteenth century again; she had always been drawn to the novel of manners, as though her own spare life was somehow validated, made buoyant, by a look at those intricate social tapestries. This time it was *Emma*. And here she observed, as she had many times before, that children were only shadows, hidden away. Not until they were marriageable or ready to take on careers did they attract the family's or the author's interest. Was childhood mortality at the root of all that cool maternal passivity? Those terrible centuries of infant and child loss. Those statistics—one child in ten surviving to the age of five. "Another kind of plague," Victor had commented once. "Oh yes, yes," she had said, clamping her hands to her ears.

She thought again of Gary, tried to visualize him. Was he in Vermont now, or New Hampshire, or Maine? He could be anywhere. Did he live in a house or a barn? Was it a one-room apartment above the convenience store in some small town, with the baby in a crib, perhaps dangerously close to a kerosene heater? Angel and Gary had lived in such quarters when they first moved to Vermont, before they found a house that they could rent. And did the baby look like Gary? Or did he have Angel's golden bloom? And were they already on their way in search of a "welcoming" place? Oh, she must do something.

It was Sunday; there was a knock on the door, and Jessica came in with the parrot. She settled herself and the cage on Sylvie's bed. "I'm going to call him Melvin," she confided.

"Why Melvin?" Sylvie asked, drawing her robe around her.

"Because it sounds right," Jessica replied.

Jessica's legs were folded under her; she was wearing a bright plaid skirt, Miss Piggy sneakers. Strands of hair had pulled loose from her ponytail and curled in a damp straggle on her neck. Her eyes were as sharp as Melvin's. She might be lovely one day, Sylvie thought, turning away.

"You're not really *too* sick, are you?" Jessica asked, bouncing slightly on the bed. There was gum on one of her sneakers and it was sticking to the spread.

"Medium sick. You're making a mess."

Jess pressed her cheek against Sylvie's knees for a moment and then sat up and touched her finger to the cage. The bird dove for it, shrieking, "Hak! Hak!" Jessica sighed. "If only he'd just say *good,* like in good day, I'd at least know he was smart. You're supposed to say things to him slowly and then give him a treat if he tries hard." There were pumpkin seeds clenched in her fist. "I hope he's not a dummy." She settled the cage on a comforter at Sylvie's feet and shouted, *"Good day, Mrs. Weyman! Good day, Mrs. Weyman!"*

Melvin screamed back, "Hak! Gak!"

SHE called Victor again on Sunday afternoon, and this time found him home. "I'm sorry, sorry . . . ," she began.

"Oh, well, no need for that," he said. His voice was reserved. She heard the click of his pipe between his teeth and imagined his spotless look, the spicy smell of tobacco clinging to his sweater. "I'm awfully busy just now. . . ." For one brief terrible moment she wondered whether he was with another woman. A younger, silkier woman who stroked his neck as she coaxed him to try another bite of her steak tartare. But the notion was too devastating to be dealt with, and she put it aside. She thought she knew him totally; still there was always another niche, a chink of surprise. Once, when he was telling her about himself, he'd said, "I should have been in research. I can see myself wild with joy at spotting and naming a brand-new nasty little bug. I should have gotten a medical degree and then headed for Washington and the NIH. I don't know how I ended up in commerce, working for an insurance company." And then he'd said, "Oh, hell, of course I know."

One of his New York uncles on his mother's side had sent for him. He was nearly ten years old when he arrived from France, a few years after the end of the war. He lived with one set of relatives and then another, growing up mostly in households without children ("Only my mother seemed to have had the knack"), feeling shadowy and uncertain, unable to take root in that well-meaning but ambivalent family soil. ("You know how people are! One of my cousins threw a fit when I used her toothpaste. She sent me a toilet-paper note written in lipstick: Go back, jerk!") At seventeen he had had enough ersatz generosity stuffed down his throat. He went to New York University to train as quickly as he could to be self-sufficient. "But weren't there grants?" she asked. Not really, not without private support, he said. Anyway, the process was too slow. He hooked up with Apollo early, and it wasn't too bad; eventually he even enjoyed his work, moving numbers around, playing seer, divining whole continents of risk.

Now he asked, "Are you . . . are you finding what you need right now?"

She said, "I met someone, Danny Baum—do you remember him? He said he recently bumped into Gary in Vermont."

"Well, it's a better lead than the Yucatan. What are you going to do?"

"I'm in a state of shock. I don't even know if I can handle it yet—seeing the baby."

MARGO came in to talk to her later that evening, "How are you doing? Mind if I barge in?"

Sylvie was in bed for the night, but she waved Margo to the chair. "I'll be all right by tomorrow," she said. "I felt dizzy, I guess. Upset. It's a personal matter. I needed these two days to pull myself together."

"Well, I've watched you, and I know at least *one* contributing factor," Margo remarked sternly. She sat upright in the recliner and folded her knees under her. Her hair shone in the lamplight, fringed and silky, the color of fallen oak leaves. Her young face was narrower than Jessica's. Her eyes were hazel, Jessica's intense blue. Her lips were fuller, more sensual; Jessica's smile held the hint of Michael's droll, questioning mouth. Sylvie had a sudden notion of Tania's baby born with an ambiguous little face and the relatives joking around: "He's the spitting image of the newspaper boy, right?" Or ironically, going the other way, "That's Larry's face all right, down to the sweet dimpled chin!"

People see what they choose to see, Sylvie thought. Cherish

their belief. Angel had found something compelling in Gary's harum-scarum look. "It's in his smile . . . his dear naked heart . . ."

"You don't eat enough," Margo was saying. "A chicken wing, some lettuce leaves. It's not enough to keep a fly going. And all that swimming every day to burn off whatever calories dare accumulate. Really, Sylvie, why do you do it? You have such a lovely figure; I wish I were as tall and, well, arresting, as you." She looked troubled. Whatever it was, it extended beyond her concern for Sylvie. "You don't have a food problem, do you?" she asked. "I mean, there's a name for that sort of thing. Something to do with self-punishment. Have you always been this way?"

"Not exactly. But at the moment, I can't bear the thought of excess. I don't know. You've heard of people talking about getting down to the bone. Well . . . I may be taking that too literally." She smiled, lifting her hands in a submissive gesture. "It's a private thing."

"But you're so *mysterious,*" Margo said. Her eyes, wide, questioning, became fixed on an architectural rendering of a Tudor castle, complete with moat, that hung above the bookcase. Sylvie had borrowed it from Louden's "Now and Then" wall. "Your interests seem so special . . . your books . . ." She was at a loss. "I know so little about you, except that you're terribly efficient and somewhat withdrawn. Michael says you're a little like the character in stories who arrives on a windswept night and stands silently in the attic window looking out. Sort of like *The French Lieutenant's Woman.* But don't get him wrong. He thinks you're terrific." She said, "I don't mean to pry." And then quickly, "Yes, I do."

Sylvie took a long breath. "I don't *want* to be mysterious." She patted the covers around her as if to root herself to the bed. Oh, why not, she thought. Sooner or later they would know. She spoke hurriedly, awkwardly. "I had a daughter who was twenty-two. She died. It's nearly six months now. Her name was Angel . . . and that's all there is to it . . ."

Margo's face shimmered in the glow of the room. Her mouth shaped itself into a small moist "Oh." She came and sat on the edge of Sylvie's bed and took her hand. "God, what agony. I can't bear to imagine it . . ." She was silent for a while, nonplussed, like a visitor in a hospital taken aback at the gravity of the patient's condition. Then she said, "What can I say? You seem so strong. I know this will sound crazy, but in a way, you seem above ordinary misfortune. You have so much darn composure . . ." Margo looked at her helplessly and said in a faintly puzzled tone, "Is that why you're here —to be away from familiar, painful things?"

"I suppose so. I hope I'm earning my keep."

"Does your being here, in a family that seems reasonably whole, with a very lively and demanding child, does it make you feel better?" Margo's voice implied an issue that ought to be settled.

"As much better as I'm likely to feel right now."

Margo said nothing. She squeezed Sylvie's hand, standing over her like a mother comforting a child before sleep. She said, "I'm so, so sorry. If you only knew." Then she said simply, "I'm glad you're here."

After that, Feliciana knocked at her door; she'd brought a small tomato cut like a flower, festooned with sprigs of dill. It remained only for Michael to poke his head in and boom something silly and personal at her. And he did. He stood on the threshold in warm-up pants and a pullover, sweaty from a bout with his exercycle. "French toast and Virginia ham for breakfast tomorrow. Zorro will serve." He blew her a kiss and was gone.

She could hear Margo's brisk footsteps retreating down the hall. The click of a door. Jessica's high-pitched voice demanding an answer to something. Melvin, rending the night with an imperious "Gak!" And beyond that, silence and the heavy thudding of her own heart.

A few days later, she took Jessica to the Museum of Natural History after school. A new space film was being shown that reproduced the sight and sensation of interplanetary flight. Margo had noticed the film in the Kids' Stuff column of the school newspaper and left a note for Sylvie on Jessica's bulletin board.

Jessica squealed at lift-off, buried her head in Sylvie's shoulder, clutched Sylvie's hand and the arm of her seat and held on to both as though she, too, could be spun away through space. Her grip loosened. She sat back and watched the rush of stars, the jettisoning of rockets, the planets looming closer like luminescent boulders—Saturn with its flaring rings, ethereal Venus, the blood-rose flush of Mars.

"What is space?" Jessica demanded. Angel had asked, *Who colors the sun? Where do the stars go in the morning?*

"It's what we're floating in, like a helium balloon only without a string to drag us back down." The question dwarfed the imagination.

Jessica wiggled closer, pretending to be climbing onto Sylvie's lap. "I want to sit in your space."

"Quiet. We're coming down into the ocean."

After the film, Jess wanted to take her through the museum to see the animal displays. The dinosaurs on the fourth floor. The huge stuffed grizzly, towering on hind legs like a victorious wrestler, on the first. A vast glass-fronted wall display showed a wolf family in its natural habitat, complete with a litter of pups.

"Aren't the babies sweet?" Jessica said. "Mr. Wallace told us that wolf mothers chew up their babies' food and spit it into their mouths." Her own mouth was pursed in a tiny bud. "Double yuk," she said.

Angel had taken her love of animals right through college. In college she visited model farms that specialized in animal husbandry. She had developed a mad crush on a local vet, a young man who walked around in knee-high rubber boots and carried forceps the size of forging tongs in the back of his car. She had helped him deliver a calf once and called Sylvie in Rosevale to tell her about it. "It was spectacular!" she breathed.

Sylvie ached when she saw Angel's enthusiasm gradually dissolve in the muddle of Gary's aspirations. They might build a cooperative, she began to say. They could start an organic food restaurant and call it Germ of Truth. They were thinking about getting the backing for a printing press and bindery and doing only the work of some very special poets and other writers. "Gary's got what it takes," she said, as though it was something rehearsed from memory. "We've got to get him on the road first; then me."

"Why in that order?" Sylvie had inquired. It was recent, each detail was razor-sharp: Angel in scuffed work boots and lumberjack clothes, saying, "We want to be self-sufficient before I get all wound up in going back to school"; Angel sending pictures of herself, a tattered gypsy in a long skirt and headband, sitting at a table in the local crafts center, making bracelets; Angel standing between Gary and Danny Baum, holding a pumpkin in her arms.

"I'm wiring money, until you get started."

"Thanks, but no. We are started. There are several couples like ourselves, and it looks as if we'll get that cooperative to fly."

THEY stopped off at the ladies' room on the third floor. "Do you need help?" Sylvie asked.

"Let's pee together," Jessica said in a giggly voice. Her eyes gleamed. She pulled Sylvie into the cubicle and slid the latch closed. "First I'll go and then you." She was undoing her overalls.

Sylvie unlatched the door. "I'll wait outside."

There was a scale near the washbasins, and stepping on the black mat, she watched the needle calibrate her weight. She had lost half a pound, eight ounces of body weight. The heaviness over her heart hadn't changed.

They took the elevator to the main floor. "We didn't see the whale," Jess complained.

"Next time. There's always a next time," she said abstractedly. Her eye was caught by two people at the far corner of the floor near the elevators. The man was in shirt-sleeves. The woman had her fleece coat wrapped tightly around her, the collar nearly concealing her small cap of hair. The man's head was tilted toward her. His hand was on her wrist. He lifted the wrist and held it lightly to his lips. The woman put her hand protectively in her pocket. She reached up with the other and picked something, perhaps lint or crumbs, from the man's beard. Her fingers brushed his lips. He left her for a moment and came back, zipping a ski jacket. They walked quickly to the door. It was Margo, of course, and who? But Sylvie knew who. Flooded with instant knowledge, she was sure it was Mr. Wallace of the museum, of the zoo. She clutched Jessica's hand and hurried her away. "I've changed my mind. One quick look at the whale and then we go."

When they were finally outside, it had turned dark. A brisk wind swept across the park, whipping up sheets of newspaper and bits of debris. Sylvie tucked Jess's scarf around her neck and scanned the street, fearful that she'd see Margo and that man.

They walked to the corner for the connecting East Side bus or, in this cold, a cab.

"Must we go home?" Jessica asked.

"What's that supposed to mean?"

"We've never eaten out," she said, the idea popping like a flashbulb in her head. "Oh, please! We've never done *that.*" She stopped in the street and opened her change purse. "One dollar and ten cents. Will it be enough?"

"Perhaps for midgets." Sylvie hurried her toward Amsterdam Avenue. Actually coffee sounded like a good idea. She was feeling faint again. There was a peculiar hollow buzzing behind her eyes.

"Oh, here," Jessica said, stopping in front of a Mexican restaurant. Stained-glass medallions tinkled from the ceiling as they opened the door. The window held vividly painted candelabra, foil stars. A cook was standing at an open grill stuffing enchiladas. Jessica ordered pinto beans, which she ate one by one. Sylvie wondered uneasily whether they were being missed at home. She went to the phone and called, but the line was busy. She went back to the table and sipped her coffee. Jessica offered her a bean. "Try it," she insisted.

"I'm not wild about beans." Jessica looked crestfallen and held her fork like a staff, with the single bean speared on top. "All right," Sylvie said. "One bean." She hadn't swum in two days, and the thought of this made her skittish with fear. She went back to the phone. Still busy. Jessica was taking forever. She had ordered a Coke and was nibbling the edges of a taco. "My teacher, Miss Formico, says tacos are higher up on the food chain than potato chips." Sylvie tried the phone again, and again the busy signal droned away. It was seven o'clock, almost two hours past the time they should have returned.

She hurried Jessica along. "We'll take a doggy bag."

"And a parrot bag," Jessica said. She lifted her hands palms up, Margo's gesture. "Let him just *try.*"

When they got home, Margo and Michael were having dinner. It was obvious that an argument had been in progress. Margo's face was pale. Michael, head bent, was shovelling food into his mouth.

Jessica dug into her pocket and dropped a taco in Zorro's bowl. "We had Mexican," she sang out.

"My God," Margo said in astonishment, "I didn't even realize that you two weren't home." She pressed a napkin hastily to her mouth and got to her feet. "I guess I just assumed . . ."

Watching her, the distraction in her face, Sylvie thought again how quickly, oh, how quickly the guard was down.

CHAPTER 12

THE gallery in question was on a narrow street in the lower part of the city. A neighborhood in transition, Margo decided, neither fish nor fowl. Light industry, still present, smogged the windows of nearby boutiques and coffee shops. Overflowing refuse cans leaned tipsily at the sides of doorways. The gallery owner was gay, clever, supercilious and in a permanent state of confusion. "Nothing is cheap, you know," he said, tossing his hands. "So be prepared for numbers!" His name was St. Clair. He wore skinny black hiphuggers, black espadrilles, and wire-frame rose glasses perched like birds at the end of his long nose. His look was a mix of Cocteau and beachboy.

"I'm concentrating on good," Margo said, allowing a little flint to color her voice.

Alessa had told her to ask about Robbie Riotson's work. "He's just beginning to surface," she said. "Now's the time."

St. Clair had some Riotson in the rear gallery. Even in the dark, the paintings lit the room. Brilliant pieces glazed to a heavy metallic sheen. There were wonderfully intricate compositions of posed women in bracelets, boas, cloches. Sophisticated ladies with heavy-lidded eyes and a faintly sinister look. There were four of them, and they were all wonderful.

"How much?" Margo asked.

"Three thousand each, and that's only because he's new."

"Too high," Margo said, focusing on the tuft of bird's down sprouting from St. Clair's open shirt. She would not be intimidated. "We have to jack up the price to include my fee and the fee of my accessories contact. I'm not just coming in off the street, you know." She paused. "How about eighteen hundred dollars?"

St. Clair whipped out his handkerchief and fanned his face. "Oh, please, we may be *close* to Orchard Street and the bargain hunters, but not *that* close."

Margo pressed on. She hoped she sounded cool, not anxious. "If we could strike a deal, I'd take all four. I have clients who could be interested." Alessa was right. These were marvellous, like stained glass in sunlight, much too good to pass up.

"You're too naïve," St. Clair was saying. "We're not whores down here, selling our favors for what the traffic will bear. This kind of haggling gives me a migraine."

"Oh, come, think about it. If the people I deal with are satisfied, I may be able to absorb whatever Riotson does. Here's my card."

St. Clair peered at her down the length of his nose. "Well, we'll just see what the artist has to say."

Outside she walked in the direction of Houston Street, where her station wagon was parked. She felt great. She felt as if she'd unearthed a perfect Minoan cup. Not quite. But the artist was good. He met the needs of a stylized New York trend without being too trendy. Passing a small Near Eastern restaurant, she went inside to call Brill at the museum; she was told he was on his way to the zoo. She called Michael instead, and his secretary put her through. "Sweetheart!" He was surprised. "To what do I owe . . . Come on over and have lunch."

"I've just had lunch," she lied. "I'm still in SoHo, Michael.

I've seen some beautiful work. If they come down on the price, I'd like to invest. What do you think?"

"How much?"

"Seven or eight thousand, I think, for a group of four. Will you stake me?" She meant to be tongue-in-cheek, but her voice had an anxious, needy sound.

"Will I stake you? Baby, does a tree bear fruit?"

"It's just a loan. I expect to pay you back."

"That's really funny. Anyway, I thought we were partners in *everything.*"

"I suppose so," she answered, miserable. She felt like a worm. "Thank you. I mean that, Michael."

She sat at a table near the window and had a pita sandwich and thick, sweet Turkish coffee. The coffee would make her heart race all afternoon. Let it. A second cup and the sight, even the thought of Brill—or of Michael, too, for that matter —might bring on a coronary. Chance, she thought; so much of her life had finally come to that. And for Michael, too, she realized, looking at the posters on the wall. A fluttery nervousness had started up in her. The posters showed minarets and obelisks behind marble walls, veiled women with piercing eyes staring into their futures, turbanned men with an alien, dangerous look. The Arabic script might have said anything: "Kill the American infidel!"

She got up and left abruptly. She wished that Michael would drop the deal in Jidda. His contacts were too shadowy. They communicated by flying a pair of messengers into New York in a private jet. They met with Michael in public places, noisy restaurants, the lobbies of busy hotels. Money was passed, not with checks or letters of credit but in green bundles stacked neatly inside a lizard travelling case. "Our arrangements, Mr. Kort, must be free-floating, like your very ingenious port systems. There are elements in this government, in any government, ill-advised factions, fanatics nursing imaginary wounds. Imaginary, you understand, because in our country there is sufficient wealth for all. So we proceed with caution . . . when you arrive you will stay at the prime minister's residence. The hotel is, ah . . . too *available*. You will have a private car and chauffeur, certain security measures to insure your comfort . . ."

"Comfort!" she had yelled at Michael when she heard all this. "They mean your life!"

"I'm constructing a port, not starting a revolution," he'd said blandly.

RIDDLED with guilt, she walked along the street, past a housing complex whose barricaded playground echoed with the screams of children playing. There was a little slide that spilled into a sandpit. Jessica still loved the slide, although she was too big to get any mileage from such a scaled-down plaything.

Margo felt a surge of longing for Jessica this minute, right here on Houston Street, wanted her small dear hand safely tucked in hers. And yet, only the other night, swamped by her own preoccupations, she hadn't even known that Jessica and Sylvie had not come home for dinner. Her lapse of concern was frightening. She had once read about a couple who, when they pulled over to the side of the road to fix a flat tire, placed their baby in its bassinet on a grassy stretch beside the car. When the tire was changed, they drove off, forgetting the baby; they'd travelled two miles before they woke up to what they'd done. She had thought then that the parents were either creeps or retards. But it was not that simple. She felt as if her own life was skidding out of control, blurring the process of thought. There was so much confusion and ambivalence. The enormous ambivalence caused by Brill. He was not yet indispensable, she reminded herself. And there was Michael looming, throwing his long, embracing shadow. Was she ready to replace that?

One of the children had slipped off the jungle gym and into a sandpit. A mother came running, a soft, anxious woman with outstretched arms. Margo had wanted another child, despite the tumult of her life, despite Brill in the wings. In her imaginings, there were always two children in the back

seat of the station wagon with Zorro between them, groggy
with love. But there was Michael's strange resistance to deal
with, his strictly pragmatic view: "I'm away so much, and
you're all involved with this new business of yours, to say
nothing of your parents' endless needs. Are we making children for people like Sylvie Weyman to take care of?" He had
looked at her sympathetically. "Of course these are only *my*
feelings. But I'd say, let's put it off for a while and see . . ."
He was partially right, she thought. She wouldn't want
Sylvie hooked into an infant's sealed environment; not an
infant's. It was different with Jessica, who had the rest of her
world to relate to. But the reservoir of grief that woman must
be coping with. No wonder the incessant swimming and
fasting. It was more civilized, she supposed, than beating
your head against a wall. But if it had happened to her, she'd
just as soon be dead.

She turned away, stopped once more at a street phone and
called Brill at the zoo. "Darling!" He had just arrived, he
said. "Where are you?" When she told him, he said, "Get on
the East River Drive and come up. I'll shove my work into
a corner, and we can be together for a while." She hesitated,
and he added, "I haven't seen you in days. There's stuff we've
got to get settled."

She met him at the north end of the zoo. A strange, barren
landscape, dun-colored in the afternoon light. Nearly extinct
animals were kept here. The prairie bison, Mongolian wild
horses. She could see the sparse herds, motionless as statuary
in the distance.

She had gone to the meeting place he'd suggested—there
were people in his office, he said, and he'd just as soon keep
his private life private. It was a partially concealed retreat off
a small path in a pocket of trees. There was a bench for
viewing the animals that might cross the simulated plain.
Place the Robbie Riotson paintings in this landscape, she
thought, and it would be a "happening." The pictures would
seem to be burning. And he was just *one* artist. There would
be others for her inventory. *Inventory.* A serious word. She

liked the seriousness of being professional, if she could just unmuddle her life, or understand it. She felt as if she were juggling flaming balls—Michael, Brill, Jessica, her parents. The doctor had told her yesterday that Celia's bone-marrow tests were again abnormal. His voice was cautionary. "Her blood count is off. But it may only be an infection."

So much to claim her. And there was Sylvie Weyman, like a Chinese riddle still.

Brill came up the path, his ski jacket open and flapping. He swooped her from the bench, lifting her toward him. His lips were hard and sweet. "Oh, Brill," she gasped in the thorny frazzle of his beard, "I don't know what will happen next."

One Mongolian horse had broken from the herd and was trotting in circles. The others ignored him. Brill was saying, "It was settled this morning. I'm going out to Butte any time between now and a month from now." He tipped her face toward his and kissed her again slowly. "I want you to come with me . . ."

"I don't know . . ."

Michael was leaving in a week or so, which was all the more reason for her to be at home. And yet perhaps she could make her own brief escape. "I've never just gone off . . . ," wondering to herself whether she had already lost the power of coherent thought.

"Don't hassle it so much. Just relax and let it happen." They took a walk through the zoo, past the Children's Zoo, where last year, in a simpler time, she'd taken Jessica to see the domestic animals, chicks to cuddle, a curly baby lamb. She said to Brill, "We have a parrot." That morning Melvin had seemed to say "Gud," and Jessica rewarded him with a little party plate of pumpkin seed.

"A parrot?" He pulled her into Bird World, raucous with the cries of birds and filled with great leafy rain-forest plants.

She said, "I saw some really good art today. All this gorgeous color is a reminder . . ."

He pressed her against him. His jacket was unzipped; she was being branded by his sweater buttons. "Tell me everything," he said.

Too upset to speak, she pointed. "There . . . with the mauve head feathers." Melvin and his ancestors were perched in a banyan tree. But Brill was already leading her out and down another path in the direction of the wolves. A bemused pack, staring out through the barricade. They seemed thin to her, not dangerous; and yet danger was everywhere. How far might Michael go as the betrayed husband? It would be a matter of pride. The other night he had come to bed with his pajama bottoms hanging low on his hips. His signal. He poured V.O. for them both, turned WNCN to high, rolled some Tía Juana Gold and passed it to her. "I don't need *that*," she said, annoyed. "Either I'm in the mood or I'm not." He glanced at her with a foolish hurt look. "Yeah, and just where is that so-called mood . . ." He might even, with his appetite for being in the right—it was a terrifying thought—try to take Jessica away from her. She was the transgressor; he could cut her off without a cent. And then what would happen to Celia and Max? But that was not his style. He was not a heartless man. Yet how could she tell what he would do when pushed, really pushed, bludgeoned?

Brill was saying, "We seem to be finding that animals in captivity, the wolf, in particular . . ." He stopped and looked at her as if all the energy had run out of him. "Oh, hell, how does any of it affect the two of us?" His arm was around her waist, and she looked to see if there were any Pritchard mothers or offspring nearby. He said in a serious voice, "It's the oldest story in the world. I just don't want to go off without you."

In the end she said she'd try. She didn't know for how long, or precisely when. But she might meet him somewhere, Santa Fe or Taos maybe. There was reason for her to take a look at the work out there. They were holding hands, both of hers in both of his. He had begun to laugh. "God, what a thought!" he said. "Real solid time together." His laughter buoyed her; it was only her heart that dragged.

CHAPTER 13

"Go away, you fiend!" It was Alessa talking to Zorro. Persistent Zorro dug his nose between her legs. "You're a crotch man, I see. Like some other guys I know."

"It's your perfume that's turning him on," Margo said.

Walking up the stairs, Alessa paused and flung open her arms. She turned to Margo, who held a deranged Zorro by the collar. "There's something spooky about this stairway . . . it's as if God lowered it for the Ascent."

"Not precisely *God,*" Margo said, "merely a self-styled facsimile. In this house we each have our own style for dealing with the stairs. Feliciana clutches the banister as though she were on board a ship. Jessica picks her way down like a little princess. Zorro usually does a belly flop to the bottom. And I duck my head and make a dash for it." Originally the rail had been made of invisible steel filaments, and once Jessica, searching for a grip, missed entirely and fell several steps. "Tear the thing down!" Margo had stormed at Michael. "I don't care if you replace it with a ladder to the second floor. At least it will be honest."

"Oh, Christ! Stop foaming or I *will* go out and find a

ladder." But he took her anger seriously and replaced the filaments with a banister of sturdy teak.

"When are you going to really furnish this place?" Alessa asked.

"Oh, when I have the time . . . and the interest." She still felt at odds with the house.

But in Margo's study, Alessa looked around approvingly. She scanned a shelf of art and design periodicals, ran her fingers over the smooth functional desk. "Very neat and efficient. I predict a dynamic future . . ." She leaned against the windowsill and sighed. "I could use a cup of tea. Something herbal. Caffeine destroys the complexion I'm told." Margo wondered who had told her. She did look drawn, all of her taut as a sheet. She was an arresting woman, statuesque. Her dark hair, swept back and gathered in a flawless chignon, framed shadowed cheekbones, a narrow prominent nose, eyes too large to quite fit their sockets. She was wearing pants, a flaring tunic, a cape seamed in a crazy jigsaw of parts, brilliant lipstick. Smudgy pencilled eyelids gave her face the pointed look of a raccoon's.

Margo went to get the tea. When she returned, Alessa was looking at the few canvases leaning against the wall. "Just for the record," Alessa said, "corporate art must be cool. It cannot be shocking, brutal, avant-garde or sexy. Riotson is not for corporate lobbies or boardrooms. He belongs over some collector's mantle."

"I guess the idea is not to offend or excite the public sensibility."

"That's right." Alessa held her hand to the light and examined her nails, glittery polished amethyst ovals. "Stick to geometric patterns, simple landscapes, still lifes. It's the way to please most of the people most of the time. You'll do fine."

"Well *you've* certainly been terrific. I don't think I could have gotten started without you." Margo poured tea for them both. Alessa had stretched out on the couch, an odalisque, brooding, steamy. They had known each other only about a year. In the park one Saturday morning, Margo had been watching Jessica on the swings while Michael did his three or four miles around the reservoir. Alessa came by with little Brett, who promptly took possession of both Jessica and the swing. "I'll push," Brett said. "I'll give you a twisty and then jump in your lap. I could sit on your shoulders."

"I don't want you on my shoulders," Jessica cried out indignantly.

"Less enthusiasm, Brett. Please! I mean, cool it."

"Your little boy's a real entrepreneur," Margo said, smiling.

"He's not my little boy. I'm minding him for someone." It turned out that Brett was the son of her current boyfriend, who happened to be out of town. "Nanny for a day," Alessa said jauntily. Her own son, Stephen, was away at boarding school.

They sat and chatted, took the children to Peppermint Park for sodas. Alessa was an interior designer and had her own gallery in Woodstock. She seemed to know everyone. And she regarded Margo as a find. "You're great, you know that? I mean, you have this air of nonjudgmental inquiry. It's special. You're the sort of person who'll seem fresh and unspoiled until the day you die." She gave Margo an approving hug.

"I wish I could bet on that," Margo said. There was so much restlessness in her, dismay and grudgingness, impurity in all her feelings, even for Jessica . . . for Michael. And there was Brill.

Alessa had been married "centuries ago." "I'm only forty, but I feel as if I've been alive since the dawn of time," she said. The marriage just fell apart. "It was my fault, I suppose. I had a brief fling with this Danish princeling I met at an antiques fair in the Coliseum. My husband found out, and that started it. I tried to smooth things over, got pregnant and felt euphoric. I thought this is the ultimate, the universal glue —marriage, children. I imagined a new, glorious beginning. Artless little dope that I was. There was the baby first, then the divorce."

Now, stretched on the couch, her long agate cigarette holder between her lips, she had the Art Deco look of one of Riotson's own women, the very women she was staring at in his canvases propped against the wall. She said, "They breathe transvestite. They'd give Trump and the others the willies."

"All right, you've made your point," Margo said. "But they *are* fun."

"I think they're shallow. They're design, not art." She drew on her cigarette, sending up thin lines of smoke. "Everything's over between Val and me, you know." Val was her current lover, a city planner. "Dark and rugged. A little bit brutish, like a gentle gangster," she'd told Margo some months before, when it all started. "What's happening between us is so powerful. It makes me believe in mythology, in *legend.*" But now he'd walked out. The heat was too much. His wife had found out about the affair and gone berserk. Shredded his clothes. Slashed her wrists, then jumped off the second-floor terrace of their garden apartment in Riverdale. "Talk about overkill!" Alessa said. "She fractured both ankles and a few vertebrae. She's in a cast up to her ears. Val said, 'Baby, we have to lay low for now—maybe indefinitely. I'm not the killer type—my conscience won't let me . . .'" Alessa examined her nails again.

"God, the pain!" Margo said.

"For who, Val? Me? Or the wife?"

"For everyone, of course. No one is exempt."

"You're right. No one is exempt. But what if *I* jumped out the window? Would *my* action be as persuasive as hers?"

"No, you're not in a priority position."

"You know, I hate it when you're being sensible. Is Brill?"

"Is Brill what?"

"Priority was *your* word, wasn't it?"

"I think you're being annoyed with me."

Sylvie had come up the stairs just then and stuck her head in the room. "I'm taking your father to his doctor's appointment." She was wearing a narrow tweed skirt that emphasized her slenderness. Her hair was pulled back and wound around her head like a turban, a style favored by Alessa. But there the similarity ended. Sylvie's reserve was like a shade drawn across a window, in contrast to Alessa's floodlit attentiveness. "I'll use the station wagon. Is that all right?"

"Yes, of course," Margo said. Michael had the Saab. She would take a crosstown bus if Brill called. Her heart leapt and then sank. Brill had only one thing on his mind: Was she or was she not going to meet him somewhere in the West.

Margo introduced Sylvie to Alessa, who sat up and extended her hand. Sylvie nodded, her pale composed face settling for an instant in a smile. She pressed Alessa's hand and left.

After she had gone Alessa pursed her lips and said, "Very special. Perhaps *too* special. Gorgeous hair. What is she doing in your house?"

"I sometimes wonder myself."

"So where does it leave you"—Alessa had lit another cigarette—"now that you have someone so remarkably efficient to take up the slack?" She got up and knelt before the Riotson women. "Double-breasted jackets with nipples in place of buttons. My lord!" She glanced up at the wall mirror and blew puffs of smoke at herself. "You ought to go out to Santa Fe. There's a flourishing art scene there, and you won't have to contend with East Coast prices. Val has something hanging over the bed by John Swiftwater of New Mexico—a cluster of women's faces, adobe-colored, with strands of hair like black grass whipping across their cheeks." Her voice slid into a lower, harsher register, and she paused to inhale her cigarette more deeply.

"Brill has been urging . . ." Margo said quickly. Alessa on the verge of tears and just a little nasty was more than she could handle.

"I know. You told me. Why don't you just go? See what's in store for you. You owe it to yourself. Listen to me, experience is everything. I've had enough of it. It's where the oxygen is."

Margo turned away from her friend, who was getting ready to leave, wrapping herself elaborately into something that looked like a fringed serape. Easy for Alessa to give advice. There were no fixed points in her life, nothing to anchor her, to make her pause. But she said quietly, "I may do it. I may just pick up and go for a week or so, after Michael leaves." If she could. If her guilt wouldn't crash the plane.

CHAPTER 14

A T a certain time in the early morning, the skylights above the pool gilded the swimming lanes below. This pool, on the roof of an East Side health club overlooking the river, was more popular than the one in Rosevale, and Sylvie, arriving when the doors opened at seven, her swimsuit already on, intended to do her laps and get back to the Korts' by eight-thirty to see Jessica off to school.

She chose her lane and swam into a path of speckled gold. Hauling herself through water, hand over hand, pulling, breathing, commanding herself to do laps . . . fifty-five, fifty-seven . . . she kept on. Weighing herself that morning, she found that she had lost another pound. Her breasts barely filled her bra. Standing naked before her bedroom mirror, she had studied her prominent shoulder blades and the blue-tinged skin—so translucent now, she could almost peer inside —that thinly covered her pelvic bones.

Sylvie realized she would have to put an end to this semi-fasting, but not now, not too soon. She swam blindly, flipping onto her back at the end of each lap, then rolling into a crawl.

The other night, the night that Michael chaotically readied

himself for his trip, there was a tapping at her door. Margo came in. She sat on a hassock, her sneakered feet turned in like a child's, smoking a cigarette, staring out at Gorham House sparkling with night lights. "Mount Everest at our elbow," she said in a sad voice. "It dwarfs everything. Michael says our major cities are being choked by badly conceived architecture. He says Frank Lloyd Wright had the right idea when he wanted to build a five-mile-high skyscraper in the middle of Central Park, and leave the rest of the city free for grass and a river view. God knows, Michael is never, but *never* wrong." Sylvie was silent. Margo squashed her cigarette into a clean ashtray and emptied the contents into a Kleenex for disposal later. "Filthy habit. I gave it up when I was pregnant with Jessica, then started in again just recently." She paused. "Who's Victor?"

"A very dear friend," Sylvie said stiffly.

"I supposed *that.*" She hesitated. "And your husband? I never asked . . ."

"Oh, dead. Some time ago. Eight years." Sylvie had begun to tremble.

Margo shook her head. "You've had your share . . ." She looked around the room as though seeking some one special thing on which to fix; finally she picked up one of Sylvie's books: *Cranford.* "These nineteenth-century women really fascinate you."

"I put together some fact sheets once for someone doing a comparative study . . ."

"I remember reading *Emma* in college and thinking, Of course they died young—asphyxiated by boredom," Margo said. "All those tinkling teacups."

"Is it so different now?" Sylvie asked.

"Oh, I know I'm being shallow; a first-class wet blanket tonight. Michael's so crazy whenever he takes off on a long trip, it makes me crazy, too. This time I feel more upset than usual." Her cheeks looked feverish. "There's wine downstairs in the refrigerator."

Sylvie said, "No, thank you."

"No. Well, at least you're consistent." She lifted her eyes. "I don't mean to be callous, but I do envy you, in spite of—everything. Well, not everything. But I envy your freedom—the very fact that you *chose* to be here." She lit another cigarette and looked away. "God, *marriage*! It's so unreal, so doomed, sort of, like a bad tribal rite that a dim-witted priest thought up in primitive times, to make the corn grow." She turned and asked, "What do *you* think?"

"I had a child. And I was primitive enough once to make do." The trembling seemed out of control. She rose and put on a sweater.

"I know. The child can be the whole point, I suppose. That's what the dim-witted priest had in mind." Margo roved around the room, pulled a book off the shelf and looked at Sylvie appraisingly. "*Villette.* I never even *heard* of this one." She sat down on Sylvie's bed. "I know we're going to lose you. I feel myself mentally preparing for it already. It's in the cards, and I'm being sorry in advance."

"But not yet," Sylvie said. "Not for a while."

"Eventually you will leave. You can get up and move whenever you please. You're free, that's the point, as soon as you feel you're ready. You have your . . . Victor . . ."

"And you have your Jessica, who you just said is everything . . . and your Michael . . ." Sylvie had gone to the window and drawn the shades against the spangled lights of Gorham House. Margo stood with both hands on the back of the recliner and seemed about to burst into tears. "Are you so unhappy then?" Sylvie asked.

"I'm too confused to know."

THE pool was filling up with other swimmers. In an adjacent lane she could see the mackerel-colored legs of a man wearing flippers. He plunged back and forth like a tadpole, mindless of the propriety of pools. When she surfaced once, he was sitting on the side ladder, adjusting one of his fins. "Never had these damn things on before," he volunteered. "I'm in training for some scuba diving off the coast of Barbados."

"I suppose this is better than training in a bathtub," she said.

She had lost the hypnotic mood, and she blamed it on those flippers, flashing by like disembodied feet, breaking the spell.

She thought of Victor. She had phoned him at his office and left a message. A day or so later, Margo knocked on her door and said, trying to keep her voice expressionless, "A Victor Severin on the phone for you."

Victor and she spoke quietly together. "I just wanted to know about you," she said.

"There's nothing more to know."

She said quickly, "I thought we could have dinner some night soon. There's a small restaurant near here . . ."

"Oh, have you returned to food? Sorry, but not just yet. I'll tell you when." She imagined his gray eyebrows lifting, his sardonic, world-weary look. And then he added in a softer tone, "I hope you're suffering less."

Later that night, Margo stopped her in the hall, touched her arm. "I sometimes think about you," she said. "I sometimes feel there's something I ought to be doing for *you.*"

"It's therapy enough just being here," Sylvie said and continued down to the kitchen to brew tea. She tried to put Victor out of her mind. The house had been in confusion all evening. Michael was having a nighttime meeting to review his plans for Jidda. The trip had been delayed and rescheduled. Margo had allowed her anger to surface. "I just have this premonition," she said to him. "Who needs it?" But he was leaving in a few days. His suitcase was being packed with all the fanfare of a Broadway opening: shirts, ties, his tiny travel clock that chimed the opening bars of the *Eroica*; his heavy briefcases bulged with structural drawings, sketches, photographs, engineering plans. His medium-weight suits had been misplaced, and storming into the hallway, he yelled, "Where in hell—"

"The cleaners," Margo snapped.

Zorro had been exiled to the downstairs bathroom with a supply of Arrowroot cookies. Melvin had regressed to a weak

"Hak, hak." Michael lashed out at everyone. People were waiting in his study. People with more on their minds than the shenanigans going on in the house. "Nothing is goddamn ever where it should be!" he said to Margo. "You're too busy with more important things, right?"

"That's a piggish exit line!"

Jessica began to cry. Sylvie tucked her in bed and told her the story of the stuffed ptarmigan who lived alone in an attic for nearly a century but who never lost heart because he believed he had a higher destiny.

"Ptarmigan?"

"A bird about the size of a duck with funny feathered legs that look as if he's wearing knickers. This particular ptarmigan was made of mattress ticking. Anyway, sure enough, in the next century he *was* discovered, and sent right off to the Smithsonian because he *had* become rare."

"I think he was rare all the time," Jessica said.

"He only sounds rare."

Jessica wiggled closer to Sylvie. The room was in shadow, the large wolf poster could be discerned in blocks of light and dark, a vague snoring buzz issued from Melvin's draped cage. "I'd like to be rare," she said.

"And locked up in a museum?"

"No, just rare, and the one and only."

"Your parents think you *are* the one and only."

She gave Sylvie her twinkling mouse look. "Do *you* think so?" But Sylvie rose, touched the child's forehead and left the room

Victor had called the following day. There were no preliminaries. He said, "Would you like to go to a movie tonight? There's something at the Forum . . ." Dressing to meet him, she put on the blue-and-emerald scarf that Margo had given her the previous weekend as a get-well gift. Margo, in a rush with Michael's last-minute chores, came briefly to her study door and said, "You look great! Cool and dangerous! It's the only way to go!"

Jessica insisted on a butterfly kiss. She brushed her lashes demurely along Sylvie's cheek. "I need to smell your perfume."

VICTOR took her to the Downtown Film Forum. The place had once been a public garage and still smelled of oil and used tires. They sat on folding chairs beneath the exposed crossbeams. Almost a month had passed since she'd seen him, and it was as though a psychological shift had taken place between them. She found herself studying his face; the web of veins in his eyes gave him a tired look. He fingered her scarf. "You look nice," he said.

"And you, have you been all right?" He was wearing a dark green jersey that clung to his ribs, and he seemed leaner than ever, his face more equine, his hair gray and curlier and all of him less formal.

He looked at her without answering and took her hand between his, shaking it as though shaking dice, then placed it lightly on his lap. "Oh, more or less all right."

The film was a Polish export done by an underground group and dubbed in English. It was only thirty-five minutes long. It had been shot in a small grimy town and showed people drifting to work at the local iron foundry. There were clusters of vacant, hardened faces, scornful remarks about the meager contents of lunch pails. "Again potato and leek stew," one man said. Someone else complained about not having eaten meat in three months. "Pig farming is all washed up," he remarked. "The last chicken I saw wore high heels," another said sourly. There were dark symbolic shots of sky and roofs and endless frozen fields. The air was granular and dark. Comic relief was provided by an effeminate younger worker who sidled up to the others and flinging his arm around one fellow's neck, pinched and goosed his bottom. His gestures were extreme enough to be farce, Sylvie thought. Either farce or psychosis. His eyebrows and lids were outlined in black. Even his mouth and earlobes were darkened. He pretended to kiss one of the men on the lips and was knocked down and kicked in the head. When he stood

up, he was knocked down again. Suddenly his prancing girlish mood changed and he staggered to his feet, unzipped his
pants and held out his penis. "Eat!" he sneered. "It's meat
enough!" He was so piercingly fierce and repellent that the
others turned slowly and walked away. In the end, one man
came forward and after closing and zipping the young man's
clothes, took him by the arm. "We are all starving," he said.

Afterward Victor told her, "The symbols were pretty
crude and obvious. It was too blatantly graphic. But don't
you think it was interesting, the way it ended? That Polish
gang, even in a confrontation like that—so morally distaste-
ful and all—walked off unsure of what they really felt."

Sylvie wondered what Victor wanted her to say. The film
was ugly but at least believable. Hungry Poles were in the
news all the time. She was silent, and finally he said, "Doesn't
the larger metaphor get to you?"

"Which is?"

"That poverty and deprivation are questions of soul as well
as matters of material fact."

"Listen," she said, inexplicably brimming over, "I don't
believe in your so-called 'soul.' It does nothing for me. I'm
too upset with everything that's happened to *me* to care."

"Ssh," he said. "No need to have a fit." He suggested a
drink at his apartment.

She hadn't been there for months, and when he switched
on the lights, the strangeness overwhelmed her. Everything
was in place, yet somehow different, as if the furnishings had
been rotated an inch or two, changing the perspective: his
spare, very modern couch and chairs, the series of Toltec
heads on the coffee table that Mona had sent from Cuernavaca just before they'd separated. There was a bulky stack
of new books on film on the floor. Perhaps that was it. He
poured brandy and drew her to the couch. "The Polish film
was a bad choice for you, I suppose . . ." He seemed defeated,
and she was sorry.

"It's just me. The film was interesting. I'll have to think
about it—that man, the androgynous one, offering himself
with such a strange Eucharistic gesture . . ."

He drained his glass and poured another. "My own little project is off to a creeping start." He shrugged, a modest dip of his head. "My favorite fantasy has me exhibiting at one of those minor film festivals . . ."

She had stared so intensely at the mottled Portuguese rug that there were spots in front of her eyes. "Victor, what am I going to do about Sean? Gary and Sean?"

"Keep looking," he said. "Let's face it, Gary is never going to come running to you. He and Angel weren't married. Think about *that*! Your claim to Sean is as strong as his. *Stronger*. He'd have to prove paternity as well as parental fitness if, for example, you ever brought him into court." She listened numbly. Her thoughts had never gone this far. "And if you find Sean, what then?" he asked. "What will you want to do?"

"I don't know . . ." It was an idea that took her breath away.

Victor put a record on the turntable and drew her to her feet. "Well, don't be upset. Things have a way of working out . . . it's the inverse rule to Murphy's Law." As they clung in rhythm to the music, her brain was teeming. She felt every knob and turning of his body. He smelled like silk. She felt her own quickening, a soft, lazy memory in the pit of her stomach, which grew heavier, as if she were being filled with sand. The film was vivid in her mind. Those men like pack dogs. And the brute, enduring posture of the other. All of it so melodramatic and banal, the way tragedy often is. How well she knew. Victor's mouth was buried in her hair, and she shook her head. "No, Victor, take me home, please."

ALL that had been last night, and now, swimming, she strove to drive the faces in the film away. Goggles in place, she searched the fissures at the bottom of the pool, imagining another face, faces, flickering as if lit by phosphorescent organisms. Had she assumed Victor would hang around forever, ministering to her moods? When he brought her back to the Korts' last night, he had withdrawn into a deeper remoteness. He dropped her off with merely a pat on her shoulder.

But she mustn't think about Victor. Not yet. Or Gary. Or Sean. She found herself reciting chores, instead. Things still to be done. Take Jessica to the dentist. Buy warm tights and a skating sweater at Macy's. Get chocolate chips and marzipan paste for Little Chefs. She had spent a full morning and part of an afternoon this week at Margo's parents' apartment, had filled out Medicare forms, paid current bills, driven Max to the barber and back. Max had received a letter from Mayor Koch, praising him for his civic interests. "You can be sure your plant-a-tree suggestion is not being filed in a wastebasket. So how'm I doing?" Max tottered around the house like an ecstatic chipmunk, waving his cane and declaiming, "There are no little people; just dummies who keep their mouths shut."

Celia was asleep almost the whole time, but when she woke, the crazed screaming began. "I saw him with his pants down. Don't lie to me!"

SYLVIE swam like an engine, pressing closer to the wall, staring into a shadowy montage. The filter pipes were like nostrils blowing water. Margo had said she wanted to talk to her this morning. She swam droning out a litany of lists in her mind: Call the meat market, pick up at the dressmaker's, set up a play-date for Jess with her school chums Charlotte and Lyle, retype Margo's letter to Bob Fleet, who was having a show next month at one of the downtown cooperative galleries and was still very new, send her letter special delivery to Cozzens, no, hand-deliver it. Five hours from New York in Margo's station wagon. Wouldn't Gary and the baby have left some sort of trail in Cozzens? Do *not* hand-deliver the letter. She was not an extremist—not in everything. But she tried to remember Danny Baum's words; she'd been so numbed, so unprepared for him, that tall, good-natured young man with those extraordinary blue eyes. The blue of Egypt, Angel once wrote in a letter to Sylvie. Angel said,

"I'm making an enamel bracelet as blue as Daniel Baum's eyes. You remember Danny. He's the one near Cozzens. The one on the small farm who's starting up a yogurt business. Remember when he helped us plow the back field?" In another letter Angel had said, "Our neighbor, Baum, may be putting in sheep."

She swam more slowly now. Her leg muscles ached. She scraped her arm on the pool wall. She might try a peanut butter sandwich for lunch. What exactly had Daniel Baum said? Was Gary going to leave again with the baby? Go to Baja California? She must see a map. Exhausted, she looked up at the clock on the wall. She'd been swimming for only twenty minutes. She hauled herself forward; she would deliver herself to the shower room in ten more minutes. It would take another fifteen to get back to the Korts'. There was a fierce rush of sound in her ears, as if oceans were pouring through her head. She couldn't think, and yet there was Gary crowding her brain, and Sean, the two on mule back, going over the top of a mountain. Perhaps they had already left Cozzens, left Baja California and gone somewhere really far away. Peru. In this vision she saw the baby sucking the thin air of Machu Picchu, his golden head turning toward a weak trickle of sun. Gary burning bridges. Whereabouts unknown.

She stopped swimming and floated face down. She was like a corked bottle in which breath was trapped. She seemed to sleep on water, her lungs stilled. How had she waited so long —five, nearly six months? The point was, Gary might be in the vicinity of Cozzens now. When she opened her eyes, the scuba diver was on his back swimming directly beneath her, as if they were partners in a water ballet. It was the last clear thing she remembered, because suddenly black tentacles were encircling her waist. She was being dragged through the water at a surprising speed, thrown against the tile steps leading from the pool and pulled out onto the apron. The scuba diver, on one knee, had flung aside his flippers and mask, shoved her head back and clamped his mouth to hers.

Flailing, she tried to push his head away. "No!" she managed. But then his lips, like suction cups, were attached to hers. He blew his warm strange breath mightily into her throat. She fought and at last tore free, screaming, "Will you stop!"

The man sat back slowly on his heels, a confused grin on his lips. "Gosh, no offense. I thought for sure you passed out."

"Well, take your idiotic hands off me," she said, quivering with fury, as she started toward the showers.

"You don't have to get so teed-off," she heard him say. "It's not as though I'm into necrophilia!"

CHAPTER 15

MARGO'S excitement seemed feverish. She had brought a canister of coffee up to her study and asked Sylvie to join her.

"There are a few things I ought to be going over with you," Margo said. "Things I'd like you to do." She spoke about taking Jess to the doctor for her booster shots, Celia to a new gerontologist at Mt. Sinai. She reminded Sylvie to make sure that Feliciana attended to her daily chores—bathrooms and kitchen to be mopped every day. "She can be a real goof-off, if she thinks no one is paying attention." Margo sighed; her mind was clearly elsewhere. She tapped her forehead. "What else, what else. Oh yes, Jess tells me she lost her gloves again. You'd better buy a couple of pairs this time."

"I know. I've already replaced them," Sylvie said.

Margo drank her coffee and poured more, her hand quivering as she lifted the cup to her lips. "Yes, of course you did. You always manage to attend to things without having them spelled out." Then she continued with what seemed like a checklist—mail to go, phone calls to the gallery in SoHo; she listed details as though she weren't going to be around. Sylvie listened apprehensively. "If St. Clair calls with anything for me—more Riotson, for example—I'd like you to go down with the station wagon and pick them up. You know, I ought to take you to SoHo this morning and introduce you to St. Clair myself." But she was sunk in a peculiar gloom. She picked at a paper napkin, tearing a fringe around its edges and suddenly said, "I want to ask you something. Now don't faint. It's none of my business, but . . ." She paused, sipped thoughtfully. "Did you love your husband? I mean did you have a solid feeling for him, a feeling you didn't have to think about or define?"

Sylvie was so startled, her cup tipped. Margo was watching her intently. "I don't know quite what to say." Say nothing, she told herself. She rarely thought about Arthur, thought of him only in connection with Angel. But Margo's silence prodded her. She began quietly: "At first I saw my husband as extraordinary, someone better than I, a model for perfect performance. I expected to learn from him forever." How she had indulged this image of Arthur. Even his idiosyncrasies had seemed special—his indifference to his clothes, the habit he had of wearing unmatched socks. "Life was exciting at first. I don't think I told you, he was a civil-rights lawyer, right in the middle of one of the most powerful movements in the country. Bull Conners swore he'd throw him in jail if he even crossed a street crooked. Bull Conners, if you remember, was the Birmingham sheriff. The one with the fire hoses." Margo was staring off into space. Sylvie continued: "I suppose the very things that made him exciting, made me seem less so. He was interested in constitutional change. The time was perfect for his kind of battle. My interests were less public. Family-centered." Daughter-centered, she thought numbly. Four days had passed since she'd met Danny Baum in the pet shop. Four days of remembering the exact tone of his voice when he said, "Oh, by the way, I ran into . . ."

"You were misplaced, I guess," Margo said, coming to life. "I know the feeling. Michael with his work and success and money. It's a weight, depressing. Nothing you try to do seems to have an impact. I can't even work up the interest to go out and buy some decent furniture. My friend Alessa thinks I'm weird." Margo smiled and instantly became sober. "She challenges my commitment to my life. Not that *she's* one for fidelity or anything as tradition-bound as that. She just thinks I ought to know where I stand." And then she said, looking closely at Sylvie, "You could have left him, your husband."

"Not really. I suppose I thought about that occasionally, but it didn't seem like an answer. I admired my husband, even though I grew to love him less. I was not being abused except by expectation."

"Expectation!" Margo shook her head. "You're extraordinary, Sylvie."

"Well, expectation varies with fashion. Madame Bovary may have longed to change her life, but she didn't really expect to be lucky at it."

"She was crazed with boredom. It's different. There was nothing important to anchor her."

Certainly not her child, Sylvie thought. Her eyes stung. She glanced at Margo, spoke as quickly as she could without stumbling over her words. "And there was Angel—an overwhelming reason for me to stay put. She loved me, but she loved her father, too. I think, for a long time, hanging on to a family structure for her, no matter how imperfect, seemed more important than anything else. Of course if someone unusually wonderful had come along, someone who was available at that moment . . . but even then, I think Angel's needs might have been decisive. And I don't think I'm talking about sacrifice, nothing as high-flown as that. It's something else. A way of being, for me at least, that seemed inevitable."

Once, when Angel was nine and Sylvie was working at the Rosevale library, she became aware of a blond, soft-spoken young man who sat for hours at a table near the window. His name was Malcolm Bolt. He was doing a research project on the uses of land in agrarian societies. "People have always been a little *religious* about land," he'd said to her as he handed in his request for a certain title. He spoke quietly, in a voice husky from too many cigarettes—and she wanted to caution him about that. One day, she went with him to the basement stacks to find a monograph. They stood close together under the green-shaded ceiling lamps, searching the shelves. She remembered saying, "It should be in this folder, I think." And then he had reached for her, and she was in his arms, and he was kissing her and murmuring, "Don't be angry. You're so beautiful, you know."

She began to run into him outside the library, and they'd stroll for a little while in the town park. Several times they met in a neighborhood coffee shop for lunch. Their conversation was impersonal, as though that wayward kiss had never happened. He spoke of his work. "It's easy to be sentimental about the nineteenth century," he told her. "It was farm and family before anything else."

She remembered answering, "Maybe in this country. But not abroad. Not the concept of family as we know it. In the novels of that time, *Middlemarch,* for example, young children are rarely mentioned. Not a word in that long busy book about maternal feeling." It was an odd little speech, and she recalled the color rising to her cheeks.

"Do you have children?" he asked.

"One," she said. "Just one fairly perfect child."

"I guessed that. Guessed she was special. You're so intense about kids."

Another day, without a word, he drove her to his house in a neighboring town, a small untidy ranch with the smell of Long Island Sound in the distance. His wife had a job in the city, he said. Their living arrangements here were temporary, just until he got his degree.

He led her immediately to the bedroom. They undressed in silence and then, slipping under the sheets, came together in a rush, and then again, and again, two mute voluptuaries, stoking flames, rampant with desire.

Later he sat up in bed, kissing her shoulders. "You have an important need," he said, full of the satisfaction of discovery. She heard the receding echo of her own sex-logged voice.

"You're wrong," she answered, getting out of bed, picking up the humiliating scatter of her clothes. What was she doing, breaking into a stranger's life? She never allowed herself to be alone with him again.

"OH God, Sylvie," Margo said, touching her hand. "I find this side of you unnerving. The side I guess that I'd call will." She had gotten up from the couch and gone for her coat. "I guess I've come to trust you absolutely." The phone rang. It was obviously Michael, calling from the airport. The last-minute good-byes. "Take care, please," Margo was saying, fiddling so brutally with a pencil that its point shattered. "Yes, yes, it's all right, I forgive . . . I know, it was just the tension . . ." Sylvie turned away and stared out the window. Across the street Gorham House rose, beautiful in its way, even though all that stone and glass blotted out sunlight. Margo had cupped her hand over the phone. She was saying, "I don't know. Maybe I will. I'm not clear about it yet. There's Jess . . . But you—well, don't take any wooden rials, or whatever. Love you, yes." She hung up and turned to Sylvie. "That was Michael, saying good-bye and urging me, by the way, to take a little trip West. I had mentioned Santa Fe once, for its art scene; just an idea . . ." She shook her head and looked at Sylvie. "Come on. I need air. Let's go downtown to SoHo. I'll get the station wagon."

"THIS is St. Clair," Margo said. "Only one name, but don't fool around with him. He doesn't bite, but what a bark!"

St. Clair looked pleased at the introduction. Margo had presented Sylvie as her assistant, and now she was saying, "If ever I'm not available, you can contact Mrs. Weyman . . ."

"Lovely," St. Clair breathed, rearranging his scarf. "As long as there's no hassle over . . . whatever." Sylvie had moved off to wander around the gallery. Blobs of color, linear abstractions. There was a new Riotson with a glossy enamelled look on the front wall. It showed two turn-of-the-century women in enormous hats and bow ties, sitting at a table in a café, holding hands. "Sappho and Friend," the caption read. It was unpleasantly stunning. She was somehow pleased that Margo was holding off on his work. Margo was leaning over St. Clair's desk staring at what must have been a price list, saying, "Absolutely not. Anything over two thousand won't budge. Not with the people I'm dealing with!" She sounded knowledgeable, Sylvie thought. A quick learner. The sort who comes off as meek but always manages to get what she wants.

Outside the gallery Margo said, "So much for St. Clair. Watch out for him, though. He sounds female-hysteric, but his mind is pure IBM." All this unburdening, Sylvie thought. She wondered when Margo planned to make her exit.

"There's a good Lebanese place nearby," Margo said. "Let's have lunch. You don't have to pick Jess up at school until three, do you? Come to think of it, I'll pick Jess up today myself and take her to flute. It will be good for both of us."

They had just rounded the corner of Prince Street when a young man came toward them. Margo stopped in her tracks as though brakes had been applied. The young man took Margo's hand and shook it gravely. "This is a fantastic surprise," he said, touching his curly beard, a bemused and happy expression on his face. "I needed some supplies—special filters, agar dishes, stuff like that. And I was told about a shop down here on Greene Street . . . all you need is a compass to find it . . ." He hadn't let go of her hand. "Who knows what I'll be able to dig up in an emergency, when I'm out there in—" But Margo had interrupted him. "I'd like you to meet Sylvie Weyman." She turned to Sylvie. "Brill Wallace. Jess's friend and mine from the zoo and the natural history museum." Yes, of course, from the museum, Sylvie thought. Margo said, "Mr. Wallace lectures wonderfully about animals—wolves, in particular, their extraordinary social organization, et cetera . . ." The et cetera made her voice sound frivolous.

Brill looked pleased. "Don't overdo it," he said modestly. "I'm just your ordinary garden-variety zoologist. Nothing to write home about." Sylvie noted that he'd finally dropped Margo's hand. He turned to Sylvie. "I think it's Jessica who's made a big-time wolf person out of me."

"Well, you're her folk hero, like Tarzan or Kong," Margo said.

"I can do better than that!" He was staring at Margo with a mischievous gleam. Sylvie moved away, gazing into shop windows. Looking back, she saw them standing together, heads down, talking.

She paused before a coffee shop. The aroma was glorious. One could OD on caffeine, just breathing the air. OD was Angel's word, not hers. "I've OD'd on maternal love, Mother . . . OK?" It had such a shocking sound. She looked back. Now Margo was talking earnestly to Brill. She wondered what Margo saw in him. He seemed a little artificial. "I'm your ordinary garden-variety zoologist," he'd said, less with modesty than with the desire to inform, to be accurately identified, as though it mattered. She'd known men like that, who were self-important in a wisecracking way. It made her uneasy. But there was the chemistry, no doubt. Good-looking, rugged, just a little unkempt, the sort who'd feel clever in torn jogging shoes. Nothing like Michael. Nothing at all.

She went into the coffee shop and bought a pound of something rich-smelling and pungent from Tanzania. If no one else would drink it, there was always Zorro. Leaning against the counter, she thought of Margo saying, "You could have left. Why didn't you?" Why didn't she? Talking to Margo, she had made it all sound so high-minded and purposeful, when in simple fact she had been bent on making something of herself and Arthur, wanted to do it for herself as well as for Angel. She'd been determined to make Arthur love and acknowledge her more than he did, and it had seemed possible, had always seemed possible until the end.

She left the shop and saw Margo coming along the street toward her. Brill was gone. Margo had a strange calm look on her face. They walked to the restaurant and sat at a little table. Margo pointed to the posters of women in purdah, of shadowy men behind a grid of Arabic script. "It makes me uneasy." And then shaking her head as if to free her mind of unpleasant thoughts, she leaned toward Sylvie and said, "I haven't told you about it yet, but I'm going off on a trip . . . for a week or so."

CHAPTER 16

*L*OOKING back, Sylvie would have to say that it happened too quickly. Michael taking off for the Near East
and Margo telling her in that little Lebanese place, between
bites of pita bread she seemed barely able to chew, that she
would be leaving on a trip West. "I'll be gone for a week
possibly. Do you think you can manage?"

"Yes, of course," Sylvie said, trying to deal with an unreasonable burst of disapproval.

Margo leaned across the table and gave Sylvie a distracted
little hug. "I know. I can't think of anyone else I'd rather
leave Jessica with."

When they returned home, Margo offered a few details.
She'd be staying at the Sheraton in Albuquerque. She didn't
know where she'd be in Santa Fe. Not yet. "But I'll be calling
home . . ." she said.

Margo left on a Wednesday night, and the next day Sylvie,
as if following deep-rooted subliminal directions, found herself in a departure mode of her own. She quietly made plans.
Margo called home on Thursday and Friday nights. She
spoke to Sylvie. "Everything on target? Good!" Then she

asked to speak to Jessica, who got on the long-distance phone and yelled, "Mommy, Miss Formico brought leftover Valentine hearts to school and we had them during Snacks. Charlotte ate *six*! Lyle is sick with a hundred and three. See you!" When Sylvie got back on the wire, Margo said happily, "No holding *her* down." The phone call on Friday night was more of the same. Just before Margo hung up Sylvie asked casually, "Mind if I take Jessica upstate on an outing for a day or so? It's a long weekend. Lyle's birthday party is cancelled, and Pritchard is closed Monday for boiler repairs. I thought we could do something, skiing, maybe, or snowmobiling."

"But where would you go?" There was concern in her voice. "And isn't it dangerous?"

"Oh, some place north, not too far. And we'd only play around on a small hill."

"I don't know," Margo said, thinking. Then she added, "I guess it's all right, Sylvie. Just use your own good judgment and be careful."

Feliciana was given the weekend off and told to come in early on Monday. Zorro, wagging and snuffling, was sent to Canine Cottage with instructions on food and drink tagged to his collar like a medical marker. Which left only Melvin to be disposed of. Feliciana, looking frightened, would have none of him. "I no can take him home. He scream too much!" Transvaal Pets said firmly that their policy precluded boarding ... "health department rules, you know. And if you move him around, make sure he's warm. Parrots catch cold." Sylvie hung up in dismay, to face Jessica, who wailed, "If we leave Mel behind, he'll forget all his words."

"Words?" But in the end Sylvie decided she would chance taking him with them. She gathered up a large wool shawl and Zorro's electric blanket, which could even plug into a car cigarette lighter, and they were on their way.

It began to snow as they moved into the New England Thruway. Sylvie turned the heater up, and the station wagon became a cozy nest. Jessica, strapped in, looked out the window through a blowy curtain of white. Melvin's drape had been thrown over his cage to simulate night, and over that the wool shawl, but she could hear him hopping about suspiciously on his perch, rasping an occasional "Fak" and "Gudma."

Three hours out of New York, the snow came down more heavily. They were near the lower Berkshires. The windshield wipers labored. Sylvie slowed the car. She had expected to do Brattleboro in six hours, spend the night at a motel and then make plans. She found it impossible to imagine what would come next. Would her nerve fail? And if she found Gary, what could they say to each other? He would surely see her as the avenger come to haunt him. And the baby, Sean. She didn't dare imagine *him*. How would she hold the frayed parts of herself together with Sean close by, Sean in her arms? Thinking, imagining against her will his look, Angel's round bright face in his, she shivered as she drove.

She stopped at a gas station, and the attendant, a teenaged boy, came puffing to the car. "We're in for it," he said, pulling his red hunting hat deep over his ears.

"What's the forecast?" Sylvie asked.

"An easy foot or more, and then into the deep freeze."

Jessica sat back in glee. She'd been lost in wonder from the moment Sylvie told her they were going on a trip. "Will we ski?" she'd instantly asked. "Will we drive a snowmobile?"

Sylvie had the tank filled, the oil checked and the level of antifreeze measured. "You're good for thirty below," the boy said, hopping from foot to foot, dislodging the shawl of snow on his shoulders, as he dug for change.

When they stopped at a diner for lunch, Sylvie realized that Jessica's flushed face was not merely a reaction to cold. They had just crossed the boundary into Massachusetts, near the small mill town of Egremont, and although Jessica had asked for a grilled cheese sandwich and a milkshake, she sat back and picked at her food. To encourage her, Sylvie ordered a poached egg and pretended to eat with gusto. The waitress brought over a gingerbread man with a sugar top hat. "This is for little girls who clean their plates."

But Jessica had laid her head on the table. "My throat hurts," she said in a tiny parched voice. Sylvie touched her lips to the child's forehead. Her skin was burning.

The cashier told her where to find a doctor. "Doc Paulson, two miles down the highway. It's a white shingle house set back from the road."

Examining Jessica's throat with a slender light probe, Dr. Paulson hummed and made little jokes to himself. "What have we here? We have a frog. No, a horse. Well, one thing's sure. We have a bonfire!" He turned to Sylvie. "Bad inflammation. Staph infection, most likely. I'll give you a prescription; but I would keep this little lady in bed for a few days."

"In bed? We're heading north, into Vermont . . ." Two hours or so away. She wanted to keep moving.

"Change your plans," the doctor said briskly. He placed his examining instruments in a sterilizer. "It's your child," he said. "If she were mine, I wouldn't want to be driving around in all this weather. I'd want her in bed with plenty of warm liquids, immediately."

"Is there a motel near here then? A Holiday Inn?" Sylvie felt at a loss. She was suddenly filled with premonitions and doubts about the whole venture.

"I have a better idea," Dr. Paulson said, impersonal and efficient once more. He scribbled a prescription and an address on a pad and said he'd phone ahead on both.

THE Sarah Croft Inn was on a side road near the main highway. It looked as though it might have once been a farmhouse, spread out and comfortably ramshackle. Sarah Croft was waiting for them. Flames leapt in the fireplace. There were deep worn couches and easy chairs around the living room, a bear rug with an enormous glaring face and heavy paws in front of the fire.

"The poor child is sick. I know all about it. Doc Paulson called ahead." Sarah bustled them upstairs to a modest twin-bedded room that looked out on a stand of snow-tipped trees. "It's the best I can do this particular weekend. We've been booked over two months on this one." She was dressed in corduroy work pants and a plaid flannel shirt, and her streaked gray hair was bundled handsomely on top of her head. "There's cold juices, and hot broth," she said turning down the covers on one of the beds. Glancing at Melvin's curtained cage, from which only the faintest rustle emanated, she said, "The parrot goes to the storeroom downstairs."

An anguished, "No!" from Jessica. "He needs to *see* us. Otherwise he won't know where he *is.*"

Mrs. Croft relented. She dug a pin out of her hair and reinserted it emphatically. "OK. As long as he keeps his mouth shut! There's a wedding going on tomorrow morning. It took quite some shuffling to get you in here. Anyone other than Paulson would have gotten a flat *no* from me." She stood on the threshold a moment longer. "Remember, I'm not a bird person!" she said, pointing a finger at Jess.

Sylvie had picked up the Terramycin on the way to Croft's, and now she spooned some into Jessica's mouth, along with liquid aspirin for her fever. The child leaned groggily against Sylvie's bosom; her waxy skin seemed to melt beneath Sylvie's touch. "You'll feel better in the morning," Sylvie promised, laying Jessica's head on the pillows and tucking her in. She removed the curtain from Melvin's cage and filled his feeder with parrot mix. He hopped around saying, "Gudma, Gudma," and she put him in the bathroom. "Be quiet!" she said sharply, as she closed the door.

In the early evening she went downstairs and sat in front of the fire. Brooding, mesmerized by the flames, fingers of light on the blackened hearth like a golden hand flexing. Her own hand opened and closed nervously. Jessica had taken a cup of broth and was asleep upstairs, with the dresser lamp on and the door ajar so that she could call down if she awoke. Sylvie felt panic gathering, tried to imagine Gary again. What if she actually found him, and he refused to see her, or to let her see Sean? No, she thought. He wouldn't dare. Did he know that she, too, had blood rights? Her panic intensified. She had not had good hard exercise for several days. Perhaps if she could do some local jogging or swimming she could dull this terrible sense of dissolution, all the scattered pieces in her head . . . But jogging was out. The roads were too snowy. Perhaps running in place . . . but with Jess and Melvin as onlookers?

Sarah Croft came in to say that dinner was ready. She would have one of her girls sit on the stairs in case Jess awoke.

The dining room was mostly empty, although a few of the next day's wedding guests had already arrived. Two couples, both young, were eating silently at an adjacent table. They had the deep pallor and translucent eyes of people who never see sunlight. There was a Bible alongside each plate, and between hurried gulps of food they would take up the book and read, their fingers like the beaks of ravening birds, picking along the pages. The women wore plain cotton skirts and buttoned-up blouses. The two men were in black suits, their faces apple-smooth. One of the young men looked up and called over to Sylvie, "Christ has blessed your dinner." His message was so intense and personal, it was as though a mysterious stranger had delivered a love note.

She ate quickly. There was a small chicken thigh on her plate and a baked potato, exactly as she'd requested, and she stared at them reluctantly, as if even this small breach of discipline would send her whole edifice of control tumbling. The potato clogged her throat, and she drank half a glass of milk and swallowed forcefully.

She checked on Jessica, who was sleeping quietly, a tiny froth of bubbles around her lips. In the bathroom, Melvin, balanced on one foot on his perch, looked as though a taxidermist had gotten to him; Sylvie wrapped the shawl around his cage.

Not ready for sleep, she went downstairs and browsed through a bucket of magazines—*Ski News, New England Traveller, Tanglewood Today, Fishing Life.* She thought of Victor dragging her off to Montauk. The crushing cold, the strange story of the man in the valise, all of it merging, layer on layer, in her mind. It was Victor's brooding and allusive turn of thought that caught her by surprise again and again. How she hated to see that web of veins in his eyes, the wounded look; she imagined her hands, gifted as a faith healer's, reviving him merely by the power of touch.

There was a wall of books—mysteries, science fiction, blockbusters. An old edition of a biography of George Sand and a volume of letters written by Elizabeth Barrett Browning, lying on their sides. There was a letter by Mrs. Browning written to the emperor Louis Napoleon to solicit sympathetic understanding for Victor Hugo. "Sir, I am only a woman . . . and you a great man . . . I beseech you to have patience with me while I supplicate you . . ." Had she been humiliated at having to write such hypocritical words? And would she, Sylvie, be so humiliated in her dealings with Gary, if a meeting finally came about?

The room had the warm patina of age. Ski racks in the outer hall threw pickets of shadow through the open doorway. Sylvie held the books in her lap and experienced a surge and fall of uneasiness. She had given herself three days to try to accomplish her mission. One day was already gone.

Sarah Croft came in from outside, rosy-cheeked with cold. She pulled a chair to the fire. "I'm beat," she said. "This wedding tomorrow is fundamentalist Christian. True believers. The menu has to be vegetarian. Believe me, if I could have predicted this kind of snow, I would never have given over the place to them. Skiers are a more profitable lot. They want hot grog. They order special steaks. You can charge almost anything." She spoke in an undertone. In her silvery insulated warm-up overalls, she looked ready for a moon-walk. "The girl's parents still live around here, and she's come back to be married. Which is sweet, I'm not saying it isn't. But her mother is just sick at heart. Doesn't think much of those spooky religious sects.

"Of course, these folks are not as weird as that Moonie gang, who get themselves married a thousand at a time, and to absolute strangers! But that's not saying much!"

The next day, Jess's fever was nearly gone. The inn was

already full of wedding guests. Sylvie heard their subdued voices rustling in the halls and on the stairs. When she and Jessica went down for early lunch, the wedding service was already under way. A sprig of holly was nailed to the mantle. There were no flowers or other decorations. Sylvie and Jess sat on the bottom step listening. Someone mentioned the beauty of self-denial in the face of worldly temptation, and there were murmurs of assent. The guests took turns reading from the apostles and citing what seemed to Sylvie to be their own homemade tracts for good behavior in the service of Christ. A little of this and so much of that, as though their lives, like loaves of bread, would rise to a golden perfection if the ingredients were right.

She remembered her own wedding day. Arthur and she at City Hall, the sense of hurry because Arthur had just been asked to represent a poverty group in Tennessee and they were to fly to Nashville together that night. After the ceremony, her parents had held a luncheon reception at a newly opened Hunan restaurant. They ate strange fiery Chinese morsels that gave them such heartburn, Arthur couldn't make love to her. "Done in by a Chinese meatball," he'd said, sitting up miserably in bed.

Now, the ceremony over, the bride in her neat gray suit was walking around shaking hands with the guests. She looked no more than nineteen. The groom stood by, holding his Bible to his chest as if it were a shield. The bride's mother accepted congratulations with streaming eyes. Sylvie was suddenly overcome with such compassion for the woman that she thought she, too, would cry. Angel had never wanted to marry Gary. Had refused to marry him. "I don't think he could handle the closeness." At another time she said, "Right now, having the baby is enough." So strange, strange, as if part of her wanted to unsettle, even shock, Sylvie.

One of the young women passed a tray of fruit punch to Sylvie. She took a glass for Jessica. "Christ thanks you," the woman said.

"Why does Christ thank us?" Jessica asked.

"For being here, I guess."

"Were we invited?"

Sarah Croft came up and said, "I have a small table for the two of you, in a corner."

Another young woman said happily to Sylvie as she started toward the dining room, "I'm a Christian, are you?"

Sylvie wanted to answer no, but she said instead, "I believe in belief."

Jessica wanted to know exactly who Christ was.

"A sort of father to a lot of people," Sylvie said. She had no personal interest in religion. She had longed to pray after Angel's death. Had repeated a verse fragment from an anonymous English poet over and over into the night—"Closer to the stars, oh, heavenly self . . ."—until Victor covered her mouth with his hand, and the words sank into the crypt of her brain.

Jessica was smiling. "Daddy thinks he's Jesus Christ."

"Oh?"

"Mommy says Daddy thinks he is."

They had carrot soup and broccoli pancakes. The dining room had a ceremonial quiet so profound it befitted a funeral gathering. The young fundamentalists read their Bibles as they ate, lifting their heads, it seemed, only to make biblical points. Their guests, subdued by so much solemnity, spoke in hushed tones. "Eat quickly," Sylvie said softly. "We have to get moving."

"Everyone's whispering," Jessica whispered with her mouth full.

"They're very polite," Sylvie said. "Polite to God." And suspicious of joy, she thought. It seemed so sad. She thought of Angel's sudden poignant beliefs in rural verities, in the art of self-sufficiency, as though she had left the real world behind for the mysticism of the church. "Blessings," she had once said in Vermont as she placed corn muffins on the breakfast table. And Sylvie had risen and gone unsteadily from the room.

Victor and she had been visiting that time, and afterward,

173

when they were alone, he asked, "Why does all of this upset you so? I think she's opted for a good, clean, perfectly sensible life, except for this business of wanting to have the child out of wedlock—"

"Oh, for God's sake, do you think I'm a fool!" she interrupted angrily. "Do you think I have something personal against rural life? Do you suppose I'm stupid enough to think it's all just hippie stuff? No! No! No!" It was Angel herself, she said—Angel, who was too restless and urban, too analytical. How long could she be in love with the soil without sticking some in a vial, or love animals without being able to give them medical care? They were taking a walk across a back field, the grass so high they seemed legless in a sea of green; she faced him, shaking. "It's that I don't see her as having made a choice. I see it all as a reaction—against me, even to the point of having the baby. Oh, Victor, I feel so responsible!"

"You're wrong, wrong," he'd said. "You're overlooking the part that's Gary. He's touched something maternal and caring in Angel. Can't you see that? He's another of her weimaraner pups." Victor had his arm linked in hers, and he was talking seriously in that way of his, as though a dozen things were going on in his mind at once. "You could let go, you know. Practice the fine art of distancing. You could just turn your back for a while and let her be." But there hadn't been enough time to practice anything.

LATER, in their room, Jessica wanted to know if they were going to ride in a snowmobile. "Not now. Maybe when we get to Vermont." If we get to Vermont, Sylvie thought, glancing out the window. A foot and a half of new snow had fallen, but she could see the cars, their roofs thatched with skis, barrelling along a highway kept whistle-clean for the winter-sports crowd.

Before they left, Sylvie put through a call to the Sheraton in Albuquerque. Ten A.M. New Mexico time, and Margo was checking out of her room. "You just caught me," she said.

"I'm driving to Santa Fe; I'll be staying at . . . well, look, I'll call *you*. How's everything going?"

"Wonderfully. We're north of Stockbridge. Lots of snow."

"Jess?"

"Fine." A very small white lie.

Jess grabbed the phone and called out, "I love you, Mommy. The snow is over my ears."

Back on the wire, Sylvie heard Margo say, "You'll be back home tomorrow, right?"

"Yes." The lie had turned gray, possibly darker.

In the station wagon, Jessica relaxed against the seat cushions. She seemed too relaxed, her cheeks tinted with a light flush. Was she feverish again, Sylvie wondered. "A few hours on the road and we'll be in Brattleboro," Sylvie said, turning and touching her hand to Jessica's forehead. She'd give it another day, and if Jessica wasn't back to normal, they'd certainly return to New York.

"Myra says she's going to St. Thomas-boro for March vacation," Jessica said, giggling listlessly. "She sits next to me at school. Last summer she went to Nantucket-boro."

"You're being silly. Are you OK? Throat hurt or anything?"

Jess shook her head. She patted the cage. "Can we take Melvin in the snowmobile when we get to Brattle?"

CHAPTER 17

THEY drove into Brattleboro and found a moderate-size motor inn, red-shingled and turreted, with its Motor Club approval sign hanging from a post. They even had housemothers on call for baby-sitting. The room had two double beds, TV, piped-in music and a tray of sterile cups in plastic wrap. "This place is gorgeous," Jessica said, unwrapping the cups. Sylvie had managed to spirit Melvin into the room and hide him behind the shower curtain in the bathroom.

Jessica lolled on the bed, not feverish after all, though she did look wan. She needed another day to allow the medicine to do its work, and Sylvie decided they would have to stay put, certainly until tomorrow.

Sylvie ordered broth and scrambled eggs to be sent in, and after the little tray arrived, they sat on the bed eating.

"Will I get to ski tomorrow?" Jessica asked. She had begun to cough—a mild, dry, hacking sound.

"I doubt it. Let's give the medicine a chance." There was a small electro-perk in the room and Sylvie started water to boil for tea. She thumbed through the phone book, a colorful affair that listed Brattleboro and a few neighboring towns. There was no Gary Markson in the book. She called the operator and asked about Gary Markson in Cozzens. There was no listing in Cozzens either. What if it was all too late? Would always be too late? She tried to think of what to do next, but her head spun. Why had she assumed that it might be possible to find him, as if all of New England were just one small town?

She tucked Jess into bed and went into the bathroom, where Melvin, behind the shower curtain, was making hoarse piteous sounds. "Be quiet!" she admonished, as if talking to a child. Jessica was drowsing on her pillow. "Why are we here if we're not skiing?" she asked sleepily. And then, "Tell me a story." She puffed her pillow with her fist. "Mommy says she bets you have a story to tell."

"Everyone has a story to tell." Sylvie glanced at the phone book again. Baum. Daniel Baum's name *was* listed.

Jessica sat up in bed and flopped back. "I expect I'll dream about Zorro tonight. I expect I'll hear him crying because there's no coffee or a minibagel or anything where he is."

"He's in a good place. Probably happy as a lark, eating puppy biscuits just like all his friends." Angel had done that —given human characteristics to animals, pretending that her pets were jealous, grieving, in love. She'd thought once that her painted turtle had developed a crush on Goldie Fish.

Sylvie gave Jess a capsule with a glass of juice. The child, languid now, was drifting off, and Sylvie covered those chubby fingers, for a moment, with her own. "I'm going downstairs, but the housemother will pop her head in every few minutes to check on you." Jess was already asleep.

DANNY Baum needed only a moment to put her in context. "Hey, this is a surprise. You never mentioned anything about coming up this way. That kid ever get her parrot? Good. So what can I do for you?"

"I'm trying to locate Gary."

He was quiet for a moment, a thoughtful silence. "OK. Where are you staying. I'll come over. We'll talk."

He arrived in about twenty minutes, striding across the cozy lobby to the fireplace corner. She was sitting on a sofa, suddenly very tired. When he came toward her, she rose. "This is really nice of you, to just drop everything . . ."

"There wasn't all that much to drop. Bread day. I've been baking with my little crew since dawn. Yesterday was yogurt. I can use a change of pace."

She liked his looks. A shadow of beard on his fair skin. Yes, very blue eyes, a straggle of reddish-brown sun-streaked hair on his forehead. He was pleasingly relaxed; there was a missing button or two on his lumberjack's shirt. He smiled an open, good-natured smile. Sylvie tried to remember what Angel had said about him. "Terrific friend. Made for country life. You can't imagine him in any other setting. Not like Gary and me," she'd said ruefully, "the way we're still in some sort of process, some method of finding out what feels right between us. No advice, please . . ." No advice, but it had sounded as if she were speaking in code, and Sylvie thought about it then—"some sort of process," as though Angel was secretly hinting at a deeper restlessness. But then she got pregnant, and she and Gary were on a fixed course.

"Excuse me a moment," Sylvie said abruptly. She went upstairs to check on Jess, who was sleeping soundly, little bubbly whistles of air coming from her mouth. The housemother was sitting in the hall knitting. "Don't worry, I'll call you if she wakes."

Back in the living room again, she settled into the sofa, waiting to hear what Danny would say.

He'd stretched hands and feet toward the fire. "Listen, I just made a few calls around Cozzens. The fact is nobody up there has seen Gary for the last couple of weeks."

"Do you think he's gone?" she asked, trying to cover the upset in her voice.

"I can drive you over tomorrow, if you like. We can see a few people. I know a lot of folks in Cozzens."

She looked up at him. He had lit a pipe—one of those long corncob types that Victor thought were such a joke. She said quite simply, "I finally have this overwhelming need to see the baby. It's as if something in me, some terrible lump of resistance, something awful that plugged up everything, has split open. I think meeting you in that pet shop helped make it happen. I really want to look in earnest now."

"All I did was buy a civet cat for my summer zoo." He smiled, his hands pressed together under his chin, a gesture reminiscent of Victor, and of Arthur, too, who long ago, when he'd been tired or thoughtful, would place the tips of his fingers together as if in prayer, as Danny had just done. Once, when he'd returned from a trip to Chicago, where he'd represented a young woman who'd placed explosives in the outdoor money machine of a multinational bank, he'd come into their bedroom and sprawled exhausted in a chair, chin resting on a pyramid of fingers. "The bastard judge cites *us* for contempt," he said. "Scott prepares a glorious, searing brief, doesn't do a fucking bit of good." She remembered wondering which of Scott's searing facts had the power to challenge dynamite in a money machine.

Angel, aged twelve, had come in, wondering if anyone wanted to go out for pizza. But Arthur had wandered off to the bathroom mumbling to himself, resifting the testimony.

"Nobody around here ever wants to do anything!" Angel complained. Later, Sylvie had found the handkerchief wrapped around the nosegay in his pocket, along with his wallet and car keys. A limp bedraggled thing. She didn't know what possessed her to pick it up and sniff. The flowers gave off a spicy, acrid scent. Assertive. A little bit like an after-dinner drink. She'd wondered, again, whether he was having an affair.

"I hadn't been seeing too much of Gary," Danny was saying almost apologetically. "Even before . . . before Angel died." He spoke firmly, although his voice wavered, lost its pitch. He avoided her eyes for a moment, and she saw that Angel's death had touched him in much more than a passing way. He said, "There was a time, after Angel was a few months along, when Gary began to get into one of his crazy moods. He's that sort of guy—you probably know, an idea would hit him and he'd lose his bearings. Suspect everyone and everything. He got off on accusing people of way-out things and then sitting back looking gleeful at their attempts at self-defense. It gave him some notion of power that he couldn't seem to get any other way. I guess he tried it on me once too often. About his unborn child—who the father *really* was and all that crap, looking me up and down as though waiting for an explanation and then pretending it was a joke. Angel was furious. Embarrassed for him. I stopped coming around after a while . . ." But Sylvie was thinking of something else, a very young Gary sitting in that foster home, jumping up every time the phone rang or the postman came by, hanging around, just waiting.

"I never really accepted him," she murmured. "Maybe that counted, after a while. Tipped some invisible balance."

"Probably not. I don't go much for invisible anything. But Gary is fundamentally OK. A little unsure of what his life is supposed to be, as though there's something hard he has to prove. I mean, here he was in Vermont, trying to be self-sufficient, work with his hands, really messianic about it, and he was pretty good—his bookbinding was good, you know. Yet all the time he was sitting on something more, some worry about where his life and Angel's were going, some dread, I guess, that he might be stalled in a backwater, might end up a hayseed at the bottom of the barrel, and Angel would walk out. It made him bitter and shrill." He paused. "Angel was something else, though . . ."

Sylvie looked at him. "I'm surprised about that. I thought Gary made a credo of disdaining a certain kind of success." He gave up on being a lawyer, Angel had said.

"Not a credo, a pose. He changed poses the way people change doctors when the ailment isn't cured."

He had her smiling. His simple straightforwardness reminded her of Victor. She looked at his wind-roughened hands. What exactly did one do on yogurt day? Last winter, when she and Victor had visited Brattleboro after a storm, they drove up and found Danny helping Gary dig a path to the house. Danny was in a snowmobile with a blower attached to the front end, standing up in the machine, tall as a pole, his longish hair hanging out of his ski hat, and he was waving at Gary, who was packing down walls of snow on either side of the driveway with a shovel. Victor watched him for a while, narrowed his eyes as though he were staring through binoculars. Danny's back arched over the steering wheel. "I like the way that guy's strung together," Victor said.

Now she said, "If Jessica feels well enough, I'd like to drive to Cozzens tomorrow, and perhaps stay for a day or two." She knew it would take time. Finding Gary was only part of it. Breaking into his reserve, his dislike of her, his suspicion, was something else. And there was Sean. That would be hardest of all. To see and touch the baby, to know that she was touching Angel, too. "If you could meet us for a while, it might speed things up."

Danny agreed. In the firelight his face had an earnest glow. His eyes were dark and noncommittal. Had he loved Angel too, she wondered. He was saying, "Sure. Let's make it eleven o'clock tomorrow morning. It's forty miles north of here. I'll lead the way."

CHAPTER 18

*T*HE trip to Cozzens took more than an hour. Jess sat in the back, as did Melvin. Jessica's fever was gone, but she was left with a cough, which Melvin was vigorously imitating. "Who's Danny anyway?" Jessica asked.

"The friend of someone very dear to me." For the moment it seemed enough.

Danny was waiting for them at the Cozzens Diner. "I called Gary's former landlady," he said immediately. "Gary stopped off to see her about two weeks ago. He and the baby. She hasn't the slightest idea where he is now."

Sylvie's disappointment was unbearable.

"Don't lose heart," Danny said. "We've only just started. There are other places to look. The people at the bindery might know something."

Sylvie parked the station wagon, and they went off in Danny's pickup truck with Jessica and Melvin crowded between them in the front seat.

Norbert Fiske, who owned the bindery, wasn't much help. "Sure, Gary worked here for a while, but then he just left. Took some tools of mine, some special ink and some damn good vellum—not that I'd go so far as to call him a thief. Maybe he thought I owed him. But I haven't any idea where he's gone." Norbert spoke in quick fits and starts. "I'll tell you this, though, the friends he'd been hanging out with recently didn't look good to me. Swift-talking guys who'd park their cars and amble in here as though they'd come from around the block instead of from places like Texas and California and Montreal. And the sheriff come over too, asking about who these transients were, and what they had to do with Gary, and if any of them had passed bum checks. The sheriff said to me, more as a joke than anything else, 'Now, Norbert, you're not using your presses here as a laundering place for dealers to operate from, are you?'

"I said, 'Oh, sure! You've got the right party, buddy.' But the fact is Gary was always short of funds. He needed stuff for the baby. Always something else—a car seat, a stash of bitty clothes. And he had to hire someone to help out when he was at work. He wanted to get away from this place, though. Move somewhere else. Said it would be easier to raise a kid where it was warm."

They asked questions around town, visited people who'd had business with him—his former landlady, the man who'd serviced his snowmobile back in Brattleboro, the clerks in the organic food store. It was his landlady who finally suggested they talk to Yvonne, the girl who'd taken care of Sean when Gary was at work. "Yvonne Dufault? Oh, Christ, I know Yvonne," Danny said. There was an off-center smile on his face. When they were in the truck, he said, "Listen, this is a bummer. Yvonne and I are—were—friends. Had something going between us for a while." He looked unhappy, pushed his ski hat up on his brow. "I don't think she feels so friendly now. Oh, well, onward . . ."

Yvonne lived in an apartment above a convenience store. When she opened the door, she looked blank for a minute. "Ye gods, you!" she said when she saw Danny. A scornful look passed over her face. She was a skinny young woman. Her small sharp features seemed diminished by the bright red of her handwoven turtleneck. A green cigarette holder was stuck in the corner of her mouth, and she smoked and puffed, talking in a tight brittle voice. "Well, well, to what do I owe the honor . . ."

"Hi, Yvonne," Danny said. He reached to take her hand, but she pulled away.

"Nice of you to come by. I mean, a girl really appreciates when old, dependable friends drop in."

Jessica had stuck her head past the threshold and saw a family of stuffed dolls sitting on the couch. "Oh, neat," she said.

The girl shifted away from the threshold. "You might as well come in—all of you. But just for a minute, please. I'm busy."

"We're trying to get some word on Gary," Danny said. "This is his . . . his mother-in-law, Sylvie Weyman." Yvonne stared at Sylvie, then turned away. The room was a showcase for handicrafts. Besides the dolls there were embroidered pillows, a loom, baskets of wool, of fabrics, a bowl of buttons on a low table near the crowded couch. There was barely space to sit down.

"Place look familiar?" she asked Danny tartly.

"Cool it, Yvonne. I think we ought to concentrate on Mrs. Weyman; she has a serious problem."

"Well, if you're going to press me about Gary, let me say right off I don't know where he's gone. Why should I? I wasn't his confidante or anything." Her sullen gaze floated past Danny, came to rest on Sylvie. "The baby's grandmother, right?"

"Right," Danny said. She drew deeply on the cigarette, then dropped the ash in a clay pot near the couch. Sylvie suddenly realized that the cigarette holder was one of a series that Angel had made last year. She recognized it with dawning shock. The beautifully carved stock, like a slender upside-down urn. Mineral green. Angel had sent a similar one to Victor for Christmas with a little card: "CAUTION: This is a for love. Not smoke!"

"The baby's grandmother, yes," she said, trying to stop the quivering that had begun in her. The girl seemed furious with Danny; her dark pupils consumed her eyes. Sylvie wondered whether she was stoned and said clearly, "If there's any way you can help us find him . . ."

"There's no way I know of to help. I wasn't his personal secretary." Yvonne's hair hung loose to her shoulders, and she tossed it back with a little animal shake of her head. Her look had turned shrewd. It was the look of someone without significant expectations. She said, "Gary was renting this trailer over near Dummerston. He just wanted to get out of Brattleboro. Get away from the beaten track. Brattleboro was death, he said. You know." She seemed to be staring at the cut-glass seraphs hanging on the wall. "All I did was some light housekeeping. Took care of his kid and such." Her face softened as she spoke.

Sylvie realized that she was very young, possibly not more than twenty. She said quietly, "Tell me about the baby."

Yvonne looked at her in disgust. "You're really something else, for sure. I can't believe I'm supposed to be answering such basic questions from the grandmother, no less. I mean, lady, I can imagine your pain. But where the hell were you these last months. We could have used you . . ." She stopped and shook her head. "No—don't tell me. I know. Gary did a wipe-out where you were concerned. He wanted to stay clear of you, of everybody."

"The baby?" Sylvie asked again.

Yvonne relented. "Oh well, the baby was OK. Gary breathed for that kid. Fussed over him. The two of us took him to a pediatric clinic over the New Hampshire line to see that he got started right—shots, vitamins and all that. We'd stick this little dropper full of liquid vitamins in his mouth and he'd suck it up as if it was maple syrup." She turned to Danny. "So how's the big bread and yogurt dealer these days? I heard you're doing chocolate chip cookies next. Gary said you've turned into a real entrepreneur with those nets of yours flung out to Boston and New

York. Planning to give Dannon and Pepperidge Farm a run for their money?"

"Gary is capable of saying anything," Danny said. His face looked hot. "In fact he *has* said just about everything."

Jessica had picked up a doll with ginger-colored braids. "I love it." She gave Sylvie her special waif smile. "Can't we . . . ?"

"No more dolls," Sylvie said.

Jessica wandered around the room, started toward a doorway off the kitchen. "I have to pee." Yvonne grabbed her and said, "Not there! The bathroom's over here!" When Jessica reappeared, pulling up her ski pants, she added, "You'll have to go now. All of you. I have work to do."

There was too much discord in the room, Sylvie thought. Too many things said and unsaid. She had a single interest, Gary and the child. She guided Jessica through the door. "Who are Gary and Sean, anyway?" Jessica wanted to know.

"My family. Sean's the baby . . . my little grandchild."

"Are we going to visit them?"

"I hope so." She held Jessica's hand and walked quickly down the steps. Vermont was not a large state, but for the moment it seemed to have swallowed them whole.

"WHAT are you going to do?" Danny asked, when they were once more climbing into his pickup truck. It had begun to snow, a heavy curtain of flakes snapping at their cheeks. Jessica, muffled to her ears in ski suit and scarf, looked snug; her cough was no worse. Sylvie had made her decision. It was impossible to rush back to New York. Not now. She didn't care about consequences. "We'll stay around here for a few more days," she said. It was Monday. She'd call Feliciana with some excuse to pass on to Margo, when she phoned.

Danny found a comfortable guest house for them; a bedroom and bath on the second floor of a Vermont colonial set in a snow-muffled glade. The owner, Maggie Friel, bustled cheerfully around them. She bent over Melvin's cage, cooing, "Here, Polly, Polly."

"His name is Melvin. He's a boy," Jess said.

Two four-poster beds spread with white linen stood against one wall. Sylvie intended to coax Jessica into taking an afternoon nap, and she slipped into bed with her. There was the fragrance of freshly laundered sheets. A small box of foil-wrapped maple sugar leaves was on the washstand, along with green-stitched towels. Victor always insisted on fresh sheets. He bought silky percales loomed in Hong Kong. Embroidered pillow slips. He preferred ironed bed linen. A down comforter. "Small eccentricities," he'd say, sliding the percale over their heads. "I want something lovely next to my skin." Her heart thumped in her chest. She wondered where he was this very minute. On leave? Working with that little production company on his film? Throwing his money to the winds? But it's only money, he would say. Only a job. Only a life, she thought, only a false marriage, an idolatrous motherhood. She could hear his voice offering certainty. "Everything can be mended," he'd said. He was the actuary second-guessing facts. She had barely understood the full depth of his hurt until recently, when she'd discovered his obsession with Kesselmann, his need to do something graphic with those few outlandish facts. She remembered the sudden blank inwardness that floated across his face when he talked about the film, the way he dispelled it by a cynical aside—*"The Banality of Evil,"* he'd said, "with apologies to you know who." He tamped some shreds of tobacco in his pipe. "I might even call it *Nazis in Love,"* he said, smiling at her astonished face.

"Tell me a story," Jess was saying, reaching out and tugging at Sylvie.

"Make-believe or real-life?" Sylvie tried to relax. She'd rest, too, and then decide on the next move.

"Real-life," Jessica said. It was still snowing hard, and the room was like a viewing chamber to the world outside. Melvin was making eerily human sounds from his post beneath the bathroom sink. "I don't thing he's going to learn anything, except 'Gudma,'" Jess said, aggrieved.

"Maybe that's all it takes to make him happy."

"If I were a parrot, it would take at least a real 'Good morning' to make me happy. At least that."

Sylvie felt herself falling asleep, tuning down, slipping away. Death must be like that, she thought.

When Angel died, Sylvie catalogued the ways to die too: gas, poison, slicing her wrists, drowning. She came to believe that she understood suicide. Not theory so much as enactment—the spaciness, as if one were etherized, except for the pinprick of the idea itself against the whited-out canvas of the mind. Seductive and irrefutable. Only Victor stood between her and the persuasiveness of the idea. "You will walk," he said, dragging her out of her house, walking her for miles through the streets of Rosevale, pulling her by the elbow past the shopping mall, the movie theatre, the local bank, to the town dock, where the pleasure vessels were moored—the large sailboats and cabin cruisers, and farther out the graceful lamina of Sunfish and Sailfish, the small catamarans, the Rhodes 19's tethered and wheeling around their buoys. "If you want to jump," he said, "then jump. I can only say it will show a disgraceful lack of curiosity . . ."

They drove into the city, and he rented bicycles. They took the path near the reservoir in Central Park. Sightless, she stared at the crenellated skyline, the silvery disk of water. Horses cantered past them. She and Victor pedalled abreast. He said, "Imagine your legs are pistons. Imagine you are an engine with a flooded carburetor."

In the park, she passed out, fell into a rush of oncoming bikes.

He dragged her to her knees. "Live, God damn you!" he shouted.

It was Victor who made her swim. In the beginning he forced her out of bed when the pool opened in the early morning and swam alongside her. "Actually, I hate flailing about at this ridiculous hour," he said. "It's a real sacrifice." His hair was slick; there was a wedge of foam on his moustache. He never took his eyes off her.

The swimming took hold. She became addicted.

When he first knew her Victor said, "I imagine your husband really did a number on you."

"In his own way, he was an important man," she said, as though lecturing on a topic of historic value. "He rode into battle. Carver Stedman, the black preacher, said he was one of three or four white people he'd ever known whose selfless passion . . . oh well, it's ancient history."

"Like hell it is. History is never ancient or finished. History repeats and repeats like a garlic pickle, my love."

She enlarged her explanation. "We were simply not one of his causes—Angel and I. He tried for a while, but gradually . . ."

"Why didn't you take Angel and leave?"

"Because it seemed worth it—my life. Because I saw us as a family. In spite of everything."

He'd have none of that. "I think there's more here than meets the eye. Self-justification, perhaps?"

"I loved him," she said angrily.

"Oh, gosh, *honestly*?"

"Victor!"

"Well, if not honestly, then *purely*?"

"I can't believe you're making this sound so corny. My *life*, remember?"

He persisted. "And he? Noble in heart, was he? No little affairs here and there? No adultery?"

She hated him for a moment, but she gave him the answer he deserved. "No adultery, as far as I know." She offered nothing more. No additions or enlargements. No sleepers for shock effect.

JESSICA'S voice was fretful. "I don't hear any stories." The child's hand slid over the coverlet, and Sylvie permitted the flutter of fingers to stay twined in hers.

"Well, there was once a little girl who loved to make necklaces. She made them from spaghetti and macaroni. She punched a little hole into Oreo cookies and Fig Newtons and made a necklace of those, too. An edible necklace. She made a necklace from pea pods and cherry tomatoes and little squares of beef, which could be barbecued when she was tired of wearing it. She strung a necklace of peppermint Lifesavers and dime-store engagement rings, which would come in handy if she ever ate an onion or wanted to become engaged quickly."

Jess giggled. Her thumb had slid into her mouth, but when she saw Sylvie looking at her she popped it out. "I don't think it's a real-life story."

"It's real enough. One day she tried something more complicated. She wanted to do a necklace of starfish and went to a place called Starfish Beach. 'Don't go into the water,' her mother warned. 'You'll get stung.' But the little girl had stopped hearing her mother."

"You're a good mother," Angel had said, fluffing her hair over her new angora sweater. "But what I was really hoping for was rhinestone earrings." It was her twelfth birthday. Arthur was taking them to dinner. He called from Newark. "I don't think I can make it. The mayor's had us on a leash all day . . ."

"No! No!" she said loudly. "I have a carton of books to read on the Mary Shelley thing, and *I* managed to put that aside . . . so don't you dare . . ." There was a rare wild sound in her voice.

He said, "Drive in. We'll meet in Chinatown."

Angel and she arrived after the peak dining hour. The place was half empty. Arthur and Scott were sitting at a table drinking shots of vodka on ice. "Happy birthday, sweetheart," Arthur said to Angel. He had bought her a satin kimono embroidered with tinsel dragons at one of the oriental shops down the street. Scott had an ivory fan with a pink tassel. Arthur bent his head close to Sylvie's and said, "Do you think I can help this? Do you think I want everything to always get so botched up?"

Scott was talking to Angel. He kept pushing his very straight hair out of his eyes. "Are you only twelve, Miss

Femme Fatale? My God!" He stared at the ceiling. "What will she be like at sixteen?"

They ordered butterfly shrimp. Angel picked up a shrimp by the tail. "This poor little thing just spread its wings and got deep-fried."

Scott swept his hair off his forehead. "What a terrible image! You're making me nauseous." Sylvie watched him play court to Angel. She had never before noticed the grace of his fingers, his faintly polished fingernails.

Arthur touched her arm. "You're going to hate this, but Scott and I have to go back to Newark tonight or the whole day will be down the drain."

"You're right, I hate it."

Driving home through the spring night, Angel said, "Wasn't Daddy funny, and Scott?" She was wearing the kimono over her coat. The fan dangled at her wrist. "Wasn't everything perfect?"

False, she thought. She'd caught a glimpse of Scott bending toward Arthur as the four of them parted in the noise and hustle of Mott Street. Arthur grinning. It was so false, the way she played the role of supportive wife, getting high on the distant vapors of Arthur's ambition, making Angel her project.

Once, she left Arthur, left Rosevale. A sudden unpremeditated move. She took a small apartment in Greenwich Village. Angel was thirteen. It was autumn, the beginning of a new school term. She was lucky enough to be able to enroll Angel in a nearby junior high at the last minute. There was some money; she did free-lance editing, continued with her few contacts in library research.

Arthur came looking for her after a while. "You don't want to do this," he said. He held her hands tightly in his. "Nothing is easy. Oh, Lord, absolutely nothing is clear or simple or fucking goddamn certain. Nothing! What I'm asking you to do is hang on." It was mid-morning. Angel was in school. They were in the bedroom. He ran his hands up her arms. Cradled her face. He smelled like bread, tobacco smoke, newly minted dollar bills. He kissed her lips and said, "I don't want to give you up." He said, "It won't always be this way . . . I can shift directions, if you can just be tolerant." He made love ardently, recapitulated their life together, made it sound like a work of the imagination. "After all, you never wanted to be *ordinary!*" he said. He started to get dressed. She said, "It's just that I don't feel central to anything that affects you anymore. I haven't for the longest time." She had his total attention. She said, "Sometimes I think there's another woman. And that Scott is covering for you. . . . And what's more, I'm not sure that I really want to know."

He looked as though he'd had the wind knocked out of him. He sat back slowly on the bed. "That kind of talk is unworthy . . . !" He studied a mote of dust on the bedroom sill. "The fact is, I do love you," he said at last. "Be patient. People pass through things . . . and then it's over."

All that he passed through was his own life, a year later, on a street in Brooklyn.

"So," Jessica was saying, "what happened at Starfish Beach?"

"Absolute mayhem," Sylvie continued in a serious voice. "The starfish banded together and made themselves into a starfish submarine and dove beneath the surf and nipped the little girl's toes."

"Is that as bad as a wasp sting?"

"Much worse."

"Zorro once got stung on his tongue by a wasp, and his tongue swelled up and hung out of his mouth like a frankfurter. I put butter on it and then we stuck it in coffee, because coffee takes the pain away. Mommy says that's when Zorro learned to be a coffee freak."

Sylvie felt on the verge of tears. The child's innocence was perfect. She pressed her cheek against Jessica's. A cool cheek now. Even the coughing had stopped.

"What happened then?" Jessica mumbled; she was slipping away.

"Nothing good," Sylvie whispered.

* * *

It was arranged. Maggie Friel would fix a hamburger dinner that evening for Jessica. Jules Verne was being serialized on TV, and Jess could see it before going to bed. Sylvie had an errand to do in the village, she said. She'd try not to be late.

She backed the car down the driveway and into the freshly plowed road. It was already dark. Stars, like frozen dust, blanketed the sky. She would take a chance on Yvonne's being home, and alone. If not, she'd sit in the diner across the road and wait.

The brightly lit convenience store looked like an oasis on an otherwise blacked-out street. There was a straggle of shoppers loading up with staples in case the weather turned really vicious. The checkout boy had an electric percolator plugged in at the side of his counter, and through the window she saw him pouring complimentary cups of coffee to his few patrons before they headed out into the night.

Sylvie climbed the stairs to Yvonne's apartment. When she rang the bell, Yvonne opened the door. She had a sandwich in her hand, and she stared at Sylvie as though they had never met.

Sylvie said, "I wanted to speak to you again."

"Oh well, I don't think so. I'm just about ready to go out."

"Only for a few minutes."

The girl said, "I don't know . . ." She seemed to consider the matter and grudgingly agreed. "All right, you can come in. But just for a sec." She finished her sandwich without taking her eyes off Sylvie. "Might as well make yourself comfortable," she said waving at a wicker chair crowded with patchwork cushions. There was a fire in the grate and a harsh chemical smell hung in the air. Sylvie's eyes smarted. "I'll get you something to drink," Yvonne said, still watching her. "Gets pretty murky in here when I'm dyeing wool." Sylvie wondered whether Sean had been allowed to stay in this chemically loaded atmosphere. Yvonne turned up the radio, went behind a partition into a little kitchen galley and came back with two glasses filled with a pinkish drink. One swallow and Sylvie's throat seemed anesthetized. "My specialty.

Don't worry, it won't kill you. It's pink tequila. So, you're here. What do you want?" Yvonne didn't seem as tight and forbidding as earlier in the day.

Sylvie looked around. "Do you live here alone?" The room they were in was meant for both studio and living quarters. The couch obviously opened to sleep two. The door off the kitchen might open to storage space.

"That's a pretty personal question, isn't it?" But Yvonne didn't seem annoyed. She seemed rather balmy and at ease, as if aware that she held some sort of advantage over Sylvie. "I've had invited guests here, you might say. People I've wanted to be in a relationship with." Sylvie thought about Daniel, and as if reading her mind, Yvonne said, "I've known Danny Baum pretty well. I guess that was obvious. Maybe he told you about us."

"Not really," Sylvie said quickly. "I barely know Danny. He just seemed to be the right person to help me get in touch with Gary and Sean."

"I had something good going with Danny for a long time. You must have guessed *that*. He can be really sweet, except when he's being superior and full of plans that everyone is supposed to fall in line with—like this yogurt and bread venture of his. Gary liked him a lot, though, and Angel too." She lit a cigarette with trembling fingers and tried to place it in the green holder. Sylvie wondered whether that holder had been a gift from Angel to Gary. "Danny worked for a bank in Boston until just a couple of years ago, believe it or not. He came to Vermont on a ski weekend just once and decided right then and there that he wanted to live a rural life. Get away from the inhumanity of cities. The same words as Gary's." She shook her head. "Grown men, and so *naïve*!"

She seemed to be waiting for Sylvie to confirm this view. "There's inhumanity just about everywhere," Sylvie said mildly. Victor had been more imaginative on the point. He'd once said the defining stroke between man and the animal world was the ability of man to relinquish his human essence if he chose. Just toss it out the window like a discarded cigarette. How tuned she was to the bittersweet edge of his thinking. Oh, she could use him now, to help her make this young girl stop babbling and come across with the facts.

But the girl continued, "He bought a small farm, and then he went about everything so meticulously. A real back-to-the land specialist. Read up on everything from animal husbandry to the economics of local villages. Gary was impressed. Angel too. We all were. But those three hung around together a lot." Her face was flushed. "Say, you wouldn't want something to eat before you go?" she suddenly asked. "I have a wedge of cheddar and some fruit." She disappeared again behind the partition. Sylvie wondered why she was hearing so much about Danny. The girl's mood was bewildering. Instead of the petulance she'd expected, she was getting a flood of confidences.

The voice of Streisand belting out "The Way We Were" filled the room. Yvonne came back and placed a dish of cheese and apples on the floor between them. "That song always breaks me up," she said, flopping on the couch, her swingy skirt spreading over the cushions, her bracelets clacking. She was still talking, almost to herself. "A business has to have an identity. It can't be both rural and commercial." She had a damp, overheated look. She had brought back another rose-colored drink for herself. Slightly drunk, she asked, "Am I right, or am I right?"

Sylvie stared off into the fire for a moment, wondering whether there was anything here for her, and then she asked abruptly, "Where do you think Gary might have gone?"

"I told you, I was just the baby-sitter . . ." Despite the sarcastic tone, Yvonne seemed to have shrunk against the couch. She held one of the dolls in her lap and for an instant Sylvie could imagine her, like Jessica, popping a thumb into her mouth.

There was a blare of music and static from the radio. "I don't think I heard you," Sylvie said. "Could you turn your radio down?"

"I said I was just the baby-sitter. And I like my music loud! Look, maybe we'd better split."

But Sylvie took another tack. "Have you been in Cozzens long?"

"How long is long?" Yvonne looked at Sylvie as though she'd said something very wise. "I left home about four years ago—Quebec, eight kids in the family, rosaries on all the doorknobs. Anyway, I ended up here. Had no romanticized ideas about country living. Why should I? Rural Quebec is as rural as you can get." She dipped a wedge of apple into her glass and sucked on it. "I thought I'd find a job as a waitress, but I did even better with crafts. I make pretty decent money on just my dolls alone."

She set her glass on the floor next to the plate of apples and looked up at Sylvie. Her eyes had a catlike sheen. "Danny and I had an important feeling for each other. Good things might have happened." She said this accusingly, as though Sylvie was somehow responsible. "We could have joined forces. I expected that. I expected to be a real part of his life. But Angel spoiled it. Angel just stepped in and made it impossible."

"Angel?" Sylvie said. She felt as if she were in a play whose script she'd totally misread.

"I'm sorry to bring it up," Yvonne said in a wobbly voice, "with all the grief and everything that came later. But there was your daughter with everything, Gary who trailed after her like a sick calf, and she growing so relaxed and beautiful each month with her baby in her, and electing not to care seriously for anyone. Not for Gary or for Danny. As though she'd made a pact, only with herself. It was Angel's idea to give birth at home."

"Angel's idea?" But how could this girl have known?

"I had the feeling, after the baby, she might just leave. Go off somewhere—and Gary wouldn't even have a claim on her.

"Of course, Daniel and I never really discussed this," she went on. "No accusations or soul-searching. He'd just come over and smoke a joint, and we'd pull the couch in front of the fire, and you know . . . But he came by less and less. And after Angel died, he stopped altogether. Today was the first time I'd seen him in months."

Sylvie's voice dropped to a lower key. She heard herself barely whisper, "I'm so worried about Gary and the baby off alone somewhere. Gary can be so paranoid, who knows what he might decide to do next. And I think it's odd that he's gone. I mean, he disappeared from Brattleboro and turned up here with Sean. And now he seems to have gone off somewhere again . . ."

"Look, all you're interested in is the baby, period. The way I heard it, you never gave a shit for Gary . . ." The sudden harshness of the girl was like snow shoved down her neck.

She got up, shivering. "I think I'm bothering you. You've been patient, and you said you had to leave." She bent to zip up her boots.

The girl turned frantic. "No, don't go yet. I didn't mean to insult you or anything. Maybe I'll think of some way to help." She scooped up the dolls, put them in a copper scuttle and made a place for Sylvie on the couch next to her. "Don't rush away. Here, sit. Do you want to try something mellow?" The girl opened a drawer in a side table and removed cigarette papers and a tin of something that Sylvie knew was not tobacco. She proceeded to roll two joints. Sylvie tried to demur, but the girl's loneliness was compelling.

"I don't think I'm up to this sort of thing. Frankly, the times I've tried it, I've felt very uneasy, spacey," Sylvie said. Like those people, she thought, who experience clinical death and hover at the ceiling, looking down on their own inert bodies.

The girl was nodding sagely. "Well, you have to appreciate feeling spacey."

She had smoked once with Arthur. It was after a party at their house. Scott was there. Angel, fourteen at the time, was having a sleep-over at her friend Molly's house. They were cleaning up the mess of dirty glasses and leftover food when Scott said, "I have some superb grass." They sat in the litter

of the living room, she and Arthur on the couch, Scott on a
hassock at their feet. They passed one joint around. She drew
the smoke into her lungs. "I'm a little bit worried about this."
She felt flakes of herself beginning to collect and harden into
a certain unnerving alertness. Every word uttered sounded
like a chime. Arthur was saying, "Well, folks, I think I'm
finally getting the *feel* of myself, and I rather like what's
there." He said, "I am very, very elastic." And she imagined
him turning to Silly Putty, stretching from one corner of the
room to the other.

Scott was smiling. He was lying on the couch, long thin
legs extended, pale graceful hands folded on his chest. She
noticed his eyes as she never had before—large, intense,
darkly liquid, in contrast to the fairness of his skin. She
remembered thinking, He's very beautiful and fine. Scott
lifted his head. She could hear his voice, the mellow rounded
vowels. She recalled wondering, Princeton, Yale? Scott was
saying, "What do you say, Artie? The stuff smells so damn
good. So *quintessential.* It's worth preserving, right?" He
disappeared from the room. She heard him in the kitchen
opening and closing the pantry door. He came back with two
bottles in his hand; B&B and Cointreau. She remembered
thinking, What in the name of heaven? He made a little
mound of pot on a dish. Pressed and fooled with it until it
took on the shape of a leaf. "That's a very expensive hobby
you have there, Scott, my boy," Arthur was saying. Scott
sprinkled a few drops of Cointreau on his marijuana leaf.
"This should do it," he said. "Entrap the scent in alcohol."
He looked very clever. Looked at them both with love.
Reached forward and jointly hugged their knees.

Arthur said, "I must say, you have a way with weeds."
Sylvie burned with sudden knowledge; went to the bathroom
and threw up. In the artificial brilliance of her mind she saw
herself on her knees, her arms wound around the toilet bowl,
hanging on. Arthur came and stood at the door, staring
in. "OK, you've made your point. Henceforth we banish

pot. . . ." He smiled at some secret amusement. "God, I feel so unbearably clever. Let's get you into bed."

"No, no," she said wildly. "Go back to Scott. I'll manage."

YVONNE lay back, blowing the dull smoke through her nose. She passed the joint to Sylvie and squirmed deeper into the couch. "Nothing ever really works out. Did you ever notice how things just stop dead, or else go down some twisty side road?"

Sylvie inhaled and handed the joint back. She nodded drowsily, felt that if she closed her eyes, she could fall asleep for a long time. She thought of Jessica at Mrs. Friel's. "Do you mind if I use your phone?"

"Oh, be my guest," the girl answered, as if from a distance. She dialled Maggie Friel. "Is Jessica asleep?"

"Sure, ages ago."

"I'll be along soon."

Back in the room, Yvonne was still talking, as if offering a prologue to herself. "You see, my father was crazy about my mother. But after the eighth child she said, 'No more, Buddy.' His name was Buddy. She literally pushed him out of her bed, she being pure Catholic and all. 'No more' meant just that. He said, 'Jetta, you're killing me.' She said, 'You've got that wrong, Buddy; you're the one who's killing me.'

"Well, one night, when my mother was at a late mass, he went into my sister Bernadette's room. I've always imagined how it was. Bernadette in bed, looking surprised, and my father just standing there dazed by what he wanted to do and furious, as though he was carrying out someone else's orders. And then Bernadette, who was sixteen and had a terrific pair of lungs, yelling. When my mother came home, Bernadette was hysterical. And when my mother understood, she went calmly into the kitchen, came back with a small paring knife, and walked up to my father. 'Nothing happened,' he was shouting, 'nothing! It's all lies!' But my mother had placed herself before him and quietly lifted her arm as though the knife was a baton and she was calling a chamber group to order, and then she sliced her own wrists. I mean right in front of him, in front of all of us, the blood spurting and he going white as a sheet. The doctor came and all. They sewed her up right away. But I left after that. I couldn't take the drama."

Yvonne was lighting up again. "No! No!" Sylvie said, refusing the joint. Her own voice floated back at her from across the room. She thought of the way she'd dealt with her "drama." Reeling away like a drunkard. Coming back. Considering the mass of it as an idea, a reality. It was so immense, it required digestion. Digestion and regurgitation. She had said nothing but remembered everything. Arthur and Scott going over a brief in the living room, Arthur's hand, motionless as a glove, resting on Scott's neck. Arthur calling from St. Louis or Denver or Detroit. In Detroit he was cited for contempt. He said, "Bastard judge! This will delay Scott and me another few days."

She took Angel out of school, and they went to California. They stayed in Los Angeles for one day and then came back. Angel was indignant. "I've missed hockey and swimming team. All for one day in Santa Monica!" Sylvie took her to Maine for a weekend, to Rhode Island for a whale watch. Each time she could barely wait to turn around and return. Angel, lifting her sweet, surprised face from the rented binoculars, had said, "I don't think you're enjoying yourself one bit." She bought theatre tickets, opera tickets, for several nights of the week, and failed to use them. She insisted on a boat ride around Manhattan. Passing the blind prison windows of Rikers Island, Angel said, "It's so scary."

Sylvie said, "It's not scary enough." She rushed forward in search of new footing. Her life had never existed. All of it had been imagined. A mirage, a nullity of her own doing. A conceit. Only Angel was real; she existed, the one small, soft flare in all the rubble. She was ready to confront Arthur. Angel was at a school play for the evening. Arthur had said, "Let's go to that new Indian restaurant in town." He was home for a few days before leaving for Memphis. At the restaurant, they ordered from the tandoor oven. A waiter in a satin turban hovered over them. The heavy spices heated her mouth. Arthur choked on his dal and gulped a glass of ice water. She sipped her ginger drink, a gambler ready to throw in her few remaining chips. "Do you want a divorce?" she asked. Arthur dipped his napkin into his water glass and wiped his lips.

He said very softly, every muscle in his face gone slack, "Only if it's something *you* have to do."

"Yes, it's what I have to do!"

YVONNE was saying that she loved her father, who had worked for a pickling factory and who would come home with the smell of bay leaves in his hair. It was terrible the way their lives just came apart, after Bernadette. She said she tried to tell Danny about it. What she really wanted was for Danny to be wiped out with disgust. But he just said, "That poor guy must have felt like shit!"

"It turned me on to him. Just that one remark. Made me want to love him on the spot." Yvonne had reached for a doll and was braiding and unbraiding its wool hair. There was something incomplete about her, Sylvie thought, as though she'd stumbled past some maturation process without allowing it to take effect. The thought of Yvonne as a baby-sitter, making decisions about Sean, was awful.

"Tell me more about the baby," Sylvie said.

"Sean? He's a sweet, quiet child. When he was four months, we started him on instant baby rice. Three or four spoonfuls a day. Gary had him at the clinic, not in Brattleboro or Cozzens. He drove fifty miles into New Hampshire and had him seen at a pediatric clinic in Manchester. He said he didn't want people keeping tabs on him. Knowing too much. Making it easy to find him." He meant me, Sylvie thought.

"Sean was strong," Yvonne said. "Lots of curly blond hair . . . like a little cherub." She had stopped playing with the doll's braids and was looking at Sylvie. "What I'd really like to do now, I guess, is to go to Mexico, to a place near Guadalajara. There's an American colony there. You can live cheaply and work. Of course, the plane fare is killing . . ." Sylvie wondered whether the shape of this encounter was coming clear at last. Were there to be facts forthcoming, but only for a price?

She was about to say, "How much would you need?" when Yvonne got up and stirred the fire. Her back was bent, and her lovely handloomed skirt swept the hearth. When she straightened up, her face was streaked with firelight.

"I would die for love," she said. "When I saw Danny and me just drizzling off, and Danny turning to Angel . . ." She picked up the cigarette holder and held it in the palm of her hand, as if testing its weight. "Angel made a few of these. She gave one to Danny. I took it from him, and he let me have it. And then I knew it was like a farewell gift . . . the very fact that he'd part with it. I knew it had something to do with his bad conscience; it was all over, and I just wanted to die. I would imagine getting into Danny's pickup some night, closing the windows and turning on the motor. And in the morning he'd find me there propped behind the wheel. Do I sound crazy?"

Sylvie sighed. "No more than anyone in pain."

Her answer displeased Yvonne. "Gosh, you're so with it, aren't you," she said. "All your feathers in place. I mean, you give the impression of being on top of everything. I bet nobody would have the nerve to walk out on you." To her dismay Sylvie realized the girl was weeping.

"You're wrong," she said. "My husband did walk out, more or less. For his career . . . and finally . . ." She paused, gathering breath. Even Victor had never heard this single fact. "He left me for a lover, who happened to be a man."

Yvonne looked stunned. "Wow, that must have been a real downer."

"Where's Gary?" Sylvie asked sharply.

The girl was frightened. Ravel's *Bolero* came in ear-splitting waves. Yvonne fiddled with the knobs turning the volume down and then up again. She came and held out the cigarette holder. "I really want you to have this . . ."

Sylvie shook her head. "A very dear friend of mine also has one. It's enough." She repeated the question, "Where's Gary?"

"Boone," Yvonne said, "Boone, New Hampshire. That's what I think. I'm not sure. He talked about Boone. Only, if you find him, you mustn't tell him I told you."

CHAPTER 19

IT was early morning, and Sylvie swam in the murky pool of the Four-Star Motor Inn down the road. Maggie said that during the week the inn didn't mind if outsiders came and used it. Jess was in the playroom alcove nearby, busy with tumbling mats and chinning bars.

The pool had obviously not been filtered or renewed, and Sylvie was finding the experience unpleasant. Forty laps, she thought. She would survive. She plunged ahead, swimming with all the speed she could manage, but the welcome blankness that usually followed extreme exertion had deserted her; her thoughts were on a course of their own.

She summoned up Yvonne, another poor squandered soul. It was disconcerting to remember sitting in front of the fire with the girl, passing a joint back and forth with such strange intimacy. Sylvie felt she had given something of herself away. And for what? Well, of course, she had finally gotten some information about Gary, but she would probably have gotten that anyway.

She looked across the tile apron at Jessica rolling around on top of a huge beach ball. Jessica sat up and waved.

Sylvie promised herself to call Bob Fleet before they moved on to New Hampshire. She reviewed her story: She was representing Mrs. Kort, the potential buyer he'd written to not long ago. Mrs. Kort would like to see slides of his most recent work and perhaps a representational canvas or two. . . . For an instant she thought of this encounter from Margo's point of view. Would the logic hold?

Jessica had come to the side of the pool, her straight little body tilting forward as she peered down at Sylvie. Her hair was stretched taut in a flawless ponytail. Maggy Friel's work. Jess had stood in front of Sylvie that morning with brush and rubber bands, her shiny head bent trustingly. Sylvie, suddenly breathless, had said, "Maybe Mrs. Friel will do that. I want to dress."

Now Jess said in reminder, "Maggie promised she'd take me out in her snowmobile if we stay around long enough."

Jess was standing on the lip of the pool. "Be careful!" Sylvie said sharply.

"I won't fall in. Anyway I can swim." She made crawling motions with her arms.

"Well don't prove it, for heaven's sake!" Sylvie climbed out, grabbed Jess and held her tightly for a moment.

"You're getting me wet!" Jess squeaked.

"Sorry."

They headed for the locker room. A quick visit to Bob Fleet and then New Hampshire. Boone was nearly seventy miles away; they would have to hurry. She wanted to get there by mid-afternoon. She had hold of Jess's hand and was tugging the child along. "When we're in New Hampshire, I promise, we'll do everything."

CHAPTER 20

S HE found Fleet on a barely plowed side road off the main highway. A red pennant with the words *Americas Cup* had been stuck on a pole in a snowbank to mark the turnoff.

Fleet had sounded very interested when she phoned him after the pool. "Oh, sure, terrific. I didn't expect to see anyone, you know, *in person.* But come on over. Just follow my red flag up the road."

He lived in a trailer in the center of a grove of pines. Behind the trailer was a large Quonset hut that looked like a space module set stealthily in the woods. Halos of sunlight crowned its plastic roof. The structure seemed so eerie, she wondered just how eccentric Fleet was and if he could be relied on as a supplier of quality art.

He bounded toward them as soon as their station wagon pulled up, full of extravagant greetings, as if they were loved ones whose death had been falsely rumored. "Great to see you! Isn't this fantastic!" He peered through the car windows. "Honestly, nobody, but nobody ever comes crawling up this trail." Sylvie stared at him. He was bald as a Buddha. Red fleece earmuffs were clamped to his skull. "No trouble, I take it, getting off the road? My Americas pennant's a proper beacon, wouldn't you say?" He bounced on the balls of his feet like a peppy handball player. Observing him more closely, Sylvie realized that his earmuffs were the headpiece for a pocket cassette player, piping music into him like an intravenous feeding. "Listen, do you want something to drink? Hot chocolate for your little girl?" Her little girl? She looked at Jess and shook her head.

Jess was opting for hot chocolate, but Sylvie got down to business. She was in a hurry. "If you'll refer to Mrs. Kort's letter, you'll see—"

"Oh, sure. I was going to send her some slides—but now that you're here, I guess I can just give them to you . . ." It was exactly what she wanted. It would make her visit, the whole Vermont adventure, seem more reasonable. "Is there a canvas or two that I can take along?"

Jessica was peering into the woods. "Are there bears around?" she asked.

"Oh, bears—well hardly." His face wrinkled into a grin. Despite the cold there were pinpricks of perspiration on the egglike surface of his skull.

"Wolves, then?"

"Wolves! Good heavens, don't mothers tell their daughters anything anymore? You have to go to Alaska or Montana, or wherever they keep wolves these days." He winked at Sylvie, opened the door to the Quonset hut. "Well, let me show you my studio."

Fleet had done a great deal of work. There were pictures covering all the wall surfaces. Blown-up photographs of sides of buildings, decayed doorways with brass knockers hanging askew, fences crudely painted with the graffiti of children. "You see, I start with a photograph, and using it for pattern, the way other artists use work sketches, I paint over it, layer on layer and just see what happens."

Sylvie thought the paintings were remarkable. Abstract, mysterious. The original photographs were transmuted into a brocade of nearly familiar shapes—the suggestion of a door or a roof appeared the way a cubist hand or foot might in an abstract canvas. "I call this series 'Surfaces,'" he was saying. Sylvie made a memo in her head for Margo.

She cleared her throat. "This is such good work, I think Mrs. Kort will be enthusiastic. Her clientele happens to think in terms of the decorative factor in art before anything else. She's forced to be practical . . ."

Fleet removed a sheet of slides from a file cabinet and held them up to the light. "Here, show her these. Anything she likes I'll ship down immediately on approval. What's more, I'll give you a canvas or two from my 'Surfaces' series, for the hard evidence." He was putting slides in a manila envelope and tearing wrapping paper for the canvases. Good, Sylvie thought. He was turning into an effective alibi.

There was a photograph of a sailboat on the wall framed in Lucite. She knew he wouldn't want to lose *that* under layers of visionary paint. Following her glance, he said, "That's my darling. *Suzanna Sue.* I sail her in summer and paint in winter. This summer we're going to fool around at the Narragansett races."

The boat looked expensive. Perhaps he would be too high in price. Or conversely, perhaps his habits were so costly that he was always pressed for money, in which case he might welcome a client like Margo who would buy not one item but several.

"We'll have to be going," she said when he had lugged the paintings out to the car. Jessica was already there checking on Melvin, whose cage was wrapped in Zorro's electric blanket. "Snug little bunny," Jess was murmuring.

"Are you heading back to New York?" Fleet asked. He had left his earmuffs back in the studio. His leprechaun look had melted away. But he still spoke in a bright, chirpy voice, and he seemed even more good-natured and purposeful than before. She hoped he'd keep his prices in line.

"No, as a matter of fact we're going into New Hampshire, to Boone," she said.

There was a vague shift of light in his eye. "Oh yes, Boone. Haven't been there for a while myself. Know people in Boone?"

"As it happens I do. Gary Markson. Have you run into him by any chance?" She wondered why she hadn't thought to ask before.

Again the shift of light. The shiny mouth seemed to freeze before it relaxed into a casual smile. "Sure, I met Gary a couple of times. He didn't live around here all that long, though. Did some imaginative bookbindings, as I remember. Stopped by once and asked me for some advice on the use of watercolor. Related or anything?" He seemed to be walking away. The snow under his boots sounded like ice being crushed for a drink. But he'd taken only a few steps backward.

"Yes, we're related, but it's a long and complicated story." The sun had gone behind a cloud bank, and she realized that she was cold.

"If you see him, send my regards," Fleet was saying. "Hell, I hope you don't find him in jail."

CHAPTER 21

THE road from Albuquerque to Santa Fe rose quickly through a desert landscape, pocked like the moon, with gullies of scrub and tumbleweed. Margo felt extraordinarily light-headed. She had left the gravity pull of normal existence far behind. Brill would be waiting for her in Santa Fe. She was suddenly finding it hard to think about him except as an abstraction, the recent lover. He seemed to have lost substance in the ten days that he'd been gone. Her life had been so full of turmoil that her mind couldn't fix and shape him, couldn't make him central. It made her wonder why she had agreed to meet him in so remote a place. It was one thing to be together in New York. But the fact that they were thousands of miles from home gave it all a new importance. Of course, Brill *was* important, she told herself. Still, she felt confused.

She turned on the radio and listened for a while to a rock station. "Baby, when I need you; baby, how I need you . . ." The music heightened her feeling of displacement.

As she sped north, the desert terrain turned gentler, the yucca and sagebrush giving way to groupings of juniper and fir. She could have phoned Brill from Albuquerque and told him that she had decided to return home. It wouldn't have been hard to find reasons—Jessica, her parents, the demands of her work, Michael's trip, which seemed so threatening now. The newspapers were full of horror stories every day about Americans abroad in hostile places, as though violence had become the norm. With Michael so persistently in her thoughts, her presence here seemed pure treachery. She would tell Brill this. Perhaps they'd be together briefly; perhaps she'd just leave. There were no commitments.

She had managed successfully in Albuquerque, found a gallery that sponsored the work of several regional artists, all of them good. In a phone call to Alessa she tried to make real those large sunstruck canvases, the blinding light in the Spanish-Indian faces, black satin hair against mahogany cheeks, and the sinister beauty of the desert always in the background, like a drug-induced dream.

"Sounds great," Alessa said, "but I don't know. What you're describing seems too romanticized for your friendly neighborhood boardroom! Still, if you love it, buy!" She did, exhausting her traveller's checks, her letter of credit. She reminded herself that her resources were Michael's. Would he have said "Buy"? Probably. Yet financial independence was what she wanted. She wanted it more than ever, now that money was no longer a problem.

The road curved along the Rio Grande, through a golden-gray terrain of gama grass and mesquite, of rocky outcroppings burnished green by lichen with the deeper green of piñon and ponderosa pines in the distance. She passed a roadside trading post and stopped. Indian jewelry literally hung from the rafters. A woman with long black braids and a band of seed pearls around her forehead was making avocado-and-papaya shakes in a blender. Margo ordered a drink and examined trays of silver-and-turquoise bracelets. There was a small silver wristlet inlaid with coral birds that caught her eye. Jess, she thought. The birds, of course, would be transformed into parrots, a chorus of Melvins. There was also a man's belt with silver medallions, each medallion depicting a scene of harvest or hunting. Not Michael's style. Brill's? She paid for the bracelet and was on the way to the car when she turned back and bought the belt.

The highway had broadened. She passed arroyos, stick fences, streams like black strings laid on the pebbly earth. There was a sign on the road that said San Felipe Pueblo. She imagined a cluster of hivelike adobe structures pressed against a hillside, the Sangre de Cristo mountains looming in the distance. Brill had told her he would be visiting a Zuni pueblo because of a particular mineral that was found in the streambeds. Brill. She waited for the spirit of him to form. Felt a nervous tingling at last. What would they talk about? He would be coming down from Montana. He had dropped her a note in care of Alessa and mentioned something about the bad management in a park's zoo near Wyoming. A rhinoceros with cataracts had been allowed to go blind. "Can't wait to be with you!" he'd written.

Beyond, deep in the mountains, was Taos. Brill had said they would have to climb those trails. "No wolves, I promise, maybe a coyote or a mountain lion." Sylvie had mentioned Taos when she heard that Margo was making a trip to New Mexico. "D. H. Lawrence spent time in Taos," she said. "He lived there with Frieda, with his lover Lady Brett in a cottage out back. Their quarrels were legendary." Margo said, "Golly! Poor Frieda must have been a basket case!" Sylvie said, "He was a strange and complicated man." And you're a strange and complicated woman, Margo had thought, wondering whether the story was true. So odd, Sylvie, with all her intellectual gifts, working in a real-estate office these last years. She felt that she had hit on something in Sylvie's nature —a certain clear-eyed, Spartan bent that she envied a little.

THERE were signs to Santa Fe, guiding her off the highway into an access road. The city was laid out before her—a village square, a Spanish church, municipal buildings; architecture the color of gold clay, of baked mud, of a material that hardened to the look of tortoiseshell. As she drove past, she noticed the stained-glass windows in a grocer's shop, the formal arcades beneath which leather and silver wares were displayed. The road meandered into the hills. Brill was meeting her at the Hacienda Manuelo. Margo came on it quickly —a low building surrounded by vine-laden verandas on all sides.

He had already arrived. The Spanish woman at the desk said, "*Sí,*" and directed her down a long open corridor. Outside were trees that looked like eucalyptus, where in summer, bats must hang in the shadows at night. She went to the oak door at the end of the hallway, knocked once and entered. Brill had been in bed napping. Mosquito netting left over from summer hung in veils from the ceiling; he tore these aside and bounded naked toward her.

SHE must have dozed, because he woke her, bent over her once more and pressed his lips to her eyelids. The room was spare as a cell with scrubbed tile floors. An oak dresser, table and trunk were placed against a chalk-white wall. "Get dressed. You've been asleep for hours," he said. "Aren't you starved? We'll have dinner at a place on the mountain road called Floritas. Tomorrow we'll rent horses, maybe get back-packing stuff, sleeping bags. . . . We can try one of the trails going toward Taos if you're in the mood."

There was an upbeat sound in his voice. He turned to see if she liked his plan, and then he was over her again. His mouth slid down her body. "Jesus," he was whispering, "oh, Jesus God." She said, "No, Brill. Please!" She had the feeling of being hurled again and again toward an abrupt conclusion. She thought she must surely die. Welcomed the idea.

He had opened the blinds and was looking out at the garden. It was dusk now, but from the bed she could see low-lying cactus shrubs, their pale feathery spikes caught and turned to silver in the last rays of light. He moved restlessly around the room, picked things up and set them down. He started to dress, brushed his hair without looking in the mirror, searched for his spectacles, which he'd forgotten were on the floor near the bed. Preoccupied now, he ignored her.

"Come here and tell me about everything," she said, patting the white stitched coverlet.

He came and sat beside her, took her hand, rubbed it against his face. The long hunting scar on his upper arm shone white as exposed bone. She couldn't bear the excitement of his touch.

He said solemnly, "Yes, we make it in bed."

"We do." She was not able to look at him.

"If only everything worked out as well."

"What's wrong? Tell me about Wyoming?"

He sighed. "These guys had private money to develop a zoo. I think the investors thought of trapping the tourist crowds that spill through the national parks. Do a Disney World of the Northwest. Are you really interested in this?"

She laced her fingers in his and said, "Just talk."

"Any real development would mean moving the creatures to a warmer climate in winter. One of the investors had the bright idea of looking into a region around Puerto Vallarta. They were honest to God thinking of a dual habitat. Hollywood talking, right?"

"I don't understand any of this. You're a zoologist, not a showman."

He lit a cigarette. A nimbus of smoke rose and settled in the mosquito netting. The room, their low voices conversing so matter-of-factly after the heat of the bed, were surreal. "Listen, they had an elephant there wearing laced leather boots."

"Is that supposed to be a joke?"

"No. The poor beast had had a fungus infection on his hind feet, and the boots were meant to contain the medication."

"Archaic, is that the point?"

"I don't know. I guess the point is, do you or do you not support the principle of keeping animals as close as possible to their natural state, as though they were still in the wild. An elephant in the jungles of Ruanda would not wear boots because of fungus disease. The other way is to establish an artificial environment—elephants on skates, bears playing tambourines, singing seals. Actually, I was pretty pissed that they thought to get in touch with me in the first place."

He looked quietly miserable. "They knew my work on wolves and offered me just about anything I wanted. Wolves in summer and project management in Puerto Vallarta the rest of the time. But it was basically weird."

"So you walked away from it?" There was something else on her mind.

"Sure. I guess. Or maybe something in me is curious. I haven't decided. Get dressed, we'll have dinner. I still can't believe you're here."

She showered, stood docilely under a lukewarm spray and thought of Sylvie off somewhere with Jess skiing. North of Stockbridge, she'd said. She hoped they were taking care. All so spur-of-the-moment. It was unsettling.

THEY sat on the glass-enclosed veranda at Floritas, in front of a roaring fire. The tables were set with floor-length cloths like Mexican skirts, like her own long wool skirt with its border of birds. There were baskets of arrowhead plants hanging so low from the ceiling that the leaves brushed her cheeks like fingertips. She felt a vague uneasiness. The waitress brought margaritas, and she drank one and then another as quickly as she could. "Watch it," Brill said. "I like you when you're conscious." There were steps leading down to an unkempt garden, to a Mexican-Indian sundial set on a pedestal in a weed-choked pond. Three goats and a pony were tethered nearby. She was charmed by the goats and thought again of Jess, hoped she was on the smallest, gentlest ski slope.

Brill was ordering for them both in imperfect Spanish. "Guacamole, empanadas con rizzo, enchiladas, and another round of margaritas."

"Hold the chili pepper," she warned Brill.

"Ah *sí,*" he said to the solemn waitress.

Margo licked the salt off the rim of her glass. They smiled at each other, allowed a silence to develop dense with unspoken thoughts. She stretched her leg and rubbed his thigh with her foot. He leaned under the long tablecloth as though to retrieve a dropped napkin and slid his hand up her leg, stirred the warmth in her. She gasped. "You're disgusting," she whispered, trembling.

"And you're a slut," he whispered back, "not wearing underpants on a cold night." Her face burned, and froze. She hardly knew herself anymore.

The food came and was too spicy. She felt the heat in her mouth and throat like a warning or a punishment. What was she doing? Why was she here? He looked past her toward the pond, where the sundial rose in a haze of corroded green. "Primates don't swim," he said, as if he were continuing a conversation. "If you drop a chimpanzee into water, it will try to climb the water and then give up." He paused and said, "You're very beautiful. That first time I saw you at Pritchard, and afterward in the coffee shop, there was something that touched me. I mean, there was no put-on and that was touching, because you seemed as uncomfortable as hell to be there with me. And I just loved every bit of it."

"Tell me more," she said. But her head was swimming. The margaritas were definitely too much.

"OK, I'll tell you more. The San Diego Zoo is sending an expedition along the Orinoco. A bird and reptile hunt. It's intriguing."

She said, "It's a long way."

He thought she meant a long way from his original interest. "Oh, there's a common enough biology among the species. My wolves have a blood chemistry not *that* far removed from, say, a cockatoo . . ."

"That's not what I meant," she said quietly.

"Are you glad you're here?"

"I'm glad to be with you."

"Well, that's a beginning, but I don't exactly trust it. I can feel the reach of your husband and little Jess and your parents, all of them, way out here. I feel cornered."

"But they exist," she said softly. "You do too. Brill," she started to say, "you were doing good work in New York . . ." A custard was being served. She couldn't touch it. "I think I need air," she said.

"But there's air all around us." He glanced into the garden, where the goats wheeled timidly.

She went into the bathroom and leaned dizzily over the sink, patting her forehead with cold water. He could shed me like old skin, she thought. His mind is filled with too many things; and I'm another hassle. She felt regret, as if it had already happened. Tears filled her eyes.

Back in the dining room, she ordered tea and lemon. He was smoking a cigarillo. There had been a ripple of happiness on his face when he saw her return to the room. He shared her tea, staring at her over the steaming cup. His eyeglasses fogged, and his beard was beaded with drops of moisture. His face reflected indecision. She wondered whether it extended to her. She realized that he wasn't at all clear about what his life was going to be. The indecision bothered her. It was like a mask that had momentarily slipped across his features, making him strange.

Her dizziness returned and with it nausea. There was some business about who was going to pay the bill. He said, annoyed, "What makes you think I'm hard up for cash?"

She had never really thought about it at all. She suddenly knew that she was going to be sick. "We'd better go!" They drove quickly down the hill toward the hotel. Once inside, she fled to the bathroom, her intestines erupting. Perspiration poured down her face. She felt faint and leaned against the sink to keep from toppling to the floor. Brill kept knocking. "Do you need help?"

"Oh, God, no. Go away. I can manage." She began to retch in deep convulsive gasps. A boulder of pain moved inside her. The last thing she remembered was the slippery tile floor coming up to meet her face.

She awoke once in the night. She was in bed, and her stomach felt as if it had been cleansed with a blow torch. Brill was bending over her with two white pills and a glass of water. "Lomotil," he was whispering. "Just sip the water slowly." She fell asleep again. Dreamed that she was in the garden at Floritas. Her mother was screaming at the goats. "They are all whores," she was saying. Jess and Sylvie were in the pond. Sylvie was ducking Jess's head, holding it under water. Margo watched nervously. Each time, Jess came up laughing for more. "No more!" Margo called wordlessly. Jess's hair was covered with snow. Why was she laughing with that snow-choked mouth? Alarmed, she tried to catch Sylvie's eye, but Brill was holding the margaritas up and saying, "They have the same blood as a cockatoo . . . the blood of the Orinoco." And then Brill became Michael in hip boots and an explorer's hat. Michael was unwrapping a gift, an enormous tambourine that resounded through the house when he hung it on the dining-room wall. "Perfect!" he was saying. A sound of bells filled her head. The sound was lethal. She wanted to protect Jess from the bells. They were running down a road. They were in the garden at Floritas. The goats had bells around their necks. Jess kissed her wrist. Even her wrist tinkled. Bells fell from her mouth. "This will make you better, Mommy," Jess was saying.

CHAPTER 22

*B*RILL was sitting on the edge of the bed, holding out a cup of tea. He had pushed aside the curtains, and the sunlight was blinding. Someone was walking up and down the outside patio, shaking a cluster of bells. "*Desayuno! Desayuno!*"

"Sip this," Brill said. "Do you think you could try some papaya?" Actually she felt fine. Hollow, scooped clean, but with that terrible nausea gone. He said, "I guess backpacking is out for today."

"I think I'd rather drive around later on and look at some galleries." She stretched and smiled. "I had such a crazy mixed-up dream last night. So much was happening, and you weren't being very nice to me."

"I'm nice to you now." He was stroking her back. He had a bottle of witch hazel and was trickling some down her spine. He pressed each vertebrae with the flat of his thumb. "I love your bones." He said the word *love* lightly, and she found she did not want to meet his eyes.

"I dreamt about the Orinoco. Only it was Michael on the river, not you."

"Oh, that San Diego stuff is pretty farfetched." He was in jeans and a white Indian shirt that drained color from his face. He needed a day in the sun. She observed his restlessness again. She recalled the way he'd been when they first met. The cheerful glint in his face when he spoke to the children about wolves; the teasing tone in which he had said, "So this is the way the *riche* live"; the comradely way he'd dealt with Spunk. And the way he had been with her that first time, on the floor, with Spunk growling nearby.

She sighed, stirred by lust. In Alessa's terms, he was an extraordinary fuck. Was any of it real?

"Did *they* let you go?" she called out as she showered.

"They? What are you talking about?" His voice had a curious sound.

Wrapped in a large towel, she was brushing her hair. "New York. The zoo. I never asked why you were—well, why you were on the road, so to speak."

"Oh, that. I'd finished my project with them." He was at the window looking onto the patio. When he turned, he seemed pained. "I'd done a little study on grief as a cause of death in animals. Pining. Depression. I'd put together a number on suicide in wolves."

"Suicide?" How, she wondered. A gun to the head?

"In one of my papers the subject, a female, kept throwing herself against dangerous objects—the chain-link fence, boulders that separated the wolf compound from adjacent animals. She rushed at everything head-on, as if bent on smashing her skull. I said it was because her cub had died. But when they produced a surrogate cub, she tried to throttle that one to death. The conclusion? Animal psychosis. You'd think they would have given it another analytic run-through. Wasn't it possible, I said, that the wolf mom was saying, 'Do you guys think I don't know the real McCoy?' "

Oh yes, Margo breathed. If something ever happened to Jess she could imagine doing something wildly self-destructive like that, banging her head against a wall to crush the pain. Despising the replacement, if it were offered to her. In the dream, Margo remembered her terror as Sylvie dunked Jess in the frozen pond, again and again. No, she'd shrieked. But it was Sylvie who had suffered the very loss Brill spoke about. Margo felt if she kept to this line of thought, she'd go crazy.

Brill was saying, "Like anywhere else, there are too many vested interests. Clearly a zoo would be very touchy about the whole notion of animal suicide." He looked at her, his light-chipped eyes shadowed with disappointment. "Hell, maybe what I really believe is that there shouldn't be zoos at all. No so-called natural habitats. Nothing! If people want to see animals, let them go on a safari. But I gave you some of this back on old Amsterdam Avenue, didn't I?"

"Not completely." She hadn't realized this side of him. So combatively antiestablishment. In the seventies he must have been a terror. He certainly would have been at the center of all the protest. But that was part of the attraction—the undercurrent of revolt.

He interrupted her thought. "I'm in tough shape. I started with animal behavior in zoos, you know—wolves and all. Not only the biology. You see, I go for the psychological. The despair of animals in an alien environment. A chimpanzee who jabs a stick in her ear and punctures her brain. I mean, it forces a moral dilemma . . . Oh, hell, why am I talking so much. It's just you and I here in the glorious Southwest." He cradled her face with both hands. "What's on *your* mind?" She didn't have to answer because there was a knock on the door, and a maid came in with their hot chocolate and fruit.

Margo poured the chocolate quickly, eager for the bitter-sweetness in her mouth. She suddenly said, "Brill, I don't think I'll stay more than another day or two."

"What! Baby, we're supposed to have—a week, ten days. Have I turned you off? All my dumb grumbling . . ." His eyes had grown tame behind his glasses, and he moved uncertainly in the direction of the hot drink.

"Oh, Brill, of course you haven't turned me off. There's no way you could. It's that I feel, oh, I don't know . . ."

He put down the chocolate and took both her hands in his, held them to his chest. "Why can't you lay all of it aside— everything back there—for a few days anyway?" He studied her, and his voice turned cold. "But you can't, can you? Too wound up in your tribal rites."

"That's not fair. I'm uneasy, Brill." She was thinking that she couldn't imagine him exiled from her life. He was saying, " . . . you'll have a dead man on your conscience." He'd made a handcuff of his thumb and forefinger and held her wrist. She looked at him and smiled; well, she might stay on—a few more days, anyway.

THE road leading up the hill was lined with a warren of galleries. Browsing, Margo found some good things. Brill hovered nearby. He was having a long conversation with an Indian selling silver trinkets and pottery in an open stall on the street. Afterward he told her that the Indian had invited them to his workshop. "It's on a reservation, between here and Taos. He has a collection of animal masks, some of them very old. Wolves and bison. I'd like to take a look."

They paused in the late afternoon for a drink. "Just ginger ale for me," she said. They were in a café with glass walls and roof that opened to the sky. From their table they could see a rosy scallop of hills.

"Maybe we'll arrange for some horses and take one of the mountain trails to his reservation in the morning. It's just a few hours there and back." She was thinking of something else. She took her drink into a phone booth in back of the café and called New York. It would be seven P.M. there. Jess and Sylvie would surely be home by now, and she ached to hear her child's voice on the telephone.

Feliciana answered. She was staying overnight because of Zorro, she said. The kennel had called and wanted someone to come and get him. "But aren't Mrs. Weyman and Jessica there?" Margo asked, uncomprehending.

"They no come back yet," Feliciana said. "They come in one more day or two. Mrs. Weyman call and say you not to worry."

"Not to worry!"

"They go to Vermont." Vermont! "Very important business, Mrs. Weyman say. She go see Mr. Bob Fleet. She say to tell you that you will like very much this business. Jessica, too, very much like this business. They come home very soon." And then she was back to Zorro, talking in little excited gasps. *"Dios mío!* The dog no eat, no sleep. You forgive, the stomach . . . he shit plenty. *Comprende?"*

"Comprende," Margo said, trying to hold it all in her head.

"I give rice, hamburger. No coffee. I do right?" she asked.

"Right." Margo paused, still muddled. "But did Mrs. Weyman leave a telephone number?"

"No, no nombre. She say everything fine."

"Well, all right," Margo said reluctantly. The thought of Sylvie going off on her own to see Bob Fleet was astonishing in a way. "Did anyone else call?" Feliciana's calm was soothing.

"Mr. Kort, he call. He good. He say tell to you, he love you." She could imagine Feliciana giggling into her hand.

"Thanks." Her stomach was doing a strange, squishy dive. "I'll phone tomorrow."

She hung up and immediately put through another call to New York. Jolene answered the phone. "How's it going?" Margo asked.

"Same as usual around here. Your folks OK. Blondell is acting like some kind of primmy donna, though. Doesn't lift a finger, not even to dust. And Gertrude, just like always. Langston every other word now that he's part of that concert in Felt Forum. Mr. Max, though, except for the strawberries . . ."

"Put Mr. Max on the phone," Margo said.

His voice boomed across the wire. "Long-lost traveller! You in California?"

"New Mexico. And what's with the strawberries?"

"For Blondell, she has a craving. We keep boxes packed in the refrigerator. When Celia was having you, it was sour tomatoes in the middle of the night." He barely paused for breath. "You said, New Mexico? Aha, from there we used to get shipments of coyote pelts. We made jackets with matching muffs. A pretty little set for you. Remember?"

"I remember." She'd hidden the jacket in a clump of bushes alongside the hockey field at school. She'd turned the muff into a tent for her doll. "How does Celia feel?"

"The worst. She got wind of Blondell having a baby, and like I told you, guess who's the villain."

"Well, keep the strawberries under cover." And then she added, "Mrs. Weyman will be in to look things over in a day or so. So hold the fort. I'm going horseback riding tomorrow, into the mountains. Remember when you took me riding, years ago . . . ?"

"Do I remember!" He had taken her for a pony ride in Central Park. She was frightened. He had run alongside the pony, holding her in the saddle. The pony had a red pom-pom that danced when it tossed its head. Max wore a rose in his lapel. She recalled the scent of the flower, the pony's mischievous darting head, the odor of ripe turf, the white crossed poles of the corral, behind which her mother waited, smiling (oh, rare moment!), calling out to Max in her high-pitched voice, "Don't let her fall!" And her sense of well-being, of daring, as she bumped along with one hand on her father's neck and one holding the pony's reins; the feeling of being loved, protected, cherished. "I'll be back in New York before you have a chance to miss me."

"Not possible," he said. "I miss you already. And Jess, where is she?"

"On a little trip with Mrs. Weyman . . . Vermont . . ."

"Ah, that Mrs. Weyman! If I were younger . . ."

"Hey, watch it, Dad. I'll report you to the gauleiter in the bedroom."

"It's no joke."

"You're telling me?" She made a kissing sound and hung up. She felt a little less anxious, as if her mind had begun to weave the loose threads. Jess missing a day or two at school —well, it was no big deal. For the moment she would concentrate on Brill.

* * *

THE next morning, they set out, following the dirt road winding up into hillier terrain. Wherever she looked, prickly pear and creosote bush rose like earth sculpture. Brill rode beside her, offering reassuring comments. "Sit high and hold your reins lightly. You're doing fine." Her horse had turned his head and tossed and snorted against the bit. "Just stay relaxed," Brill was saying. "Fear in humans produces an acid scent which animals pick up; it makes them uneasy . . ."

"You want me to control my scent?"

"Don't get funny."

They moved into a slow trot. Margo felt confident. She reached forward and patted the horse's long powerful neck to emphasize her sincerity. "Good girl." Brill was saying something about the need to woo the animal. He touched the hind flank of her mount, and the horse sidestepped skittishly.

She caught her breath. "Listen, you woo yours, and I'll woo mine." She leaned forward, whispering nonsense sounds into the horse's mane.

The stable manager had promised the ride out to the reservation would take two hours, not more. He had assigned a "pussy cat" of a mare to Margo. "Give her her head, and you'll get there, no time at all."

Brill's horse fell into a trot, and she followed trying to hold the rhythm and her seat. It had been years since she'd ridden a horse. Once, before Jessica was born, she and Michael had gone for a weekend to a dude ranch in the Adirondacks. It was a kind of celebration. Michael had just gotten his engineering degree as well as a new job. He would be doing stress studies for an outfit that had had a hand in building the Verrazano Bridge. "Can you believe it?" he'd said, his face flushed with triumph.

His enthusiasm was so young, so boundless. He trusted in the infinite reach of his powers. He said, that day, "Sweetheart, you're looking at a man who is going to move ahead in quantum leaps—nothing less." For their morning ride, she was given a little pinto. He had chosen the tallest horse in the stable, a big red with flaring nostrils. Margo remembered thinking that she would need a stepladder to mount that horse. But Michael managed a fairly awkward leap into the stirrups as if he were John Wayne—or perhaps Mel Brooks imitating John Wayne, she thought privately. He chose the longest trail. They flew beneath trees and across meadows. At one point they even leapt over a little brook and Margo, heart in mouth, clung to the pinto's neck. She tried to hold him back, but the animal refused to be left behind. She screamed at Michael to stop, but her words were whipped away in the rush of air around them. They finally reined in, gasping, in a grove of trees, their horses dark with sweat. She started to say "Never, but never . . . ," when Michael reached out and shackled her arm with his hand. "OK, now that we've got the hang of it, we keep going," he said.

BRILL kept glancing back now and then to see how she was doing. "This is pretty good for a couple of amateurs."

"Think so? My bottom feels raw."

"Uh-oh. We don't want any damage *there.*" He reined in his horse and hers, and they slid to the ground. "Stretch your legs and walk up and down a little," he suggested. Instead they clung together, not speaking. After a while he helped her climb back onto her horse.

They stopped once more to eat the sandwiches and fruit they'd brought. Ahead, in a flat tawny region sliced by a river branch the width of a brook, was the reservation. Rows of wooden buildings, barracks style, were set within the empty landscape. There was a parking lot with some old cars and a tour bus off to the side, reclaiming its handful of passengers. It was early afternoon. The stableman had been all wrong about the time. Brill reminded her that their visit would have to be brief. He didn't want to risk being out on the trail after sundown. They tied their horses to a post and went in search of Brill's Indian.

The crafts shop was poorly lit. There was one dirt-streaked window, through which a thin wash of light passed. A low-wattage lamp stood at one end of a long trestle table, on which the familiar silver jewelry was displayed. There were pottery bowls and urns whose ochres and burnt crimsons seemed to have been ground from desert light. An Indian blanket hung in the shadow of one wall. On the floor was a marvellously intricate basket, with symbolic food gatherers woven into the design. The Indian nodded in solemn recognition when they entered his shack. Now he watched them handle the objects spread out on the table. Margo whispered to Brill, "I like the basket." She was imagining Michael's collection of teeth displayed in this mysteriously adorned vessel.

Brill responded cryptically, "Later."

She chose a string of hishi beads and feathers which looked as if it had ceremonial significance, as a gift for Sylvie. Brill was in a corner of the room talking in a sober voice to the Indian.

The Indian went to a trunk in back of the shop and brought out several wood carvings. Brill shook his head. The Indian lit a cigarette and offered one to Brill. They smoked for a while; then Brill leaned forward and spoke in low earnest tones. "I live among animals," she heard him say, as if offering credentials. The Indian stared at him impassively. Brill spoke on, but she could not hear him. She looked out the small window; there was nothing on which to focus, just the few derelict cars. Even the motionless air beyond the window seemed emptied of sound. She was suddenly struck with apprehension and turned, shivering, to Brill. "I want to leave."

The Indian offered her a cigarette. She took it, accepted Brill's light. "We have another two hours on those horses . . ." She seemed to be talking to herself. She felt a nameless terror at the sinister depth of the silence, the immobility of the Indian's face. Was the tour bus a mirage? Surely there must be someone in the other buildings, someone making corn bread and reaching for a Coke. She felt they could disappear off the face of the earth. A search party could come to the reservation and inquire, "Two people on horseback?" and the Indian would shake his head impassively. Who would know? She thought of Jess, bereft; she thought of Michael.

Brill's gaze was on the Indian, who had gone back to the trunk and was leaning over it. When he returned, he was carrying several masks carved of bark, all of them replicating the heads of animals in caricature, with one or two characteristics sharply distorted: a bear's head, a bison or buffalo mask with a silver-hinged jaw that seemed to settle into a smile, and the very large head of a wolf, carved of pearly white bark, inlaid with lumps of turquoise for eyes, its partially open jaw revealing perfectly formed ivory teeth.

Brill was bargaining for the wolf. The Indian was shaking his head, offering the bison or the bear. "These two are not what I want. It's the other one, the older mask . . ." He lifted the wolf and stared directly into its turquoise eyes.

"Look, Brill, I'm going to wait for you outside . . ." But she couldn't move. They had begun a ritual of offer and refusal.

"What will you take?" Brill asked.

"The wolf has been in my clan since the time of my fathers." The Indian's expressionless voice gained in volume.

She thought she heard Brill say, "But I am worthy . . ." And then he was telling about a visit to Northern Canada, to the region of the Cariboo Mountains, of camping out alone, of being encircled by a family of wolves that roved the perimeter of his campfire. In the night, their hunger drove them to leap the flames and break into his tent, looking for food. The leader tore his arm. Here Brill rolled up his sleeve to show the long white scar. He, in turn, grabbed a hunting knife and tried to scare the wolves off. He stabbed the leader in the hindquarters and blood spurted on his hands. He licked his hands clean, just as the wolf had licked his teeth. He was now blood brother to the wolf. And then—it was very strange —his powers became great. He could run long distances without tiring, his mind was capable of new vibrations. Turn-

ing to glance at Margo, he said, with straight-faced persuasiveness, "I became like a prairie dog with women." He was
mocking them, Margo thought, suddenly furious, averting
her eyes from the Indian, who seemed carved into the clay
of the hut.

The Indian's expression had relaxed. His mouth softened
into something that distantly resembled a smile. "You are no
blood brother to the wolf," he said emphatically. But he
capitulated anyway, as though the game had run its course.
"Cash. One hundred and seventy five," he said, wrapping the
mask in a newspaper and handing it to Brill.

THEY were silent at first as the horses picked their way back
along the trail. Brill seemed in good spirits, but a leaden
sheath lay over her heart. She would certainly return to New
York tomorrow. The question was whether she was glad of
this decision or not. The sun had disappeared behind a layer
of clouds, and every tree and scrubby bush seemed to stand
in a pool of shadow. The mist pricked her throat, making her
cough. She said, "Listen, old brother to the wolf, just what
was all that craziness back there supposed to mean?"

He smiled at her. "I was trying to crash his vibes. And I
didn't do badly, either. In fact, I amused him." He sounded
so smug and self-congratulatory that she turned away in
dismay. "Vibes." She wished he wouldn't talk that way. "Oh,
Brill," she murmured, "I'm . . . surprised."

"Surprised at what—who do you think got the better of
whom?" The drizzle had turned into a light rain. The trail
seemed to have taken new twists and turnings as it pitched
downward. It had grown cold. She wondered nervously
whether they were on the right road. Brill was beside her,
talking and not watching where they were going. He held the
wolf mask protectively under one arm. He was telling her
about the mystique of animals in early societies. He wiped the
rain from his face as he spoke. "People needed reassurance
in the face of natural calamities . . . earthquake, famine,
death. And so they gave beasts supernatural powers and felt

safe. Made gods of lions, wild boars, wolves, and expected protection. It was like a tribal mafia to help them deal with the cosmic force out there. When those guys put on their animal heads, they *were* the beast!" He made a face at her, his features glossy with rain, and she knew that he was jabbing at her for her own self-centered place in all that he was describing.

She recalled once telling him how hard it was to sell good paintings. "I'm new at this, and I usually have to deal with some corporate purchaser who hasn't the vaguest idea of the value of anything, and who says things like, 'Get something big and green for the wall over the reception desk.' " She had meant to imply that it was a challenge, a chance to develop her taste and pass it on to someone else. But his answer had been cryptic and surprising. "Did you ever think that if people want art, they ought to make it themselves?"

"What kind of statement is that?" A little flash of hurt made her voice wobble.

He was silent for an instant and then said, "I'm sorry." And once he'd said of Michael, "So he builds ports. Real big deal! A little extra pocket money for the sheiks, or the South American generals, or what the hell . . ." None of his criticism had mattered, of course, in her breathlessness at how imaginative and free and authentically connected to a larger life he was. She was simply grateful that he'd singled her out.

It was raining hard, and she heard the low grumble of thunder off in the distance. She buttoned her sheepskin jacket to her throat. Brill threw his poncho over her head. "We're lucky. This could easily have been snow." Then he said, chuckling to himself, "Of course, the Indian back there was playing a pretty sharp game with me. The mask was never in doubt—with or without my story. He was just trying to get me to pay his price."

"The basket!" she said. She'd forgotten to bargain for the lovely straw bowl.

"We could drive over tomorrow if it's that important," Brill said. She shook her head. Michael would do without.

Michael, the tooth fairy, who just liked the idea of teeth; not only Jessica's but Zorro's first incisors were part of his collection. "Because teeth are indestructible," he had said. "They *endure*! So if Dr. Finkleberg ever pulls one of your molars, I want it, baby, for posterity, in the vault alongside the securities and mortgage papers and the family jewels, if we ever get to have family jewels." Wasn't it unfair of Brill to be so condescending about Michael simply over the issue of money? Surely he could see the possible arguments in favor of wealth.

Another flash of lightning tore the skies. It had grown very dark. The next burst of thunder brought with it lashing sheets of rain. Brill led the way to a rocky overhang and helped her dismount. "Pretty freaky this time of year, but it's only a squall, nothing important. We'll sit here and wait it out." They crawled under a canopy of stone. Rain beat against the rocks and trees. The trail had turned into a muddy rivulet boiling in front of them. She heard the tethered horses whinnying and stamping in a darkness made more ominous because it had closed in on them so suddenly. Brill pulled her toward him and buried her head in the shelter of his arms. "This is turning into a real downer," he said. "We should have been sensible and just driven over by car."

"Well, you didn't exactly command the rain."

She meant to be funny, but he said quite seriously, "I hadn't intended to . . ."

Despite her exhaustion, she burst into laughter, but everything ached, her bones, thighs, hips. Would she ever be able to climb back onto that horse? "We're not lost, Brill, are we?"

"In the literal sense, no. Once the rain stops, it's about an hour or so back to the hotel." The sky had turned blacker still. The rain was an opaque curtain sealing the lip of the ledge. He held her, murmuring "Ssh . . . ssh . . . ," as though she were a child. There was a vast booming sound overhead, as if bowling balls were being rolled across the sky, and then the smack of a tree, splintering apart in the grove below them. She shuddered and grabbed for him.

He had leaned away from her for a moment, and when she lifted her head toward his she found herself staring into the face of a wolf—ghostly elongated jaw and glinting eyes set into a flat marmoreal skull. She screamed, a howl of terror ricocheting in her brain. And then she was running down the trail, blinded by rain, ankle-deep in mud. Demented, she ran faster. She cried out as a branch caught her cheek, stumbled and fell face down on the trail. She pulled herself to her feet, but Brill had caught up to her and pinned her against a tree. "Are you crazy?" he yelled. "Are you fucking out of your mind?"

He was drenched, filaments of hair were pasted to his forehead, his glasses were opaque with rain. He said, "Good God, will you take it easy. I'm sorry. Please. Listen. I'm a dumb clod. I didn't want to frighten you. You know how much you mean to me . . ."

But she didn't know, didn't want to know. He paused for breath, made a supreme effort to lower his voice until his words were only an undercurrent in the hissing leaves. "I was just being silly, cute. Putting on that mask meant I was your dumb-assed protector, nothing else. See—I'm drawing you a diagram. Oh, God, you're furious. You're livid. Only please quiet down and let's get back to the ledge, unless, oh, Christ, unless you want to be split down the middle by lightning!" Not lightning, she thought, not again.

When the rain let up, Brill rode beside her, holding her reins with his own. Speechless, they reached the inn. As if in a dream, Brill filled the bathtub with hot water and sponged her down, massaged her legs and arms with hot suds. She felt like wood, whittled away, inert. He treated the bruise on her face with antiseptic powder. They spoke in whispers, as if they were in a sickroom.

"Here, let me wrap you in towels. You're going to have some shiner."

"You're shivering," she said. "What about your own bath?"

He threw their clothes in a heap on the floor. His mud-encrusted shirt and sweater, her battered jeans. Then filled the tub for himself. Later she felt the warmth of his body next to hers, his hand resting on her towel-encased hip. They slept. When they awoke, it was night. The sky glittered like a Persian canopy held high by slaves.

She said, "I'm sorry about all that back there, about acting like a kid having a nightmare."

"It was my fault." He seemed genuinely sorry. "All that mystical talk, the thunderstorm, the isolation of the reservation. I think what I expected when you saw me in the mask was a little spoofing around. 'Oh, please, Mr. Wolf, don't eat me . . . well, not yet . . .' I guess I didn't perceive that in those particular circumstances, it was no joke."

He was unwinding the towel and throwing it aside. His own body was naked and gleaming. He had earlier unwrapped the wolf mask and placed it on a table. In the subdued light, its chalky features, the long, powerful muzzle and extravagant eyes were once again mere artifact, something to ponder at a distance. The way she was pondering sex with Brill, the enchanted labyrinth he'd led her to. He started to kiss her, moving his hand along her thigh. "These poor aching parts," he said softly. She'd begun to tremble. He sat up. "Wait, I'm going to make tea for us."

"Now?"

"The Indian gave me some stuff, after we'd sealed our bargain. A medicinal powdered root that grows in this region." He was boiling water in an electric teapot provided by the hacienda. "The Indian said, when you drink this, the universe will open like a mariposa bud. His very words. He said we'll know everything that needs to be known."

She said, "Brill, one thing I do know is that I'm flying out of Albuquerque tomorrow . . ."

"Ssh, we'll talk about it later . . ." He was pouring the brew into ceramic cups.

She would remember what happened next as a form of death and resurrection. She thought of miners buried alive and rescued moments before their hearts gave out; she thought of victims of clinical death being exploded back to life by electroshock.

They sipped the tea, which had a surprisingly pleasant scent—honeysuckle came to mind, and hibiscus. This may be curative, she remembered thinking; but she couldn't hold on to what she wanted to be cured of, couldn't keep her thoughts from slipping off the glassy sides of her mind. They started sitting upright in bed, smiling at each other, holding hands. Two friendly passengers in an ark, but the climate quickly changed. The ark became a raft, flying dangerously through surf. The bed tilted, and she was being dragged beneath a foam of sheets. Brill was rocking her, cradling her in his arms. Her eyes were closed, but she saw his face reflected over and over in the corridor of mirrors behind her lids. His eyes, his ruffle of beard magnified a thousand times, the image of teeth like ivory stelae toppling toward her; his tongue filled her head, making her gasp for breath. She thought, is anyone in control here? Her body rushed toward her, flayed, the bones laid bare. There was a soft center which he plucked at with tweezerlike precision, the beak of a bird probing for the succulent center. He plunged into her, clambered up her slippery sides, hung on. She came again and again. Screamed for mercy. No more, Brill! Bits of memory were snatched up and swept away, a flash of Celia, of Jess caught and held in a web of capillaria, of Michael, sinking into the murk of her mind. She called to Brill, but a polar cap divided them. She shivered until she thought her bones would break. Perspiration poured out of her. She was alone. She was the last woman on earth. She was an infant screaming for help, begging to be allowed to live, promising that she would learn to live. The wolf mask opened its jaws and leered. At one point they seemed to be returning to sanity. Brill's voice circled the shell of her ear. She thought he said, "When trapped, you see, the plains boar fucks to kill . . ."

"Are you trapped, Brill?" But how could he be? His species, unattached male, in love with his state of "unattachedness," was not threatened by extinction.

"Are you?" he asked. But she didn't feel trapped. She felt judicial, like a judge and jury moving toward a verdict. But something was happening to time, to minutes ticking. Brill seemed to be thundering toward her in his lonely avid quest. Was this, then, to be the kill? She went blank. Only her muscles, tissues, molecules were violently alive. She seemed to be again crying, "No!" Too late. A cataract of sensation rose to decimate her in one long, reverberating sigh.

CHAPTER 23

THE explosion burst over him, gathering substance, entering his head as if through an open door. A whoosh of sound, a tail of sparks, then nothing. His eyes fell shut, and he plunged through darkness. Now he was swimming upward in something more dense than sleep. He tried to sift the debris in his head. Had the driver taken a wrong turning? Jamil, the minister's boy. Jamil with the slippery mouth. Habib had been more than gracious. Pressing his hands together as he spoke. Girlish hands. Clear white skin. "Jamil will drive you to the residence and wait until it is time for the airport. We will not take chances."

But which airport? Jamil had left the boulevard, turned the Mercedes into an unfamiliar street, followed a serpentine path. Serpentine. His very own word. An offshore port lying flat as a serpent on the surface of the water. No need for a conventional dock; any strip of shore would do. Cargo moving smoothly to shore and back. In this case oil. Habib had clapped those lily hands. The deal was as good as made. "*Extraordinaire,*" he'd said, a reminder that his schooling had been at the Sorbonne. As for the cost? "*Mon Dieu,* the treasury is limitless."

He tried again to force his eyes open. Had someone sewn his lids together? There was a flash of panic and then the deep backward sprawl into fogged darkness, and again the slow climb upward. Like an infant on hands and knees. He could blame it on Jamil, the dirty sycophant, bowing before Habib. The Mercedes worming through some back alley. "What's this, Jamil? Why have we left the boulevard?" Jamil stopping the car, jumping out in front of a curtained shop, his tunic flashing. "A moment please"—the elastic mouth stretching into a smile—"if the gentleman doesn't mind . . . cigars have been requested by the minister . . ."

But the gentleman damn well did mind! The gentleman didn't dare risk missing his plane. And back alleys were definitely not on the agenda.

A wave of anxiety broke over him, receded. He had to get back to New York. Where was Jamil? That trumped-up story. Habib requesting cigars to be picked up on the way *to* the airport? Why not on the way *from*? But then there was Jamil appearing at the entrance to the shop, peering out, stepping away. And the motorcycle roaring through the alley, the blinding Cyclops eye of its one headlight fixing him as it came abreast of the car and seemed to hover for an instant. There were two men in black leather masks and army fatigues, a burst of fire and then the sudden dark, as if a sack had been thrown over his head. How strange. The words clanged in his skull. "How strange, how strange . . ." And how strangely language changed its shape. The words had become, "Mr. Kort, Mr. Kort . . ." But he was too far away to answer.

"MR. Kort." A woman's voice was calling him. "Now, if you please, Mr. Kort, you must wake up." The voice was closer now, but the pain in his head was immense. Again he tried to open his eyes without success. He lifted one arm as though it was on a cable and pulley and tried to touch his face. "Sir, if you please," the woman's voice said, "your eyes are bandaged, as is your jaw and one side of your face. You mustn't be alarmed."

He sank mercifully into darkness again, but the next time he awoke his head had cleared somewhat, though the pain was like a helmet, reaching to his neck. He knew he was in a hospital because of the antiseptic smells, the sound of instrument trays being rattled, the rustle and moan of patients in the beds nearby.

"Mr. Kort"—it was a man's voice now—"how are you feeling?"

"Pain," he managed, because in fact the pain seemed to be dissolving the side of his face.

"Yes, but now that you're awake, they'll be giving you a narcotic to kill the pain." The man leaned closer. He smelled of cigarettes and Brut. He introduced himself as Tom Nearing, an embassy representative.

"And I am here, too. This is all so terrible. *Douloureux.*" It was Habib's voice.

He felt his arm being swabbed, caught the fragrance of the nurse as she bent over him. "Mr. Kort, this will not hurt—it will help the pain . . ." There could be nothing for this pain. He felt as if part of his skull had been hacked away. He lay dazed, waiting for an explanation. He had caught only a flicker of Jamil in the doorway—and then the screeching brakes of the motorcycle as it came abreast of the car.

"Mr. Nearing," he called out, "will you tell me what the fucking blazes has happened?"

He heard Habib jabbering on the other side of the bed. "As minister of internal development, it is my duty to explain, to apologize . . ." He blew his nose and cried softly, "You see, Mr. Kort, there was a terrible accident . . ." Michael tried to absorb the nature of the accident. Although his arms were folded over his chest, he seemed to be clutching the bed. The pain had become a distant commanding thud. Habib spoke rapidly. "You seem to have been the subject of an attack, a grenade flung at the car—well, fortunately you were not on the driver's side or the damage could have been worse . . ."

Worse? Michael wondered about the nature of the damage. He tried to lift his hand to his head but realized that both arms were restrained. He could elevate them to the neck but no farther. "Mr. Kort," the nurse was saying, "the doctor advises you will be so good as not to attempt to touch your face and head . . ."

And then the doctor himself was at his bedside. Michael heard the squeak of shoes, felt a shift in the composition of the atmosphere, caught a whiff of alcohol and sterile soap. "Good afternoon, sir." The accent bespoke Oxford. The doctor was subdued, bored, professional. "The damage has been confined to the right eye, with deep lacerations to the temple and cheek." He took his time, seemed to yawn between words. "The lacerations will heal in time with plastic surgery, perhaps some bone replacement to the forehead . . ."

"The eye!" Michael shouted at him.

"The eye, yes. It is not clear what the outcome will be there. We have done the preliminary surgery to stem bleeding and remove shattered tissue." Shattered tissue! He felt consciousness beginning to slip.

"Are you saying that I will lose the eye?" He was floating away, willing his mind to go blank. He would be blind in one eye? In both?

"It is possible that will happen. The injured eye—well, we must wait." Possible? Probable? A sure thing?

Nearing was standing close to him once more. He was saying, "The embassy will make arrangements to have you flown home. The whole business is so damned ticklish. Thank God you weren't killed, old man. What a flap, if you were . . ." The nurse was jabbing him with a needle again.

WHEN he awoke, Habib was at his bedside. He felt hungry, angry.

"What happened to Nearing?"

"He has gone to work out the details of your departure. It is delicate. In our country such an event is not typical . . ."

"When did all this happen, Habib?"

"It is not yet three days. You have sustained a concussion as well as, yes . . . as well as . . . But you are alive. What more can I say?" His voice floated on little gasps of sympathy and remorse, then turned instructive. "You see, even in our country, there are partisan groups who press for participation in government. Here, there are occasional antireligionists who are fired by a socialist point of view. . . . Well, let me say they represent a rabid mentality. There was an incident, a few months ago, at our new computerized electric power installation at . . ." His voice, which had faltered, rose. He placed a hand in camaraderie on Michael's shoulder. "With all our social reforms, education, health, new wage-earning possibilities, it is never sufficient. You can see how it goes. Prosperity brings discontent. That is clear. And very dangerous. Look at Iran . . . the voices of the impoverished, it is true. A religious revolution. But still, who would imagine they could dethrone a king. In our case, what these factions want is representation. A voice in how money will be spent. The millions that we expect to allocate for your port are obviously a magnet for multiple grievances."

Habib must surely be waving his hands, fluttering the long lashes of his very dark eyes. Oh, God, eyes. "Well, these small-time insurrectionists have an occasional fierce sting." His voice sounded as if he were drawing breath from a collapsed lung. Michael could imagine him, his dark goatee quivering as he sought the most tactful expression for the facts. "One hopes," he continued, and now he must be leaning forward solicitously, one knee bent in a small curtsying movement, "that this terrible act against a citizen of so respected and mighty a country as the United States would not affect the mutual respect developed, arduously and at such profit . . ."

"Oh, quit the bullshit, Habib. Has my wife been informed?"

"That is Mr. Nearing's responsibility. Perhaps he will suggest that you inform her yourself, by cable or phone. The media have not been apprised. You see . . . such publicity . . . well, you can certainly understand."

Tom Nearing had returned again and gone. His family

would be informed. He would be leaving Jidda that evening. The surgeon here had suggested he go directly to one of the eye centers in New York. "You see how unfortunate it all is," Habib said. "These despised events. The troublemakers are inspired by foreign elements. They are like children who see a movie of violence and then go out and practice similar deeds As for Jamil, there will be no mercy." Habib wheezed his good-byes. His hand—was it the one with the twenty-karat star sapphire?—grasped Michael's shoulder. He bent to kiss him on the cheek, wishing him a safe return to his home. And of course the project would go on. A month or two of rest and Michael would be fit. There was, after all, the example of the famous Israeli general with a similar wound, whose name shall go unmentioned. And they would yet construct a port more ingenious than the hanging gardens of Babylon . . . Habib's voice was receding. "Be well. I will visit you in New York in two or three months, and we will continue with our plans." He closed the door behind him.

The good news was that they were putting him on a plane for home, with a nurse and a medical assistant, that evening. They obviously couldn't get him out of the country fast enough. Three days had passed, they said, nearly four. Five before he'd be home. What would Margo think? The answer to that was nothing. He doubted she'd been informed. He was not in the habit of phoning home often or leaving a detailed map of his whereabouts when he was on these trips. His office was in communication with him. It was enough. He'd bet his office hadn't been told of the so-called accident. Habib's patriotic sense of diplomacy would have forbidden it.

And, of course, Margo would be away. The thought resonated off-key. When she first spoke to him about setting up a small business of her own, he had endorsed it, even encouraged it. OK with him, as long as he called the shots, kept everything in balance, policed the borders of their life, held on to the purse strings. "A new couch, at least, for the living room," she'd said, voicing her thoughts aloud. But it was not an ultimatum. And he wasn't especially interested. Didn't want them suffocated by material acquisition all at once, buying, spending. Let the money accumulate for a while, harden into sheltered funds, into solid securities. Maybe then it would seem real. And then they'd do things with a bang, if that's what they wanted. At the moment, his affluence felt suspect. He didn't entirely believe in it. A few bad deals, and his company could go down the drain. Look at this business in Jidda. Habib would probably pull back. The princes would announce a new multimillion-dollar child-care program and another mosque for the devout. The port? Habib might worry about *how* the port would be perceived. There was the example of Iran, he'd said . . .

Not that he couldn't land on his feet. Anyway, as he'd told Margo, they could always live on fixed income like most of the world. And not to worry about her parents. He'd be there to provide for them.

She'd laughed at that scenario. "Oh, what a funny song you sing. You know there's no way of keeping you down."

True, he supposed. He always went for big, the hardest jobs, the most difficult assignments, as if scale was what counted. If he was going to win, he'd win big. Even as a child he'd gotten a certain kind of message when he was taken to California by his uncle and saw the Golden Gate Bridge for the first time. They had parked the car and stood on a grassy palisade, staring across the water. "How does it stay up?" he asked Uncle Arnie that day.

"You ask me how it stays up?" Arnie looked both confused and scornful. "Look, there are laws to things like that. One thing affects another. You learn what affects what, and it stays up."

He would go to engineering school, he told his father, who was a bookkeeper for a plastics company in Queens.

"An engineer? Isn't there an engineering glut?" Kennedy had just been assassinated, and his father saw it as a prophetic symbol of decline. "Better civilizations than this began to go under for less. You should be in something that isn't subject to recessions." He recommended plastics. "Everything in the world will soon be made of plastic." Or frozen orange juice. "The floor could drop out of the stock market, people could be jumping off skyscrapers, and they'd still drink orange juice." His boss's nephew was doing splendidly at Tropicana.

But he stayed firm, went to Rensselaer Polytech, took a graduate degree at Columbia. And when Margo came along, he explained it all to her, sitting in the Greenleaf Bar on Broadway, sipping ginger beer, as she listened to him discuss his ideas on structural balance and how the advent of new synthetic metals was going to create a universe—goddamnit, a whole galaxy—of possibilities. "You know, you can do anything," she said seriously.

Margo filled his thoughts. Maybe it was that so much had been left unsaid recently. A kind of low-grade domestic boredom had dogged them, as though the demands of their separate lives had become more persuasive than their life as a couple. Well, in his case it was the tyranny of work. But in hers? She'd gone off to New Mexico. What did it mean?

His head was beginning to throb again. "Nurse," he called, feeling the terror beginning to break through. Would he . . . had he lost an eye? There was a rustle at his bedside, and this time the needle went into his thigh.

But he refused to relax. Margo was insistently before him, as though finally demanding equal time. How he wished she were here beside him. She had had a presentiment about this deal in Jidda: "Camels with diamond nose clasps!" she'd said disdainfully. Her presence seemed so real that he groped across the coverlet, almost expecting to touch her, to touch the smooth cap of hair with its glint of straw frosting that gave her face a frail, indefinite look. She was not an indefinite person, though. She was able to steer a middle course, he knew that all too well. Who was the manipulator and who the manipulated, when it came right down to it? The way her hazel gaze fused with its object, and then yielded ground rather than endure conflict. He played on the fact that she could be managed. Deployed, if he was intelligently persuasive. "That stairway is *not* kitsch," he'd said in answer to her complaints. "I'm told it's a perfect example of Bauhaus modern and safely usable. It's only Zorro who keeps falling down the stairs."

"Oh, well, as long as you don't expect me to walk down it wearing nothing but a fan."

Still, still . . . She was true to her nature in her dealings with Sylvie Weyman: deferential, secretly admiring, anxious to please, as if *she* were the one who might someday need good references. And she was a damn good daughter. That madhouse—how she willed it to survive. He saw her lovingly through the clear pane of his imaginings, and yet there was something amiss. He hadn't seriously believed that she would go off on that trip to New Mexico and leave Jess behind with Sylvie. It was out of character. She was so serious about Jessica.

"But this was purely business," she would say. "And that's why we have someone like Sylvie Weyman."

Purely business. But she hadn't even begun to mine the local New York scene. Something didn't click. Or possibly something did. There was that time he went through her pocketbook for a quarter and found . . . but he couldn't focus on what he'd found. His mind reeled dizzily away.

Mr. Nearing was at his bedside. "Mr. Kort—Jesus, fella, you look as though you're in a lot of pain."

Actually, the pain had receded, had taken on the monotonous rhythm of surf lapping at the shore.

"Man, you have a real tight look on your face. Just relax, we'll be flying you out of here in a few hours. I've come by to tell you that personally. The staff in New York will call your wife and alert her about making hospital arrangements."

Alert her. But where would she be? And why was she there? "I want Manhattan Eye and Ear." The strangeness of being so helpless appalled him. He was in an air-conditioned space beyond which—beyond his window, beyond the paved center of the city—the vastness of the desert lay. But she had her own desert. New Mexico. Why, exactly, was she there?

"Yes, of course, alert her," he said, his voice suddenly shrill, as if he were sounding alarms.

CHAPTER 24

THE ambulette snaked through the traffic of Eighth Avenue and pulled up in front of the Felt Forum. Max, heady with excitement, needed to sit still for a few minutes and catch his breath. He didn't dare stand up. Not yet. His cane was insufficient, like a toothpick propping a giraffe. The ambulette was the size of a pickup van—the same shape as the delivery trucks used by La Brava Furs, years ago, to transport their garments. Then, even Alexander's bought a few pieces from old man Bravalinsky. Fred the Furrier, with his "Hi, Nancy," "Hi, Alice," hadn't even been born. This conveyance, painted white with red crosses, looked like a souvenir from World War I, but it delivered. Delivered old bodies from one place to another. For him, it had come to that.

He was sitting next to Jolene, who was as gloomy as ever, and across from Gertrude, who was wearing a Persian lamb jacket of not bad quality and a satin turban. For her, no matter what, it would be a night of triumph. Blondell sat facing him, next to Celia in her wheelchair. Celia, who had somehow been lulled by the motion of driving, came to life as the van pulled to a stop. She looked around suspiciously. "Where are you taking me?" she cried out accusingly.

"Just calm yourself, sweetheart," Gertrude said, leaning over and patting Celia's blanketed knee. "You going to have one dandy time. Wait and see!"

"I think what we're doing is plain crazy," Jolene remarked. Now that they'd arrived, she lit a cigarette and stuck it in the corner of her mouth. She was the worrier and complainer: She thought things out ahead of time, took on extra burdens and didn't let anyone forget it. "Mrs. Kort is going to pop a blood vessel when she gets wind of this."

"Listen to Miss Killjoy!" Gertrude snapped back.

Max raised his cane. "Enough with all the quibbling! Mrs. Celia won't know what's going on!"

Celia lifted her head. "Don't think you're going to put anything over on me," she said furiously.

Max hoped this outing was worth it. Just being here would cost Margo a pretty penny. The ambulette alone was one hundred and twenty-five dollars. But he had been caught off guard. Caught with a longing. Gertrude had presented the case so convincingly. She had waved the tickets in his face. "My Langston has provided me with these, and he said, 'Bring the folks you work for to the concert. It will invigorate them in a real beautiful way.' "

"The music is not too loud?" he had asked, going through a minor ritual of inquiry, although his mind had been made up instantly.

"Not so's I know," Gertrude said. "Anyway, if the sound gets too big, all you have to do is turn off your hearing aid."

He would have liked to discuss the matter with Margo, who had gone West somewhere. Santa Fe—a place that sounded mysterious and foreign, like Samarkand, where yak skins for rugs were shipped from. He'd once been as far west as Denver to visit a cousin. But Celia had never been interested in general travel. To her mind, if it wasn't Florida, it wasn't on the map.

He looked across at Blondell, who had clapped her hands like a child when she heard about the tickets, Blondell, so round and lush like a honeydew. She reminded him of the dark-skinned gypsy girls who had lived in storefronts in the Brooklyn neighborhood of his boyhood. All those sentimental thoughts crawling in his head, visions of long ago—girls with dark hair to their waists who moved barefoot in the streets in summer, their bracelets and strings of beads jingling. Girls whose mothers and aunts read tea leaves and appeared suddenly in the doorways in the evenings, with large bellies and glorious engorged breasts that floated as if alive beneath their gauze blouses, who teased him because he couldn't tear his eyes away.

He'd always liked women, thought about them, daydreamed about them, dizzy with the vision of bosoms and thighs, marvelling at them. As a young man, he loved to be in love. When Celia entered his life, he gave up the chase. It was time. He'd known plenty of women. He was thirty-eight. Celia was thirty. She was a picture then, his Celia. Brown eyes and light brown hair like honey, a future gift to Margo. Who could know that after they were married, the gloom would settle in, the terrible moodiness, the depressions, all of it made worse when his retail fur business went under during the war. That time, both the source and the market dried up in the same moment. Women were walking around in cotton stockings to protest Japanese silkworms. With the Germans swarming into Russia, you could get stoned for flaunting a fur coat. Secretly, he hadn't cared all that much that the business was gone. He had wanted to be doing something different all along, something more exciting, daring. Wanted to trade in pelts, make killings in the fur auctions of Leningrad, dash overseas and haggle for bundles of sables and lynx. In those years he imagined himself a captivating mix of pirate and chevalier, leaving the drudgery of conversion—the cutting, piecing, fashioning—to others.

They had been married ten years when Margo came along. At first, Celia was fine. And then her moods changed again, up and down. Still, it hadn't been too bad, his life. He had never made it to the great fur auctions, but he'd gotten along decently enough, working in small shops, matching, sewing, even a little designing thrown in. When Margo was five, he'd made a fur jacket from muskrat tails for her. When she was sixteen, he'd managed a three-quarter coat in curly lamb. "Nobody I know wears a fur coat," she said, in tears, as if he'd told her to put on a tail and horns for school. With Celia it was a red fox stole, a broadtail coat, a leopard muff. And sometimes, if she was in one of her happier moods, she'd swivel in front of the mirror flirtatiously, signalling that she'd be warm and welcoming in bed. Who could afford to complain?

BLONDELL was fixing a shawl around Celia's neck. "Stop fussing with me," Celia cried out, staring around with that wild, unfocused look. In Khomeini's court, the Iranian prisoners had such a look. Thank God for TV. He felt he was still abreast of the world.

"OK, folks," the driver said, opening the rear doors, unfolding a little ramp and wheeling Celia down. "I'm going to park around the corner. Whenever you guys have had it with the rock and roll, just come out. I'll be waiting for you."

"We'll be out when the concert's over and not a minute before," Gertrude said. Jolene puffed hard, then stamped her cigarette on the sidewalk. "We'll be out when Mr. Max tells us!" she shot back.

The auditorium was packed. Young people mostly, in boots, skintight pants, shirts as bright as neon, with crazy jewelry hung around their necks, stuff that he, even as a young man, wouldn't have been caught dead with. There were a lot of older people in the audience, but they, too, wore a kind of uniform: men in T-shirts and bush jackets; women in gaucho pants, bulky sweaters, shoes that laced up to the knee like a Roman stable-boy's. He had put on his red checked vest for warmth. But now, as he opened his jacket, he felt stylish.

Gertrude was leading them down a side aisle toward the stage. She told the usherette, who was hurrying to keep up, "My son is performing tonight . . ."

"No wheelchairs in the aisle," the usherette said.

"Who says!" Gertrude asked, glaring at the woman, who was hugging a stack of programs to her chest.

"The fire marshal says, that's who!" For a moment, with a flicker of relief, Max thought it was all over and they'd be escorted back up the aisle and out into the street, where the ambulette waited.

But Jolene took charge. "Lady, let's not give these old folks a hard time, OK? They been looking forward to a night out, and we aim to see they get satisfaction." She suggested placing Celia in an aisle seat and removing the wheelchair to a cloak room. "We don't intend to stay to the very end," she added, giving Gertrude a threatening look, "so we can claim the chair and leave before the rush begins."

Seated, Max leaned close to Celia. Jolene, Blondell and Gertrude sat in the row behind them. "Isn't this nice?" he asked. Celia shook her head. One hand lay like a stone in her lap. The other clutched the armrest as though she were in a speeding vehicle. "Don't sweet-talk me," she said, staring at the crowds flowing toward their seats. Two young men in cult clothes—chains, straps, boots—had climbed over them to take their places farther down the row. "Something fishy's going on. I can smell it. Are you trying to get rid of me? I want the truth!" Her voice had taken on a thin wailing sound.

"Calm yourself." Max squeezed her arm. "No one's getting rid of you. If you see chains around here, it's the latest style. In a minute you'll hear Gertrude's son with the drums."

The stage was nothing more than a large platform, bare except for a mesh of wires hanging from the ceiling with microphones, and a darkened wreath of spotlights suspended by invisible threads. He remembered the musical theatre of forty, fifty years ago. The Yiddish stage, bright with color and life, the actors pausing after every line until the laughter died away. Later on, he and Celia took in *Oklahoma!, My Fair Lady, Fiddler on the Roof.* It was during a long stretch when her personality was upbeat. Celia would come home and stand in front of the bedroom mirror, singing. Three times in one year she changed Margo's piano teacher in her search for the best. They hadn't been to the theatre in years. He wasn't complaining. "Age is the great democratizer." Who said that? Roosevelt? Churchill? "Everyone's horse heads for the stable in the end." That, he knew, was Gary Cooper. So who was he to feel singled out? But since her stroke, it hurt his heart to look at her. As though her personality had been picked apart and only the worst elements remained. More suspicious and enraged then any living person had a right to be.

Bolts of light suddenly crisscrossed the stage. A few bar stools were being grouped in the center. A piano was wheeled out and drums and an instrument that looked like a brass table on wheels. And suddenly four men were standing on the stage, glittering as if they'd been dipped in gold. They wore rhinestone belts with gold-tipped revolvers. They were called The Trains. And the audience roared, "Trains! Trains! Choo-Choo Trains!" Gertrude let out little shrieks behind him. She leaned forward and squealed into his good ear. "The second from the left is my Langston. Isn't he gorgeous!"

Max turned and said, "After the performance, I'll give you a critique." The costumes alone could light up the city of New York.

Celia dozed beside him. Her mouth had fallen open, and with her dentures shoved forward she had the look of an animal baring its teeth. The image disturbed him, and he gripped her hand, feeling light-headed and disoriented himself as he glanced around at the last of the crowd heaving itself down the aisles of the packed auditorium. He pressed Celia's hand to his lips. It was time he felt his age in an appropriate way. But as it was, he'd turned his back on the darkness, on the demon waiting in the wings.

Now the floodlights were concentrated in a large oval that drenched the four performers on the stage. A gigantic wave of sound rose and burst in splintery vibrations. He turned his hearing aid way down. The performers were singing, strumming, twisting like belly dancers. Their shirts were slit to the navel, exposing dark hair, glistening chests. Max felt shame and looked down at his shoes, polished but old, seamed with lines like his face. When he looked again, Gertrude's Langston was hunched over the drums, jerking his shoulders and feet. Rising on his little gold stool, he yelped and fell back again, his sticks beating on a brass kettle, as if he were subduing a beast. Behind Max, Gertrude was yelling, "Go to it, Langston honey. Give it to us, baby doll."

The audience screamed approval, whistled, slapped each other with rolled-up programs. He was trapped in sound. If he wasn't careful, he could drift away on a raft of sound, lose his bearings. Too much commotion. This concert wasn't such a hot idea, after all. He doubted Margo would have approved, or even Mrs. Weyman. When Sylvie Weyman dropped by a few days ago to pick up the doctor's bills for Medicare, he had purposely said nothing, although he'd already made the arrangements, hired the ambulette. She did the paperwork and looked things over, decided that Celia seemed pale and asked Jolene to fix a protein milk shake. And Jolene did her bidding without back talk for once. There was something in Mrs. Weyman's manner. A solemn individual with such glorious hair—like a Madonna, if only she wouldn't pull the hair back so tight, and if only her mouth wasn't so . . . so strict. Max spoke to her with care. "A woman as tall as you could carry sheared beaver very well."

She'd smiled. "Nobody in my family ever owned a fur coat. I guess we weren't fur people . . ."

"Ah ha, it's the old debate—should you kill animals for their skins or let them kill each other because of overpopulation." He quickly added, "I'm not talking about the endangered types now or clubbing baby seals over the head. And I'm not exactly Mr. Gun Lobby, either. When I was in the industry, I campaigned for humane methods of trapping animals."

"I'm sure you did." Then she said, "A member of my family was very interested in animals. She thought about being a veterinarian for a while . . ." A she? Max would have liked to know more, but the tone of Mrs. Weyman's voice seemed to end the conversation right there.

Margo, too, had loved animals. There had always been a dog in the house when she was growing up. He saw to it, even though Celia was squeamish about dogs. "They eat dirt and then lick your face. It's disgusting." He wondered how Zorro was making out. Margo didn't seem to have much time for anything these days. She was too busy rushing, stretching herself thin. He wondered whether she was unhappy. It was his private view that unhappy people threw themselves into a frenzy of activity in direct proportion to their unhappiness. She wasn't the same old Margo. This new person was constantly preoccupied, a little forlorn. Like someone with one foot out in the cold, which was foolishness, considering that Margo had more money now than she could ever use. Margo and Michael. She was always careful to tell Max that it was Michael's money that provided for them all so well; Michael's good business sense, his talent, his luck, as though she were just an interested bystander. He wondered uneasily whether Michael was "fooling around." A little bud of indignation burst in his chest. He cautioned himself not to jump to conclusions. There seemed to be a common thread, though, connecting Sylvie Weyman and his Margo, something repressed, unspoken, sad. Maybe that's why Margo hired her. If only he could help. But that was the burden of old age—to be perceived as less than one was, to be seen as just an ancient child.

Another musical number had ended, and there was thunderous applause around them. Whistles and shrieks from the audience. People were on their feet, stamping and cheering. From the row behind, Gertrude had leaned forward and flung her arms around his neck. "Couldn't you just die," she sobbed. Again the chant "ChooChoo Trains! ChooChoo Trains!" hung in the air, a huge ballast of noise pressing down on him, entering his body like electric shocks. He turned his hearing aid off for a moment and then tuned it to its lowest range.

Celia stirred. Her eyes flew open, and she gave him a frightened look. "Why are we here?" she asked.

"It's the music, a lovely concert," he answered, ducking his head as if he needed to hide. Behind him, he heard Blondell saying, "You have one talented son, Gertrude." And Gertrude answering, "You can say that again!"

Celia was pushing at his arm with her elbow. For an instant she looked strange, sweetly young, her white hair like uncarded cotton blossoming in tufts around her face. *"Trains! Trains! Trains!"* roared over them. "Is this the right place for us?" She was making herself heard despite the bedlam. "The right stop?" she asked hoarsely. "Will Margo know where to find us?"

"She'll know." He felt his heart swell; there was sandpaper in his throat. He grasped her hand tighter still and squeezed it. The shawl had slipped, exposing her neck, frail as a chicken's. In her good moods, she'd been vain, spent more time and money on herself than on Margo. Always managing to eke out a new outfit, another piece of lingerie. They'd fought plenty. He thought of all this now with a sweet patience. "Shouldn't we have more than one child?" he'd asked her long ago. "But we started so late," she answered. And she was right, and anyway there were her moods, the swings from up to down. Down had been so terrible; she would sit in the dark, wring her hands, refuse to get dressed for weeks on end. So it was only Margo, their family; and from her, Michael and then Jessica. Thank God for that. Wasn't family what life was all about?

He said to Celia now, "For us there's no such thing as a right stop or a wrong stop. If we like where we are, we stay."

She was staring at the scene, her shoulders bent, her head tilted. "Did Margo come?"

"No, my love. Margo is away somewhere on business."

A conspiratorial tone had crept into her voice. "So who's here, then?"

He laughed as if it were a private joke, resettled his cane so his knee could rest against hers. "The whole world is here.

Look around. They call this a concert. But it's like Union Square. A mass demonstration."

"Isn't there someone here we know?" A trap he fell right into.

"Sure. The girls are sitting right behind us. Jolene and Blondell. Gertrude, too. Don't you remember? Her son is one of those noisemakers on the stage." A little joke. He waited for a smile, a reserved twitch of the lips, sad and faraway, the way she was sometimes when the fog cleared.

"The girls?" Now she was looking at him as if she suddenly understood his true nature. Hitler on her doorstep! Goebbels! A bitter wedge of anger flattened her lips. "Rotten bastard," she growled. "You bring your concubines here for the whole world to see?" Her voice gathered volume, rose in fury. A tatter of foam hung from her mouth. "Is there no respect?" she screamed at him.

"Shush. You don't understand . . ." The clenched fist of her good hand was pounding the armrest.

"I know more than you think. I know it all . . . all your filthy secrets, all your lies . . ." He looked around desperately, but the intermission was over. The Trains were gathered in a rosy spray of light to begin their next number. Jolene and Blondell were on their feet clapping. Gertrude, half dead with excitement, was leaning forward to embrace them. The audience whistled, booed, shrieked. *Trains! Trains! Trains!* In the din, he alone could hear Celia's voice screaming in rhythm, "You should all be dead . . . dead . . . dead!"

CHAPTER 25

SYLVIE tried to imagine Gary. She summoned up his thin defiant face. Summoned him up as he had been in the hospital waiting room that last time, huddled on the visitors' couch in the watery dawn light—he must have been there for hours—as waxy and inert as if his blood and vital organs had been removed by embalmers. She and Victor had received the phone call from one of Angel and Gary's friends —Daniel Baum?—but shivering in the dark, she'd failed to ask who. Victor was sitting up in bed, clearing his throat; thank God it was one of his nights at her house. "Do I understand you're suggesting we leave immediately for Brattleboro?" she said into the phone. "But why? What's happened?" There was a pause at the other end, a blurred response, and not daring to hear more, she said, "We'll come at once."

It was after midnight, but they dressed quickly. A few things in her overnight case. Toilet articles selected in a daze. Rain boots for both of them. Was Angel having the baby earlier than expected? She wasn't due for three more weeks. Had she caught something and been ordered to bed for the last part of her term, with instructions for a relative or some-one to come and take care of her? She was grasping at straws. Her blood knew. The sticky receptor threads in her nerve endings knew. Nothing minor had happened. Nothing that would linger and then benignly disappear.

Victor drove, speeding along the empty highways, one hand moving from the steering wheel to her knee from time to time.

"Victor, I'm terrified."

"Anything, any number of things are possible."

"They pulled us out of bed for just anything?"

"Maybe it's Gary, not Angel. Maybe he's having some kind of crisis. If it's Gary, the range is infinite. You've said so yourself." But Victor's heart wasn't in his words.

A five-hour drive. Ninety miles out of New York, it started to rain. In lower Vermont, the streambeds overflowed the roads. It had been raining heavily for days. On Route 9, they followed a straggle of cars the rest of the way through the downpour. Pulling up to the hospital, in darkness diluted by the first seepage of dawn, a milky swath of stars blinking weakly through the falling drops, she felt the breath being squeezed from her. Victor was clearing his throat again and saying, "OK. So now we'll see . . ."

Inside the hospital, the elevator crawled to the third floor. The waiting room. And there was Gary, dragging himself to his feet. She was shocked by his devastated face, the hoarse cry, like the scream of an animal, that he gave when he saw them. "Oh, God"—he clutched Victor's arm—". . . if only it had been me!"

Victor seemed to totter, sat down. She remembered the bread-and-butter simplicity of the waiting room, the molded plastic chairs, their everydayness a reminder of how com-monplace disaster is. Gary continued to cling to Victor's arm. "It came so suddenly. She wasn't due for weeks. We pan-icked, but it wasn't that. There was supposed to be a nurse-midwife, and we couldn't get hold of her, but it wasn't that either." He was staring at Sylvie, entreatingly. "It would have been all right, but on the way to the hospital we were blocked by a truck that had skidded and overturned. We couldn't get around it. She just lay there in the back of the station wagon and bled." He dropped Victor's arm and stared up at the single light bulb as though it were a governing presence. "God, why?"

She felt herself sinking under the weight, heard Victor, his lips against her ear, commanding, "Sylvie!"

THEY'D crossed into New Hampshire. Along the road were signs alerting skiers—Mt. Sunapee, Hellcat Gorge, Cranmore Mountain. Jessica had been dozing in the back seat of the car. Now she was awake and and wide-eyed.

"*Now* where are we going?" she asked, exasperated.

"I told you at breakfast. Don't you remember? New Hampshire. A place called Boone."

"Like Daniel Boone?"

"I don't know."

Jessica dragged Melvin's cage onto the seat next to her, unwound the shawl and said, "We're going to Daniel Boone, Melvin."

The town came at them suddenly. The snowbanked road narrowed, rounded a bend, and when it straightened again, a large shopping center straddled it like a spread butterfly, with bowling alley, movie theatre, every type of store imaginable. In the near distance she could see a grid of streets, houses, a church spire, a denser cluster of buildings—the business section, presumably—and farther on, the tiers of snow-capped mountain peaks in the distance. The town was just five miles from Concord, but it had retained its back-country character, except for the one or two motels they passed that advertised skiing on the premises. They checked into one of those, a neon-lit affair with its AAA-approval sign swinging from a post.

"How long will we stay here?" Jess asked, perking up when she saw the ski lift and two or three children out on the hill.

"I'm not sure." Sylvie had no exact plan for her next move.

She would inquire among the printers and ask at the library where a small collection of handbound books might be kept.

Sylvie unloaded their suitcase and ignoring the No Pets sign, grabbed Melvin's cage and quickly darted into the room. "One of these days," she said, looking at the bird, "there'll be a knock on the door, and a man with hand-cuffs—"

"Be quiet," Melvin said with dignity.

"Did he just say something?" Jessica asked, startled.

"I think he was telling us off."

Jessica rushed for the pumpkin-seed treats, pleading, "Now say, 'Good morning, Mrs. Weyman,' pleeease!"

Sylvie scanned the phone book for printers or bookbinders. There was one printer, no bookbinder. They drove into town past the local library, and Sylvie decided to go in there first.

"But I want to *ski,*" Jessica complained.

"We will, we will," Sylvie said absently, reading a poster that informed her that they'd just missed a book exhibit featuring hand-worked bindings.

The librarian was helpful. "There are a few volumes still on loan that the craftsperson hasn't picked up yet. I'll give you a private showing." She cheerfully marched off, returning with an armful of books. They were extraordinarily beautiful, covered with homespuns in deep, rich colors— burgundy, dark cerulean blue. One was bound in muslin. And one, a children's book, had a little tooled-leather door in the cover through which an accordion of cutouts could be pulled out and examined. Sylvie went back to the muslin and fingered it. "I like the one with the door," Jessica said. "Do they sell them?"

"Are these the work of someone named Gary Markson by any chance?" Sylvie asked.

The librarian looked surprised. "Oh, then you've seen his bindings before?"

"Yes."

"I wish he'd do more. Particularly the children's books. It would be interesting for a small-town library like ours to have this kind of work on permanent exhibit."

"Do you know how I could get in touch with him?"

"Oh, well." The librarian was suddenly reluctant. "I'm not sure. I really don't think he'd be too easy to contact right now."

"Why?" Sylvie asked. "Please, I'd be grateful for any information."

The librarian merely shook her head.

"We're . . . we're . . . related, you see . . ."

"Well, I don't know," the librarian said at last. "I'm not one for passing rumor from one to the next, but it was only yesterday I heard about Mr. Markson from someone who lives in Concord. Seems he got himself into plenty of trouble up there. This person I know told me about his trouble." The librarian looked at them in a worried way. "If you're interested in the young man, I guess you had better go see the police in Concord."

WHEN they returned to the motel, Sylvie sat on the bed and pondered her next move. "If we go to jail," Jessica said, "I could tell everyone about it in Show and Tell." But Sylvie wondered; could she simply present herself to the Concord police with a string of careful inquiries about Gary? She heard herself facing up to it, addressing a sheriff or marshal or whatever law official was appropriate. "This young man, my . . . my son-in-law . . ." What was it that he was supposed to have done? And what *had* he done with the baby? She considered calling Danny Baum for advice but decided against it, remembering what he had told her about Gary's accusations.

It was time for lunch, and in the coffee shop Jessica solemnly ate bacon and tomato on toast and stared at Sylvie from time to time with an injured look. Sylvie had a tuna melt on English muffin. The pool had slipped away, and with it all her other disciplines. Jessica rose from the table with a crust of toast in a paper napkin. "I guess I'll just have to go and feed Melvin," she said.

It was only one o'clock. They could probably ski for an hour and *then* drive over to Concord. Sylvie said, "There's a ski shop next door. Shall we rent?" Jessica clapped her hands, and Sylvie added, "First a phone call home, to Feliciana."

"It looks like we'll need another day or two up here," she told Feliciana.

"Oh, *sí* . . . another day? Mrs. Kort, she say . . ."

"Yes, but everything is fine. Tell Mrs. Kort, not to worry. I'll explain when we get back."

"You explain to Mrs. Kort . . . ?" Feliciana sounded perplexed.

Jessica was saying, "Ask about Zorro."

"Ai, Zorro—he is home from kennel now," Feliciana said. "He sleep a lot, no eat much."

"Well, Jess is wonderful. Tell Mrs. Kort . . ."

When Sylvie hung up, Jessica said, "I want to go home too. After we ski, I want to go home and take care of Zorro." There was a misty look in her eyes.

"Of course. I want to get back too," Sylvie said. She was suddenly overcome by lassitude. The lack of swimming was making her sluggish. And she was eating too much. It was all getting so complicated.

On the little slope, Jessica in her rented skis watched the other children and then leaned firmly against the T-bar and allowed herself to be pushed to the crest of the hill. Once there, she pointed down, in snowplow position, and glided toward the hut at the bottom. When she fell, she picked herself up, turned and waved to Sylvie.

Sylvie, doing lazy stem turns behind her, wondered what sort of trouble Gary was in. Imagined a list of possible crimes —a bad check, drugs, breaking and entering (impossible). Actually, she couldn't see him doing any of those things. Well, drugs, maybe. She assumed he smoked pot, but he was too haphazard to be a drug dealer. And as for the rest—petty crimes, small larcenies—none of it suited his aggrieved though basically moral personality. Perhaps the librarian was wrong, the information false. Such a gritty, unyielding man. How had Angel ever come to him?

The midday sun had given the snow a soft granular crust. Like the Italian ices sold from corner carts in her youth. Her father would stop at such carts and buy lemon ice for her and her brother, Jeffrey. "Done," he'd say, after paying the vendor, as though all his acts, however small, carried equal weight.

Victor was the other side of that coin, coming out of a similar background with his sweetness intact, Victor with his dry little tables of consequences and penalties and his polished elegance. She wanted desperately to talk to him, find her way back to an earlier time, when she'd handled him so lightly, with such assurance. "I think I rather enjoy being your slave," he'd said, taking the pins from her hair, burying his fingers to the scalp, pulling her gently until she sank beneath him. "Only if you insist . . ." she'd said. How had she dared? It was only last year that they had driven out of the city one weekend to Pennsylvania, to Doylestown, where there was an inn on the canal. "The history of this place is so marvellous," he said in anticipation. The inn had several front parlors, low-beamed ceilings, slanted floors of pegged oak. "The bed," he said, "ah, the bed." It was neither too small nor too large and was covered with goosedown comforters, under which one could safely hibernate for a century or more. How did he know, she'd asked. Oh, well, he'd been there once, with Mona, he said. Yes, years ago, before the outside world informed her of his imperfections. Washington was said to have walked the banks of the Delaware in this very region, he added. Even Mona appreciated that. History as theatre; a general sloshing through river bottoms and snowbanks to make the impossible real.

"We'll do everything," Victor told her that weekend. He fished for river bass. She had a volume of Russian stories, which she read dreamily, rocking in the porch swing. They drank too much wine with dinner and collapsed in each other's arms beneath that fabled comforter, which proved to be everything he'd said—a cave, a nest for prolonged and, despite the wine, exuberant love-making. He said, "I think we can have a very decent, slightly amphibious life here for at least a week, without moving an inch."

"You're talking to a woman with a fully grown daughter."

"Yes, yes, I know," he'd said happily. That weekend was the first time they spoke about getting married.

She wanted desperately to see him now, see him close by. Are your feelings the same, Victor? Oh, God, tell me they are. Perhaps she would call him tonight. Victor, I'm here. Don't be angry. She might have something to tell him about Gary.

SHE climbed to the top of the hill and observed Jessica below, pointing her skis downward and making wide, confident snowplow turns. Sylvie wondered what Margo would think if she saw her child in this snowy carefree scene. She imagined a dialogue:

"This isn't dangerous, is it?"

"Not really. Children ski almost by instinct."

She wondered where Margo was now, wondered at the attraction of opposites, the perverse attraction of someone like Brill drawing Margo away from the safety and warmth of her environment. And what went into Margo's thinking? Did she imagine that Michael was dispensable? Sylvie had come to admire Michael in the nearly two months that she'd been living in their house. He was a man of sweeping gestures, of optimism. And he was honest. There was none of the high-handed phoniness often seen in people who were rich.

She had grown fond of Margo, too—she hoped Margo wasn't acting like a fool.

Looking down the side of the hill, Sylvie suddenly saw Jessica bunched and unmoving, a blotch of navy and red on the slope. A wave of terror seized her. She skied quickly to her side. The child's face was buried in the snow. "Jess!" she cried out and quickly turned her over. Jess screamed, "Surprise!" Her hair and lashes were crusted with snow. Her nose was moist and pink. "Did I scare you, Mrs. Weyman?" she asked, licking snow from her upper lip.

Sylvie cradled the child in her arms, rocking her back and

forth, feeling waves of relief wash over her. "Oh, baby, baby," she whispered. "Don't you ever . . . !" She brushed the snow off the child's face and kissed her cheeks and eyes again and again, hugging her tightly until her own beating heart became quiet. "You must never do that again. I was so frightened."

"Why? Because I'm precious?"

She looked into those teasing eyes and shook her gently. "Yes, because you're precious."

CHAPTER 26

THE police station was off the main street in the center of Concord. There was a scattering of police cars, shiny and serious-looking, lined against the curb.

Sylvie felt a shudder of dread, but Jessica was exuberant. "On *Hill Street Blues,* the sergeant gives out peanut-butter cups if the kids come in with their moms. Did you do something wrong?"

"Maybe." Maybe many things, she thought. If one could return to the start again, was it possible to run a different course? "I'm just trying to find someone," she reassured Jess.

Inside the building she asked to speak to the officer in charge. He listened without a trace of expression on his face. "What's your relationship to the person in question?"

"Mother-in-law. Is there information about him?"

The sergeant took her name and address and asked for identification. Then he got up abruptly and went into a rear office. He left the door ajar, and Sylvie caught sight of a man behind a desk in white shirt-sleeves with the tinny glitter of an official badge on his chest.

Jessica had gone to the side of the room and sat on a bench. "What about the peanut-butter cups," she mouthed.

"Later," Sylvie whispered. She didn't know why she whispered. The atmosphere was courteous and unthreatening. But she was filled with premonitions. The sergeant beckoned. "If you sit here and don't move," Sylvie said to Jess, "we might do a little tobogganing this afternoon."

The office was so thick with smoke that the man in shirtsleeves looked submerged. Sylvie waited politely, trying not to cough. After a while, he looked up from a manilla folder in front of him and acknowledged her. "Ma'am?" The desk marker said Captain Lothrop. "Mother of Gary Markson? Sit down, won't you."

"Mother-in-law." She moved a chair closer to the desk and sat down.

He leaned back and looked her over silently for a while. She was about to speak when he said, "Well, I don't know if you're aware of this, but your boy is in trouble. And it's serious stuff. Hasn't he been in touch with you?"

"I haven't seen him in months. As it happens, I drove up from New York to look for him. Someone in Boone told me to check with your office. Frankly, I'm in shock." Her hands were sweaty. She kept repeating to herself that whatever the problem was, it belonged to Gary. Her only interest was in Sean. She looked at Captain Lothrop, whose attention seemed to have wandered. "Did he come in with a child? He's the father of an infant."

The captain looked at her. "No child mentioned here. We've got most of the facts." He glanced down at the papers before him. "Mrs. Weyman. Mother-in-law. I think your daughter, wherever she is, was looking for trouble."

"My daughter is dead. Don't you have that in your records?" She spoke conversationally. They might have been discussing a news item in the local homicides column. She wondered if she sounded like one of those victims of disaster on TV who dazedly describe how several members of their family were wiped out when the mine collapsed.

"My sympathies. No, we were just told his wife wasn't living with him." He came around the desk and pulled up a chair to face Sylvie. There was an aura of sweat and pragmatism and fatigue about him that was not unappealing. "Well, here's what we have. It's not a bedtime story . . ."

Gary had been picked up on a charge of statutory rape. "Now that's damn serious business," he said. "A serious felony. No fooling around with that one, especially around here. Good New England folk in these parts, up in arms about the Young Turks who've been drifting in here these many years—the type that tries to bust up the town, shock the natives. Mostly we pick them up on drugs, disturbing the peace, such. But with statutory rape, the whole fucking— pardon, ma'am—legal machine moves into gear."

"I don't understand." Gary was not the type. She had always seen his helter-skelter activities as a cover-up for a deeply passive and searching nature. Statutory rape! "Are you sure?"

The captain was continuing to inform her. "Now I'm going to give you more details than you can use," he said, settling back. "Your boy got mixed up with a minor, fifteen years old. No father, working mother, but her uncle is something else. Unfortunately for your Mr. Markson, the uncle is one of our more influential citizens. This has become an issue with him. His niece assaulted and defiled. Defiled—can you believe it, with what kids are into today?" He looked at the ceiling and blew smoke. "The man's not only coming up for reelection to the state senate, but he has his hand in one of the more prominent newspapers in this region. So I would say it's a stacked deck. Against your Mr. Markson, that is."

"And your records do *not* indicate that there's a baby? Gary Markson's child, a little boy?"

"No. That information isn't pertinent to the case. In any event, charges were placed against him five days ago. You'll find out at the state prison. I'd advise you to go there and have a little talk with him. See if he's been assigned a public defender yet."

THE first thing she did when she returned to the inn was to call Danny after all. She needed help. She needed someone who knew Gary, who was sympathetic to her, whom she could trust Jessica with. "It will take me a few hours, but I'll get started immediately," he said.

Upstairs, Jessica was jumping up and down on the bed yelling for tobogganing. "Daddy took me once in Van Cortlandt Park. And you promised!" Jessica cried, landing on her head.

"Stop it!" Sylvie shouted. Jessica could injure her neck on the mattress, she could break an arm on a toboggan. Everything seemed to have gotten out of hand. And there was no end in sight.

"Now look," she said, trying to sound as calm as possible, "we may have to stay here a day or two longer, so I expect you to behave!"

Jessica had grown still. "I'm missing school and flute. Is that allowed?" She had the tone of a co-conspirator.

"This once it will have to be allowed."

"My mother hates me to miss anything," she said, plucking at the tufts of candlewick in the bedspread. She placed a tiny fluff of white on her upper lip and blew at it.

"I'll see that you make up everything when we come back. We'll even bring a jug of maple syrup for Mrs. Beerbohm, to sweeten her up." But Sylvie wondered what she could ever say to Margo to explain all this, or to Michael. On the other hand, what could they do? Fire her? But she *did* want to be responsible. That's what proximity did to one. Brought oneself and others into clearer focus. She liked Margo, liked the way she went about things with so much energetic fervor, fingers crossed, no doubt that everything would come out all right. A certain elemental decency about her, no matter what she was up to. Sylvie didn't want to disappoint her.

"If we're not going out in the snow, then I'd like a hot fudge sundae in the coffee shop, and I want you to have one, too."

"I might possibly have a dish of ice cream."

"I just love it when you eat the same things I do," Jess said. Danny Baum arrived after dinner. Jess was ready for bed.

"I'll be downstairs in the lobby talking to Danny," Sylvie said.

Jess had her nose pressed to the door of Melvin's cage. "Good morning, Mrs. Weyman," she was saying.

"Be quiet!" Melvin said.

DANNY whistled under his breath as Sylvie explained the situation. "I can barely see Gary in the role of a seducer, let alone a rapist," he said. "Maybe someone got it all wrong. Maybe the girl said, 'Let's do it,' he said, 'No,' and she jumped him." Sylvie didn't even smile. She couldn't begin to measure the extent of Gary's guilt and despair, or of how dangerous he could be to himself and others. "And if he's in prison," Danny continued, "that means that the legal proceedings have travelled a certain distance. He had to appear before a magistrate, who must have decided that there was merit to the charge and that a trial was in order. Bail was probably set at a figure beyond his reach. Poor guy, he must have felt really isolated and humiliated not to try to get it from the people he knew. Yvonne, for one. And me."

He was slouched low in a chair near her, chewing on the end of his pipe stem, his long legs in laced boots stretched in front of him, a stubble of beard like cinders on his chin. "Yvonne is very fond of you," Sylvie said suddenly.

He didn't respond at first, and then, "I was fond of her, too, for a while, until I realized things about her . . . that dream world of hers. With Yvonne, even spreading peanut butter on a slice of bread becomes a meditation."

CHAPTER 27

THE prison was two miles from town. Low brick buildings enclosed by a high stone wall with observation towers on top. Inside, as she walked toward the steel gate at the end of a tiled corridor, the feeling of threat was so palpable that she turned to the marshal at her side and asked, "How long will I be able to stay with the prisoner?" *Prisoner!* It was making no sense at all.

"The visitor's clerk will tell you all about that, ma'am."

The visitor's clerk, a crew-cut young man with a pink face, handed her a pen and an information card and said, "Go to it, lady." She filled in the required information and showed identification. "Visiting has already started; you've got two hours."

A police matron took her pocketbook and jacket and ran her hands up and down Sylvie's body, then said, "You can pick up your belongings when you leave." Sylvie nodded. She could imagine Gary's state of mind in this environment. She hoped for his sake he hadn't come in wearing eccentric clothes.

She sat on a bench at the side of the room. Two or three

other people had arrived and gone through the formality of registering and identifying themselves. She wondered if everyone felt as undifferentiated as she did and realized suddenly that her fists were clenched.

It was neither harder nor easier than she expected. She was shown into a room that was several times the size of her own living room in Rosevale. There were tables and chairs scattered around, a TV in the corner, a few shelves with paperback books, and a guard in uniform at either end of the room.

When Gary entered and saw her, he stood absolutely still; one arm jerked involuntarily at his side. He stared, then turned, and she thought he would leave.

"Gary, please come and talk to me," she said.

He looked dazed. His jaw moved stiffly, as if it were wired shut. But he came and sat near her at a table.

She said quickly, trying to control her own trembling, "Are you all right?" He was wearing jeans and a pullover. His hair, though long, was neatly combed.

"As all right as I'm supposed to be under the circumstances. I guess you've been told about the *circumstances*. What about you? You beginning to get yourself together?"

"In a way, I guess. Slowly. I don't know."

He sat back and tried to meet her eyes. "So you're here. I knew one of these days it would happen. We'd be face to face."

"Well, we are," she said encouragingly. "Face to face."

"How did you get here? I mean New Hampshire. How did you know where to look?"

"I came to Brattleboro and asked people . . ."

"Well known in Brattleboro, right? Good luck Charlie."

He was silent for a while, gazing past her at one of the guards, who was yawning just then. "Why? I mean why come here now? Did something happen? Did you hear voices in the night or something? A fairy, maybe, saying, go out into the world and find Gary. He's in the fuckingest goddamned trouble." He was looking at her now, bitter but uncertain of how far he dared to go. She felt that any sudden act on her part

—if she reached over and touched his face, for example— would make him collapse sobbing on the table. "Or was it the baby? As if I need to ask."

"I met Danny Baum in New York," she said quietly, "and one thing led to another. I began to realize I had to do something. We'd made attempts to find you. Followed some false leads. I knew I had to gather the strength . . . really search in earnest . . . find Sean and you. I began to worry the two of you would just go off somewhere . . . disappear. . . . What about Sean?"

He said, "Yeah, you got here just in the nick of time." Then he said, "So Danny's been leading you around. Good old Danny. Got his hand in everything. Right? How's his peanut butter, or is it chocolate chip cookies . . . ?"

He looked thinner than ever, his features sharper, more pointed, his skin bone-white. She thought she saw tears glistening in his eyes, and she said hurriedly, "We're wasting time. Tell me what this is all about?"

He banged a fist into the palm of his hand. "I'm being framed, that's what I think. I'm being used as an example. It's as simple as that. This kid . . . well, I took a chance on her. I was at Red Charlie's, ten miles out of town, drinking a few beers, listening to music, relaxing and feeling good for a change because I'd begun to work again, doing jobs at a local bindery—some gluing and cutting. A gallery in Manchester was even talking of showing a few of my better pieces. Temporary work, but that was OK because I'd already decided to move on again. Anyway this kid Cindy comes up to me at Red Charlie's. A big, well-developed girl. Buxom as all hell and anxious to show it off. We had a couple of beers, and she hung around. When we danced, she practically crawled into my pocket. Well, I took her out to my wagon because it seemed to be what we both wanted. I'd been miserable for so long, I'd stayed away from everyone I knew. I didn't want anyone's sympathy. Sympathy's just another way for people to get off on feeling superior and smug." He stopped talking and rubbed his hands across his face. "You must be thinking

I'm a real crud. You have a revolted look; the look of someone who's trying to step around a pile of dung."

She whispered, "No, Gary."

"You're thinking of the past—of each and every time you
told Angel to get the hell out of Vermont and get on with her
life—get on with all the goals and achievements." He pulled
a handkerchief from his jeans and blew hard. "The truth is,
you know, she didn't want to be like you—stoic calm in the
face of God knows what. She thought you had it all wrong.
'My mom, the Prussian princess' she called you, meaning
that she was going to try for another model. Easier, less
hidebound."

Sylvie felt as though the breath had been knocked out of
her. She said, "Tell me the rest of your story, Gary."

"Oh, that—there's no end in sight. The girl was one of
those high-school sluts. A come-on artist. Sorry to be crude,
but it turned out she'd been laid by practically every kid
around. Of course, the courts don't know that, or care. The
townie boys know it. But who's going to testify that they
banged an underage tart whose uncle is way up there in
politics. And even if they did speak out, it doesn't make her
any less underage."

"But why did she set you up?" Sylvie asked.

"A matter of timing. With me, it seemed, she wanted more
than just fun. There happened to be coke around. She'd run
out of her allowance. She wanted money from me. She said
she'd given me a good time, right? She was just a poor girl
who needed eighty bucks. I should have come through, but
hell, I still hadn't paid for the stuff I'd gotten Sean. I told
Cindy to lay off. I said, 'Look, I never but never *pay* for it.'
It was an insensitive thing to say, and it made her boil." He'd
made a sunshade of his fingers, shaded his eyes. "Don't ever
underestimate the boiling point of any woman, of *any* age."
He extended his hand, and for an instant Sylvie thought he
was reaching for her and felt a strange, sad feeling in her
chest, but the hand came to rest on the table, and he continued. "She went bawling to her mother and her uncle, and

the next thing I know it's statutory rape. I didn't think any-one would believe her. But the town prosecutor has a broom-stick up his ass. And the newspapers around here are cloned right off the Moral Majority. And look at the thirty-thou-sand-dollar bail they slapped on me! Some guy shot his mother and sister last year and had to come up with far less."

Sylvie was barely breathing. "My mom, the Prussian prin-cess." What had Angel meant? But she was looking at Gary; he seemed so bowed by the weight of all of it.

"What about the baby?" she asked abruptly.

"Sean? I've been waiting for you to get back to Sean. I've got a picture of him here." He fished in his wallet and came up with a color snapshot. It burned in her fingers. Sean was round and pink with a cleft in his chin like a nail print in butter, a toothless smile, ringlets. Suddenly tears were run-ning down her cheeks. She patted them off with the palms of her hands. "You hate me," Gary was saying. "Don't be polite about it. You're just pretending, trying to do the decent thing. Or maybe you've come up here to grab Sean and let me go hang. You've always let me see what the score was, so don't turn goddamn hypocrite on me now."

She felt an unexpected rush of compassion for him. "Look, Gary," she said, "we'll talk about the baby later. When I came up here, I had no way of knowing . . . all this. I never expected to be lucky enough to find you. I simply felt stronger, strong enough to make a real attempt . . ." She said this softly, as if not to interrupt a train of thought. "I want to help."

Her heart was skipping beats. Had she eaten that morning? She tried to remember. Jessica had had oatmeal, and then they'd gone back to the room to wait for Danny. She thought she'd had coffee. She hoped she'd had coffee. She took a deep breath and asked, "Where's Sean now?"

"Look, I don't want to discuss Sean's whereabouts. Not now, not while I'm in here." His voice had a conclusive sound, as if he was bringing an interview to an end.

She rose abruptly. "Gary, this is pointless. Don't play

games with me, please! I *need* and *want* to see the baby. I have a *right* to. You can't interfere with *that*. For heaven's sake, tell me where he is this minute!"

His head was bowed. He lifted his clasped hands as if to ward off blows. At last he said, so quietly it was as though he hadn't spoken at all, "He's with Yvonne Dufault."

"Yvonne?" She wasn't sure she'd heard correctly. "Yvonne in Cozzens?"

"Yeah, Yvonne in Cozzens."

"But how. . . . ?" Her mind was spinning. The baby certainly hadn't been in the apartment that night. Or had he? It was such a small, crowded place. But had she only *assumed* it was small? Yvonne had been so impatient to get rid of them, passing through all her attitudes—belligerence, hurt and anger at Danny, a pseudo-chumminess with Sylvie. And the radio blasting; the closed door off the kitchen . . .

"Does Yvonne know you're in this trouble?"

"She's the only one. I had to tell her because of the baby. Not that you can keep a story like this quiet."

Sylvie was standing close to him, "I'm going to post your bail, Gary, but I want to see the baby immediately . . . if it's not too late . . ."

"What do you mean too late?" He too had risen to his feet.

"I don't know what I mean. Yvonne has her own ax to grind." She tried to deal with the sudden anxiety threatening to overwhelm her. "Danny Baum has offered to get decent legal help . . ." As she said it, she knew that she shouldn't have.

Gary instantly flared up. "You're giving me the same old shit. Coming here and interfering. I don't want that fucker anywhere near my kid. Is that understood! He has no right —no business. I don't care if anything or nothing went on between him and Angel. That kid's my territory, only mine . . ."

The matron was coming toward them. The time was up. Sylvie said, "Good-bye." She touched his arm, but he pulled back. She whispered, "Trust me."

He made no response.

Half stumbling, she followed the matron to the door to collect her things.

"I want to get back to Cozzens immediately," she was saying to Danny. They were sitting in her room at the inn. Jessica was trying to describe the snowmobile ride that Danny had taken her on.

"There was this farm," she was saying, "and Danny was looking at some yogurt stuff. And then the man on the farm wheeled out this snowmobile from the barn." Her face had a polished, wind-burned look, and Sylvie automatically tested her forehead with the back of her hand.

"Why are you so anxious?" Danny asked.

"Because I don't believe we'll find the baby at Yvonne's." She hadn't expected to say that, and the words frightened her.

Danny whistled. "Look, Yvonne may be hard to handle, but she's awfully young to be interested in kidnapping."

"Big Bird's brother was once kidnapped," Jessica said.

"I didn't exactly mean kidnapping," Sylvie said. She thought of Yvonne's angry face, the impression she gave of having been bitterly cheated. "But maybe something in-between. Some sort of rationalization for strange behavior. I mean, she pointed me toward Gary in the first place. She should have known there was a good chance he'd tell me that Sean was with her . . ." Her voice trailed off.

"Even so," Danny said, "you're doing some heavy speculating."

"Will you go to Cozzens with me, right now?"

"You'd better, or we might kidnap *you*," Jessica said.

"I'll follow in my truck," Danny said.

CHAPTER 28

S PEEDING down the highway toward Vermont, Sylvie didn't know what to think of first. She would somehow raise money for bail and at least get Gary out of that awful place. Then there was the question of lawyers. Her thoughts were whirling. There was Sean. What would she do about Sean? And there was Jessica. She looked at the child, lolling dreamily in the back of the car, one hand anchoring the parrot's cage. "I want to go home and see Charlotte and Lyle," she had said a few minutes before.

It had turned bitterly cold. The little towns they passed seemed to have shrunk in on themselves. "Are you warm enough?" Sylvie asked.

Jessica called out, "I'm warm as a bug in a fried-egg sandwich."

"That's pretty warm."

"Are you warm enough?" Victor had asked on the beach at Montauk, the salt air like a snapped towel across her face, Victor whispering, "Come to life."

"Wouldn't it be funny if I kissed Melvin on the mouth and he turned into a prince," Jessica said, giggling. "Then I would be a princess . . . "

"Don't build up your hopes," Sylvie said.

My mom, the Prussian princess! My mother, who deliberated on her life and then made a cause of it. Her head ached.

They were entering Vermont. More mountains, highways like strips of satin. She must get to Yvonne quickly. Had Sean really been there all along? And what about Gary? Not only his legal problems, but his future plans. Daniel had said he'd be responsible for getting a lawyer. She'd begun to regard him as the stable factor in all of this, and for a moment she allowed herself to wonder what Angel really thought of him. Her beautiful and defiant daughter. What did she think when she saw Danny, so lean and confident, moving toward her across the cornfields?

Jessica spoke from the back of the car. "I'm hungry, and I have to pee." They had just turned into Route 9 and a diner loomed ahead. "It's coming out," Jessica wailed. Sylvie pulled into the parking lot, threw the electric blanket over Melvin's cage, locked the doors of the car with a spare key and rushed her inside.

After the bathroom the child reminded her that they'd skipped lunch. "That's why I'm so hungry, silly." It was late afternoon, and the diner lights splashed yellow and pink in the ice-littered parking lot: Jessica ordered a cheeseburger, steak fries and a chocolate shake. Her eyes were on Sylvie. "Aren't you hungry?"

"Yes, I think I'm hungry. Very."

"Then eat!" Jessica shrieked with glee. Sylvie stared at that bright little face, suddenly pert with knowledge. It was true. She had been hungry for days.

The waitress tapped the menu in her hand. "So what's it going to be?"

"I'll have the hamburger," Sylvie said. "Rare."

"I'm going to tell my mother that we ate very well, and we had fun."

"And your father?"

Jessica was playing with the saltshakers. She twitched her shoulders in an old lady's shrug. "All I hope is that he keeps his promise and brings back some gnu teeth." It sounded like "new" teeth, but Jessica was ready for her. *"Gn,* as in gnawed a bone, silly. My grandfather Max thinks he once made jackets out of gnu."

IT was late afternoon by the time they were settled in again with Maggie Friel. At five o'clock Sylvie put through a call to Victor's office. She was told by the receptionist that he had not been in that day. A rush of hopelessness. She dialled his home phone. The answering tape announced, "Victor Severin here. Please leave name and phone number . . . " She said, "Victor. I'm away for a while. It's about Gary." But what else was there to say. He had fallen out of her life. "Are you all right, darling?" She allowed herself that.

She was wondering what to do next when Danny arrived. "Listen, I think we'd better hurry. I don't like a few things I heard." What he had heard was that Yvonne's studio had been locked for the past two days and the sign on the door said Closed. Leaving Jessica with Maggie Friel, they started out in Sylvie's station wagon.

Climbing the stairs to Yvonne's apartment, Sylvie tried to plan a strategy. What if the girl was there but insisted that Gary was lying and she didn't have Sean. A more devastating thought presented itself. What . . . oh, God, what if Gary had disposed of Sean—a foster home or an adoption agency—and was afraid to tell her. But no! He could never do that. His own childhood weighed on him too heavily. Still, the notion took her breath away.

Danny's informant had been correct. Her door was locked. The little sign hanging askew said Closed. Danny called out, "Hey, in there, Yvonne!" He kicked at the door frame. A mouse scurried along the hallway molding, squeaking, and disappeared.

"She's not here," Sylvie said, turning away.

Walking downstairs, Danny put his arm around her. "Look, don't think for a minute that this is it. She has a string of friends. We'll contact every one." It had grown dark, but the convenience store was still open and doing business when they came out into the street. The clerk, a tall young man, was joking with the few remaining shoppers. The coffeemaker still bubbled at his elbow. He had the wind-scored face of a skier and a big open smile only partially concealed by his floppy moustache. As she watched, he poured coffee into a Styrofoam cup and drank.

"You wait in the car; I want to try something," she told Danny. She went into the store, picked up three tins of tuna and waited until the clerk was free. "I wouldn't mind some coffee," she said as she slid the tuna toward him.

"Sure thing." He poured for her. "Having a good day?"

"Perfect. The snow was wonderful. I'm here with my child, and we did everything from downhill to snowmobiling."

"Nothing like it when there's real snow. You can take all that machine-made stuff and shove it." He was jokey and pleasant, lounging against the counter, legs sprawled, having coffee himself. Her purchase was in a little plastic sack.

She said casually, "I can't imagine where the girl upstairs can be—Yvonne Dufault."

"Yeah—well, Yvonne—she locked up the day before yesterday."

Sylvie shook her head, feigned a look of exasperation. "I can't believe her. I think she forgot that I was coming all the way from New York today to see her on business."

"Hey, that's too bad. For both of you, I guess." The boy smiled sympathetically.

"You can say that again," Sylvie said in as steady a voice as she could manage. "I planned to do some heavy buying. My outlets in New York are really hungry . . . Oh, well, I'll have to scout the rest of the area. There are good crafts people all over the place. If you see Yvonne, tell her I was here and —well, she wasn't." Sylvie gave him her warmest, fullest smile.

"Look, wait." Perplexed, he grabbed her arm. "I happen to know where she is, but I'm not supposed to give out information. Yvonne is that way. Very private. I respect that. Hell, I wish she had a phone so I could check this one out."

279

He smiled down at her. "But you look good. Better than good. Anyone ever tell you that you look like what's her name—Meryl Streep? Anyway, I hate to see Yvonne lose out on a chance to make some money."

YVONNE was living in a friend's trailer in a clearing out on County Road 4B, not more than three miles from Route 30, he said. Sylvie couldn't miss it. She hadn't dared to ask him if there was a child with her. But she urged Danny to get back to his place on his own. She would go the rest of the distance herself.

There was a low hanging haze in the clearing. It seemed appropriate, spooky enough to make her blood rush. The trailer, set back from the road on cinder blocks, threw out pockets of light in the dark. Sylvie, driving into a space in front grooved with cleats of ice, hoped she had the advantage of surprise. She switched off her motor and emerged from the car like a prowler. At the entrance, she knocked sharply.

The girl within called out uncertainly, "Who is it?"

"*Me.* I want to talk to you, Yvonne."

"Who the hell is me?" Sylvie said nothing. There was a long silence, and Sylvie was about to bang on the door again when Yvonne opened it and stood there in the pink, low-wattage glow, looking dazed, her mouth slack with wonder. "I just don't believe this," she said. She seemed about to slam the door in Sylvie's face, but Sylvie said, "You'd better let me in."

It was like entering a train, bare and smelling of engine oil, alcohol and Mr. Clean. They were standing in something that looked like a kitchen, with a stove, refrigerator, small table. Sylvie took in the wheat germ, vitamin drops, jug of vodka and vase with a sprig of dried mountain laurel on a shelf above the stove. Cuttings of fabric, probably for dolls' clothes, were on the table. On the shelf behind the mountain laurel was a baby's plastic bottle turned upside down on wax paper, as if it had been scrubbed and left to dry. She felt like a miner who glimpsed a vein of gold at last.

"So what's up?" Yvonne asked. "Ever find Gary?" She was barefoot, wearing ski pants and a battered tweedy pullover that hung to her knees. Her eyes were puffed from lack of sleep; a new, shaggy haircut gave her the look of a troll.

"I found him."

Yvonne looked at her. "Look, let's go in where it's warmer. But you can only stay a minute or two. I'm expecting friends."

They moved on, as if passing narrowly over a train coupling and into a space where a kerosene lamp sent out a penumbral halo of warmth. The portable stereo was on, and music, country rock, jittered in the room. If Sean cried, if he was crying now, how could anyone know?

"The guy who lives here has a kiln in town, but he's down in Boston right now, doing the galleries."

Sylvie said, "Oh yes?" Had she imagined a doll's sleeve or was it an infant's sweater in the basket with the buttons?

Yvonne was stalling for time, clearing her throat and stuffing a cigarette into the familiar green holder. Sylvie envisioned the tiny diamond drill that had scooped and shaped the crystal, and she had the urge to reach forward and slap it from Yvonne's hand. Yvonne was saying, "OK, you think I'm a shit. Right? You want to know what's going on, right? But we've got to speak fast because a few of my friends are dropping by for a bash . . . "

"I'm trying to understand your motives," Sylvie said.

"My motives?" Her voice had a jagged sound; Sylvie assumed she'd gotten a head start on her friends because the cap was off the jug of vodka on the drain.

Sylvie pushed the breath out of her lungs. "Where's Sean?"

"Sean? I don't know what you're talking about. Gary has him. There's probably someone in Boone looking after him right now. Don't come to me."

"That's not what Gary said."

"I don't care what Gary said. Don't tell me he sent you after me, because I won't believe it." Her eyes had a rigid, focused look, like those of an animal stunned by the glare of headlights.

"He said the baby was with you," Sylvie said, speaking in a monotone, cautiously. "I don't think he knew that you had —well, changed your address. But I'm confused. First, that you never mentioned Sean when we were together at your other place, and second, this sudden move of yours." She gazed around at as much of the trailer as was visible. There was an arched doorway in the living room wall that seemed to lead nowhere. She paused. Yvonne was blowing rings at the ceiling. She looked insolent and frightened and pathetic all at once. The DJ was saying, "Our next number is a honey! 'Cornflower Blues'!" A whack of sound, strings and horn, crashed into the room. A blurry scarf of smoke encircled Yvonne. The sympathy Sylvie had felt for her during their first meetings was gone; now she simply wanted to accomplish what she'd come for and leave.

Yvonne, who had flopped to the couch, got to her feet. "Look, I really want you out of here. I've got tons of things going on before my friends arrive. Anyway, this is crazy. I don't believe Gary would even talk to you."

Sylvie persisted. "He had no choice. Look, Yvonne, it's a tricky thing you're doing. It could be mistaken for something else—kidnapping, for example?"

"Kidnapping? Only Gary could accuse me of *that,* if he had a reason. Which he doesn't. Oh, shit!" Her face flamed with emotion. "Now really, get out!"

Sylvie controlled herself. "You're wrong. I could accuse you, too!"

"I don't believe what I'm hearing. Not one word!" The girl poured vodka and took a long swallow. She wrapped herself in a mohair scarf, a chrysalis of threads and hair that nearly concealed her face. She had begun to shake, to clutch herself and rock back and forth. Sylvie realized that she was crying. "Why is it necessary to—well, to hide out this way?" Sylvie asked. Then she said softly, "I thought we understood each other a little. We had a pretty confidential talk the other night. I told you things I never talk about to anybody."

The girl lifted her eyes and said, "Oh, Christ!"

She dragged herself to her feet. "Just a minute," she said and disappeared through the arched doorway. After a while she came back, tottering a little, clutching at things as she moved. Sylvie could imagine the amount of vodka she'd consumed. But she seemed to have gotten a second wind. "Just how long are you going to keep this up?" she asked, facing Sylvie. "I mean, how long do you plan to hang around here bullying me after I said I want you out of here?"

Sylvie said, "I want to know why. Why have you taken the baby? Where is he? I'm not leaving, Yvonne, until I know."

"I'll call the police."

"I don't think you will."

Yvonne began to sob. "Oh, God, if you want to know, I just couldn't bear it anymore, not any of it." Tears poured out of her eyes. "You up here waiting to snatch the baby away, or if not you, then Gary, as soon as he beats his own rap." She raised her tear-smeared face. "I've seen it coming with him. Before all this happened in Boone, he'd talked about a cooperative out on the coast—Salem, Oregon. Soy beans and fish oil. To hear him, he was going to be Moses in the desert, pulling nutrition for everyone out of thin air. I asked him what made him go sour on bookbinding. And he said, 'Because I can't control what goes into the books.' That's Gary! But in his plan he and Sean would take to the road, all romance and idealized shit." She drained the vodka so shakily that it dribbled down the front of her scarf. "Hell, oh bloody hell."

Sylvie reached for Yvonne's scarf and pulled her gently forward. Her head, as if disconnected from the rest of her torso, bobbed just an inch or two in front of Sylvie's face. "Sean's in here," Sylvie said. Then they both heard the sound of feet stamping.

People were pushing open the trailer door. "Hello in there!" Three couples were pulling off their boots, shrugging jackets from their shoulders. "Hey, Yvonne! Where are you, baby? We brought over some new tapes . . . " Yvonne went out to the kitchen and said, "Pour yourself, will you," and handed over the vodka. "I'm just finishing up some business in here."

She turned back to Sylvie, who was saying, "Sean . . . somewhere behind all the this racket . . . "

"It is my absolutely private view," Yvonne said thickly, "that Sean isn't even Gary's baby. He's Angel's, yes, but I believe he's Danny's, too. And sometimes even Gary thinks so. Only sometimes. When he's in the mood for self-torture. I kind of like the idea, Sean being part Danny." She raised her bleared and anguished eyes to Sylvie. "Are you shocked?"

"Not shocked, curious." But she was more than curious. She was frightened. The girl was clutching her glass so tightly it seemed in danger of splintering. "Is that why you left with the baby?"

Yvonne was crying again, great heaving gasps. "I don't know. I didn't want to make it too easy for anyone—not Gary and especially not Danny. Let them worry a little." She stopped and blew her nose, but the tears kept flowing. "I'm no thumbprint to be rubbed away as if I never existed. I had something sweet going with Danny. We were in love for a while, I swear it. I'd go over to his place and help him figure out what new thing to put in his yogurt. I'm the one that came up with Cinnamon Cider. My hair was long then, and he used to call me Rapunzel. And then Angel moved into the scene. So cool and beautiful and spoken for." She wiped her eyes with the hem of her skirt. Fumbled for a joint. Lit it. Sylvie slapped it out of her hand. "You're in no condition . . . "

Yvonne's mouth fell open. A deep flush spread over her face. "What right . . . " she sputtered. But then her friends were crowding into the room. "What's going on in here, Yvonne?" Someone said to Sylvie, "Hi, there!" Another joint was passed, and Sylvie was included in the circle. She puffed but didn't draw the smoke into her lungs. One of the girls said to her, "Are you related to Yvonne? You look a little like her." The air in the room was syrupy thick, faintly sweet. The scene, those soft undulations of sound and space around her, was like something viewed underwater. One of the young men had put his arms around Yvonne and swayed with her as if rocking her to sleep. She seemed asleep, drooping on his shoulder, her head flung forward like someone rescued from the sea.

Sylvie saw her chance and slipped through the curtained arch, down a hall as narrow as a pencil holder, past tiny bedrooms. The first two were empty. In the third, she found a string hanging from the ceiling and pulled it. The room filled with watery light. Motes of dust like constellations of larval moths clouded the air. A chair, a bed, a low chest of drawers, no window. But in the corner was a barricaded area —a mattress of folded blankets fenced off by soup cartons weighted down by books. The baby was motionless behind the barricade.

Sylvie got down on her hands and knees, whispering to herself, *Don't let him be dead!* She turned him on his back. He was in a blue-and-yellow coverall. A parade of ducks circled his collar. She shook him gently, and he stirred; his forefinger crept to his mouth; he let out a long whistling sigh. Music rose and swelled in her. She sat on the floor and took Sean in her arms, held him against the labored thud of her heart. This golden child, with ringlets matted from sleep and baby sweat, fawn skin. She opened his fist and examined the dimpled flesh. His nails were too long, and she searched his face for scratches. She was waiting for him to open his eyes. And when he did, it was like looking into a clear pond; she breathed in little sobs, but there it was. Angel's wide flat brow, her pointed chin, asymmetrical mouth with one lip full, less shapely than the other. The baby was staring back at her in startled concentration; then slowly his lower lip trembled, and he began to cry.

"Oh no." She held him to her breast. She saw herself

tunnelling back in time. Angel everywhere—the sweetness of her, long golden hair, head dipped in listening, eyes flooded with inquiry. "Now, let's just get this straight, Mother!" Arms around Sylvie's neck. "Oh, Mommy, Mommy . . ." Arranging her games in graduated sizes. Putting ID bracelets on her dolls' wrists. Her brow furrowed, concentrating, an invisible aura like a force field flowing around her, her own ease with herself becoming a moat, something to hold her apart. Coming home from school and asking, "Where's my good daddy?" Chewing on a piece of hair, sucking it until it looked like a whittled stick. "I think I need my daddy." And lost in thought, the child-mind masked by its own innocence. "Now, I just don't know." Hands on little hips.

When Angel was a baby, she, too, sucked her forefinger instead of her thumb, and it gave her a pensive judicious look, as if she were coming to grave decisions. Her daughter. Her calm quirky child. Driving off in the family car at the age of eleven, as though she could do anything. Baking brownies and selling them in the school lunchroom for thirty-five cents, undercover, lest the lunchroom manager find out. And afterward sending away for the famous Soleri bells as a Mother's Day present, because Sylvie had admired them at the Museum of Modern Art. Watching the whales in the steamer off the Rhode Island coast. A long solemn gaze: "Do you think they know they're being watched? Do you suppose they're putting on a whale ballet just for us, seeing who can spout highest?" And after a bit, "Do you think Sloppy is watching us from somewhere?" And older, a young lady, a woman, standing back, making a space between herself and Sylvie, casting off on her own . . . "Gary's different from you and Dad, the way Dad was right up until he died. Dad always knew what he was. And you managed; you *made* yourself manage. And I know why. And just knowing *why* is like being born under a star or a cross." Jerking away fitfully. "Oh, Mom, you . . . Anyway, Gary's the kind of guy who needs proofs, all the time. He's always asking himself, 'How can I be sure that . . . ' There's something in him that needs, well, the hard evidence, or else this dark lost thing comes over him. But I've got it under control. Stroke him, love him, and he's alive." Her vision: "What does it matter? Ultimately we get some of what we want." She had said, "I want the baby for me."

Sylvie quickly threw some baby clothes, Pampers, baby wipes, bottle, whatever she could find, into a plastic bag lying nearby and stuffed Sean into a sweater and snowsuit; he had decided not to cry and looked astonished instead.

All at once Yvonne was in the doorway. "What do you think you're doing?" Music floated from down the corridor. Jimi Hendrix singing.

"I'm taking the baby with me."

"You have no goddamn right—I'll call the police."

"The police? Yvonne, think of what you're saying. You don't dare. And it's not only the baby. One sniff of the air in this place, and they'll take all of you in for possession." She tried to push her way out of the little room. "Frankly, I can't understand Gary leaving the baby with you. I'm aghast . . . You don't have the emotional strength. Not now! I mean, the baby in a back room and you working your way toward a coma . . . " Yvonne was blocking the doorway. "If you interfere with me," Sylvie said, "if you try to stop me, you'll be in more trouble than you ever bargained for."

"That's not fair! Nothing you're saying is fair. I always knew what I was doing. I mean, you're so uptight, how do you know what it takes to get into a coma?" She was talking through a flood of tears. "I thought you were someone I could *relate* to—who would understand. Now you walk in here like a raider. How do I even know Gary wants me to let you have the baby? He can't stand your guts." She paused to breathe and then screamed, the sound bursting out like air from a pressurized container. "Well, how the fucking hell do I know anything?"

"You'll have to chance it," Sylvie said.

No car seat. She wrapped Sean tightly in a blanket and laid him on the floor of the car as she drove. He had begun to cry. At the first gas station, she called Danny. Talking in an outside booth, cradling Sean, she removed her glove, and let Sean suck on her pinky finger . . . all the tics and reflexes of motherhood intact, the memory tracings.

"How did you make out?" he asked, sounding worried.

"It wasn't easy, but I have what I came for." She moved her finger in the baby's mouth and touched a hard toothy knob beneath the gum; felt idiotic with pleasure.

"I was sorry I let you go on alone," Danny was saying. "Yvonne can be so bitchy when she gets it into her head that people are doing her in. She doesn't believe that any one person, besides herself, has a stake in any given situation. Poor mutt."

"You sound condescending, Daniel. I'm surprised. The girl's in pain, for heaven's sake. You should know better than anyone."

"Well, honestly, I never promised her the moon or goddamn stars. I swear it."

"We're wasting time. Do me one more favor, please." She didn't know what one thing to ask for. She hugged the baby closer; he'd fallen asleep on her shoulder. "Will you please get someone to drive you over to the convenience store. It's just too dangerous for me to continue on these roads without a car seat for the baby."

"Jesus, I don't believe it. She let you have him?"

"Yes, she *let* me."

He was at the convenience store almost the minute she drove up. He'd come on the run—parked his pickup at Maggie's and hitched a ride the rest of the way. He climbed into the station wagon beside her and gathered the baby against him. The car was sitting in a small wash of light, and Sylvie could watch the action in his face. "God, you're sweet," he was whispering. He had unzipped Sean's hood and was rubbing his nose on the infant's cheek. "Know how sweet you are?" He was crooning a love song, Sylvie thought. He lifted his eyes to her and said, "Well, how do you like your grandchild?"

"How do you?" In the rusty light his head seemed almost Indian, motionless, calm, unsmiling. The color of his skin was nearly taupe. He looked older than his years. Even the wrinkles around his eyes had deepened. He had opened his parka to get closer to the child, had removed his ski cap, and his ears seemed bleached, like shells that had been lying out in the sand too long. She reached up and touched his face, touched the chilled rims of his ears. He caught her hand and turning it over brought it to his lips.

She gathered whatever remnants of voice were left and said, "Was it just chance that we met at Transvaal Pets?"

"It was chance then, but I intended to look you up. I thought it was time that I got to you and started some interest going in Gary and the baby. Rub a few twigs together. I had your phone number in Rosevale. Actually, I was stunned when I recognized you in the shop."

She said, "Danny, is this child yours?"

He looked at her, the illuminations of the street were condensed in his eyes, and he spoke so slowly that she thought he'd lost control of speech. "Angel told me that he wasn't mine."

They sat together for a while before she started up the car. Danny had put a cigarette in his mouth but didn't light it. She had bought some apple juice and a baby bottle at the convenience store, and Sean was making noisy, satisfied, sucking sounds in Danny's arms, his eyes open and focused on Jessica's red earmuffs hanging from the mirror.

She said after a bit, "I don't think you ought to see the baby again. It would only complicate things. Gary would mistrust me if he thought you were hanging around."

He removed the dead cigarette, tossed it out the window and said, "I think you're probably right."

They drove back to Maggie Friel's without saying much. There were a few remarks about Gary. Danny said he was sure he'd be able to get a decent lawyer on the case. A problem about bail had cropped up—the kid Cindy's uncle was pure bastard and was pressing for no bail at all. But Danny was sure the uncle couldn't get away with *that*. This wasn't some Latin American country where they bang out a new set of legal precedents whenever the spirit moves them.

Gary, the poor slob, didn't knock the kid up: nothing that serious had been put forward. He took his piece of cake like a lot of others. Of course, no one ever said that justice necessarily comes to the deserving. Oh, maybe someone did—a Mormon or some other minion of God. He guessed she was going back to Boone, to the prison, tomorrow. And she said, of course. There were several matters that she had to straighten out with Gary, and then she'd head straight back to New York with Jessica before the heavens crashed there.

Danny got out of the station wagon in front of Maggie Friel's. He had Sean in his arms. He waited for Sylvie to back more securely into her parking space, but she was thinking of Gary and what she had to do next, and she buried the rear bumper in a snowbank. Not serious. She was watching Danny snuggle the baby and kiss him. "You're some beauty," he was saying. Then he bent down quickly and touched his lips to Sylvie's cheek. He handed Sean to her and said, "You're pretty much of a beauty yourself, lady. You must have been a damn good mother, too . . . "

She was shivering from head to foot. "I doubt if Angel thought so."

"She thought so," he said earnestly. "I remember her saying once, sort of exasperated but loving, too, 'She's my lodestar, my mom, whether I like it or not.' I remember the word *lodestar* because it sounded important, like destiny or fate." He'd gotten into his pickup, and she realized that her eyes were spilling over, tiny drops crystallizing on her cheeks, and the baby, sensing something, was kicking his legs inside his snowsuit and beginning to whimper.

She climbed the steps toward the lights in Maggie's front parlor. When she opened the door, she saw Jessica skipping toward her and Maggie Friel sitting on a hassock near the fire with a box of Godiva chocolates open on her lap, and Victor. Victor was walking toward her, jaunty in a red bushwhacker's shirt, reaching for her and the baby and saying in a voice filled with wonder, "Well, well, what do we have here?"

CHAPTER 29

MARGO had to believe in retribution. Only the avenging furies, their poisoned darts hurled in her direction, could have made her feel so threatened. She wanted to fall on her knees and vow eternal goodness. I'll be a saint, she promised silently, wringing her hands, if only things come back to normal again.

Her plane arrived at Kennedy in the late afternoon, and she took a taxi home. Feliciana met her at the door. Sylvie and Jessica were still gone, Feliciana said. The hallway seemed to buckle toward her, and Margo leaned against the wall for balance. She had awakened nauseated that morning in Santa Fe, her stomach doing a long slow glissade. She'd rushed for the bathroom and toppled over the bowl, vomiting. Afterward in bed, Brill had stroked her saying, "Again? Poor baby. Do you think it was the empanadas this time?" —saying it in a solemn way, his eyes fastened to her face as if focusing a beam of thought so strong she would be forced to change her mind about going home. "I'm going back to New York today, Brill, that's definite. For a lot of reasons. I'm just too uneasy."

On the plane, she vomited again, a sudden, embarrassing throwing-up that spattered her seatmate, an elderly man from New Orleans, and sent both of them staggering to the bathrooms in the rear of the plane. Inside the tiny cubicle, as she splashed water on her neck and wrists, the stunning thought occurred: She could be pregnant! She did a hasty calculation. Yes, actually, she was three weeks late. She sank dizzily to the toilet seat and pressed her forehead against the wall. She couldn't think, didn't dare to think.

Now she cried out at Feliciana, who stood in the hallway smoothing and smoothing her apron, her ribbon-braided head bowed like a Madonna's on a Mexican candlestick, "But why are they gone this long? It's absurd! The child will have missed at least three days of school!" She was outraged.

Feliciana had begun to weep. "She call all the time. She say no worry. You no leave phone number. She no leave phone number . . . "

Zorro snivelled at her ankle, and she nudged him away. "When exactly did you last speak to Mrs. Weyman?"

"Yesterday. She say she coming home to New York right away."

"So where is she, then? Where was she calling from?"

"Some town, she say. Some town is in the Vermountains."

"Vermont. Bob Fleet. That much you've already told me."

Feliciana sighed. "Is so." Margo had Fleet's number in her office and, lifting her travel bag, headed in that direction. But Feliciana was touching her arm. "Is more I have to say . . . " She seemed about to stuff her handkerchief into her mouth. "Is Mr. Kort—"

"Michael? A letter—a cable from Mr. Kort?"

"Is Mr. Kort in hospital."

"Hospital!" Margo clung to the banister. "Where?"

"He come by plane this morning. They call and say. Is here in New York. The hospital for the eye and ear."

Running up the stairs to deposit her things, Margo made a brief call to Fleet before she went to the hospital. His jovial voice poured forth. "Hey there, Mrs. Kort. Serendipity! I've just sent some more stuff to you. Gave your assistant two large canvases." She asked him about Sylvie and Jess. "That nice lady with your pretty little girl? They were here a day or so ago. I had the impression they were heading on up to New Hampshire." *New Hampshire!* The telephone had turned to stone in her hand. "About my work now—I'll have more to show this summer after I get finished fuddling around with the Americas Cup . . . " But she had already hung up.

WALKING the slick corridor toward Michael's room, she found herself making pacts with assorted deities: if . . . if . . . please don't let him . . . But even so, these bargains could never contain her rampant sense of guilt. She prayed that whatever had happened wasn't dire. There was a nurse coming out of his room.

"I'm Mrs. Kort," she said. "How serious is he . . . ?"

"Dr. Packard will give you the details." The nurse walked away, a figure of snow evanescing into a bank of white at the busy nursing station down the hall.

Michael looked diminished in the bed. He was connected to intravenous tubes and bottles, like a spaceman hooked up to life-giving substances. The upper part of his head was covered by a helmet of bandages; his nose and chin had been swabbed with something pink. "Michael, can you hear me?"

The merest shifting of his head, and then his hand shot out from beneath the covers. "Margo? Oh, God, what a relief you're here!"

She placed her hand over his lips. "Don't talk, Michael."

But he pushed her hand away. "I'm in a hell of a mess, darling! Just don't say you warned me."

"Not a peep."

He moved his fingers over her face and said again, "I can't believe it's you. I thought you were still way out, wherever . . . " Then he added, "The consulate man, Tom Nearing, was supposed to contact you from Jidda. Did he get through?"

"No." Margo was weeping. "Someone spoke to Feliciana. I just got back from New Mexico today."

"Well, I had them make the arrangements from over there. I'm at Manhattan Eye and Ear, right?"

"Yes, oh, Michael, tell me . . ."

"What's to tell? A sophisticated little firecracker, aimed at my car window. Christ! And the minute that happened, I was shit to both the Saudis and our own guys in the embassy."

"The injury?" She was afraid to ask.

"My eye." His voice turned smoky and dim. "I may lose an eye. That's a very real possibility." He lifted the arm with the IV and set it down carefully. "I'm dealing with it. I'm dealing with it." He tried to smile but gave up. "Anyway, I'm here, and that's no small feat. The original objective of those gorillas was not to have me walk out of Saudi with just a little head wound." His voice faded. "I'm exhausted."

Dr. Packard came in and escorted her into the corridor. He spoke quickly, in flat pragmatic tones. "We advise surgical removal of the eye. In fact, there is no other choice. The damage is too severe—choroid and vitreous tissue, retina, have been extruded; the zygomatic bone of the socket is fractured. In fact, if all goes well, he'll need plastic surgery to restore the socket and upper lid for an artificial eye." She reached out and steadied herself on his arm, this distant, nondescript man in a dark suit and loafers, whose tangled stethoscope hung indifferently from his pocket. He was still talking, cataloguing possibilities. "The possibility of infection; sepsis into the brain cavity, for one thing. The brain is connected to the eye by means of the optic nerve, and in that sense brain and eye are one."

"The other eye?" She was feeling nausea again, and she folded her arms over her abdomen to contain it.

"About the other eye," Dr. Packard was saying, "we haven't done a full evaluation. There's no discrete evidence at the moment of anything negative going on. But there's always the possibility, quite likely remote, of what we call sympathetic ophthalmia." She looked up at him, barely listening now. "Surgery, then, tomorrow," he said. "No need to worry." He patted her shoulder and walked off.

In the room, Michael dozed briefly. She watched him come awake. "He says surgery tomorrow."

"Yes, I know."

"Are you frightened, Michael?"

"Not frightened," he paused. "Not frightened so much as . . . well, dismal. It's that I feel so funny about my body, as if it were a house that I was being forced to vacate for a while —forced to allow someone else to occupy. I have all this nostalgia."

She wanted desperately to tell him about Jessica and Sylvie; she needed his support, wanted to hear some sensible advice. But she didn't dare add to his burden.

She left the hospital in the early evening. Feliciana had already gone home. There was nobody to answer the phone if a call came in. But she didn't want phone calls. She wanted to see Jess asleep in her own bed. She hadn't allowed herself to think of Brill.

Upstairs, she wandered from her bedroom into Sylvie's. Everything was neat, the shades drawn. A copy of Sylvia Plath's letters to her mother lay open on the night table. She began to rummage among Sylvie's things, not really knowing what she was looking for. There was an address book on a shelf, and she scanned that. She came to Severin. Victor Severin: office, home. She called his home. An answering machine intervened. She said, "This is Margo Kort, and this is an emergency. Please phone me immediately."

She wandered down to the kitchen and made coffee. Poured a little into Zorro's dish. The dog gurgled with delight. She tossed him a dog biscuit, and he slopped it around in his coffee before gobbling it.

A half hour later, she called both the Vermont and New Hampshire police. She explained the problem, described the green station wagon, the woman, the child, and asked for an All Points Alert.

* * *

WHEN she awoke the following day, she could barely summon the will to get out of bed. Nausea again. Michael was being operated on in mid-morning. She phoned his room, heard him fumbling with the phone. "Luck, darling," she said.

"*Ciao,*" he mumbled. The nurse picked up and said he'd been sedated in his room before surgery; afterward there'd be a deep postoperative sleep lasting several hours. She was advised not to come to the hospital before the late afternoon.

Margo thought she'd go mad just sitting and waiting. Feliciana had come in, weepy. "No hear yet from the Vermountains?" Her hair was wrapped in a white napkin because she'd stopped at her church to light a candle.

It was still early in the day. All those hours ahead. Then the phone rang. Margo rushed to pick it up. "Yes," she said breathlessly. It was Blondell with a bulletin on her mother. "She's been acting real droopy, in a funny way. I think somebody ought to look at her."

"I can't come now! It's absolutely impossible! But I'll send a doctor over," Margo said. She hung up and burst into tears.

CHAPTER 30

MARGO remembered when she was a child being taken far away to an uncle's house for a visit and waking up in the dark, in a strange room where she had been put to nap; remembered the curtains billowing at the window like ghosts, the long deformed shadows of the furniture lurking against the walls, and the sense of terror as palpable as the ruffled spread under which she hid. She felt that terror now, and moving frantically through the rooms of her house, purposelessly climbing the stairs again and again, tried to deal with it.

It was mid-morning, and Feliciana brought coffee and toast, but merely looking at the food made her rush to the bathroom to be sick. She went to her bedroom and sat there, willing the phone to ring, imagining scenarios, one more doomed than the next. She thought of Jessica off somewhere out of reach, of Michael inert beneath the surgeon's knife, and waves of feeling—hysteria, nausea—rose to engulf her. She finally threw on her clothes and, leaving Feliciana to man the phone, took a cab downtown to the hospital.

The small surgical waiting room was crowded. But the

sounds around her were like white noise, a distant, thrumming background to the chaos of her own thoughts. Vermont. New Hampshire. Had there been *something* all along in Sylvie, a warped thread somewhere that she'd failed to see? And there was Michael upstairs, trapped in the bright glare of an operating room. She couldn't bear any of it.

Suddenly Dr. Packard stood before her. He held her hand and massaged it vigorously as if trying to revive her. "It's over, and your husband will be fine," he said. "We did what had to be done. But there was nothing unforeseen, no complications. We'll have him on his feet in no time at all."

"I'm glad. I'm glad," she said distractedly.

He was looking at her closely. "You seem tired. Why don't you go home? He won't be out of recovery for another three or four hours. I suggest you come back then."

She left the hospital. At a street-corner phone, she called Feliciana. Nothing. "If anyone calls, *anyone,* write down phone numbers, messages, *everything.* I'll keep calling in to check." She realized that she was crying again, decided she must keep moving, hailed a cab and directed the driver over the bridge to Queens.

"MY darling stranger!" Max said as Margo walked through the door. "Am I glad to see you!" He reached out and grasped her.

"I can only stay a little while," she warned quickly. "I've got to get back."

But he chattered away. The doctor's assistant had popped in and taken some of Celia's blood. Gave her an injection to pep her up. "She'll be OK," he said, turning his head for a kiss. She bent toward him. Family ties, she thought. He was beaming a steady signal at her through those thick lenses. Weren't one's obligations to society supposed to begin at home? Home meant Jessica, and she intoned silently for the hundredth time, Oh, let them return *today.*

She looked in on Celia, who was asleep in her wheelchair. Deep steady breaths. Decent color in her cheeks. When she was back in the living room her father said, "So tell me all the news. Don't leave anything out." Blondell came out of the kitchen, drying her hands on a dish towel. "She just scared me to death, your mother did, that's all." Blondell's long dark hair shone as if pressed between sheets of glass. Looking at her, Margo wondered when she was due. "You're not carrying twins in there, are you?" She asked. "I haven't seen you for just a couple of weeks, but, well . . . !"

Blondell turned away smiling. "The doctor say I better stop eating for a while—but I'm so hungry all the time." Margo thought of Sylvie, who was never hungry . . .

"So, in New Mexico, with Los Alamos and Alamogordo, they should have even more worries than we do in New York," her father was saying. His poppy-colored scarf was wrapped several times around his neck, and the fringed bottom flared like a Spanish dancer's. He tapped her on the shoulder with the cane. "Only two days ago I received word from Mr. Caspar Weinberger."

"Oh, really?" Was it too soon to call Feliciana again?

Max was holding up a letter on official stationery. "I wrote and said where ICBMs are concerned he is like a drunken cowboy with twitching fingers." He peered up at Margo, full of mischief. "I thought for sure the FBI would pay me a little visit."

"There must have been a more dignified way of saying the same thing," she said distantly.

"I should mince words? Does your husband, Michael, mince words? Michael once told me that when some professor in engineering school was telling him about new steel girders they would use for bridges, and how if you balance them with a certain type of cable, they could take a wind force of two hundred miles an hour, Michael said to him, 'Mr. Professor, I beg to differ. Those girders will come down if you just fart in their direction.' "

Margo said, "Oh, *please* . . . "

Her father was reading aloud: "Dear Mr. Sondheim. We value the opinions of all our citizens, but—"

Margo said, "Michael is in the hospital. He's had surgery."

"Oh ho?" Her father was folding the letter and patting it into his pocket. "Something serious?"

"I don't know." She'd crossed her fingers, under her folded arms. "He's injured his eye."

HER mother drowsed over her breakfast tray, one hand arrested in midair, clutching a piece of toast. "How do you feel?" Margo asked.

"As if I have one foot in and one foot out."

"In and out of what?"

"In my grave and out of my life," her mother said, looking at Margo as if seeing her for the first time in years. A sprinkle of tears started down her cheeks.

Margo reached out and held her hand. "Don't say that, Mother. You look as pink as a baby."

"Some baby!" But her mother's face did have an iridescent newborn glow.

The pink of baby skin. She'd have a pregnancy test as soon as she could, but she already knew the verdict. Along with the nausea of these past two days, her breasts had become tender and hard. All of it a puzzle, in a way, but only in terms of whether she wanted this baby or not. She could imagine Alessa exclaiming, "Darling, *quelle* dilemma! Well, *now* you've tied the Gordian knot!" But this was no mystery baby. Except for that first time, when it was Brill who had slipped a condom on at the last minute, she had been the one to take precautions, using a diaphragm meticulously each time she'd been with him.

But with Michael there had been a lapse, once, twice, particularly in recent weeks, before his major trips.

Once, weeks and weeks ago, he'd been staring at her all through dinner. "Have you been out in the sun?" he asked. "You have such wonderful color." Reaching past her for cream, he allowed his hand to touch her breast. Rising from the table, he had said in a sweet and sappy way, "I sort of feel like stretching out." He'd wrapped an arm around her waist and pushed her up the stairs. For a while, they hadn't been together that way all that much. Sometimes she had used the simple, tried-and-true headache ploy. She hated the idea of two men bedding her at once and tried to rub the image from her mind. On that particular night, Michael had locked the door, shoved her on the bed and undressed them both. One lamp was lit, and he left it on. "I really want to get a look at you, darling. We always seem to be scrambling around in the dark."

He was nuzzling her as he spoke, licking her cheek and neck with long strokes of his tongue. Like Zorro, she thought moronically. Michael was murmuring from her lower regions. Foolish babble. Not his kind of talk, and she felt a dip of fear. Was he giving out some kind of code? He said, "You smell like apricots."

She observed, "I'm told the sperm of men who eat only vegetables has the taste of peach."

"I could give up meat for *your* pleasure . . ." His voice was like smoke in her ear. He settled on top of her, a long dreamy, attenuated fuck. She remembered her diaphragm in the bed-side table a million miles away. Too late. The racketing inside her had begun. She couldn't reach out and stop the proceedings now. Anyway, maybe in her own perverse way, she'd meant to generate the larger complication.

Her mother's head was nodding, and Margo asked softly, "Mother, are you OK?" Margo glanced at her watch again. Only fifteen minutes had passed.

Celia seemed to be falling asleep, but then she suddenly said, "When you were born, it was nice. We had tried for years. I thought that Max was doing it with all the girls at Bravalinsky's, underneath the pelts. Making his sperm weak. All the machine operators were getting pregnant but not me."

"Did you really think *that*?" Her mother seemed so sad and clear.

"Once he went to a wedding, and they mistook him for the groom. It was in Lower New York before we were married.

Everyone had gotten drunk before the ceremony. It was my opinion he slept with the bride."

"Now, that's really wild!" There were old photographs in sepia gravure of Celia's and Max's parents and grandparents on the wall, anchoring them all to lineage. She closed her eyes.

"Then later you came along, such a lovely child. It was a miracle."

"Tell me more. Tell me how lovely." She craved to be transported to a more innocent time. Should she call Feliciana again? No, she would simply go home and wait, pace, climb walls. Later she would go back to the hospital. Celia was speaking now of cunning baby shoes, later dipped in bronze, of sweaters knitted with big needles for bulk, and diapers laid to dry in the sun.

"I did everything willingly," her mother said, "no matter how Max remembers it. I practically chewed up your food and put it in your mouth like with a little bird."

"I was a real valuable kid."

Her mother swallowed drily. "So why doesn't all this go on tape, with Stanford?"

Margo shook her head. "I don't have my tape recorder today." Celia's useless hands made an odd motion, as if she were shuffling invisible cards. Her cheeks looked unusually bright. A circle of rose was planted on either side of her hawkish nose. Margo wondered, had she loved her mother? She supposed so. But now she was already letting go. Preparing herself. Conceiving of her mother whispering away, crossing a dark divide alone. And she sanctioned it. Perhaps she was being punished for *that*.

Gertrude came in for the afternoon shift, and Blondell prepared to leave. Margo took Blondell aside. "When exactly is your due date?"

"The doctor says June." The large mound beneath her dress quivered as she bent for her coat.

"Do you have what you need?"

"Yes. Mr. Max always asks. He's really good."

Gertrude was saying, "My Langston is getting closer to the big time every day." She pulled out a photograph that showed Langston and four young men in purple satin windbreakers with *THE TRAINS* scrolled across their chests.

Margo said tiredly, ". . . really, taking them to the Felt Forum in an ambulette! I'm surprised you didn't go to a disco afterward."

Max had come stumbling in, and now he interrupted. "Don't blame the women. I had a taste to see the world." He leaned toward her on his cane, staring at Celia, who was nodding off to sleep. "Nothing worse than usual happened."

Margo steered Max back into the living room, made another phone call to Feliciana. "No one person called," Feliciana said in her small frightened voice.

Her father was saying, "I bet you're thinking your mother looks terrific right now. But looks deceive. The doctor has his eye on something. When her face gets rosy, it's not roses. It has something to do with extra blood cells."

Margo had something else on her mind. "Has Sylvie Weyman been around? Doing her job?"

"Last week, two times. She paid the women, ordered a case of incontinent pads . . ." He offered a list of odds and ends.

"How did she seem?" Margo asked.

"Like a sweetheart. How did you ever come across her?"

"I wish I really knew." She wanted to mention Jessica to him. Wanted to say, "Daddy, I'm so frightened, and Michael's in the hospital with this dreadful surgery. . . ." She touched his cheek, said, "Now I *really* have to go."

They were standing at the door, his perky, talcumed face at eye-level with her own. "I know we cost you a bundle," he said.

"It's OK, Max. It's only money."

"You're a good person, sweets. I mean it," he said.

She bent to kiss him and said, "Oh, sure."

CHAPTER 31

MICHAEL felt himself crawling up the side of a cliff. There was an eagle on his head tearing at his face. He tried to shake it off and plummeted back again into scorching dark. His head, his face were scorched. The eagle continued to tear away. Michael flapped his arms and careened backward, passing through elemental gravity; hung upside down. Dragging forward, he pursued the upward climb. Birds swooped, pecked at his skull. The eagle's claws were bracketing his ears. He climbed faster, flailing at the bird. Swifter, into sweeter air, softer air on his nose and lips. The smell of vanilla was all around. He was passing through a vanilla-tinted cloud. There were whispers in his head, a voice calling, "Michael, Michael." The bird hung on.

He thought he'd answered, shouting across a ravine, his voice thudding in his ear: "Here I am. I'm here."

"Michael, you must wake up now. You can't keep falling asleep. You've been out of recovery for hours. It's four o'-clock."

Margo's voice. He heard but lost it, climbed toward her once again. Closer now, but not close enough. He slept.

Awoke again to hear her calling him still. "Come on, Michael, please wake up." She seemed to be inside his ear.

He coughed, dragged out the syllables, "All right, I've got it." The pain was staggering. He groped for her hand. "Fucking pain . . ."

"It's going to be all right . . ."

"All right my ass." The fact was, he'd lost an eye. He slept again. This time when he awoke his head was clear. But he was overwhelmed by the dark. "Margo!" he shouted in terror. She took his hands. "Am I blind?"

"No, I swear it. It's only one eye. The doctor said the other would be as good as ever. They'll start taking the bandages off in a few days. You'll see for yourself."

The next time he awoke, he found she'd adjusted the bed so that he was partially sitting up. The radio was playing chamber music behind him. The pain was like a storm cloud lurking in the distance. She held a fruit drink to his mouth.

"All the comforts of home," he managed.

"Not quite." She didn't say anything about Jessica and Sylvie.

He was quiet. Then he said, "When this is over . . ."

"Yes, when this is over," she repeated, wondering what he meant.

A nurse stepped into the room—ebony skin, hair done in an elaborate tassel of braids. "Your private duty," she said. "The name's Miss Pink."

Margo went out into the hall to call Feliciana. Nothing new.

Back in the room, Miss Pink had gone for Michael's medication. "Miss Pink is not so pink," Margo said, whispering in his ear.

He managed a smile. "Screw Miss Pink. I'm sort of hungry, but not for her." His lips were regaining color, and she bent to kiss him. "I wouldn't mind a roast beef sandwich. I don't really know what I want. How's Jess?"

"OK, Michael . . ." She hesitated—but it was still not time.

"Actually, I feel queasy from the anesthetic. There's a Ferris wheel in my head that's still doing its number."

"I know." Her own stomach was churning. "I have some saltines in my purse."

"Saltines? Are you making it with squirrels, these days? What time is it?" he asked.

"Six o'clock. Michael, there's something I want to say." There was a stillness in her voice that frightened him, and he hoped she wasn't about to turn confessional in the middle of everything else. He just didn't have the strength to go through that right now. Dealing with words. Hearing details.

That day he'd rummaged in her pocketbook looking for a quarter for the parking meter, he saw it. A pale blue compact. It looked as if it might have held a powder puff, but he knew there was no powder puff inside. It held her diaphragm. He lost a pulse or two when he took it out, touched it, as if it were the skin of a private part.

"You have a lot of clutter in your purse," he'd remarked that evening.

There was a breath of silence between them and then her clear-eyed gaze. "I was at my gynecologist's . . ." He felt foolish, didn't want to hear anything more. Didn't want to know. A man has a right *not* to know.

"Don't you want to listen?" she was asking now. She was still nibbling on that cracker; he could hear the crunching sound.

"Hey, I can keep you in croissants, remember?"

When he fell silent, she seemed to understand. "All right. No more talk. Whatever I had to say will keep."

This time when she called Feliciana, there had been a phone message. A Mr. Victor, Feliciana said. "He sorry he missed you."

"Victor Severin! Did you tell him I'd phone him right back?"

"Yes, but he say he leaving for out of the town. He call again."

Back in the room, Michael seemed to be sleeping. His

mouth had fallen open, and she could hear the silky rustle of his breath. She sent Miss Pink out for her supper and sat close to Michael, looking at him. Strong chin, full, bitten lips; it was his habit to make a point and then chew his lower lip, waiting for what he'd said to sink in. Brill's lips curved naturally into a smile.

That last morning in Santa Fe, he'd held her arms behind her back and kissed her hard. He was going on to San Diego, he said. "But who knows? I might end up back in the Bronx with my wolves." Would she be glad? he asked. She closed her eyes against the image of his face so close to hers.

How do you walk away from a good man? It sounded like a song of Lena Horne's. She could see her belting it out, hanging over a microphone in a patch of glitter, sobbing.

Had she ever seriously thought of walking out on Michael? she wondered. She didn't know. With Brill, it was like trying to cement the pieces of a dream together and make it real. Impossible. Walk out of one life and into another? With another unmanageable man? A seminomadic life? And where would Jessica fit into all of that? Or Michael? She wasn't "current" enough for such goings-on.

She wasn't exactly sure how she had gotten involved with Brill; he seemed to be showing her the other side of a coin, the other side of herself. He made her feel lawless, and she liked it. But there could be no future for her with Brill, because the best of her would be buried in his life. She'd be another relic signifying the variety of his interests, something to be lovingly handled when he returned from his river trips or his wolf studies at some zoological station. Yet another travelling man. In this image she'd be den mother to Spunk. Jessica was nowhere on the scene.

Michael shifted, started awake, said, "Margo?" and fell off to sleep again. In a way it had all proved simple; it was not just the fact of her being pregnant that gave a lambent glow to the problem. It was something else—she didn't have the talent, strength, or taste to despise herself.

Miss Pink came into the room with an assortment of pills.

"Bedtime snacks," she sang out in a chummy voice. Michael woke again, propped himself up to swallow the pills. He called Margo's name.

"I'm here."

"Come over where I can touch you." She sat down on the bed. "I think you ought to go home now . . ." He fingered the bandages around his eyes. "This awful thing . . ." He pulled her face down to his, murmuring drowsily, "When I'm out of this, what I think . . ." His tongue couldn't shape the words. ". . . there's Jess and you . . . ," he seemed to say before he slept.

She had barely entered the foyer when the phone rang. An official-sounding voice said, "Mrs. Kort? Vermont police, here. If you can come on up to the station in Brattleboro, we have something for you."

CHAPTER 32

IT was falling into place. She would borrow Victor's Rabbit and drive over to Boone to talk to Gary once more. No matter what the outcome in Boone, she and Jessica and Sean would leave for New York that day.

Maggie was rattling around in the kitchen with both children. Jessica had asked for blueberry muffins, and their sugary fragrance wafted through the house. Sean was in the laundry basket with a bottle of milk. Melvin, underneath the kitchen stove, was nibbling on a parrot-seed cake. At the moment, Victor and she were alone in the bedroom. Victor was gazing out at new snow blanketing the driveway, the entire scene tinted mauve because the early morning sun had not quite penetrated the pine trees. "Snow makes everything seem so new," he said. "Even decaying houses look as though they've been given a fresh coat of paint."

"Yes, they do, don't they," she said, feeling pleased and full, as if she'd painted the scene for him herself.

When she'd walked in and seen him last night, it was all so strange. There was the fuss and bustle over Sean. Maggie ran for a large laundry basket. Jessica stood by solemnly

observing that Sean smelled funny. They'd all hung around
the kitchen sink and bathed and changed the baby. Jessica
wanted to do the powdering (Maggie's talc). Sean stared at
them each in turn, looking dazzled but fearless in the midst
of the small commotion. "His tummy has a shape like bread,"
Jessica said. His tummy. The silky whorl of navel and below,
the little knob of flesh quivering on its frail stalk. This little
boy holding gravely steady under her gaze, transmitting messages. Angel's.

Maggie had given Victor a bedroom under the eaves. Sylvie
went to him after Jessica was asleep, taking Sean, also asleep,
with her in the laundry basket. Victor had gotten into bed to
wait for her, and she slipped in and wound her arms around
him. "Pretty much of a detective, you are," she said.

"You left clues. That artist fellow in Cozzens was a help.
Maggie was just pure fate. I was looking for a room for the
night, and someone at the diner down the highway pointed
me at her."

"Why?" she said after a moment.

"You mean why am I here?" He moved restlessly, rubbing
his toes slowly back and forth across her ankles. He fiddled
with her flannel nightgown, pushing the long sleeves up
above her elbows. "All this downy stuff," he grumbled. He
bunched the hem of her nightgown in his hand. "Let's see.
Do you have those woolly leg warmers on underneath . . ."

She twined her arms around his neck. Sean hiccupped and
turned in the basket. She said to Victor, "I wasn't all that
surprised to see you. I mean, I didn't anticipate it, and yet
when I saw you, I thought, of course!"

He pulled her tightly toward him. "I was getting worried.
There was that freeze between us. And I didn't know what
your emotional state had come to. And then there was a
miniseries on TV about a woman who leapt over a cliff. I
forget exactly why. But there was a lover who walked out,
shattering whatever was left of her ego. They interrupted to
sell Ragu Spaghetti Sauce, but I wasn't fooled by the script,
the old actuarial bloodhound on the trail. Girl meets boy, girl
loses boy . . . Anyway, I had the bizarre notion that a pro-

longed silence from me would be the final straw for you. Actually, it was Feliciana who steered me to Vermont."

"You're slightly mad, as usual."

"Do you approve?" Not mad, she thought again. All this dear buffoonery. His way . . .

The window shade was up, framing a patch of stars. He was on his elbow staring at her through veils of moonlight. He tapped the collar of her nightgown. "Do we really need this thing in bed with us?"

"Well, since you mention it . . ." Wrapped in each other's arms, she cautioned him not to make noise. "Maggie Friel's bedroom is right below us. And let's not wake Sean."

"I'm not one of those Indian levitators, you know." But he pulled her beneath him, fitted himself over her, mouth to mouth, like people dragged from a smoking ruin, resuscitating each other. She was almost his length. "Victor," she breathed, "you are just right."

They must have slept. At one point she opened her eyes and found him sitting up in bed. She stretched toward him and said, "Oh, I'm glad you're here."

He kissed the tips of her fingers slowly. After a while she asked, "The film. How's it going?"

"Oh, well—it's proving to be an experience. Everything moves so slowly." The production company he'd hired was just beginning to put together props, script, a cast . . .

"And the substance of the film?"

"Well, there . . ." He hesitated. "I don't know. We get Kesselmann's wife into the hospital, lugging that suitcase. She has a face like an iron horse. But when she enters his room, the predetermined elements in the script just fall away." He banged his pipe on the ashtray. "I thought of this film as something like describing the family life of the killer wasp. But somehow that wasp . . ." He turned and stroked her hair. "Enough of that. You. What do you plan to do?" She explained once more about Gary and how she had found Sean.

"You haven't answered my question."

"I want the baby."

CHAPTER 33

GARY greeted her with sullen reserve. Except for the guards, they were alone in the visitors' room. "I was thinking about you all night," he said coldly. "You just turned up out of nowhere. Lady Bountiful offering bail money and good advice and a lot of phony concern."

"I'm sorry, Gary. I didn't mean to be phony."

"Oh, sure! Suddenly you're goddamn in love with me. You can't do enough. You've gone biblical. Your heart is spilling over with sympathy. You're choking on it. *Me!* The guy you hold responsible for everything . . . How was it? How did you say it back there in the hospital a million years ago? Never mind what you said, it was the way you looked at me. That *look*—like putting a mirror inside my brain and reflecting what was already there, because I was looking at myself the same way."

"You're not going to hold that against me? A look?"

"You're fucking right, *a look*! Listen, I felt your scorn from day one. Angel must have told you once that I was beginning to write poetry. Because you wrote to her soon after, a letter full of sanctimonious shit. You said, 'To be *good,* an artist, or anyone else, has to be committed to an *ideal* of himself.' Implying me, of course, meaning me as some kind of vermin metamorphosing backward into an even lower form."

"I don't remember that. I never thought of you that way. Angel told me about the hard times you had when you were a child, and I felt sorry."

"For *her,* being mixed up with a whacked-up clod."

It was going all wrong. She didn't want a major confrontation, not here, not now. She felt sick but tried again. "Angel was an only child. The one steadily good thing for me. She was what kept me going during some terrible years of my own. I wanted so much for her. So much more than I'd been able to achieve. Mothers are legendary for that . . . some of them. I wanted to see her be her full self. I guess I held on too long, said too much. It's not a defense. But I can be frightened, too."

"No, lady, not you. You always knew where the triggers were, and which ones to pull to set off something negative between Angel and me. I swear to God, if I didn't know better, I'd even think you planted Daniel, the friendly neighbor, in the middle of our back meadow . . ."

"You give me too much credit . . ."

"Visiting us with your boyfriend, Victor, all spruced up like ambassadors from a very snazzy country examining the life-style of a minor cultural group." He stopped suddenly and looked at her. "Anyway what did *you* have to be frightened about?"

"Think about it for a while." She started to reach out her hand to touch him, saw his face and withdrew. "Let's be objective, Gary. I don't think we have any choice but to be friends."

She told him what was being done to get him released from jail. She would guarantee the bail. He'd have to take it from there, work it out with a lawyer, but there was money to help him. Some money of hers that had belonged to Angel and now ought to go to him.

"Not to me. To Sean," he said. "You saw Sean over at Yvonne's yesterday?"

She didn't bother with the details. "Yes."

"So what did you think? A honey, isn't he? Angel's skin and hair." He pressed his fists to his eyes and then looked up blinking. His mouth had softened to the small shadow of a smile, and she imagined that smile offered tentatively to strangers, when he was a child.

"He's a miracle, Gary. But I'm surprised you'd leave him with someone like Yvonne, someone so . . . so unstable."

"Oh, Yvonne—she's mostly OK. Anyway, it was only temporary; she never had him all that much. I was on the scene, keeping an eye on things—until I got messed up with this . . ." He looked sharply at her. "All right, let's have it. What's going on in your head? What are you cooking up?"

She took a deep breath and plunged ahead, speaking quickly. "Listen, Gary, you ought to let me have Sean for a while, until you get your current problems untangled. At least until you straighten yourself out and manage to get your life together in a more permanent way. Next to you, I'm the one who cares about him most, not those sitters you pick up all over the place, people like Yvonne."

He had half risen from his seat; his eyes had begun to flash. He said, "Like hell!" And her heart sank. "I knew this would be your next move. I was waiting for it. But let's get this straight. The baby's mine. He's *my* kid. He stays with *me.*" He looked her over for a minute and then said in a lower voice, "Look, I want an honest answer on this one. Did Danny put you up to this—coming here and trying to take the baby away?"

She allowed herself to be angry. "That's absurd and insulting! Danny's not in this at all. He has nothing to do with Sean. For God's sake, don't let your imagination eat you up!" She paused, and then said clearly, "And Gary—the baby's *mine,* too. Remember it. So let's not be adversaries; I don't think you have anything to gain if we are."

He sat back slowly, his eyes fixed on her face.

She said quietly, "It's simple common sense; it's what's best for Sean. When all of this is over, if it's Oregon you want, well, go out there. Try it for a while and see if it meets your expectations before you think about dragging the baby across the country. Meanwhile let him stay with me. When you're ready for him, we'll work it out." She didn't say, I have a blood claim. I will look much stronger in court, Gary, than you. Even with your name on a birth certificate, you would have to prove parenthood, fitness, worth. She kept the pressure low. She knew he was like celluloid, inflammable, and she blew softly to cool the potential heat.

In the end it was the reasonableness of her argument that finally brought him around. He cracked his knuckles in succession twice. "You're right, I suppose, for now anyway," he said at last. "I guess Sean will be better off with you . . . with family . . ." There was a stitch in his voice. "But it's temporary; be sure you understand that!"

She kept her mouth steady. Her eyes felt warm. She said, "We'll be in Rosevale, Gary, whenever you're ready."

CHAPTER 34

THEY were on the highway heading south, Sean in a car seat that Victor had bought in a local K Mart after Sylvie phoned him from the prison, Jessica belted in beside him. Sylvie was tensely scanning the road, worrying about the late start they'd made, when she suddenly heard sirens building up behind her. A state police car signalled her to the side of the road. She knew she hadn't exceeded the speed limit. Victor, when he'd left for New York earlier, had said, "You have a lot of precious cargo there, so drive carefully."

She blew him a kiss. "Do you really think I need to be reminded!"

The trooper pulled in behind her, leaving his whirling lights on. He walked around the station wagon to examine the license plate. She was digging into her wallet for her driver's license, but he didn't seem especially interested in that. He looked into the back at the children and said, "OK, lady. Nothing funny now. Just start her up and follow me."

SHE thought how tenuous the line was between sanity and the absurd. She was standing at the sergeant's desk, holding Sean to her shoulder and Jessica by the hand, all of them still bundled up in ski clothes, Melvin out in the car wrapped in his electric blanket. She had on the earmuffs Jessica had made for her; no wonder she was having trouble hearing what the sergeant had to say. She pulled the earmuffs off and unzipped her jacket and the children's. Her hair, which hung in a loose knot on her shoulders, had come undone, and with it her composure. The sergeant was aiming a ballpoint pen at her. "We have an All Points Alert on you . . ."

"On me?" But then she knew. Margo had returned.

"Look! I can clear this up. I have to make a phone call immediately." She tried to present an authoritative image.

The officer continued to concentrate on the papers in front of him. "We'll have to book you until identification is made. Then we'll have a magistrate look at the charges." He stared at her, dubious, but standing fast. "You'd better figure out how you're going to prove who *that* baby belongs to," he said, indicating Sean. "We know you're under suspicion of kidnapping the little girl. You sure have been a busy lady."

"Am I kidnapped?" Jessica asked, delighted.

Sylvie, rattled now but earnest, tried to explain to the officer. Surely the man wasn't a fool. "No one has been kidnapped. The little girl is in my care. I work for her parents."

"We know that. That's why you're here." His voice was elaborately patient.

"But this is a misunderstanding," she persisted. "The baby is Sean Markson, my grandchild. The little girl, Jessica—"

"Jessica is the object of a two-state search." His voice had become sharp. "Now you just relax and attend to those children until we have some additional data on you."

"Wait till Charlotte hears this," Jessica said, all smiles. "All she ever got was run over by a grocery cart in D'Agostino's."

TIME passed slowly. Sylvie had someone send out for a hamburger for Jessica, milk and a jar of baby food for Sean. The three of them had been placed in an office with a matron standing by. The matron sipped coffee and looked them over carefully from time to time, as though they might dematerialize. "If you want, I'll hold the baby for you a little bit," she offered. Sylvie politely refused. Jessica curled into a chair and fell asleep. Sylvie fed and changed Sean, who was fascinated by the activity around him.

Nearly three hours passed. Sylvie asked to be allowed to go out to the car and check on Melvin. He seemed unduly quiet, his little scimitar of beak pressed tightly shut. She unplugged his blanket and brought him back into the building with her. "You asking to bring that bird in here?" the sergeant said. "How do I know he's not diseased or something?" But in the end he merely turned away, muttering.

And then Margo was suddenly there. She had flown from New York to Boston and taken a limousine the rest of the way. She rushed in and saw Jessica first, "Oh, baby, baby! Oh, my God! Thank heaven!" Then she turned to Sylvie and immediately loosed a geyser of rage. Her small frame was quivering. "How could you have done such an unbelievable thing. What was in your mind? You said you'd be gone for a day or two. You were going to the Berkshires, you said, then suddenly you were in Vermont, and then New Hampshire. Who gave you the authority? I really want to know that! How could you have assumed that you could simply travel around New England with my child for five days without expressly receiving instructions from *me*? It was as good as kidnapping. It was the same thing—taking someone else's child, doing what you pleased . . . !" She clutched Jessica to her, shaking with emotion.

Sylvie let her speak and then tried to explain, but Margo had burst into tears. "I think you are a very disturbed woman," she said, "and I'm not interested in your explanations. I don't know what I could have been thinking of, allowing you to be with Jess." She had sunk down on a bench, drawing Jessica into her lap. Jess was enumerating the high points of their trip. "I was on a snowmobile," she said. "And

I saw a yogurt factory; they were making blueberry . . ." The matron poured tea from a thermos and urged it on Margo, who took it and sipped, tears running down her cheeks. "I just don't know what to say. I feel so *betrayed*. I feel like pressing charges. Maybe I will. And whose baby is that?"

Sylvie came over, sat on the bench beside Margo and turned Sean toward her. He had just finished his bottle, and he had the trancelike inwardness of a small Buddha. "My grandson," Sylvie said. "Everything that's happened stems from him."

Margo looked at her and then at Sean, who was now examining his fingers, making slushy sibilant sounds of approval. "All right," she said, "let's have this from the beginning."

LATER, driving toward New York, Margo said, "You never told me how your daughter died. And I never knew, of course, about the child. You're a very private person, Sylvie, and I tried to respect that." Sylvie glanced at her. She had been so full of determination with the Brattleboro police, had held her ground before the sergeant, talking rapidly, clearly, her voice at a higher pitch than usual. She said there had been a terrible misunderstanding on her part. She had been out of town and had misinterpreted certain events. She wanted to drop all charges. "Well, listen, madam"—the officer was blustery with annoyance—"you don't reverse the wheels of the legal process all that easily. Not in this state you don't. Now this woman is booked, and she stays booked."

"But it was *my* mistake," Margo insisted. "It had nothing to do with her." Then someone from the magistrate's office arrived and reviewed the situation. At Sylvie's request a call had been put through to Victor, who had just that minute walked into his apartment. There were discussions back and forth. Other parties were contacted, including Gary in Boone. The relevant New York police precincts were reached to see if Sylvie had a previous record. In the end she was released on Victor's recognizance until the charges were officially dropped; a matter of paperwork, she was told.

Now Sylvie said, "I had never really allowed myself to think about Sean." She glanced in back of the car. Everyone was asleep. "It was a way of hanging on, I suppose, not thinking, not letting my mind crawl into a no-man's-land. Swimming served a purpose, and not eating. And of course, taking the job with you. I suppose it was a conscious effort to stay slightly exhausted and draggy and estranged from everything I knew."

Margo was nodding her head.

"But then in Transvaal Pets, I met a man who'd known them—Angel and Gary—and everything rushed in. I was terrified that if I didn't act quickly, Gary and Sean would disappear forever. We'd made efforts to find them before, but now it seemed especially urgent. I could imagine them dissolving in thin air, disappearing completely as if they'd fallen through a crack in the earth."

"Fallen through a crack in the earth . . . it has its positive side," Margo said. "Just being able to seal yourself off from everything." She told Sylvie what had happened to Michael.

Sylvie stared at her. "You're lucky," she said. "Losing Michael like that would have been a real disaster. Particularly with you away and all . . ."

Margo murmured, "Sylvie, please don't." Then she added, "I'm not the best person. I guess you've figured that out."

"Why *should* you be? And who do you imagine *I* am to judge?"

"I create a certain impression. Agreeable. A good sport. But even *I* don't know what I'm capable of." She was silent for a while, then turned, and for an instant her gaze held Sylvie's. "I believe I'm pregnant, on top of everything else— or maybe because of everything else."

The highway unwound before them like a coil of wire. Sylvie said sharply, "Watch the road!"

After another silence Margo said, "I *know* it's Michael's child."

* * *

THEY were on the lower Taconic Parkway when Sylvie remarked, "It's come to an end."

"What has?"

Jessica, suddenly awake, asked, "What happened to my pizza? Didn't Victor promise me pizza?" and promptly fell back to sleep. Sean slept so silently it seemed he wasn't breathing at all.

"My career as household assistant."

The car swerved, and Margo leaned forward through the dark as though trying to penetrate a dimly perceived vista. "Jesus. I hadn't really thought that through." She seemed taken aback. "Still, maybe not. Maybe we could rearrange the whole thing. Design new specs for the job. I could get additional help for both of us. You'll need help with Sean. Maybe we could combine forces on several levels, work, kids. Don't make any hasty decisions, Sylvie. Promise me that. Look, I've barely gotten to know you!"

Sylvie was thinking how strange it all was. She was in a time warp still, but now she could imagine herself reaching the outer boundaries and catching up.

CHAPTER 35

ANOTHER autumn. The air shimmered with heat and early September sounds: an endless vibrato of beetles, jays screaming in the mimosa branches that overhung the roof. Sylvie had been reading on the screened porch. She was doing a research assignment for Michael on architectural visionaries. Michael had moved from offshore ports to more generalized "technologies of living," as he put it. He spoke of great translucent domes—"If only Bucky Fuller were still alive!"—enclosing miniature cities, where the elements of day-to-day life would be dealt with in extraordinary ways.

In a book called *Eccentric Spaces* she read that cities seem to be the oldest things on earth, "making us feel that life was here long before hills, woods or the sea." The author implied that cities give a continuity to life, to consciousness, without which the notion of landscape alone dwindles. She wondered how Michael's vision of domed communities would fulfill that need—the need for continuity. If she could run a thread backward through her own life, she would stitch it to everyone who had mattered—Arthur along with Victor, Gary, Sean, Angel, Angel above all. And she would wind herself in that thread, a cocoon of her history, her own archeology, through which she might one day be deciphered.

Meanwhile it had begun to rain, a distinct tap-tapping on the porch roof, as if each drop had been minted separately and flung earthward. Sean's yellow plastic wading pool was lying face up on the lawn. His little horse on wheels was on its side; so was the musical pull-toy duck. Gary had brought the duck when he'd come by three months ago. Sean had just begun to take a few tentative steps. The duck played "The Farmer in the Dell," and Sean dragged it along the floor behind him, crowing with pleasure. Gary had said, "He's such a terrific kid."

"He surely is," she'd said, praying that the tense equilibrium between them would hold. Gary was on his way to Oregon. He said he'd been put in touch with a small press and bindery in one of the coastal towns. Blue Falcon Press. He wanted to try his hand at writing and then printing and binding his own work. "A little cottage industry. Any comments?" He gave a self-deprecating laugh. "There are things inside me that just ought to surface, somehow . . . I don't know. Maybe everything that happens in a person's life is his own fault. Do you believe that?"

"No. I think fate or chance weighs in heavily, and then comes free will."

"If Angel had lived," he said, "I bet she never would have stayed with me. She would have gone off eventually to be a veterinarian or a biochemist . . . something like that."

His face went blank, and Sylvie said quickly, "On the other hand, if she had gone, she might have wanted you to go too."

Victor was saying, "If Oregon is disappointing, there's always the lively East. Less laid back, more adrenaline in the air . . ." Sylvie noticed that he, too, was purposely focusing away from Sean.

Gary seemed lost in thought; then he asked, "Heard from Danny Baum?" She pretended he'd asked a nonsense question and answered in kind. "Oh, sure. All the time. Sometimes twice in one day." Actually she had heard from Danny only once, a brief note. "I think about you and Sean all the time, and how things have worked out, and how Angel would have approved, for now, anyway . . ."

Gary said to Sylvie, "Look, I'm grateful you went to all that trouble for me in Boone. At least I'd like to think it was for me." He spoke slowly as if each word were hard for him. He'd received a suspended sentence with a few strings attached. But no real sweat, he told her, "not even the months they made me spend in a work program." He looked at her more closely. "Everything that I'm doing now is aimed at straightening myself out for Sean. You understand that, don't you?"

She said, "Yes," and it seemed to comfort him.

When Gary took off for Portland a day later, he said nothing more about Sean or himself except, "I'll write." Her sense of reprieve was so great, she shivered for half a day.

She still swam each morning, fifty-two lonely aggressive laps, her mind hollow and resting, the towel attendant in her glass cubicle still gazing out at her from time to time but watchful now in a less serious way. The floor of the pool yielded nothing, and she swam not as an explorer of anguish but as a traveller from the realm of the curious.

Tania said when she visited, "Nothing like a baby around to make you feel fifteen years younger. Right?" Wrong, Sylvie thought. She felt ancient, slippery as a stone rubbed smooth by time, but resilient, too, her ear tuned to the small grenades of memory nesting in her. Perhaps all the swimming had put her in condition for the new daily assault on her energies— Sean, up at dawn, in perpetual motion.

"I rather like playing mom and dad," Victor had said. He had finally given up his apartment. His belongings were merged with hers. In the downstairs hall closet his Burberry scarf was draped over a hook like a heraldic banner. He now had a video camera and cassette recorder. He was filming their progress—the three of them.

Tania's baby had arrived prematurely three weeks before. She called from the hospital and chatted as if they were at lunch at The Perfect Carrot. "I was working on a deal in Farms and Acreage; the office was planning a baby shower; Louden had hinted at something especially lucrative for me. And lo! The prince arrives!" But her voice was full and happy. "The baby's going to be just fine. We're naming him Nicholas. Little Nicky. And Larry is absolutely delirious."

"Everything pretty stable between you two?"

"Like a rock, for now anyway. But I'm a fatalist! If we fall apart again, at least there'll be the baby." Her voice became conspiratorial. "When my mother saw Nicky and asked who he looked like, Larry piped in, 'Are you blind or something? Who does he look like? The kid has my nose! My mouth!'

"What do you think, Sylvie?" For a moment the chirpiness had evaporated. "I keep imagining that somehow you-know-who will find out and want to come around and bother us. Order a blood test, something. I get so frightened."

"Leave it alone, Tania."

"Sylvie?"

"Maybe someday you'll tell him."

VICTOR had come out on the porch. "Are you ready for the preview?"

"Just about. I wanted to finish a few more index cards for Michael. Sean still asleep?"

"He's good for another hour. I'll call you when I'm ready." He reached over and kissed the top of her head. "Christ," he said, "I feel as if I were seventeen again!" He bent jauntily to light his pipe. "I think the film will blow your mind," he said and went back inside.

She gathered up the index cards and notebooks and placed them in a folder marked "Michael Kort." Her admiration for Michael had grown enormously in these past months. When she saw him after he returned home from the hospital, she tried not to let her feeling of shock at his appearance show. He was resting in a chair. Part of his face and head was bandaged. He was in a sweat suit and sneakers, and he looked diminished, reduced to sharp planes and angularities. His shoulder blades stuck out like rudders. "Michael, Michael," she said, abandoning any pretense of formality.

"Come on, Sylvie, you can throw up your hands and scream. I've told Margo to do it. Margo, scream for Sylvie." It was a weak joke, but he stayed with it. "They say the damage is not as extensive as it first appeared. My face will merely look more 'rugged' than before." He breathed deeply and looked away.

Jessica giggled. "I'm making an eye patch for Zorro," she said, "and a little one the size of a Velamint for Melvin." Jessica had grabbed Sylvie's hand and clung to it the moment Sylvie came in. Zorro rushed in circles around her feet, making ecstatic snuffly sounds.

"I have to recover from 'insult to the corpus totalis,' according to my asshole doctors," Michael said. Then he added, "Forgive me, Sylvie. I guess I can wait the two or three months they say it will take before the old machine is running again. And be grateful, too."

Later, sipping orange juice in the kitchen, Margo said, "I can see his mind working. He has this thing now about environment and humanism. Well, it's pretty lofty stuff!" She lifted her hands in bewilderment. "How can that possibly *not* become global, sooner or later? You tell me!" It was the end of her second month, and her face had a soft dewy bloom.

Glancing through the doorway into the dining room, Sylvie saw a tooled-leather belt with silver medallions hanging on the wall near the bowl of teeth. Margo, watching Sylvie, told her she had bought it in New Mexico. "It was so dandified and macho, the way the early Spaniards must have been—the way the toreadors are today," she said. "I couldn't pass it up. Michael thought he'd feel too self-conscious wearing it. But he said, 'Let's hang it anyway, as an artifact.' "

"Is he happy about the baby?" Sylvie asked.

"He's quiet about it. He never really wanted more than one child. He said to me, though—it was strange—'Any kid of yours is a kid of mine.' I picked up with, 'Any kid of mine would have to be a kid of yours.' We could have followed that with a soft-shoe routine. 'Yes, sir, that's my baby!' Oh, hell, Sylvie. He's no fool. But no questions asked. We just left it at that." She studied Sylvie's face. "That man from the zoo —Brill Wallace; I've been—well—in touch with him once or twice. He's going away soon. Something came up in San Diego, a study of the psychosocial nature of wolves. He has this thing for wolves, you know. Apparently they gave him an offer he couldn't refuse—so it's good-bye New York." She turned the glass slowly in her hand. After a while she said, "Well, he's going to San Diego, and I'm going to have my baby."

Jessica pulled Sylvie into the atrium, where Melvin sat on an open perch among the dieffenbachia. He gurgled, "Be quiet, Gudman!"

"I think he will always be defective," Jessica said. She pursed her lips and shrilled, *Weyman,* you dumbo!"

"He sounds mysterious and interesting," Sylvie said.

"He sounds as if his head is stuffed with peanuts," Jessica retorted. "Do you think he's defective?"

"No, just independent," Sylvie said.

MARGO had called Sylvie almost continually when they had returned. "I need you more than ever now, at least until Michael gets back on his feet." They arranged for Sylvie to come in from Rosevale with Sean three days a week and be driven back each of those nights in a hired limousine. Feliciana's sister Lucia was taken on for Sean. Margo was rarely in touch with her friend Alessa these days. "We've always been on different wavelengths, you know," she said, as though it would be news to Sylvie.

Sylvie continued to help, of course. Along with the research she was doing for Michael, the gathering of facts, bibliographies, monographs, cassettes that people like Fuller, Venturi and Wright had made, she continued to attend to Margo's affairs. She kept records, read art journals. Suddenly she knew who the interior designers of new commercial buildings were and what sort of budgets they worked with.

The main foyer and public spaces of the AT&T building alone could absorb half the gallery offerings of Madison Avenue, to say nothing of the requirements of the Trump Tower. She was personally responsible for the sale of a painting to an IBM reception center. Margo, lyrical with enthusiasm, said, "I feel like your younger sister and darn lucky!"

IN late July she had gone with Margo to visit Max in Forest Hills. When they entered the apartment, Max tiptoed toward them, balancing on his cane. He had his finger to his lips. "The baby's sleeping. When she wakes, God forbid my hearing aid should be on. What lungs!" Blondell came from the kitchen and greeted them. She had had the baby in June, a month after Celia died. Margo had called Sylvie immediately and told her about Celia's death. She said it felt redundant. She guessed that some part of her had mourned that ruined and wasted life for so long that the death itself seemed predigested somehow. Jolene, who had taken a job in a hospital, was let go because of "poor attitude." Her defense, "I don't let nobody use me for a footstool!" She dropped by afternoons to give Blondell a hand, first going into the bathroom for a quick smoke before emerging to offer a lot of free advice. Gertrude sometimes came in on weekends, high as ever on Langston, who had bought himself a Subaru dealership after The Trains split up.

Blondell took care of Max. She lived in with her baby, dark-eyed Ingretta. She and Ingretta had the room that was formerly Celia's. Max insisted on continuing in his old small room. "Like a monk's cell, you should pardon the expression. Only God and I know where every little hanky and pair of socks is."

Blondell had put on weight. She seemed more imperturbable than ever, moving through the rooms of the apartment as if she glided on water, fussing over Max as if he, too, were a baby. "Eat your stew, man," she admonished. "I made it real soft and good. No fat, so you don't get the burps."

Max lifted his eyebrow at Margo and Sylvie. A bottle of

Alka-Seltzer was on the table next to the salt and pepper. "Goat stew and plantain pudding. When in Rome . . ." There was the hint of a twinkle behind the smudgy film of his eyes. In his own way he had surmounted his mortality; he still cared about the world. He had written to Gromyko and warned, "No more stockpiling. Here, at issue, is nothing less than all of human existence!" Then he sweetened him, he said, with a few words of praise for the Russian lynx.

When they left, Max stood in the doorway holding Ingretta gingerly in one arm. Swaying on his cane, he said to Margo, "If Celia could see me now!" He looked at the ceiling. "Poor thing, maybe she *can* and is bursting her pipes up there over all of this." The baby had started to cry, and he jiggled her. "The way I see it, it's like starting from scratch."

GATHERING material for Michael, Sylvie realized that she was doing some private research of her own. She began to call it the hidden woman. She'd discovered these women, hidden in the sociology of their time, existing unannounced in commerce, arts and the professions. The late nineteenth and early twentieth centuries were filled with examples. Not fabulous luminaries, but women of large accomplishment, unnoticed because of the mischance of being born in a prefeminist time. She began to see herself doing a glossary or dictionary, using biographical sketches: Abby Porsche, who created and ran one of the largest breakfast-cereal companies in the country; Fanny Palmer, who helped keep Currier and Ives in business; the sculptor Dorothy Burnham, whose heroic statues— heroes on horseback, soldiers in bronze raising victory banners—can still be seen in the parks and plazas of large cities. And Lucy Lapino, suffragette, who lost four children in a tenement fire and managed to turn her grief into another form of energy. She saw the project running like a river through her life. All the garnered bits of wisdom that made those women survive, the unbending spine of courage, somehow affected her directly. It was the quiet conquering of their condition that interested her most.

She gathered up her books and file boxes and carried them into the house. Through the intercom that Victor had rigged up, she heard Sean's breathing.

Victor called out, "We're set to go!" He had been fussing in the wings all these months, taking a day off here and there from Apollo. "It's taken forever, because my production crew—well, this is just moonlighting for them." He spoke about the film as "my ego trip." He said he wasn't apologizing for it. Some men spend a ton on their hobbies—scuba diving, race cars. This was his indulgence. The little off-hours film group that he'd hired eventually pulled the pieces together. He had purposely not researched the story too closely. "It's an impressionistic work," he said. "I don't want to be crowded by reality." He had a video copy, and now he was ready to project it on their TV screen.

The living-room blinds were drawn and the sofa repositioned so that it faced the TV. Victor's face was flushed, and he darted about, adjusting sound, fiddling with the dials on the cassette recorder. "Later on we'll relax with some new stuff on Sean." Victor looked younger and more intense than ever.

"The way I see this thing, it's a sort of passion play," he said. "In the Middle Ages, you know, the passion play was invented as a ritual to appease the plague. Like crossing yourself a dozen times over. A vow was made to do the play every ten years for eternity, if the rats would just go away." He intended to submit the film to the Venice Festival and see what happened. He suddenly said, "Did I ever tell you that when I learned exactly how my mother died—skin experiments, Birkenau; she was slowly peeled like a plum until her body fluids leaked away—well, I went out and strangled Judith. I put a grain sack around Judith's slippery head and tied the sack with a rope and pulled with every ounce of strength—poor little porker, all that wild squealing—until she sagged, fell to her knees. Then I took my pocket knife and slit her throat through the sack—not one slit, but many, again and again. It was weird and awful. Where did I get the

physical strength? But I felt so cool. The executioner. In my
deranged, little boy's mind, there was no way that Judith
could live." He smiled, a passing glint against the friendly
map of his face, as if reminiscing about a fictional character.
"Madame Michaud was disgusted with me. 'Victor!' she
howled. 'Judith is too young for slaughter!' I think we had
her for dinner that night anyway."

Sylvie shivered. "Victor, I can't imagine you doing something so brutal. It's incredibly unlike you."

"Unlike? What's *that* supposed to mean."

She had thought she knew all there was to know about
Victor. Obviously there was always another crumb or two to
be served up. Had she told him that when she found out
about Arthur and Scott, she made a wild bundle of a few of
Arthur's clothes—shirts, a jacket, a pair of shoes—and flung
them into the fireplace, where they smouldered for hours. It
was right after the dinner at Rosevale's Indian restaurant.
Angel had come into the room, sniffed and said, "What's that
funny smell?" Among the smoky acrid odors, Sylvie imagined a high-pitched floral essence, perhaps lavender drenched
in brandy. Looking through the fire screen, Angel had said,
"Ye gods, are you burning Daddy's shoes?"

Thinking of Angel, Sylvie realized that her agonized de-
tachment had been replaced by an interest in day-to-day
matters. She found herself considering the relative merits of
a small microwave oven and a conventional toaster-broiler.

Victor started the recorder and then came and sat next to
her. "Well, here goes!" The film was called *Quandaries,* sub-
titled *A Fable in Two Moods.* There was a long somber shot
of a building on a narrow city street. The building had once
been a fortress, and there were tiny windows on the upper
floors, through which one could imagine cannon poking. It
was 1976, and the building had long since been converted into
a hospital. Three walls encompassed an inner court, into
which ambulances and other vehicles drove. Inside, the halls
were relatively silent. Here and there was a nurses' station,
a small cluster of doctors conferring, a visitor or two timor-

ously opening and then closing a door. Sylvie wondered what Victor had paid to have actors just standing around that way. A white-cowled nurse moved as if on wheels in and out of rooms. In one large, dimly lit room, a hospital bed stood in the center as though on display. The frail body of a man was outlined beneath the thin coverlet. The camera lingered on him—the once-notorious Kesselmann, who in his unspeakable heyday entertained friends and henchmen, even Adolf Eichmann, at his palazzo on the Via Castellano. His hands on the coverlet looked like the fossilized claws of an extinct bird. A woman came into view down the hall. She seemed to be walking through a tunnel, walking from darkness into a lighter zone. The hospital walls bent around her. Very interesting, Sylvie thought, the way the camera did that, giving the walker instant deeper significance. As she walked, one saw that she was carrying a very large bulky valise, like a steamer trunk. It banged against the calves of her legs, but she was oblivious to the discomfort. She was tall and broad. Her free hand hung at her side in a clenched fist. She was, perhaps, in her mid-fifties and her hair, a watery gray-blond, was drawn back and braided in a coronet. She was wearing a dark suit, flat oxfords and a cape that partially hid the valise. Her expression was neutral, the expression seen on statuary done by sculptors interested only in the physical details, not the soul of their subject.

A nurse met her at the door to her husband's room. There was a military guard posted there. The nurse said, "Ah, Mrs. Kesselmann, it is good that you are here."

"I've brought a few things for him," the wife replied. She hesitated and then said clearly, "This may be the last time that I will see him."

"The nurse was neither surprised nor bewildered," the neutral voice of the narrator said, picking up the thread. "She perhaps wondered about this woman who married Kesselmann, a life-term war criminal, only eight years ago. What she didn't know was that the wife had begun writing to him in the late sixties, when his case flashed briefly into the news over the issue of Nazis still in hiding. At least *he* was under lock and key. She wrote her first letter to him and then another. It seemed they came from the same city, had childhood friends in common. After a while he answered. They exchanged views of the world. They emptied their hearts. She had been widowed some years earlier, and she had a meditative attitude toward life. His former wife had divorced him immediately after the trials."

In one letter, Kesselmann asked her if she believed that more than one soul could occupy a body. She said she didn't know. She was not religious, but she rather liked the idea. Renewal instead of redemption. To her, renewal implied something beyond guilt, she said. After a year or two, she suggested that they seal what had become a deep emotional bond with marriage. All this was shown in flashback—snatches of Kesselmann and his future wife with heads bent over their writing tablets, the strange music of their voices hovering in the foreground as they poured out their thoughts.

"But why do you say the last time . . . ?" the nurse asked.

The wife had a quiet, conversational manner. She said, "There is some question of whether the government will allow his body to be shipped home when the day comes . . . In any case, for now, I have not arrived empty-handed." Inside the room she opened the valise, whose coffin-shaped shadow reared up across the wall. Down cushions, comforter, alpaca shoulder-throw, heavy bathrobe, pajamas, fleece slippers tumbled from its depths. The nurse held up the slippers and whispered, "But he doesn't walk too much anymore. Of course, some days are better than others . . ."

Mrs. Kesselmann shrugged. "So on the bad days, he will look at them." She had also brought tins of food, chocolate, a special coffee and tea that she thought he still liked. And books of history and philosophy, which, on his good days, someone might read to him. "He has an interest in philosophy," she told the nurse. She stared over at the bed, where her husband's even breathing indicated that he was asleep.

"Your son isn't with you this time?" the nurse asked.

"Not this time."

The camera moved closer and focused on Kesselmann, whose eyes were now open and staring at his wife. She was bending over him, whispering. She emptied the valise and arranged the contents in the drawers and on the dresser top. Biscuits and jams next to gauze, swabs, a kidney-shaped pan. The nurse had left the room, and drawing a chair close to the bed, the woman bent toward her husband, and they talked quietly together. The sound track caught the low murmurous sounds. Her son Heinrich was mentioned. "It is too crazy," Kesselmann said.

"You are not to worry," the wife answered.

"I have long ago given up *that* luxury." He raised his voice a trifle. "I would like a piece of chocolate in my mouth."

She picked up a wrappered bar (Sylvie saw that it was Toblerone, her own favorite), broke off a piece and placed it between his lips. "The nurse will be here in a few moments to give your injection. Perhaps I will allow her to see me reading a little Schopenhauer to you."

He rose on one shaky elbow. "In the end it is all rubbish," he said. Not rubbish, Sylvie thought. She was having a hard time keeping these people connected to their past. When the nurse came back, she found Kesselmann's hand clasped in his wife's. The wife was reading aloud to her drowsing husband. Her voice was calm. "Unselfish intellect rises like a perfume above the faults and follies of the world . . ." Rises and stays afloat, Sylvie thought.

Kesselmann woke. "Whose world?" he rasped. The nurse pulled back the coverlet and gave him an injection in the skimpy flesh of his thigh.

She turned to Mrs. Kesselmann. "This will hold him for four hours. After a while he will sleep." She seemed to have forgotten that she was dealing with a war criminal and his wife. The film was having trouble remembering, too. Among the scatter of personal effects in the dresser drawer was a photograph of a more innocent time. A boyish Kesselmann in white shirt and Tyrolean shorts, on a mountain trail. He was laughing. The camera drifted, as if unanchored, from drawer to dresser top and studied a tin of cookies. The painted shepherd girl on the cover, ankle-deep in violets, was also laughing. Sylvie believed the thread was being lost. The reading from Schopenhauer seemed an overly intellectual touch that muted the starkness of what went before. For her part, she knew she didn't dare think about the faults and follies of the world.

But in the next scene things moved swiftly. The woman was again walking down the hall with her valise, but this time away from the darkness of the room toward the glow of light from the stairwell. The weight of the valise pulled her shoulder downward. The military guard came after her. *"Per favore,* do you need help to the elevator?"

She gracefully refused. "Oh no. I can manage well enough. I'll ride this thing down the stairs. It's only two flights." She moved on, forced her body erect; her resolve was Herculean. The guard went back to his post. At the foot of the stairwell there was a side door to the street. Outside a limousine waited in a pool of shadow just beyond the street lamp. A tall young man with a dash of gray at his temples hurried toward her and lifted the valise. Together they placed it on the back seat of the limousine and sped away.

The scene faded, but in the next shot the narrator remarked that a half hour had passed. The nurse could be seen coming through the door and standing in the empty hospital room, staring around in disbelief. She touched the rumpled bed covers as if they were unreal, then ran to the telephone and excitedly sent out an alarm.

Meanwhile the limousine sped north through the Umbrian night. Heinrich turned on the radio, and the music of an American dance band filled the car: Frank Sinatra singing "Melancholy Baby." Finally Heinrich pulled the car to the side of the road, and they removed the valise, whose lid had been propped open to allow Kesselmann to breathe. Heinrich lifted his stepfather out of the valise and braced him against the seat pillows. Kesselmann, half asleep, protested, *"Nein!"*

In the back seat, mother and son quickly dressed him. Pants, jacket, shirt, sporty argyle socks, a dark fedora on his head. Mrs. Kesselmann put rouge on his cheeks, a touch of it on his lips as well, steel-rim glasses on his nose. They wrapped the alpaca throw around his shoulders, packed the valise into the trunk compartment. They were on the outskirts of Florence when the music was interrupted and the first bulletins were heard. In a garble of Italian, the words came clear: "This evening, Rudolph Kesselmann, notorious war criminal, was abducted from his hospital room in Rome." The announcer sounded bewildered: "It is believed his wife transported her ailing husband out of his room in a valise." More static and then another string of words: "The woman is described as having the build of a sumo wrestler . . ." In the car, Heinrich looked back at his mother and shook his head in disgust. Sylvie too felt indignation on behalf of the woman, who, though broad and strong, did not merit such a description. The announcer continued, "There are roadblocks from Rome north. The borders are covered . . ."

Heinrich said to his mother, "What do we do now?" Do *something,* Sylvie breathed. She realized she was rooting for the wrong team, but she could not help herself. Victor's arm was around her shoulder, his hand digging into her flesh. Heinrich swerved the car off the road, took the valise and buried it in the bushes. A car with the glaring letters *Polizia* pulled off the road behind them. Heinrich pretended he had been urinating in the bushes. The policeman got out of the car and Heinrich walked toward him, ostentatiously zipping his fly.

"You are having trouble?" the policeman asked. He peered into the car and saw Kesselmann dozing. The fedora slipped rakishly to one side of his forehead.

"Attending to a call of nature," Heinrich said.

"Who is the old boy?"

"My uncle. We're returning from a wedding in Arezzo." Heinrich shrugged and laughed. "I'm afraid he had a bit too much wine." The mother smiled at the policeman.

The policeman was noncommittal. "Your destination?"

"Bologna, if possible." He sighed. "It is already so late." Heinrich spoke flawless Italian. Sylvie imagined him studying the language obsessively. She saw him accompanying his mother on the twice-yearly visits to his stepfather; imagined him speaking only Italian the moment he crossed the border, as if enacting rites of a secret and dangerous order.

On the screen, the policeman said, "Well, then, on your way!" Heinrich sauntered to the car. Made himself pause to light a cigarette. He waved to the policeman and drove away. Sylvie sank farther into the cushions of the couch, but Victor's hand still clutched her shoulder. Her sympathies floated free, like a weather balloon blown off course. "The man is still a Nazi," she hissed at Victor. "Despicably vile. Damned. And the wife, I'm afraid, damned by association." But whom was she trying to convince? Surely not Victor. She added, "That the wife has heroic will is something else." She thought, a woman like that could lead governments—she would never in any time have been a hidden woman.

Now the car was stopped at a roadblock near the town of Pistoia, sixty miles from Bologna. The flashing lights of the *polizia* gave a theatrical touch to the landscape. They could hear sirens in the distance. In the back seat, Kesselmann had lifted his head. His wife pressed a stimulant between his lips. His eyes were like black holes. "Are you in pain?" she asked. *"Nein."*

"Heinrich and I are taking you home. It is just a matter of hours. Do you have to relieve yourself?" Again he said no. She placed a pipe, which Heinrich had lit, into his hand. "Just hold it, my love, as if you were smoking." Up ahead, cars were lined up at the roadblock. The occupants were being asked to step out of their cars. Mrs. Kesselmann pretended she was asleep against her husband's shoulder. When the police came to their car, Heinrich jumped out jauntily. He was told to open the trunk compartment and said with humor, "At your service." Another policeman stared at the occupants in the back seat. They saw an elderly woman asleep, an even older man smoking a pipe and nodding. "My aunt and uncle," Heinrich said. "She, poor thing, suffers from excruciating migraine. At last we've doped her up sufficiently to make her sleep. I'd be grateful if you wouldn't disturb them. As you can see, they're both out of it . . ."

"Identification," the officer said, as if he hadn't heard a word. Heinrich showed him the driver's license he had carefully provided before they left Germany. Paulo Lampioni, age thirty-eight . . . "Oh, and passports . . ." He dug into the glove compartment and came up with three Lampioni passports.

The policeman examined the photograph in each passport and then glanced into the back of the car. "We're heading for Bologna," Heinrich said, lighting a cigarette and blowing a puff of smoke over his shoulder. "Although we'll probably call it quits in Pistoia and bed down there."

The policeman was staring at Kesselmann. "And where in Pistoia?"

"Oh, the Casa Appennino, most likely," Heinrich said, infusing a note of condescension into his tone.

"So you'd better hurry," the policeman said. "They predict a heavy rain." As the car moved through the roadblock and sped away, Sylvie was flooded with relief. She knew that her feelings were being dragged every which way and wondered whether that, too, was the point. She was about to question Victor but was captured by what was happening in the film. The car flew through the night, past the turnoffs to Prato and Pistoia, through the mountains toward Imola. It began to rain. The windshield wipers flashed like knives. It was clear that they would drive forever, if necessary. They stopped once at a *gaseteria*. While Heinrich filled the tank, Kesselmann's wife offered her husband hot soup from a thermos. He opened his mouth like an infant. His desire for food was disarming. After the soup, the wife pulled a small urinal from a bag under the front seat, and groped in his clothes. "Surely *now, Liebling.*" But he shook his head. They pressed on. They passed Modena, Parma, Cremona. Northward to

Milano and from there . . . Sylvia caught her breath. She did not dare to hope. The darkness was diluted by filaments of light. It had stopped raining. The outlines of trees and houses were more distinct. The scene changed from velvety black to violet to rose. They had travelled like bandits through the night.

It was almost dawn when they passed through Como. Switzerland was in sight. There was a certain amount of revelry in the car. Heinrich reached back and pinched his mother. He grasped his stepfather's hand and held it tightly. Kesselmann had a glimmer of a smile on his face. But there was another checkpoint. The most important one. Again Kesselmann and his wife pretended to be asleep. His chin sagged to his chest. But this time there were not only local police but military officials as well. This was the border, after all. A short span of road, perhaps two hundred feet, and they would be on Swiss soil. Two uniformed individuals approached the car and asked for passports. Unfortunately, due to certain embarrassing events, there must be an interrogation. They apologized for the inconvenience. *"Terroristi* again?" Heinrich asked in disgust. He had gotten out of the car and started to move off with them, but they stopped him. They must question the two in the back as well. Heinrich protested, "What, those old ones? They're under the weather, you can see that." The military officials were adamant.

Mrs. Kesselmann opened the car window and told Heinrich to be quiet. She was well enough, and so was her husband. There were fields in either direction, tall grass, a thick fringe of stubby trees. The officials were standing with Heinrich on the driver's side of the car. Mrs. Kesselmann removed her cape, her hat. She reached in and pulled Kesselmann toward her, his features stunned in wonder, his head as loose as a rag doll's. In a sudden motion, she lifted him, cradled him in her arms and then started to run. Now the film went into slow motion, her body in awkward but miraculous flight. She dove into the tall grass and began to thrash her way forward, her husband clinging to her, his arms around her shoulders. Her hair had come undone and streamed behind her. In the dawn light, she looked as if she had been beheaded, as if her head were on a pike. She was making for the trees, for the multicolored guard station, seen through the wood, at the Swiss crossing. It took a moment or two for the group at the car to realize what had happened. Heinrich was the first. He turned screaming, "Let them be!" Then he too tried to run for it, shouting "Mama! Mama!" But the officers quickly subdued him. There were orders and confusion. A bullhorn covered the field with its boom of sound. *"Attenzione! Attenzione! Reparto!"* At some point an order was given. *"Attenzione!"* the bullhorn barked. Rifles were raised. Shots peppered the landscape. The camera's eye seemed to blink at each fusillade. There was the sudden clarity of the field in the morning light and again the deleting blink. When the lens finally remained fixed, there was a quiet landscape. A few tourists had driven up to the checkpoint and were being allowed through. Heinrich was standing between a pair of Italian soldiers. Two others were walking slowly toward the taller grass with their guns raised, like gamesmen who have bagged partridge.

SYLVIE breathed deeply. "Well!"

"Well?" Victor had removed the cassette. He looked strange, as if someone had arbitrarily rearranged his features.

"It provokes thought, Victor. Can villains lose their villainy before your eyes? I want to say no!"

"Then say it!"

"It's too confusing."

"Well, some emotions mix you up. You don't think it turned into soap opera, do you?"

She sat back, still shaken, as if she had gotten off a roller coaster and needed to test her footing. "Victor, I think . . . I think it's extraordinary . . . in a terrible and paradoxical way. I was absolutely mesmerized."

He said, "Ah," as though he'd just been kissed. "Ah . . . ," the sound of relief. "Well, at least you weren't bored."

"God, no! But the fact is, the film gives Kesselmann a human dimension, even a context—and I don't want to know about *that*. I really don't. The way you stripped him down to a kind of common mortality. Made him eat, drink, suffer cancer, die. Very manipulative. It disturbs the simplicity of pure hate."

"Yes, it does, doesn't it?" he said dreamily. The cassette was back in its container. Everything was tidied up. But then he looked at her so sharply that it was like being speared by a lance. "It's just this: Hate is so devitalizing, it drains you of humanity." He picked up his pipe, knocking the ash carefully in a tray. "And so does a lot of other stuff—grief, for example. Better to divest yourself as soon as you can; commit some minor mayhem, like crashing your car into a street lamp or putting in time as a hooker, and then say 'Enough!' "

Victor's pragmatism. She supposed he was telling her that her decision to work for the Korts had been on the right track after all. He got up and stretched until his fingertips seemed to graze the ceiling. He said, "I feel as though I've really done it. Shaken the bones of something that has plagued me forever. Turned it upside down. And now I can put it aside. Don't ask me why, how. I just feel so—so airy."

She wanted to say that she, on the other hand, still carried a sense of weight. She had only to think of Gary or Angel . . . Gary—it would always be hard to see him. She would always wonder what he would do next, and how it would affect Sean, and what her own reactions must be. If only she could wish him away, wish him into a prolonged limbo. Go to Katmandu now, now, she thought.

"Airy is just too . . ." she began. Too ethereal, too separated from matter. But Victor had taken her arm and was walking her through the rooms of the house, then on into the garden to tour the perimeter of her small Rosevale grounds. It had grown dark. He picked a zinnia and stuck it in her hair. He was high as a kite. They went back into the house and then out again.

"We may be walking all night," he said.

"Or forever," she answered.

Sean dreamed aloud over the intercom. Gary would come to claim him one day. And she would try hard to be just. She would.

ABOUT
THE AUTHOR

MURIEL SPANIER was born in New York City and was graduated from Hunter College. She has worked as an adjunct lecturer at Queens College and written copy for book publishers. Her short stories have appeared in *Redbook, Sewanee Review, Saturday Evening Post, Colorado Quarterly* and other magazines. She is married to the electrophysicist N. Marcuvitz and has two grown children. She lives on Long Island. *Staying Afloat* is her first novel.

SUPERIOR FICTION *from the* FINEST CONTEMPORARY AUTHORS